D1007086

By Darcie Chan

The Mill River Recluse

The Mill River Redemption

The
MILL RIVER
Redemption

The MILL RIVER
Redemption

A Novel

DARCIE CHAN

Ballantine Books Trade Paperbacks
New York

A Ballantine Books Trade Paperback Original

Copyright © 2014 by Darcie Chan
Reading group guide copyright © 2014 by Random House LLC

Published in the United States by Ballantine Books, an imprint of Random House, a division of Random House LLC, a Penguin Random House Company, New York.

BALLANTINE and the HOUSE colophon are registered trademarks of Random House LLC.
RANDOM HOUSE READER'S CIRCLE & Design is a registered trademark of Random House LLC.

ISBN 978-0-345-53823-9
eBook ISBN 978-0-345-54156-7

Printed in the United States of America on acid-free paper

www.randomhousereaderscircle.com

2 4 6 8 9 7 5 3 1

Book design by Donna Sinisgalli

For my sisters, Carrie and Molly, and our parents, Linda and Dennis, who gave the three of us the gifts of one another.

The
MILL RIVER
Redemption

Let parents bequeath to their children not
riches, but the spirit of reverence.

~ PLATO

PROLOGUE
A New Beginning

December 1983

JOSIE DiSANTI WAS STARTING OVER.

In the wide backseat of her station wagon, with her aunt Ivy behind the wheel and her daughters, Rose and Emily, asleep beside her, Josie bit down on her lip to keep awake. It was two in the morning, and although she couldn't see much out of the window, she peered through the glass anyway. To maintain her grip on reality, she needed to remember everything about this day.

The past week had been a terrifying blur, and she was fighting to emerge from the fog of grief that enveloped her. Her husband, Tony, was dead. All of their possessions were gone, but she and her girls were *together and alive*. Right now, that was all that mattered.

Every so often, in the illumination of a passing car's headlights, Josie met Ivy's gaze in the rearview mirror, but she didn't know her aunt well enough to be able to guess her thoughts. Ivy's presence in Josie's life had been erratic, a sequence of brief appearances years apart. The last memory Josie had of her aunt was Ivy pressing a slip of paper into her hand as her mother's casket was being lowered into the earth. "I'm all you've got left," she'd whispered. "So, if you ever need me, call."

Now, she and her girls were going to live with this aunt Ivy.

Tony didn't have any immediate family, and it wasn't safe for them to stay in New York. Their home was gone. Josie didn't know whom else she could trust. They had no other place to go.

They'd been driving north for several hours. Josie didn't know how much longer they'd be in the car, but she hoped they didn't have too much farther to go before they reached Mill River.

Josie looked down at Rose, her four-year-old, and smoothed a strand of blonde hair from her cheek. She shifted slightly under the weight of Emily, her two-year-old, whose little head of red curls rested against her side. They were just babies. She wondered how much of the whole horrible mess they would remember.

It had been just a week since the fire. Each day, Emily wandered over to her several times with wide, blue eyes, saying, "Where Da-dee?" Each time, Josie felt a renewed crush of panic and despair. Her heart racing as she struggled to control her emotions, she would take her toddler in her arms and whisper, "Daddy is gone now, but Mommy is here and loves you very much." Emily usually just scampered off to play afterward.

Helping Rose understand what had happened was more difficult. "Daddy died," Josie had explained to her. "There was no air to breathe in the kitchen, only smoke, so his body stopped working." There was no way she would explain to her older daughter how Tony had truly died. Hearing that the fire had claimed her father's life was difficult enough for Rose.

A week ago, the four-year-old's knowledge of death extended only to the occasional bug that found its way inside the house, and she had been a happy and carefree child. Now, Rose was unusually quiet and withdrawn. She refused to let Josie out of her sight. Despite Josie's explanation, she continued to ask, "When is Daddy coming home?" Josie kept repeating, as gently as she could, "Daddy's not going to come home, because he died. But he loved you and Emily and Mommy very much, and we will always love and remember Daddy."

After hearing this several times, little Rose grew angry and her eyes filled with tears. "I want Daddy!" she'd screamed. "Why did you leave him in the fire, Mommy? Why didn't you get him out, too? I hate you!" Josie was at a loss for words. She could only hug her older daughter tightly, restraining Rose's flailing arms until her little girl gave up and slumped against her.

Josie knew when the questions and outbursts were coming simply by the expressions on her daughters' faces, and the pain she felt when she stared into those innocent eyes was unlike anything she had ever experienced. Somehow she reassured her girls, keeping her voice steady and the chaos held inside.

While Rose and Emily were awake, Josie pushed the memories of her husband into the dark recesses of her brain. She refused to even *think* his name. It was only after both girls were sleeping soundly that she allowed herself to cry.

Late at night, she would remember Tony's face and how his incredible blue eyes rendered her speechless the first time she saw him. "Love you, always," she could almost hear him whisper in her ear. If she stood motionless, she could still feel his arms around her, the warmth of his hands on her skin.

The memories came faster at those times. How he used to walk his fingers over her belly when she was hugely pregnant, and sing "The Itsy-Bitsy Spider." How he held the girls as colicky infants, swaying and bouncing them, until, miraculously, they fell asleep. How he grabbed up the girls in a huge bear hug each night when he came home from work, how he made faces and used silly voices when he read them bedtime stories. And, more recently, how he sat with Josie on the sofa late into the evening, talking, no, dreaming aloud about the day they would finally have enough money saved to move their family from the cramped, rented row house into a home of their own.

Remembering him brought a cruel, faint glow of happiness. When the happy memories stopped, as they inevitably did, the terrible ones began. Grief again took hold of her, torturing her with images of bloody clothing and flames shooting up into the sky.

Her aunt's voice, coming from the front seat, jarred Josie. "We're pretty close now," Ivy said over her shoulder. "We crossed into Vermont a ways back. We're only a few miles outside Mill River."

Mill River. It was a relief to focus for a moment on those two words and nothing else. She asked in a whisper, so as not to wake the girls, "What's it like?"

"It's a pretty nice town," Ivy replied. "Small and friendly. Close enough to Rutland and the ski resorts to keep things interesting, but far enough away to give you plenty of peace and quiet, if that's what you want. You'll be safe there."

Lost in her worries, Josie sat quietly. What would the locals think of her, a widow with two young daughters and an accent shaped by a lifetime in the Bronx? Could Rose and Emily be happy growing up in such a place? Would she be able to find a decent job? How long would she have to rely on the kindness of this aunt whom she barely knew?

"We're coming into town now," Ivy said as she slowed the station wagon.

Josie squinted out the window and saw the sign, WELCOME TO MILL RIVER, VERMONT.

"We're on Main Street, where most of the businesses are," Ivy said. "Too bad it's dark now, or you could really see what a cozy little place this is. But you'll see it soon enough."

Even though it was so late, there were a few Christmas and other lights on. Josie noticed a cute bakery, a hardware store, and a brick post office. Just after the road curved a bit, they passed St. John's, an old stone church with a small parish house behind it. They stopped at an intersection, where a white town hall building stood across the street on the left side. Beyond that, Josie caught a glimpse of a well-lit police station before Ivy made a sharp left turn off the main thoroughfare. They made another left turn a few moments later.

"Here we are," Ivy said. They had pulled into the driveway of an attractive house perhaps two or three blocks off Main Street. In the headlights, Josie could see that it was a two-story 1930s-style bungalow with a big front porch. A walkway cut straight through the yard, past a large sign that read THE BOOKSTOP.

"I've got the attic bedroom all set up for you. Let me come around and take Emily. You can get Rose and some of the other things you need to bring in right away," Ivy said as she grabbed her coat and opened the driver's side door. A blast of frigid air burst into the car. Ivy cursed and muttered something that sounded like "balls off a brass monkey" before the door closed again. Josie shivered and pulled a blanket up around Emily, who was still sleeping soundly. Rose stirred on the seat beside her and opened her eyes.

"Mommy," she said, still half-asleep, "where are we?"

Maybe it was the sudden stillness of the car after hours of driving or a combination of emotional and physical exhaustion. Maybe it was feeling her soul crumble, day by day, beneath the weight of her grief. Whatever the reason, Josie's emotional fortress disintegrated, and the tears refused to stay in her eyes. She gathered Rose against her left side while holding Emily. If she survived, it would be solely because of her children. Her girls were anchors in her sea of uncertainty.

She would never let them go.

She would give anything, do anything, to make sure that they grew up safe and happy.

"Rosie, baby," she said, "we're at Aunt Ivy's house in Mill River. We're home."

CHAPTER 1

2013

O n a Saturday afternoon in early May, Father Michael O'Brien knocked at the front door of the tidy house next to The Bookstop. It opened immediately, and he found himself face-to-face with Ruth Fitzgerald, the longtime owner of the bakery-café in town.

"Hello, Father," she said, holding open the door. "Please come in."

The elderly priest walked into the house and surveyed the scene. The place was quiet even though several people were gathered there. At the far end of the living room, Ivy Collard leaned on her cane and adjusted the position of a bronze urn on a small table. Surrounding the urn were several bouquets of flowers and some framed photographs of Josie DiSanti.

He watched as Ivy wiped her eyes and glanced around toward him, then at Rose and Emily, Josie's two adult daughters. They, too, were crying, though they stood apart from each other on opposite sides of the room. It had been a long time since he had seen Josie's children, and even longer since he'd seen them together. They were older and sadder, but other than that, not much different from how he remembered them.

Rose's appearance was impeccable. Her blonde hair curved just above her shoulders, and she wore a simple but elegant black dress. She wore quite a bit of eye makeup, but her tears did no appreciable damage to it.

Rose stood beside her husband, Sheldon, an older, balding ex-investment banker with a slightly bored but properly solemn expression. Their nine-year-old son, Alex, was dressed to match his father in a perfect black suit. The little boy neither fidgeted nor whined. He stood silently between his parents, rubbing away the occasional tear that shimmered behind his glasses, and took it all in. Rose kept her gaze focused on the urn and occasionally dabbed at her eyes with a tissue.

Emily stood alone, as far from Rose and her family as was possible in the small living room of Josie's house. She was as striking as Rose, but her appearance couldn't have been more different. Her natural beauty was only accentuated by a face devoid of makeup, a smattering of freckles high on her cheeks, and her soft red curls pulled back in a loose ponytail. Tears ran from her huge blue eyes—eyes *exactly* like her father's, as Josie had said so many times. Emily, too, was dressed in black—a simple skirt and top with a black cardigan two sizes too big. She stood with her arms wound tightly around her middle, as if to hold herself up.

"It's good to see you, Father," Ivy said quietly. "I guess we're all ready now. Everything's just as she wanted."

"Yes, thank you so much for coming, Father," Rose said, throwing her shoulders back and raising her chin. "You remember my husband, Sheldon Frye, and our son, Alex?"

"Of course." Father O'Brien shook hands with both of them. "It's good to see all of you again," he said with a glance over at Emily, "although I wish it were under different circumstances."

Rose eyed Emily before continuing in her elder-in-charge voice. "I know Mom thought the world of you, Father, and she was so grateful for your help over the years."

"Yes, she did, and she was," Emily said softly. "We appreciate your being here."

"Your mother was a wonderful person." He walked carefully to the table where the bronze urn and photos were displayed. He bowed his head, said a silent prayer, and made the sign of the cross before turning back to the group.

"I still wish we could've had some sort of viewing," Ruth said. "But Josie's instructions were clear. She always hated the idea of herself in a coffin, with everyone staring down at her. Never wanted that to be the last people saw of her." Ruth's voice broke, and she quietly excused herself to the kitchen.

"The poor thing." Ivy shook her head as she lowered herself onto the sofa. "She's right, though. And I expect we'll have quite a houseful today. Everyone in Mill River loved Josie. Lots of folks from Rutland knew her, too, since she sold so many houses over that way."

"I still can't believe she's gone," Rose said. "I talked to her just last week. She never mentioned anything about not feeling well or having any sort of heart problem."

Emily sniffed and glanced over at her sister but said nothing.

As an awkward silence filled the room, Father O'Brien saw Josie's daughters make brief eye contact with each other.

"With respect to the burial," he said gently after a moment, "I understand Josie wanted it to be a private family affair. Perhaps later on, after everyone has left, we could sit for a few minutes to decide on the timing and details? I don't have anything else scheduled today."

"We probably won't get to it today, Father," Ivy said before either daughter could respond. "I know it's unusual not to have a burial scheduled right after a wake, but that was Josie's doing. She wanted the girls to take care of something first." Ivy looked at him for a moment with raised eyebrows and a strange gleam in her eyes, as if there were more that she wanted to tell him.

Father O'Brien nodded, but he eyed her suspiciously. He knew Ivy well—in fact, he'd known her since sometime in the early seventies, when she'd first moved to Mill River with her fiancé,

Thomas Dearborn. They'd finally decided to give up their hippie sort of lifestyle and put down roots, and the friendly Vermont town had seemed to them to be the perfect place.

Ivy and Thomas had bought a little house and opened The Bookstop in the front half of it. They appeared to be happy in the beginning, and certainly, their little bookstore filled a niche and thrived. For reasons unknown to Father O'Brien, though, Thomas broke their engagement and left her a few years later. Ivy stayed behind and became a loud, loving, quick-witted, slightly bawdy, big-hearted fixture in Mill River. She knew everything and everybody. It was difficult to keep a secret from her, and once she knew a secret . . . well, she found it almost impossible not to reveal it.

Looking at Ivy, Father O'Brien realized she was sitting on something—something having to do with Josie's girls—but he didn't have time to mull over what it might be. The townspeople had begun to arrive for Josie's wake, and before long he found himself moving through a crowded living room, visiting with those who stopped by.

Joe Fitzgerald, the police chief of Mill River, entered the house wearing his uniform. Fitz clapped him on the shoulder after he'd spoken to Josie's daughters.

"Hullo, Father," he said. "I guess everything is going well?"

"As well as these things can go," Father O'Brien replied. "Ruth's in the kitchen. She's having a rough time," he added.

"She's been upset ever since we got word. She and Josie were two peas in a pod, I tell you. Ruthie was almost as close to Josie as she was to her own sister." Fitz shook his head sadly and turned toward the kitchen. "I'll go spend a few minutes with her before I head back to the station."

A constant stream of visitors came through the front door. They made their way around the living room, signing the guest book, pausing to gaze at the urn and the pictures of Josie, stopping to shake hands and speak with Josie's daughters and Ivy. Kyle Hansen arrived with his daughter, Rowen, and Claudia Simon, an elementary-school teacher in Mill River whom he'd been dating for several months. Father O'Brien watched as Kyle and Claudia spoke with Emily, then Rose and her husband, and as Claudia knelt to speak to Alex.

The front door opened again, and another group of people filed into the house. He nodded to the Wykowski, Pearson, Burnham, and Lowell families as they passed him, but there were several people he didn't recognize. He was caught up in conversation when he felt a friendly tug on his elbow. He excused himself and looked down to see Daisy Delaine smiling up at him.

"Father, oh, am I ever glad you're here," she said in her familiar singsong voice. The little woman tossed her gray curls away from her face, revealing a large, port-wine birthmark that curled up onto her cheek. "You know, Josie was one of my best customers, and I feel so sad for her daughters. I made up a batch of my special grief potion for them. It's the same kind I made after Mrs. McAllister died. Do you remember?"

Daisy's words awoke a great sadness in his heart as he remembered the recent loss of his closest friend, but he did his best to smile and focus on the present situation. "Ah, yes, Daisy, that was quite a potent brew."

Daisy looked delighted. "Wasn't it, though? It helped me feel better, so I was thinking I'd give them each a big jar of it." She leaned closer to him and opened the top of her purse wide enough to reveal two large Mason jars full of a greenish liquid. Her voice dropped to a whisper. "I'm a little worried. I haven't seen either of them in a long time, you know. They might not remember me."

Father O'Brien smiled and patted Daisy's shoulder. "I'm sure they'll remember you," he said. "But, it's tough at a time like this, when Josie's daughters are sad and having to be good hostesses for all these people. Maybe you should wait to give them the potion until almost everyone else has gone home. That way, you'd have their full attention."

"That's a good idea, Father," Daisy said. "Thanks! I guess I'll go see what's in the kitchen while I wait. I heard Ruth brought some pies for refreshments."

He thought of Ruth Fitzgerald's fabulous tart cherry pie . . . and how he hadn't had any recently, since the bakery-café had been undergoing renovation. He turned to follow Daisy to the kitchen, but he found himself face-to-face with Ivy. She pulled him by the arm into the corner of the room, away from the clusters of mourners.

"Father, I didn't want to say anything earlier, in front of the girls," Ivy said in a low voice, "but I need to meet with them privately before this is over, and I was hoping you might sit in when I do. It's something their mother arranged, and it isn't gonna be pretty."

Sure enough, he thought, he'd been right about Ivy. "I'm happy to help however I can," he said. "If it's a personal family matter, though, shouldn't it just be between you and the girls? I wouldn't want to intrude."

"Well, you know how they are, Father. And what I've got to tell 'em, well, I know it'll go over like a frog in a punch bowl. Having you there will help them keep control of themselves and maybe even stay civil toward each other, because they're still as far apart as the sun and the moon."

"I gathered as much when I first came in," he said. "When and where will you have this meeting?"

"Rose and her family will be driving back to New York this afternoon, and Emily has an evening flight back to California, so I suspect they'll be itching to leave here as soon as they can. I thought I'd pull the girls aside once the crowd thins out."

Father O'Brien nodded. "Just let me know when."

Once most of the visitors had left Josie's house, he saw Ivy go first to Rose, then to Emily. The women looked perplexed, but they excused themselves from their conversations and made their way toward Josie's office, off the living room. Ivy looked up and caught Father O'Brien's eye from across the room. It was time.

He signaled his understanding with a small nod. As curious as he was about the reason for Ivy's meeting, he doubted very much that it would be a warm family chat. In fact, something in his gut told him that he was being sucked into a very uncomfortable situation.

CHAPTER 2

1983

LATE IN THE MORNING AFTER THEIR ARRIVAL AT THE BOOK-stop, Josie was awakened by a giggle and a little hand squeezing her nose. She opened her eyes to see Emily's smiling face two inches from her own.

"Morning, baby girl," she said, returning the smile. She reached over to tuck a strand of red hair behind Emily's ear. For a moment after she opened her eyes and looked into Emily's sweet face, all was well. There were no nightmares, no waves of sadness or nausea, no horrible memories. It took only an instant, though, for the serenity to be snuffed out and reality to settle in. Josie steeled herself for another day inside her emotional fortress.

On the other side of Emily, Rose stretched and yawned. "Mommy?"

"Yes, Rosie?"

"This is the best bed I've ever been in. It's huge!" Rose sat up and then flopped back down, flailing her arms and legs.

"It is, isn't it? Did you girls get a good sleep? Are you hungry?" The good smells of coffee and bacon wafted up into the bedroom. She sat up and rubbed her eyes. Once she and the girls were dressed, Josie led them downstairs to the kitchen. Plates of bacon and but-tered toast and a pitcher of orange juice were laid out on a small breakfast table, and Ivy stood at the stove cracking eggs into a bowl.

It was the first time in years that Josie had gotten a good look at her aunt in the daylight. Ivy was six years older and quite a bit heavier than Josie's mother had been. She was wearing faded flared jeans and a tie-dyed shirt with a matching headband. Her dark hair was shoulder-length and streaked with gray. When Ivy turned to greet them, Josie had a strange feeling of déjà vu. Although her aunt's facial features were different from her mother's, the smile was very much the same.

"Good morrow to you, fair ladies," Ivy said. "I've got paper plates in the cupboard there," she said, gesturing with her chin as she whisked the eggs, "and there's silverware and cups already set out on the counter. Come make yourselves at home."

"What's a morrow?" Rose asked. She stared up at Ivy with large round eyes.

"It's an old-fashioned word that means 'morning,'" her aunt replied. "It can also mean a new day or time ahead." Ivy paused to meet Josie's gaze and give a reassuring wink. "Did you all sleep okay? The insulation up there's not the best. It can get nippy in the winter."

"Yes, it was very warm and comfortable. Thank you." She felt awkward, standing in a strange kitchen with her children, having breakfast cooked for her by someone she barely knew. It was a relief that Ivy was so welcoming and easygoing.

"Thank you for the big bed," Rose said, while Josie smiled and Ivy chuckled with delight.

"You're welcome," Ivy said. She poured the eggs into the hot frying pan, and the butter sizzled. "You girls and your mom will probably be here with me a while, so I'm glad you like it up there. It's a nice big space, not like this little one-butt kitchen."

Josie raised her eyebrows. "A one-butt kitchen?"

"Oh," Ivy said, "that's just what I call a kitchen so small there's only enough room for one person to be working in it. More than that and you'll have butts bumping into each other. Do you girls like scrambled eggs?"

Rose nodded, and Emily yelled, "Eggs!"

After breakfast, Ivy showed them around the house. "I have a garden out back, but you can't see it on account of the snow." She moved from the kitchen into the next room. "And this used to be a dining room, but I made it my sitting room so I could use the front part of the house for the store. I never needed much space."

Josie glanced around. There was a disorganized desk against one wall. On the other side, a mismatched sofa and armchair faced an RCA television set. A miniature Christmas tree stood on an end table next to the sofa.

"I don't really watch television," Ivy said, "but the set works fine. You're welcome to use it anytime."

"Mommy," Rose said, tugging at Josie's hand. "Can we watch *Sesame Street?*"

"Sure," Josie replied. "And Mister Rogers, too."

After they had passed by the doors to Ivy's bedroom and bathroom, Ivy unlocked a heavy door separating the sitting room from the rest of the house.

"This leads into the store. Go ahead in."

Josie shepherded her girls through the door and gasped. The front room of the house was the largest, other than the attic, and every inch of space was occupied by books. Tall bookshelves lined the walls. There were stacks of books on the very tops of the shelves and in piles all over the floor.

She looked nervously at the books crammed into the shelves, thinking how so much paper in such a small place surely posed a fire hazard. She wondered if Ivy kept a fire extinguisher within easy reach.

The room smelled like warm paper and ink mixed with a faint aroma of breakfast that drifted in from Ivy's kitchen. Interspersed among the books were several small tables and squashy-looking chairs in various colors. A small writing desk and chair were shoved into one corner, and the center of the room was covered by a multicolored, well-worn throw rug that read WELCOME TO THE BOOK-STOP.

Ivy followed Josie's gaze down to the rug. "I had that made special when I first opened this place," she said, and then stooped down to speak to Rose and Emily. "Do you two like books? Look over there." Ivy pointed to the far corner of the room demarcated by small, colorful beanbags, where a sign on the wall read KIDS' CORNER. "There's a big stack of 'em just for you."

Josie held her breath, fearing that perhaps the books would remind Rose of bedtime with Tony and upset her. Her eyes welled up as she remembered how Tony used to make a big deal out of bedtime with the girls, even on nights when he had to bring extra work home to finish after he tucked them in.

"Time to pick your books," he used to say in a booming voice that sent Rose and Emily scurrying to their little bookshelf. He would settle himself on Rose's bed, and after jostling for positions on his lap the girls would sit, transfixed, while he read.

For Rose in particular, those few minutes with her father were a highlight of her day. Josie had been amused and, at the same time, a little hurt when her older daughter told her one evening, "Hurry, Mommy, say good night and go downstairs so Daddy can read!" The playfully triumphant gleam in Tony's eyes hadn't helped.

After she and the girls had been released from the hospital, they had stayed in a hotel paid for by the Red Cross. Josie had tried to maintain some sense of normalcy by buying some new books and reading to the girls at bedtime, but she hadn't made it past the first few pages before Rose dissolved into tears, asking for her father. Now, instead of reading, Josie crawled under the covers with Rose and cuddled with her until she fell asleep.

In the front room of The Bookstop, Josie was relieved when Rose squealed with delight and ran toward the children's area. Emily toddled along after her. *Maybe being in Ivy's little store will help them heal,* she thought, as the girls plopped down on the rug and began going through the colorful picture books that were piled there.

"There used to be another bedroom up front here," Ivy said, "but I knocked out the wall to expand this room. It's a little more cramped in here during the winter. When the weather's nice, I move some of the books onto the porch." Josie could see the front porch through the windows on either side of the front door. "People seem to like sitting out there and browsing through the new titles, especially in the summer."

"It's lovely," Josie said, "all of this. Your home, the store. They're very inviting and comfortable. I can see why people like to come here."

"It's not easy keeping the place going," Ivy said. "Speaking of which, it's almost opening time. Books aren't the most profitable thing to sell, not by a long shot. And I can't stock everything I'd like to, since I don't have the budget or the space. But I try to cater to the folks who come here, and they come from all over—not just Mill River."

"I expect people appreciate having a bookstore here," Josie said as Ivy went to the writing desk and removed a calculator and a pad of receipts from the top drawer.

"They tell me that all the time," Ivy replied. "I can order pretty much any title, if someone is willing to wait a few days for it, and I buy and sell used books, too. People can bring books they've already read, and if they're in good shape, I'll give them some credit for 'em. Whatever works, you know. That's what I do. I'm not a fancy person, so I don't need much. As long as I can pay my bills, I'm happy."

Their conversation was interrupted by the sound of the porch door opening and closing, followed by a loud knocking. For a moment, Josie was overcome with fear that she and the girls had been followed from New York. She relaxed when Ivy peered out the window and smiled. Her aunt flipped a sign hanging in one of the windows so that OPEN faced out and answered the door. A man in a winter postal uniform and a fur hat stood in the doorway.

"Hey there, Larry," she said. "Whatcha got for me today?"

"Looks like more inventory. You must be stocking up for last-minute shoppers." The mailman picked up the first of several boxes stacked on a hand truck next to him.

"I suppose I am," Ivy said. "Let's set them over here. Maybe I'll get them unpacked before people start showing up."

"Sure thing," Larry said. He hefted three large boxes into the front room of The Bookstop before picking up the last box, which was smaller and lighter than the others. "There might be some mistake with this one," he said as he examined the shipping label. "It's an Express Mail package with your address, but it's . . ." His voice tapered off, and an odd expression came over his face. He cleared his throat. "It's addressed to a Mrs. Josie DiSanti."

"That's me," Josie said quietly.

"Oh, how rude of me," Ivy said, looping her arm through Josie's and pulling her forward. "Larry, this is Josie, my niece. Josie, meet Larry Endicott, the nicest mailman in Mill River."

"The *only* mailman in Mill River, since the rest of 'em are ladies. The ones who cover the delivery routes, anyway." Larry smiled at Josie. "It's nice to meet you."

"Likewise."

"Josie and her girls over there will be staying with me a while," Ivy said. "So you might see some more things addressed to her."

"Ah. Well, here you are, then," Larry said, handing Josie the package. "I hope you like our little town. I've got to get going. The truck's really loaded today. Holiday rush. See you Monday!"

"See ya, Larry," Ivy said. "Keep warm!" She closed the door and turned to Josie. "That was weird, don't you think? Sort of a hasty exit? He was acting so awkward there in the end, and—"

As she clutched the package she had been handed, Josie didn't register her aunt's voice stopping mid-sentence. She stood staring at the box in her white-knuckled hands.

"Josie, what is it?" Ivy asked. Her aunt walked over to her and squinted to read the package. "Oh," was all she said.

"I can't . . . can't deal with this . . . not now. Not until after the girls are in bed," Josie choked out. She glanced at Rose and Emily in the Kids' Corner. They were blissfully unaware of her distress.

"Here," Ivy said in a low voice, and she gently pried the box from Josie's grasp. "I'll put this away until later. It's definitely not something the girls should see."

CHAPTER 3

W HEN HE REACHED JOSIE'S OFFICE, FATHER O'BRIEN SAW that Rose and her family were already seated on the long sofa against the wall. Emily had backed herself into a corner of the room, and Ivy sat at Josie's desk holding a folded piece of paper in her hands. Father O'Brien was surprised to see that Jim Gasaway, a local attorney and an old friend, was in the room as well.

"Jim, it's good to see you," he said. "You must've slipped past me earlier. I didn't see you come in."

"What in the hell is going on, Aunt Ivy?" Rose demanded. She glared at Ivy with her arms tightly crossed.

"Would you mind closing the door, Father?" Ivy asked. After he had done so, she straightened up in her chair and looked at Josie's daughters. "I know neither of you wants to be here for any longer than is necessary, so I'll get through this as quickly as I can.

"You both know that Mr. Gasaway is handling your mom's affairs. That said, Josie left this letter with me to read to you girls in case anything happened to her. Jim has a notarized copy of it, so he knows the details."

"She wrote the letter earlier this year," Jim added quietly.

"Please, just read it," Emily said in a small, tired voice.

Ivy unfolded the paper in her hands, cleared her throat, and began.

To my girls, Rose and Emily,

If you are hearing these words, it is because I have passed on. I trust Mr. Gasaway and your aunt Ivy will handle my memorial service as I requested. Also, I hope that you are not burdened with grief at my passing. I'll always be with you, and the only thing I've ever wanted for you both was happiness.

In fact, your happiness, or lack of it, is my simple reason for writing this letter. You girls were my life. I worried about you and loved you from the time you were born. If your estrangement from each other was not the cause of my death, I daresay that it must have been at least a contributing factor. Now that I'm gone, you have no immediate family left but Aunt Ivy and each other.

I know what happened was horribly painful for you both, but I also know that time can heal even the most serious grievances. For years, I asked you, begged you, to try talking, therapy, anything to repair your relationship, but you refused. So, I'm taking matters into my own hands, and from the grave, no less.

From the time we moved to Mill River, we lived frugally. I worked as hard as I could to provide for you and save what little was left. Over time, those savings multiplied, and getting into the real estate business helped me learn how to invest and grow my money. You might not have known it until now, but each of you girls stands to inherit a substantial amount from my estate.

There is a catch, however.

You know that I own several rental properties. Two of them are across the street from my house and Ivy's place. You'll remember those houses, I'm sure. One was owned by the John-

son family, and the other by the Weiders. You girls used to go over and play on their kids' tire swing and trampoline. The houses are small and simple, but they're clean, comfortable, and nicely furnished.

Of course, I can't predict when during the year you'll be reading this letter, but I expect each of you to move into one of the houses no later than two months after you do. Mr. Gasaway can meet with you to choose a move-in date. You can work out between yourselves who gets which house, or Mr. Gasaway can flip a coin, if you can't manage even that.

Inside each house or on each property, I've left a clue for each of you to find. The clues are two different objects. One will reveal the location of the key to my safe-deposit box, and the other is something that will help you obtain it. You'll have to cooperate to find the clues and use them to locate the key—which is, in fact, the key to my treasure, and to each of you sharing in it. (I admit that this plan sounds childish, but perhaps that's appropriate, given that I am trying to remind you of the bond you once shared.)

I put in my safe-deposit box a copy of my last will and testament, which directs that my estate be divided equally between you. You will have two months to work together to find it. In short, you'll be neighbors. You'll also be partners in a sort of treasure hunt. It may not be pleasant or easy for you, but it is my great hope that you'll uncover good memories to help take away the bad. Ideally, you'll come out of this experience on speaking terms, and maybe even as real sisters again.

If you both do not follow my instructions and present Mr. Gasaway with the key to my safe-deposit box by the two-month deadline, or if you both attempt to challenge my wishes in court, I have directed him to execute the second *version of my will, which distributes my estate in its entirety among a variety of worthy charities. If only one of you refuses to follow my instructions or attempts to challenge my wishes in court, Mr. Gasaway will execute the third version, which leaves my estate in its entirety to the other sister.*

I know what I'm asking of you. You will have to uproot yourselves and move back to Mill River, at least temporarily. I also know you should both be able to manage this. Rose, dear, you've told me many times that Sheldon's income alleviates the need for you to work, so there should be no job preventing you from coming. And Emily, honey, you've always been self-employed, and you're good at so many things. I know you'll have no problem finding a temporary job somewhere nearby.

When it comes down to it, girls, I can't force you to do this. I also know that, even if you do as I ask, the end result might not be the reconciliation for which I fervently hope. But I pray that you two will spend some time together and see reason, or at least come to understand what I'm trying to do for you. You might think I was a foolish old woman, but know that there isn't anything I wouldn't do for you. I've loved you both so much from the moments you were born. Even now, with what I've arranged, I have only your best interests at heart.

Your loving mother,
Josephine Collard DiSanti

For a long moment, no one spoke.

"This is complete CRAP!" Rose screeched, before lowering her voice to a hiss. "There is *no way* that we'll go along with this— this *little treasure hunt* or whatever the hell Mom called it."

Emily looked at Jim Gasaway. "Can she . . . could she really insist on this?"

"Yes, ma'am," Jim replied. "I will say that your mom's is one of the more unusual estates I've seen, since she's effectively put everything in a holding pattern for now, but it's all legal and binding. I'm confident that it would stand up in court, if it comes to that," he added, looking pointedly at Rose.

"Girls, you should know that Jim's the best lawyer around, and he's an expert in handling complex trusts and estates," Father O'Brien said quietly.

"So, we're just supposed to drop everything in our lives and move up here to *look for a key*?" Emily said. "I can't believe Mom would do this to us."

"Maybe she was losing it," Rose agreed. "And what about her precious brokerage? Who'll be running it until her estate is finally settled?"

"I'll be monitoring the books, and there's an associate broker on her staff who has the authority to approve transactions," Jim said. "Your mom was pretty careful to have contingency plans in place."

Sheldon sat up straight and turned to Rose. "Look, I think this is a total crock, too," he said in a low, pleading voice. "But, we've got two months. We can look into this further, get another legal opinion, once we get home. Let's just do what we need to do, and then we can get out of here."

"I think Sheldon's approach is reasonable," Ivy said. "Jim, maybe we should just decide on a move-in date, give each of them a set of keys to a house, and let them go for now. They can think it over for a while and still have plenty of time to make arrangements once they come around."

"Fat chance," Rose snapped.

"You will," Ivy said with a sweet smile.

Emily rolled her eyes and turned to Jim. "Whatever," she said. "Doesn't matter to me which house I get."

"WE should get the bigger house," Rose said. "We're a family. She's just one person."

Jim Gasaway fished around in his pants pocket and removed two sets of house keys and a quarter. "The houses aren't all that different in size," he said. "But, it's probably best that we consult Mr. Washington. Why don't we let Alex call it? Would that be all right?"

"Could I?" Alex asked with a hopeful grin. He looked at each of his parents. Rose said nothing, but Sheldon bent to whisper something in his ear. Emily shrugged her shoulders.

"Okay, then, Alex," Jim said, "heads or tails. On the count of three—ready? One, two, three!" He tossed the coin up high, almost to the ceiling.

"Heads!" Alex yelled, and the room was silent except for the sound of the coin landing on the wood floor.

"Looks like it's tails," Jim said as he peered down at the quarter, and Father O'Brien saw Alex frown and shrink back against the sofa. "Emily, which house do you want?"

"I suppose I'll take whichever one is *bigger*," she said, smiling. She reached out her hand for the keys that Jim held out to her.

Rose jumped quickly to her feet. "You get the keys, Sheldon," she said. "I'm going to gather up our things in the living room." Rose rushed out of the office.

"Well, that went better than I expected," Ivy muttered to herself.

"As for your arrival," Jim said to Emily, "I assume the more time the better, for both of you. Today's May fourth. Why don't we make it easy and just say you and Rose will both be back here on the first of July?"

Emily stood with one arm across her middle as she stared at

the small set of house keys in her hand. "Whatever. I will try to do what Mom asked," she said in her a sad voice, "but honestly, I don't think it will make any difference. There are some things that just can't be fixed, and with what happened between Rose and me . . ."

Sheldon sighed and shrugged. "July first." He gently squeezed Alex around the shoulders before accepting the keys that Jim offered. "We should be going," he said. "We've got a long drive ahead of us, but I'm sure we'll be consulting our attorney—"

There was a sudden loud crash somewhere outside the office, followed by Rose shrieking, "No, no, oh my God, Mom!"

"Oh, dear," said Father O'Brien. He opened the door quickly, and the four of them hurried out of the office toward the sound of the commotion.

The tidy, solemn living room had been transformed. At one end, Ruth Fitzgerald and the few remaining people who had come to pay their respects stood in a group. At the other end of the room, the small table holding Josie's memorial display was lying on its side. Covered in a mixture of ashes, broken glass, and a greenish liquid were the opened bronze urn, the photographs of Josie, several floral arrangements, and Daisy Delaine.

"Miss Rose, I'm so sorry, Miss Rose, I was only trying to give you a jar of my grief potion," Daisy stammered, trying to get to her feet.

"Oh, my God," Rose said again. She blinked and stumbled backwards. The front of her black dress was now covered in gray powder, and her stiletto heels made sharp cracking noises as they crunched down on bits of glass. She brushed at her face frantically and glared at Daisy. "How did you . . . do you realize what you've done?"

"Oh, Miss Rose, I lost my balance and fell against the table," Daisy tried to explain. The stout little woman was on her hands and knees now. She gasped when she pushed herself into a kneeling position and looked down to see a piece of glass protruding from the palm of her right hand.

"You clumsy *idiot!*" Rose screamed down at Daisy. "I swear, Ivy," she continued, whirling around. "Couldn't you have gotten an urn with a screw-top? Or at least seen that whatever cheap container this is was properly sealed?"

"But Miss Rose, I never would've . . . I didn't mean to do it. I'm so sorry, Miss Rose," Daisy cried, cradling her hand. Tears began leaving darkened streaks down each side of Daisy's ash-coated face.

Father O'Brien and Jim hurried toward Daisy, stepping gingerly through the mess until each of them could grab one of her arms. Together, they eased her to her feet and helped her over to Ruth.

"Daisy, dear, come with me. Let's go get a better look at that cut," Ruth said, putting her arm around her. "Are you hurt anywhere else?" Jim kept his hold on Daisy's other arm and walked with them to the kitchen.

"Rose," Ivy said, "I know you're upset, but it was an accident. There are fresh towels in the bathroom. You can wash up while I find something clean for you to wear." She approached Rose and reached out to touch her elbow, but Rose jumped away.

"I don't need your help," Rose said. "Move it, Sheldon!" She marched to the front door, threw it open, and walked out.

"I am so sorry about that . . . about everything," Sheldon said to Ivy. "You know how worked up Rose can get. She's been upset for days, and today was especially tough. We had better get out there, but please let . . . Daisy? Please tell her, from me . . . from us, actually . . . that accidents happen, and there is nothing to forgive." After a final glance around at the mess in the living room, he put his hand on Alex's head and gently steered him out the front door.

"I'm sorry, Aunt Ivy." Emily slipped an arm around Ivy's shoulders. "I know you went through a lot of trouble to try to make this nice for Mom. To do what she wanted." Emily paused a moment, and her eyes filled with tears as she looked down at the ruined ashes. "I don't have to leave for a few hours. I'll clean this up."

"Thanks, kid," Ivy said, and Emily left in search of cleaning supplies. Ivy looked at Father O'Brien and shook her head. "What a disaster."

Father O'Brien nodded. "And poor Daisy, bless her soul, she never meant any harm. She's probably beside herself, and she may need to see a doctor for her hand."

"She's still in the kitchen with Ruth," Ivy said, as Emily returned lugging a bucket of cleaners and paper towels, along with Josie's old Kirby vacuum. "Would you check on her? Em and I can tackle this mess."

"Of course," he said. Before he left, Emily pulled the table back into an upright position and tenderly picked up the bronze urn and its lid.

"I didn't pick out that urn," Ivy said bitterly to her great-niece. "It's one your mom chose for herself, years ago, when she decided it was time to get her affairs in order."

"It's more like a vase. It doesn't have a threaded top like it should, but it's still beautiful. Let's try to salvage what we can of her ashes. That way, we could still use it, like she wanted," Emily said. "And, don't let Rose get to you. I know she can say horrible things, but trust me . . . what comes out of her mouth isn't worth a damn thing."

CHAPTER 4

1983

WHILE IVY GREETED CUSTOMERS AND DID HER BEST TO reduce her holiday inventory, Josie spent the remainder of the day in a haze of misery. She held herself together until Rose and Emily were asleep in the attic bedroom. Quietly, she came downstairs and found Ivy settled into the recliner in the living room.

Ivy looked up from the book she was reading. "They fell out okay?"

"Yes." Josie sank into the sofa across from her. "I think I'd like to open the package now."

Ivy nodded and left the sitting room. She returned a moment later with the box that the mailman had delivered for Josie earlier in the day. "I'll be in my room, if you need me," she said quietly.

When her aunt was gone, Josie looked down at the package. With a trembling finger, she traced the words on the shipping label—PACKAGE CONTAINS CREMATED REMAINS. PLEASE HANDLE WITH CARE AND RESPECT. The return address was for a funeral home in the Bronx.

She stood up and took the package into the kitchen to cut through the tape. The cardboard shipping container held a sealed envelope and a rectangular metal box, which she lifted onto the table. Josie opened the envelope and unfolded the paper it held, but she saw only "Certificate of Cremation" and "Anthony Paolo

DiSanti" before her eyes filled with tears and the paper slipped from her fingers.

Josie couldn't breathe. She found her wool coat on the rack by the side door, stumbled outside, and started to walk.

The sidewalk was covered with a dusting of new snow, and Josie's shoes were the first to leave footprints. She pulled up her hood and occasionally used the sleeve of her coat to wipe her face. Two blocks ahead, at the intersection with Main Street, the glimmer of Christmas lights caught her attention.

When she arrived at the intersection, the white town hall building was on her left. To her right, the small row of shops she remembered seeing the night before ran along one side of the street. Across from them, set back off the road, was St. John's. It was after eight o'clock, and the shops along Main Street were long closed, but she thought she saw a few lights on inside the little stone church. Emotionally exhausted, her face numb from the frigid air, Josie crossed the street and walked up the steps of the church to the front door. To her surprise, it was open.

Josie entered cautiously, easing the door closed behind her and enjoying the warmth that met her cold face. She was in a small, dark foyer. Ahead of her were two large double doors that led into the sanctuary. She could see that the altar was well lit, but the light faded gradually so that the pews in the row closest to the door were almost completely shrouded in darkness. Josie slid into one of them and sat down.

She was grateful to be alone in this quiet, warm, dark place. Time was irrelevant. She wanted to somehow slip into the darkness and escape her grief, but when she closed her eyes, she was haunted by the words "cremated remains." As she slumped forward, tears dripped onto her lap. Josie didn't hear how her gasps and sobs echoed slightly in the sanctuary. She focused only on trying to survive the seemingly endless torrent of agony that poured out of her.

Josie didn't know how long she had been sitting there crying when she heard the pew creak under the weight of another person. She turned to see a priest seated next to her.

"I didn't mean to startle you," he said quietly. "I was just getting things ready for tomorrow's mass when I heard you. I wanted to see if I could be of any assistance. My name is Michael O'Brien. I'm the pastor here."

"Oh, I'm sorry, Father, I didn't . . . I mean, you're probably closed. I was just out walking and got cold," Josie stammered. She stood up abruptly and wiped her eyes.

"If I'm here, the front door is always open, no matter the time," Father O'Brien said. "I can see you're upset. Perhaps you were meant to find my open door."

Josie glanced down at Father O'Brien. He was tall and lanky with a receding hairline and looked to be older than Ivy. Although she had made up her mind to head back to Ivy's, there was something about this priest that kept her from leaving. He seemed to radiate compassion. Josie hesitated only a moment longer before she lowered herself back down into the pew.

"I'm not sure why I came in here," Josie whispered. "I haven't been in a church in . . . well, I can't remember the last time."

Father O'Brien smiled. "Everyone is welcome here," he said simply.

Something about his voice, his presence, was so comforting. Josie looked at her hands clasped in her lap. "My husband died last week," she whispered, "in a fire. We . . . I . . . have two little girls, and the fire took almost everything we had, so I came here, to Mill River, to stay with my aunt." Josie took a deep breath. "I'm so afraid, Father. I'm lost without him. I feel like I'm sinking lower and lower. And my aunt . . . the one we're staying with . . . I don't even know her. She's all the family I have left. She's been so welcoming, but I still feel like a horrible burden to her, being such a wreck and bringing my kids to live in her house. I don't know where to go from here. I have to take care of my girls, and I don't know how I'm going to be able to do that. I feel like I'm drowning." It was as if every thought that had tortured Josie since Tony's death gushed out along with her tears.

"I'm so sorry, my child," Father O'Brien said. "Could I . . . could I ask your name?"

"I'm Josie."

"Josie." Father O'Brien paused a moment, perhaps to collect his thoughts. "I know you're hurting right now. The way you're feeling is very normal after the loss of a spouse. You're still in the earliest stages of the grieving process, and feeling overwhelmed and afraid is very much a part of that."

Josie bit down on her lip, trying to keep some semblance of composure.

"It's always harder for people who have lost someone during the holidays, too," Father O'Brien continued. "I'm so glad you came here tonight. It's important now that you have people around you to support you. You say you're staying with an aunt here in town?"

"Yes, my aunt Ivy. She runs a little bookstore a few streets over."

"Ivy Collard is your aunt?"

Josie nodded.

"I've known her for years," Father O'Brien said, smiling. "She's . . . what is the word I want . . . feisty? Sassy? But, you'll not find a more caring, giving person."

"She seems that way. Ivy is my mother's older sister, but she and my mom never got along. Before yesterday, I hadn't seen her since my mother's funeral, and I've never really spent any time at all with her. Until now."

"You needn't worry about being a burden to her. I know Ivy well enough to know that she would never feel burdened by helping you and your girls, especially at a time like this. You should try to open up and talk to her. Give her a chance to be there for you."

Josie thought about those reassuring words. Perhaps this kindly priest could answer a question she had asked herself what seemed like a million times during the past several days. "Father, how long will it take until I can get through a day without falling apart? Until I can think about my husband without feeling as if my heart will explode?"

"It's different for everybody," Father O'Brien said, "and impossible to know. But, I can tell you that time will ultimately help ease the hurt. It may not take it away completely, but one day, you'll feel strong again. You'll be able to remember all the wonderful things about your husband and feel happy to have created those memories with him." He hesitated for a moment, smiling a little to himself. "Part of Psalm 34, which is one of my favorites, says 'the Lord is close to the brokenhearted, and saves those who are crushed in spirit.' I truly believe that, Josie. And I think that maybe in this fragile time, you and your daughters ended up in Mill River for a reason. Your wonderful aunt is here. The town's full of kind and loving people. It's a good place for children to grow up. And the natural beauty of the area! In the fall, I sometimes think that the good Lord takes a paintbrush and colors the trees one by one." He placed a hand lightly on her shoulder. "I've been the parish priest here in Mill River since I was a young man. I know the town very well. As hard as it is right now, you've come to a place where you *will* heal. It will take time, but you're not alone. Ivy will be there for you, and so will I, anytime you need me."

Josie sat very still, taking in Father O'Brien's words. "Thank you, Father," she finally said, and she rose, a bit unsteadily, to her feet. "I should get back. I left after my girls were asleep for the night. Ivy's there, but they don't know her very well yet. If they wake up and I'm gone . . ."

"Of course," Father O'Brien said. He stood up as well and walked the few steps to the front door with her. "You'll be in my prayers."

"Thank you again, Father," Josie said. She managed a small smile as she pulled her hood up over her head and slipped outside.

Back at The Bookstop, Josie let herself in through the side door and hung up her coat. She retrieved the certificate of cremation from the floor where she'd dropped it and lowered herself onto a chair at the breakfast table. Her hand was unsteady as she ran it over the box of Tony's ashes. Carefully, she slid the box from the table and hugged it against her chest.

"Josie?" Ivy's hushed voice carried into the kitchen.

"In here," Josie said.

Ivy appeared in her bathrobe in the doorway to the kitchen with a look of pity on her face. "I was a little worried when I realized you'd left," she said, coming to sit in the chair next to Josie. "I figured you needed some air, maybe some time to think."

Josie opened her mouth to say something, but she was suddenly overcome. Unable to stifle her sobs, she tucked her chin down until it rested on the top of the box in her arms.

"Oh, honey," Ivy said, as she moved closer. Josie leaned into her aunt's arms as Ivy held her, stroking her hair, rocking slightly, in much the same way as Josie had comforted her daughters so many times. "I know this was a hard day for you," she said after a few minutes. "You're gonna have lots of hard days, but you're gonna get through this. And I promise I'll be there to help you every step of the way."

Her aunt's words and the thought of what Father O'Brien had said about Ivy only made Josie cry harder. When she was finally able to speak, she looked at her aunt through her blurry eyes. "I don't know what to do, how to go forward," she whispered. "Honestly, I feel like it's such an imposition on you, having the girls and me here. We're pretty much strangers to you. And I keep worrying about raising the girls on my own, being able to provide for them. I don't know how I'm going to do it without Tony. Every time I think of him . . . I can't think about him. It hurts too much."

"Look here," Ivy said. "First, we may not know each other, which is a damn shame, but it's something we're gonna change. And you're still my family. Right now, there's nowhere else you and the girls belong except here with me. You're no burden. Second, did you and Tony have anything saved? Did he have life insurance?"

Josie sniffed and nodded. "The insurance check is being processed," she whispered. "And we were trying to save enough for a down payment on a house."

"All right, then," Ivy continued. "You don't have to worry about working right now. If you're here with me, you won't have much in the way of expenses. You should be able to get by on what you have for quite a while. Plus, your girls are so little, and they're going through a lot, too. They'll need you around 'em for the time being. We'll figure out what you can do for work once you're ready. But right now, you're not. Right now, you're raw and grieving, and you've got to give yourself time to heal."

Josie was starting to feel a bit calmer. At least she was no longer breathing in ragged gasps.

"And the last thing," Ivy said, in a quieter tone, "is that you *have* to think about Tony. Talk about him, too. It'll hurt something fierce, but you have to allow yourself to cry, to feel. You can't keep it all bottled up and expect the sadness to go away. It won't. If you keep it inside, it'll eat away at you until there's nothing left."

"Rose and Emily hate seeing me cry," Josie began, but Ivy was already shaking her head.

"With children, you've got to tell them the truth in terms that they can understand. Teach them that crying's natural, and okay.

Tell them you miss their daddy and you feel sad, and crying helps you feel better. In time, you'll cry less and they'll understand why you do when you do. It's just a part of life. It's how you'll get through this, for yourself and for the girls."

Josie could feel the memories and the grief swelling behind the emotional barrier she was maintaining, and deep down, she knew her aunt was right. The empathy and emotional engagement of her aunt were surprising to Josie because her own mother had had little of either. When Josie was growing up, her mother's answer to almost every difficult situation had been to pour herself another drink and retreat to her bedroom. As she listened to Ivy, Josie found herself marveling that someone could be so closely related to her mother and yet so different.

"You know, you're very good at sorting things out," Josie told her. "Mom could never make sense of difficult situations. She always left that to me. I guess I learned after a while how to get *her* out of trouble, but I've never had to do that for myself."

"Abby was a good person underneath, but her drinking kept her from doing a lot of things," Ivy said. "Kept her from coming home to visit, from keeping a good job and being the kind of mother you should've had. And that kept me from getting to know you while you were growing up."

"Well, as you say, we've got the chance now," Josie said. She used her sleeve to dry her eyes. "We've got a lot of catching up to do."

CHAPTER 5

At the hotel back in Rutland, a shower and a fresh change of clothing did little to help Rose's mood. Two martinis in rapid succession at dinner and a Kahlúa mudslide for dessert helped take the edge off, but even as Rose and her family resumed the drive back to Manhattan, she was still fuming.

As usual, Sheldon was behind the wheel, and Alex was in the backseat with his nose stuck in a book.

"Aren't you going to say anything?" Rose asked her husband. "You've been staring straight ahead for hours."

"What do you want me to say?" He didn't turn his head or meet her gaze, which only infuriated her further.

"Something. Anything. How about, 'Gee, it really sucks, what your mom decided to pull. It's a good thing we don't need her inheritance. We can just tell her to go to hell, if she isn't already there.'"

"Rose," Sheldon sighed. "I get that you're sad about your mom's death, and it's coming across as anger. You're pissed about the whole scheme she's concocted. And then the whole mess with the ashes. It was a bad day." He paused, seeming to consider his next words carefully. "The thing is, I don't think I can say what you'd like me to . . . because I don't agree with it."

Rose cackled. "Surely, you're not serious! Oh, that's rich, Sheldon, truly." She waited for his reaction, but he sat very still in the driver's seat, moving only to steer the car through the curves of the highway. Rose felt a realization creeping into her alcohol-numbed mind, the kind of realization with life-changing implications.

"Sheldon," Rose said, sitting further up in her seat, "what do you mean, you 'don't agree with it'?"

"If we're going to be completely honest here, we do need that inheritance. We need it very badly."

"What?" Rose felt her mouth open, but she was too shocked to figure out how to close it or what else to say.

"It's been almost three years since the bank went under. We're well into our savings. My unemployment ran out a long time ago. The occasional consulting gig isn't enough to pay for everything. Our mortgage is killing us, and we can't unload the condo because it's underwater. Our investments have come back some, but not enough to make up the losses, and a huge percentage of what we had disappeared with the company. I've cashed out some of what I can because the bills keep coming—the nanny, the housekeeper, the credit cards, school fees." Sheldon rattled off these things as if they had been circling through his mind. "There are ten, twenty guys like me out there for every open position, and no one will touch me once they learn where I worked and how high up the ladder I was. We're just about out of options."

"Why didn't you tell me before now? Didn't you think it's something I should know?"

"You've never taken much of an interest in our finances, and I wasn't sure you wanted to hear it. And," Sheldon added, more quietly, "I kept thinking that things would get better soon."

Rose struggled to process this information. "What's left of the savings?"

"Enough to cover things for another few months, maybe six if we cut out all the extras. Long enough for you to go up to Mill River for the summer and do whatever you need to do to get your share of your mom's estate."

"It can't be that bad, Sheldon."

"It is."

Rose clenched her teeth. She was starting to feel a little nauseous, imagining herself living in a tiny old house surrounded by good ol' New England country folk. Escaping that dump of a town was the main reason she had moved to New York City. "And if I go? What will you and Alex be doing?"

"I'll keep looking for work and taking consulting gigs as they come. Alex will have to go to Vermont with you. We can't afford to send him to camp or keep Clara on for the summer. If I'm working, even sporadically, you'll need to take care of him. Which means," Sheldon continued after dropping his voice to a stern whisper, "that you're going to have to lay off the booze."

"It's all right, Mom," Alex said. "I won't be any trouble. I'm almost ten. I can practically take care of myself."

Hearing her son's voice softened Rose. She turned around and looked at Alex. He smiled hopefully. She couldn't help but smile a little in return before the scowl crept back onto her face. Rose faced the front again and sighed. Leaning back against her seat, she tried to ignore her throbbing headache and the inevitably ugly summer ahead of her.

THE LONG JOURNEY BACK TO CALIFORNIA FROM VERMONT reminded Emily just how much she hated being stuck in one place. She was trapped in the middle seat on the six-hour flight from Boston to San Francisco. To her left, a man slept with his head against the window. The poor fellow's snoring would grow louder and louder until he snorted and grunted himself awake to start the cycle over again.

To her right, a tiny woman with braided gray hair and half-moon spectacles knitted at a feverish pace. The clicking of her needles combined with the snoring was almost enough to drive Emily mad.

While she sat still with her eyes closed, Emily thought about the arrangements she would have to make. Her current job was scheduled to be completed in late May or early June, which was ideal timing. Since her mother's plan was sheer lunacy, there was no telling what would happen or how long she might be living in Mill River. She would drive, not fly, back to Vermont, in late June. *In fact,* Emily thought, *maybe I should just pack up and take everything.* If she ditched the few pieces of furniture she owned, she could fit all of her other stuff into her car. She liked not being tied down or burdened by material possessions. She could pick up and move on her own anytime she wanted.

Although she loathed the idea of living next door to Rose, she knew her sister would be far unhappier in Mill River than she. If Rose acquiesced to their mother's wishes, there was no way she would pass up the opportunity to watch Rose leave her fancy life in the city to fester and squirm in "Hicksville," her sister's name for Mill River.

Emily recognized that schadenfreude was not the primary reason she was willing to go along with their mother's plan. Her first reason for returning would be to honor their mother's wishes, to show respect and gratitude for all she had done. She would make a good-faith effort to do as her mother requested regardless of how unpleasant it might be for her personally.

Secondly, Emily was tired of living like a ghost. Since the horrible accident years ago, she'd drifted from one city and failed relationship to the next. She'd gone first to Pittsburgh, then Chicago. She'd left the Windy City for San Francisco, where she'd lived since. She liked the city and its myriad neighborhoods. The weather was good there—never too hot or too cold. There was plenty of work for someone with her skills. Besides, save a move to

Hawaii or Alaska, she had run out of country. She was at the edge, as far west as she could go.

Still, she was slowly coming to the realization that she no longer wanted to be alone. Instead of disappearing anonymously into city crowds, she wanted to *live* someplace and not merely exist as an unknown among the masses. After years of dating losers and living thousands of miles from the few people she was close to, she craved real companionship. She needed *connections* again—to people, to a smaller, familiar place where she wouldn't feel lost.

If that place was Mill River, with all its good and also painful memories, she would have to accept it.

Perhaps her mother had known what she was doing.

Perhaps not.

Thinking about her summer plans temporarily diverted Emily's focus from her mother's death. The reality circled back around fast, bringing with it a deep sadness. She missed her mother terribly. She even missed the nagging and the lectures about her situation with Rose, and the phone ringing at four in the morning when her mother used to call forgetting the time difference. What she wouldn't give to receive one of those phone calls again.

The man sleeping beside her snorted loudly and shifted in his seat. Emily couldn't see his face completely, but his hair color and profile reminded her a little of Sam Kiper, a guy she'd dated years ago, in Pittsburgh. Sam had been her first relationship after the accident, and in the beginning, she had had high hopes. Gradually, though, certain things about him began to give her pause. Sam had no problem holding a job as a mid-level manager, but he was too lazy to care about advancing further. His sense of humor was dry with a mean streak. He didn't care much for kids or animals. And nothing she did infused any energy or warmth into his personality.

After Sam, there'd been Riley Woodson in Chicago. He was a young trader in the Mercantile Exchange, full of frenetic energy and the ambition that Sam had lacked. Riley wasn't handy at all, though. He'd confessed to her when she first came to work in his Lincoln Park row home that he'd never so much as touched a hammer. As much as he'd enjoyed her unclothed appearance, he'd frowned every time she donned her work overalls and tool belt.

In San Francisco, she'd dated casually, but nothing serious had materialized. Maybe she was too afraid to get deeply involved again. Maybe she was tired of trying to remedy the faults of the men she dated, to tweak and mold them into her perfect match.

That perfect match didn't exist anymore.

She had been lonely a long time. Through the years, her mother had always been there, encouraging her, listening, loving. Her mother was the one person who truly understood the kind of loss the accident had caused her and how difficult it was to try to reassemble the fragments of a shattered life. A few tears escaped from her closed eyes and meandered slowly down her face. The clicking of the knitting needles beside her stopped. She opened her eyes to find the woman with the braid watching her with a concerned expression.

"I know it's none of my business," the woman said, "but, are you all right?"

Emily wiped the tears from her cheeks and nodded. "My mother died a week ago, and I'm on my way home from her wake." She was surprised that her words spilled out so quickly.

"I'm so sorry," the woman said, her expression turning from concern to pity. "It looks like you loved her very much. I have three girls myself, so I know how there's something special between a mother and a daughter. Of course, my kids are close as sisters, too. I'm glad they'll have each other when I'm gone. Do you have any siblings?"

"I have one sister," Emily said. She began to wonder if her mother had somehow managed to plant this woman in the seat next to her.

"Well, at least you have each other, then. That, and time, will make things better," the woman said. Emily managed a half-smile and was thankful when the woman resumed her knitting.

Maybe time will help, Emily thought. Summer would be the beginning of a new stage in her life. She would honor her mother by trying to do as she had asked. It would be wonderful to spend some more time with dear Aunt Ivy. And, if Rose showed up, well, she wasn't sure what would happen—although it would certainly be something to see her Park Avenue–apartment sister living in the old Johnson house.

CHAPTER 6

For Josie, her first week at The Bookstop passed slowly. Each day was a blur of looking after the girls and trying to follow Ivy's advice to not suppress her feelings. Josie realized that she felt a little better if she stayed with her aunt in the front room, helping with customers and listening to Rose and Emily entertaining themselves in the Kids' Corner. It was a taste of normal life, and it provided just enough of a distraction to keep her grief at bay.

She clung to that small bit of normalcy two evenings before Christmas as she stood in the upstairs bathroom getting ready to go out. She'd curled her hair and even put on a little makeup. Lipstick added a touch of color to her pale face, and a bit of concealer under her eyes did wonders to hide the dark circles and puffiness from fitful sleep and frequent crying. It seemed like a long time since she'd taken any special care with her appearance. Tonight, though, Ivy was dead set on taking her and the girls to Mill River's annual holiday pitch-in. Looking at herself, she was surprised to realize that getting fixed up actually made her feel a little better.

Rose and Emily were already decked out for the occasion in new, matching red and green velvet dresses. She had splurged and purchased them during a shopping trip to Rutland the day before. They had new black patent-leather Mary Janes, too, which they discovered made a distinct tap on the hardwood floor of the attic bedroom. Before long, the girls were stomping, giggling, and chasing each other from one end of the room to the other.

"What's all that ruckus?" Ivy called from the kitchen. "You all about ready?"

"We'll be down in just a minute," Josie said. She sprayed a quick veil of Aqua Net over her hair and left the bathroom.

In the kitchen, Ivy was removing a large casserole dish from the oven.

"Something smells wonderful in here," Josie said. "What did you make?"

"My famous chicken biscuit pie," Ivy said. "It's always a hit at pitch-ins. It's like chicken potpie, but I put the filling in a casserole dish instead of a pie crust, and then I put homemade buttermilk biscuits to bake on top. Learned how to make real biscuits years ago, when your mom and I were growing up in Nashville. Thomas used to rave about 'em. There are folks up here who can really cook, but I've never had biscuits as good as they are in the South." Ivy placed a sheet of aluminum foil over the steaming casserole dish and crimped down the edges.

"It looks wonderful," Josie said, wondering who "Thomas" was, but she decided that now was not the time to ask. "The only place I've ever had biscuits is Kentucky Fried Chicken."

Ivy laughed. "Colonel Sanders makes decent biscuits, but they're not as good as mine." She carefully lowered the dish into a canvas carrying case. "All right. It's only two blocks to the town hall, so it won't be a long walk."

Josie repeatedly glanced over her shoulder as they made their way down the sidewalk. Each time she did, she saw only cozy little houses and businesses awash in light from the lampposts and holiday displays. The cold night air smelled of snow and spruce, with just a hint of wood smoke, rather than auto exhaust. Once they were on Main Street, she looked up and saw a great, white mansion on a hill overlooking the town.

"That old house has been here longer than I have. It's almost like it's watching over all of us, isn't it?" Ivy asked, following her gaze. "I know you're nervous being out, but you don't have to worry anymore. No one followed you here from New York, and only the detectives and the funeral home know where you are. I know it might take you a little time to believe it, but you and the girls are safe now."

They'd reached the white town hall building. Josie opened the door for Ivy and the girls and smiled at the scene that greeted her. The large meeting room was already full of people. Garlands and strings of lights were hung across the wood-paneled walls while white paper snowflakes hung from the rustic exposed beams in the ceiling. A cassette deck on a table in one corner played traditional Christmas carols. The room was packed with row after row of tables and chairs, and several long tables positioned end-to-end against the far wall were filling up with covered dishes. Ivy headed that way to deposit her casserole while Josie took the girls and found seats.

Her aunt knew almost everyone in town. As they were eating, Ivy pointed out or introduced her to more people than she could ever remember. When it was time for dessert, Josie watched as Ivy worked her way from the food tables back through the crowd to their seats. Her aunt handed each of the girls a beautifully decorated gingerbread man and set a slice of pie in front of Josie. "I've been hearing about this tart cherry pie," Ivy said, looking at the piece she'd brought back for herself. "The new police officer they just hired, what's his name? Joe Fitzgerald? His wife made it. People are raving about it." She sat down, took up her fork, and scooped a bite into her mouth. "Holy crap." She closed her eyes and chewed slowly. "Try it, Josie. It's the duck's nuts, I tell you! I've got to get this recipe."

"It is fantastic, isn't it?" Hearing a voice she recognized, Josie looked up to see Father O'Brien standing next to their table. In one hand, he held a plate bearing a large piece of cherry pie. In the other hand, he held a plastic spoon, at which he was staring intently. As if to snap himself out of his thoughts, he shook his head slightly and then looked down at Ivy with a sheepish smile. "I'm pretty sure it's the best I've ever had. This is actually my second piece."

"Oh! Hi, Father!" Ivy said with her mouth full. She swallowed quickly. "Have you met my niece yet? This is Josie DiSanti, and her daughters, Rose and Emily. They just came to Mill River and will be staying with me for a while."

Josie looked up at Father O'Brien, and he met her gaze with a question in his eyes. She realized that he didn't know whether it was all right to divulge the fact that they had already met.

"I actually met Father O'Brien last Saturday night, while I was out walking," Josie said quickly. She saw a flicker of relief cross the priest's face. "I ended up stopping by the church to warm up, since the door was open, and we had a nice talk." She looked down at Rose and Emily sitting next to her. "Girls, can you say hello?"

"Hello," Rose said dutifully. The little girl looked curiously at Father O'Brien's black attire and white collar, and Josie wondered whether questions about them were forthcoming. Emily stared up at the priest without speaking before turning to hide her face against Josie's side.

"Em's a little shy sometimes," Josie said.

Ivy picked up her empty dessert plate and stood up. "Why don't you take my seat, Father? I'm done eating, and I've been meaning to go introduce myself to Ruth Fitzgerald. I want to ask her about her pie recipe."

"Thanks, Ivy, that's very kind of you." He set his pie on the table and sat down as Ivy headed across the room. "I'm glad to see you here," he said to Josie, smiling at her and the girls. "You look like you're doing a little better."

"I'm trying," Josie said. "I really didn't want to come here tonight, but Ivy insisted. It's actually been easier than I expected. Even a little bit fun."

"You should try to go out every day, if you can. Getting fresh air and meeting people will do you good. I was actually hoping to see you here, since I have something for you." Father O'Brien reached inside his jacket and withdrew a padded, sealed envelope. He offered it to her. "It's a Christmas present for you and your daughters."

"A present?" Josie asked. The envelope felt lumpy and uneven, and she heard a muted jingling noise when she took hold of it. "For us?" She turned the envelope over in her hand, but there was nothing at all written on it. "Father, I . . . I don't know what to say. I would never have expected you to get us anything!"

"Oh. Ah, well, it's actually not from me. It's from someone in town, someone who wishes to remain anonymous but who wanted to do something to help you and your children. Her only request is that you wait to open it until Christmas morning."

"What's inside it?" Josie asked.

Father O'Brien pursed his lips and smiled slightly before answering her. "I would be in serious trouble if I told you that."

Josie stared at him. His eyes twinkled with delight, but he did a good job at maintaining a poker face in every other way. "All right," Josie agreed. "I'll open it on Christmas morning."

"Mommy, can I hold it?" Rose asked. She reached out her hand, but Josie carefully slid the envelope into her purse.

"No, Rosie, we don't know what's in it, so Mommy is going to put it in her purse for safekeeping." She turned back to the priest. "Father, would you please thank the person for us? And tell her that I was truly touched that she would think of my girls and me?"

"Of course. I would be happy to," he said as Ivy finally made it back to their table.

Ivy was flushed and slightly out of breath. "That Ruth is just a darling, but she won't say a word about what's in that pie. I'll have to figure out some way to weasel it out of her."

"I'm sure you will," Father O'Brien said. He prepared to tuck into his second helping just as the doors to the town hall burst open. A man dressed as Santa Claus strode into the meeting room shouting, "Ho, ho, ho! Merry Christmas!"

"It's Santa Claus!" Rose yelled. The four-year-old was already down off her chair and jumping up and down. On each side of their table, children of all ages were rushing past. Josie saw that the Santa had opened a large bag and was handing out candy canes and small packages to each of them. "Can I go up, Mommy? Please, can I?"

"Go ahead," Josie said, and Rose streaked away from her. "Try to get one for your sister, too," she called out. It made her happy to see Rose acting like her old self, and not the clingy, withdrawn girl she'd been since Tony's death.

"That one's not shy at all," Father O'Brien said.

"Nope," Josie agreed. "Never has been."

"That's Doc Richardson up there in the Santa suit," Father O'Brien said as they watched the mob of children receiving presents. "He's the only doctor in town, has been for years. He's very good."

"He plays Santa each year for the kids here and at the hospital up in Rutland," Ivy added. "He's a good doctor and a good person. Everybody loves him."

Josie noticed a slight wistfulness enter Ivy's voice as she spoke those few last words. When she looked up, her aunt's pensive expression piqued her curiosity. Josie followed Ivy's gaze across the room to the man in the Santa suit and realized again just how little she knew about her.

ON CHRISTMAS MORNING, JOSIE WAS SHAKEN AWAKE BY ROSE.

"Mommy! Wake up, wake up! We have to go see if Santa came, Mommy!"

"All right, Rosie, hang on," Josie said. On the wide bed between them, Emily opened her eyes and stretched. It took only a moment before she, too, was up and yelling, "Santa!" Josie made the girls put on their holiday slippers before they all went downstairs.

Ivy was already up filling the coffeepot with water. "Merry Christmas!" she said as they entered the kitchen. "Boy, you girls sure got lucky this year. Santa left you some pretty spiffy toys out under the tree."

Rose rushed into the sitting room. Josie followed, carrying Emily, and she was shocked by what she saw.

Ivy's tiny Christmas tree was almost completely buried in presents. Wrapped boxes and several stuffed animals were piled around the base of the table that held it. Two filled stockings hung from the edge of the table, while some smaller gifts and books were stacked around the tree itself. Only the top of the tiny evergreen was visible.

Josie was so fearful of exhausting her limited savings that she'd bought just a few gifts for the girls and Ivy during the past week, but nothing compared with the display before her. She turned and glared at Ivy.

"Let's see what you got, girls," Ivy said, with a wink at Josie. "I think I see some Strawberry Shortcake dolls!"

"I can't believe Santa brought so much," Josie said. She set Emily down so that she could join Rose in looking through the presents and then said, much more softly, "Santa didn't have to do all this."

"But Santa wanted to," Ivy replied in a hushed voice. "Looks like he even brought a few things for you." Smiling, she reached over, took two of the wrapped packages from the tree table, and handed them to Josie.

"Ivy, you really shouldn't have done this," she whispered.

"Nonsense. I wanted you all to have a nice Christmas. I know it's hard this year, but you need every little bit of happiness you can get right now. Just look at them."

They watched the girls for a moment. Emily was pawing through the toys, oblivious to everything else, while Rose was sitting off to the side, pulling the scented Strawberry Shortcake dolls from their box.

"You should open those," Ivy said, looking pointedly at the gifts in Josie's lap. Josie sighed and slid the paper from the larger of the packages. It was a book, a heavy hardcover edition of the complete works of Shakespeare. A ribbon was placed as a bookmark in the middle, and when the book fell open to the marked page, Josie saw a highlighted passage from *Macbeth*:

Give sorrow words. The Grief that does not speak
Whispers to the o'erfraught heart, and bids it break.

She looked at her aunt with tears in her eyes as Ivy took her hand.

"It's what I told you, about how it's important to talk about things," Ivy said. "This'll remind you how to heal and help you remember that I'm here for you. And, it'll help you fall asleep at night, if you need it." She chuckled. "Shakespeare's gorgeous stuff, but I can only read a little at a time before it wears me out. It's real good for insomnia, you know?"

Josie laughed and shook her head. "Thank you, Ivy. I just . . . I can't tell you how grateful I am to you for this. For everything."

"It's nothing. Now, open the other one."

The second present was small, in a box only a few inches across. Josie removed the paper and lifted the lid to reveal a gold, oval locket nestled in a bed of cotton.

"Ivy, I can't accept this. It's too much," Josie protested, but Ivy wouldn't listen.

"No it isn't, not at all. It's something that belonged to your great-grandmother. She gave it to me years ago, since I was the older of her granddaughters, for me to pass along to my oldest daughter someday. Since I never had any kids, it's just been sitting in my dresser drawer. It's a family heirloom, really, so it's something you should have." Ivy reached over, picked up the locket, and gently popped it open. "There's space in here for pictures of the girls. Maybe wearing it will remind you to keep going when you're feeling sad."

"They . . . and you . . . are about the only reasons I've made it this far," Josie said. She reached over to hug Ivy.

"Mommy?"

Josie turned around to face Rose. "Yes, sweetie?"

"Are you crying because you miss Daddy?"

Josie took a deep breath. "Mommy is crying right now because she feels happy and sad at the same time. Happy because it's Christmas and we're all together, but sad because Mommy still misses Daddy very much."

"I miss Daddy, too," Rose said, and Josie saw her little face start to crumple. "I like the new toys, but I really wanted Santa to bring Daddy for Christmas."

"Oh, sweetie," Josie choked, "not even Santa can bring Daddy back, even though I wish he could."

"You know," Ivy said to Rose, "it's okay for you to miss your daddy, and to cry when you feel like it. But you know something? Your daddy wouldn't want you to be sad *today*. He'd want you to play with all your new things and think about all the happy times you spent with him."

"That's right," Josie said. "Today, Mommy is going to try very hard to remember all the fun we had with Daddy, because he loved us all very much, and he wouldn't want us to be sad on Christmas."

Rose looked at them with her chin quivering. She put down the doll she'd been holding and laid her head in Josie's lap. "I'll try hard, too, Mommy," she said.

After a minute, Rose straightened up with an excited expression. "Mommy, what about the envelope?"

"What envelope?" Ivy asked.

"Oh," Josie said as she remembered the mysterious envelope Father O'Brien had given her at the holiday pitch-in. "I completely forgot about it. Just a minute, I'll go get my purse." She dashed back through the kitchen and up the stairs to the attic.

"I guess it slipped my mind," she said as she returned with the sealed envelope. "Father O'Brien gave me this at the holiday dinner. He said it was a gift from someone who wanted to stay anonymous. I was supposed to wait until Christmas morning to open it."

"Strange," Ivy said. "Let's see what's in it."

Josie ripped open the end of the envelope and reached inside. She withdrew two small keys on a ring, a business card, and a handwritten note, which she opened and read aloud.

Dear Josie,

I have recently learned of your arrival in Mill River and the reason for it. Let me first express my condolences for the loss of your beloved husband.

I understand that a house fire took your husband's life and most of your belongings. The keys that accompany this note are for the house next door to the home of Ivy Collard. It is a modest house, but it is in very good condition. If you find it to be a suitable home for you and your daughters, I would be honored if you would accept it, along with a modest sum for the purchase of some new furnishings, as my gift to you.

Paperwork to transfer ownership of the house to you has been prepared by the Gasaway law office in Rutland, listed on the enclosed card. You may schedule a time to sign the appropriate documents at that office at your convenience.

I wish you and your daughters a very Merry Christmas.

Best wishes,
A resident of Mill River

Josie stared at the note, blinking. *This can't be real,* she thought as she turned the keys over and over in her hand.

"Well, I'll be dipped—" Ivy started to say, but Josie was already heading through the kitchen. Even though she was still in her pajamas, she slipped on her boots and exited through the side door without her coat.

The Bookstop was on a corner lot with only one neighboring house, so Josie plowed through the snow in the front yard until she stood before the home next door. It was white with green shutters and about the same size as Ivy's. A Realtor's FOR SALE sign protruded from the snow at the edge of the lawn.

The walkway leading to the front door of the house was freshly shoveled.

Josie went to the front door and inserted one of the keys. As she turned it, the lock opened with a quiet *click.* She took a deep breath and pushed the door open.

Someone had obviously been by to turn on the heat, because it was comfortably warm inside. The entryway opened up into a living room on the left and faced the bottom of a staircase on the right. Josie slipped off her wet boots and walked cautiously across the living room carpet. On the far side, there was a fireplace and a door to a small room that could be used as an office or for storage. Toward the middle, the living room connected with a dining area, which led, in turn, to the kitchen. A door under the staircase on the right side opened to reveal a small bathroom.

Josie backtracked to the entryway and climbed the stairs. The second floor was much smaller, consisting of two bedrooms, one larger than the other, with a bathroom in between. The whole house was painted and carpeted in neutral shades and seemed immaculately clean.

She came down the stairs and went back through the living and dining rooms into the kitchen. Through a sliding glass door, Josie could see a nice yard surrounded by a white privacy fence. The kitchen already had a refrigerator, dishwasher, and range. *It's not huge, but there's room for more than one butt,* she thought to herself with a smile. Finally, Josie opened the door at the far end of the kitchen and entered a small mudroom. A new-looking washer and dryer were there, as well as a utility sink and a built-in ironing board. An exit from the mudroom led into the small attached garage.

Could someone have really given her this house? It was perfect. Not too big, but with plenty of room for the girls to grow up. Rose and Emily could share the big bedroom upstairs, and she got teary-eyed when she realized that they would be able to play to their hearts' content in the fenced backyard. It was close to Ivy, in a safe little town where amazing things happened for no reason. Josie felt a little light-headed.

With one hand against the wall for support, she went back to the living room and noticed a small Christmas card propped open on the mantel of the fireplace. Inside, in the same handwriting as that of the letter she had just opened, was written "Welcome home, Josie."

Josie sat straight down on the floor. She was trembling and

crying, trying to make sense of it all. *Who could possibly do something like this? Who would?* She wondered whether Tony had somehow managed to do this from wherever he was now. If it wasn't Tony's doing, it was staggering to think that a stranger could show her such benevolence.

At that moment, the front door opened and Ivy came in with Rose and Emily in tow.

"Mommy!" Rose said, as they all rushed over to her.

"Josie, are you all right?" Ivy asked. She leaned forward with her hands on her knees while Rose and Emily jumped into Josie's cross-legged lap.

"I'm fine," Josie choked. "Just a little overwhelmed, that's all."

"Well, it's happened again, I guess," Ivy said, shaking her head.

"What's happened again?" Josie asked.

Ivy straightened up. "The secret gift thing that happens every so often in Mill River. It seems like just when folks in town really need something, it just appears. Or sometimes, it's given to 'em, anonymously, like this." Ivy smiled. "It's happened for years, but nobody has figured out who's behind it. Nowadays, most people just accept the random gifts as part of what normally happens here."

Josie didn't answer. Her mouth was having trouble forming words.

"This house has been on the market forever," Ivy said. "I guess it was just waiting for you to get here."

"Mommy, is this going to be our house?" Rose asked.

Josie squeezed a daughter in each of her arms and pulled them against her. She noticed a new feeling building in her very center, a small, reassuring spark of something. Hope? Optimism? Maybe even the beginnings of a realization that everything was going to be okay? Whatever it was, it started because of a stranger's gift of shelter. She would draw on the spark, build on it to go on, to give her girls a safe and happy life. And even after they were grown, even if someday she could afford to move to someplace bigger or newer, she promised herself that she would continue to live in this house as a humbling reminder of the miracle she had been given.

"Yes, baby," Josie said with her face nestled in red and blond hair. She closed her eyes. "This is our house. This will always be our house."

CHAPTER 7

Early in the afternoon on July 1, The Bookstop had a flurry of customers. The date was not lost on Ivy, and she had been keeping an eye on the houses across the street to see whether Rose and Emily would show up. When she finally had a spare minute, she fixed herself a glass of iced tea, plopped down in her porch swing, and hung her cane over the armrest. It felt wonderful to slip her feet out of her sandals. She was still there, holding her empty glass, dozing and humming to herself, when a male voice spoke to her.

"Hey there, Ivy, how are you?"

She opened her eyes to see Kyle Hansen, his daughter Rowen, and Claudia Simon coming up to the porch.

"You look comfortable," Claudia said with a smile.

"I'm good, and I am," she said. "Anything I can help you all find?"

"Well, I guess we're not sure yet," Kyle said. "Rowen's birthday was last week, and she wanted to come by and see what's new."

"Dad and Cla—I mean, Miss Simon, gave me twenty dollars!" Rowen said. "Ten dollars each, because I turned ten years old."

"And it's been burning a hole in her pocket," Kyle added with a laugh.

"Well, the most recent book in the Greek demigod series you love just came out," Ivy said. "I've still got a few copies left. And there are some other good titles, too. Have a look, and holler if you need anything."

"Awesome!" Rowen said as she pulled open the front door.

Claudia followed close behind and turned to Kyle. "You coming in?"

"Nah," Kyle said. He sat down in the swing next to Ivy. "But take your time. I'll wait here for you and keep Ivy company." Once they had entered The Bookstop, Kyle turned to Ivy and grinned. "Women and their books."

"Women?" Ivy said.

"Women. Believe me, Rowen's ten going on thirty. Sometimes it freaks me out how fast she's growing up."

Ivy's attention was suddenly drawn to a sleek black BMW sedan that pulled up along the curb across the street. It was followed by a U-Haul truck, which parked directly behind it.

"That'll be Rose and her family," Ivy said, more to herself than to Kyle. "I *knew* she'd come." She'd heard from Rose only once since the wake, to offer an apology for her comment about the urn and ask for a copy of Josie's letter. Her great-niece hadn't given any indication that she intended to spend the summer in Mill River. Ivy was gratified that her feeling that Rose would show up had proved correct.

"That's your niece, right?" Kyle asked. "I think I remember her from Josie's wake."

"Great-niece, yep, one of 'em," Ivy said. "The other one's Emily, and I expect her to be along any time."

"I've heard bits about the situation from Fitz . . . something about their mom setting up some sort of plan to force them to start talking to each other?"

"Yes," Ivy said, and she glanced over at Josie's quiet house next door. The shades were drawn and the lawn was in desperate need of its weekly mowing. She hadn't gotten used to seeing the house so still, with no sign of habitation. She gave Kyle a quick summary of Josie's plan to explain why the sisters would be spending the next couple of months in Mill River.

"Well, it's unusual," Kyle said. "I don't know whether you can ever force two people to like each other who don't, even if they're related. In fact, some people who don't get along are best left separated."

The sounds of car and truck doors slamming came from across the street. Ivy and Kyle watched as Sheldon, Rose, and Alex filed through the front door of one of the little houses that faced The Bookstop. After a few minutes, they came back out with Sheldon leading the way and Rose's screeching bringing up the rear.

"Sheldon, can you really not grasp how bad this is? Or, maybe it just doesn't matter to you, since you're not the one who has to spend the next two months in a shoe box with no air-conditioning!"

Sheldon seemed to be doing his best to ignore Rose's ranting. He kept his back to her as he unlocked the U-Haul, slid up the metal door, and began unloading boxes. Even though she didn't have a great view from across the street, Ivy could have sworn she saw Sheldon flinch when Rose started up again.

"So what if the truck's due back tomorrow? You could stay the night and still get it back in plenty of time. It's not like you have a job or anything else to get back to."

Ivy sat up a little straighter. Rose's comment was worrisome. If it were true, it might explain the reason behind Rose's return.

Kyle whistled low under his breath. "Sounds like one happy family. Fitz told me what happened with Rose at the wake . . . you know, with the ashes . . . and I sort of thought he was exaggerating. But now . . ."

"He wasn't," Ivy said. "Rose is one hot mess, that's for sure."

At that moment, Claudia and Rowen came back outside with a few books apiece.

"How'd you make out?" Ivy asked. "Find everything all right?"

"Oh, definitely," Claudia said. "I think we could spend hours in there."

"I could *live* in there," Rowen said. "Miss Ivy, I got the Percy Jackson book you told me about and the first one in the *Wimpy Kid* series. A lot of my friends at school are reading those."

"I know you'll love both of 'em," Ivy said as she got out of the swing and slid her feet back into her sandals. "Let me ring you up."

After she had completed the purchases, Ivy grabbed her cane. "Since my bum knee seems to be behaving today and I haven't taken a lunch break yet, I'm going to walk across the street and visit with my niece and her family."

"Did Alex come?" Rowen asked. "The boy who was at Mrs. DiSanti's house?"

"Yep, he did," Ivy told her. "Looks like he's going to be here with his mom for the summer."

"Can we go say hello, too?" The little girl looked up at Kyle. "Please, Dad? I'll bet he doesn't know anybody his age but he probably wishes he did."

"Sure, that'd be a nice thing to do," Kyle said. "We don't have anything else going on, anyway." He raised his eyebrows at Ivy and said in a whisper, "Told you. Ten going on thirty."

Ivy led the way toward the moving truck. Rose came out of the house and saw them just as they reached the sidewalk.

"Hi, Aunt Ivy," she said. Rose wore skinny jeans and a black tank top. She pushed her dark sunglasses up onto her head and wiped the sweat from her nose as she approached. "I was going to knock on your door once we got everything inside. Sheldon has to get back to New York tonight."

"That's okay, honey. I had a little break and thought I'd come over." Ivy kissed Rose on the cheek and squeezed her in a tight hug.

"You doing all right? I'm glad you decided to come. Your mom would be happy."

"Yeah," Rose said in an irritated tone. She lowered her voice. "Trust me, this isn't something I'm too happy about."

Ivy fought the urge to laugh. "I know. It's probably selfish of me, but I'm glad you'll be so close by for a while. Alex, too. Hey, you remember Kyle Hansen, one of our police officers, and his daughter? And his friend, Claudia Simon? They were over at The Bookstop when you pulled up. Rowen wanted to say hello to Alex."

"And we wanted to welcome you, too," Claudia said, extending her hand to Rose. "I've lived in Mill River for only a short time myself, but it's a wonderful place."

Ivy watched Rose's smile falter for a moment before it quickly reappeared even wider than before. "I actually grew up here," Rose told her, "and it really hasn't changed much."

"Well, Claudia lives just over on Main Street, next to St. John's, and Rowen and I live in an apartment above the bakery," Kyle said. "We're all close by, if you need anything."

"That's very nice of you," Rose said with the same fake smile. "My son is inside getting his room set up, but I'll tell him you asked about him. I'm sure he'll be happy about that." She gave a cursory glance to the books in Rowen's hands. "Alex loves to read, too, so you've got something in common."

"You know, I couldn't help but notice your car up there is parked alongside a fire hydrant," Kyle said. "I'm not sure who's on patrol right now, but Fitz is pretty strict about people parking near hydrants and in handicapped spaces. I'd hate for you to get a ticket on your first day here. You could swing around and park across the street, at least until the truck's out of here."

Rose stared at Kyle, blinking, for a moment before she answered. "Fitz's wife was my mom's best friend. I highly doubt he would let anyone ticket *me*, especially when I'm trying to get things moved inside. Which reminds me, I've got to get some stuff unpacked before my husband leaves. Would you excuse me?"

"Of course, honey, go on," Ivy said.

"Nice seeing you again," Claudia added.

"Likewise," Rose said. She squeezed Ivy's hand and smiled before she walked back to her house.

No sooner had the front door closed behind Rose than another car pulled up along the curb and beeped its horn. Ivy turned around to see Emily smiling from behind the wheel of her old hatchback.

"Right on time," Ivy said. "Well, you all might as well stay for a few more minutes and say hello to my other niece."

Emily's old Subaru stood in contrast to the BMW parked further up the street. The Impreza's faded silver finish was scuffed and had several dents in various places. The engine rumbled loud enough to be heard a few blocks away, and the interior of the car was crammed with boxes and bags. A large dog with floppy brown ears and a brown-and-white-splotched coat sat in the front passenger seat with its head stuck out the side window.

"Aunt Ivy!" Emily said as she climbed out of the car. Her younger niece caught her in a huge hug so exuberant that Ivy had to lean on her cane to steady herself.

"I'm glad you made it all right. I was a little worried about you, driving cross-country all by yourself in that old car."

"Aw, my car's fine. Needs a new muffler and probably a new clutch, but I'll get all that taken care of once I'm moved in. And I wasn't by myself." Emily opened the front passenger's door and clipped a leash to the dog's collar before it jumped down from the seat. "This is Gus. Gus, meet my aunt Ivy, and"—she looked at everyone standing next to her aunt in turn—"Kyle, was it? And Rowen? And, I'm so sorry, I can't seem to remember your name, but I remember you were at my mom's wake, too," she said to Claudia as her cheeks turned a bright pink.

"I'm Claudia Simon."

"Claudia, that's right! I should have remembered. Anyway, I found this big boy years ago at a shelter in California. The staff had him in the kitten room while they were cleaning out cages, and all these tiny babies were climbing all over him, jumping on his head, chewing on his ears, and he just lay there with his tail wagging and let them do it." Emily reached down and massaged the dog's ears while she spoke to him in low, drawn-out manner. "Dis big boy jus' wuvs wittle kitties. Who wouldn't fall in wuv wif such a sweet puppy?" Gus whined in reply and thumped his tail against the ground.

"Oh, can I pet him?" Rowen asked.

"He seems gentle, but it's up to Emily," Kyle said.

"Sure," Emily said. "Just let him smell your hand first, so he gets to know you a little." Rowen gave her books to Claudia and approached Gus cautiously with her hand outstretched. The dog stood up, sniffed and then licked her hand, and lowered his head a little as she began to stroke him.

"You didn't bring all that much," Ivy said. "Not compared with your sister, anyway." She jerked her chin up toward Rose's U-Haul and rolled her eyes. "They got here just a minute ago."

"I didn't know whether she'd come," Emily said, "but the truck? Not surprised." She leaned back against the Impreza. "This is all my stuff. The lease on my apartment was up next month, but since I was going to be here for a while, I didn't renew it. I just packed up and brought everything with me."

"Hey, why don't Claudia and I help you get your things inside?" Kyle asked after they were all silent for a few seconds. "Since you've got just a carload, the three of us could do it pretty fast."

Ivy saw Claudia's eyes widen for a moment as she looked up at Kyle. "Uh, yeah," Claudia said quickly. "Maybe Rowen could hang out with Gus while we unload?"

"That would be awesome!" Rowen said. "Could I?"

"Wow, thanks, guys," Emily said. "Sure, Gus'll be fine here for a few minutes. I'll tie his leash to the side mirror so he can't run off, but he probably wouldn't anyway." She looked down at Rowen and smiled. "He really loves belly-rubs, you know."

As if he were following the conversation, Gus whined, dropped to the ground, and rolled over onto his back.

Ivy let out a loud snort as she laughed with the others. "He's a smarty," she said. "I'd better get back. You'll come by once you're all settled in, won't you, Em?"

"Sure thing," Emily said, and she kissed Ivy's cheek. "You care if Gus tags along?"

"Nope," Ivy said, as she started across the street. "Not so long as he's house-trained. See you all later."

CLAUDIA GAMELY CARRIED SEVERAL ARMLOADS OF CLOTHING AND boxes into Emily's house. Soon, the only thing remaining in the car was a large, flat wooden crate marked FRAGILE. She had no idea what was inside, and she watched Emily struggle to pull it from the hatchback and lower one end to the ground.

"Looks like a two-man job," Kyle said. He rushed over and grabbed one side of the box, and he and Emily lifted it together with some effort.

"I can help, too," Claudia offered, but Kyle shook his head.

"Nah, we've got it. It's so wide that a third person helping wouldn't fit through the door, anyway." Claudia stiffened, automatically reacting to what she once might have considered an insult. *But not anymore.* Kyle and Emily maneuvered the box up the front steps into the house. It was several minutes before they reemerged.

"Well, that wasn't so bad," Kyle said as he wiped his brow.

"Excuse me, Kyle?" Ivy's voice called from across the street. A UPS truck was leaving the front of her house, and a newly delivered stack of cardboard boxes was on her porch. "I see you've gotten into the moving business. Would you mind giving an old woman a hand with a few heavy boxes?"

"When it rains it pours," Kyle said with a good-natured smile. "No problem, Miss Ivy," he called back to her. "I'll just be another minute," he said to Claudia before loping across the street.

Claudia watched him for a moment and then looked at Rowen, who was sitting in the grass next to Emily's car with Gus's head in her lap. "Wow," she said to Emily, "it looks like he's found a new best friend."

"Yeah, I don't think Gus has ever met a kid he didn't like," Emily agreed.

Claudia smiled. She was unsure what else to say. It wasn't just that she barely knew Emily. She was intimidated because Emily was striking. Even with her curly red hair in a disheveled bun, a makeup-free face, and clothing wrinkled and stained from her cross-country drive, Emily was easily the most beautiful woman Claudia had ever seen in person.

And yet, she seemed friendly and down-to-earth, certainly much more so than her sister. *Being new in town wasn't easy,* Claudia thought. *Is there some way I could help her feel welcome?*

"So, do you know anyone else in Mill River?" Claudia asked. "Other than Ivy and your sister, I mean. I've lived here less than a year myself, but once you're settled in, I'd be happy to introduce you to some of my friends."

Emily's face brightened at her words, but before she could reply, Rose burst out the front door of her house. Although Claudia thought she saw Emily's sister glance in their direction, Rose did nothing to acknowledge their presence. Instead, she walked briskly to her BMW, started it, and wheeled it around to park on the opposite side of the street. Then, again ignoring her and Emily, Rose exited the sedan, came back across the street, and climbed up into the driver's seat of the U-Haul.

"What the hell?" Emily muttered. As if to answer her question, the truck's engine roared to life, and the red brake lights on the back of it lit up.

Gus startled and stood up, pulling Rowen along with him.

"Rowen, honey, come over here away from the truck," Claudia said. She reached out a hand as Kyle's daughter and Emily's dog came to stand next to her.

"Surely she's not going to try to drive that thing," Emily said.

Again, on cue, the truck started to move. Instead of pulling closer to Rose's house, though, the U-Haul lunged backwards into Emily's Subaru.

The loud *thump* reverberated up and down the street.

"My car!" Emily said.

Claudia pulled Rowen closer. The truck inched forward until several feet again separated it from the silver car. Within a few seconds, the engine was cut and Rose, looking exasperated, came around the side of the truck. Emily was already inspecting the front of the Impreza.

"Look, I'm sorry," Rose began. "Some of the stuff we brought won't fit in the house, and I was just trying to pull the truck up a little so it'd be easier to load."

"And so you put the truck *in reverse*? I can't believe it. The very first day we're here, and you wreck my car?"

"What do you mean, 'wreck'? I just tapped your bumper is all."

Emily's mouth dropped open. "Tapped? Don't you see this?" She pointed down toward her car. "The bumper is all pushed in, and the grill is cracked. I don't know how much all this'll cost to fix, but I expect you to take care of the bill."

"Whatever." Rose rolled her eyes and snorted. "Frankly, I can't believe you're still driving such a tin can. But since it's already got so many dents and scratches, what's the big deal about a few more?" She reached into the pocket of her tight jeans and withdrew a folded stack of bills. "Here," she said, peeling a few bills off the top and handing them to Emily. "This should be plenty to fix whatever you say was just damaged. Frankly, I'm not sure the bumper and grill weren't already like that."

"I just saw you smash into them!" Emily yelled. "And Claudia did, too, didn't you?"

Emily whirled around, seeking her affirmation, and Claudia gave a quick nod.

"This two hundred dollars won't even cover the deductible," Emily continued. She took another step toward Rose, waving the bills as her voice grew louder. "Maybe I should just call the police and file a report. And tell them to run a Breathalyzer while they're at it."

Claudia thought she saw Rose give a small shudder in response to Emily's threat.

"Whoa, what's going on?"

Hearing Kyle's voice sent waves of relief through Claudia, and she felt even better when she saw him coming back across the street. Only then did she look around and notice the large audience watching Rose and Emily's altercation. Ruth Fitzgerald and Ivy were standing together on the front porch at The Bookstop, along with several other people she didn't recognize. On the sidewalk a little ways away, both Daisy Delaine and her little gray dog stared in their direction. Two kids on their bicycles had pulled over along the curb, and a mail carrier was taking his time climbing the steps of a house two doors down, all the while craning his neck to see what was happening.

"She backed the truck into my car," Emily told Kyle as he

reached them. "I'm glad you're here, because I think I'd like to file—"

"Emily, Rose and I are very sorry for the damage to your car." Sheldon had suddenly appeared, and he stepped in front of Rose to speak with Emily. "I saw it happen from the house. Rose was trying to move the truck because I asked her to, and she probably wasn't used to the gearshift. I know she didn't mean to hit your car."

Sheldon's soothing, conciliatory tone seemed to catch Emily by surprise. She stopped yelling and listened.

"Of course we'll pay for any necessary repairs," Sheldon continued, and Claudia noticed that he held a black checkbook in his hands. "If you'll let me know the amount of your insurance deductible, I'll give you a check for that today. And then, once you get an estimate, if there's a balance beyond the deductible, you let me know, and I'll also cover the additional cost. Would that be okay?" Sheldon removed a business card from the checkbook and handed it to Emily. "Here's my contact information."

Claudia was surprised at how quickly the tension in the air seemed to dissipate.

"Well, yes. I suppose that would be fine," Emily said. She accepted the card from Sheldon. "I've got to check my policy to be sure about the deductible. If you want to come over to my house for a few minutes, I'll look up the information."

"Looks like everything's settled, then," Kyle said.

Everyone seemed to take his statement as a cue that the show was over. The kids on the bikes pushed off and started pedaling. Daisy and her little dog resumed their walk, and the folks at The Bookstop went back to browsing. The mail carrier walked past and nodded as if nothing out of the ordinary had happened.

Claudia watched Rose head back to her house while Sheldon followed Emily to the one next door. She couldn't imagine what had happened to ruin the sisters' relationship, but Rose's taunting treatment of her younger sister was disgusting. Claudia remembered well how it felt to be treated poorly, and her heart went out to Emily.

ONCE THE MESS ACROSS THE STREET HAD BEEN SORTED OUT AND the last of her customers had left The Bookstop, Ivy fixed herself another glass of tea and reclaimed her spot on the porch swing. She watched as Sheldon came outside to put a few boxes back into the U-Haul before climbing into the truck and driving away. Rose moved her BMW across the street, to the parking space in front of her house where the U-Haul had been. All was quiet then. It was just the two houses, side by side. The two cars parked in front of them, the shiny Beemer and the dingy Subaru, like Cinderella and an ugly stepsister. And the two real sisters inside the houses, who had finally caved in to their mother's wishes to come back to Mill River and hunt for the treasure she'd left them.

It's working so far, Josie, Ivy thought with a sad smile. *I just wish you were here to see it.*

CHAPTER 8

1985

O<small>N A CRISP</small> T<small>UESDAY MORNING IN</small> S<small>EPTEMBER,</small> J<small>OSIE</small> swung her station wagon back into her driveway. She and Emily had watched and waved as Rose boarded the school bus, and afterwards, she had dropped Emily off at the nursery school that operated out of the basement at St. John's. This new routine had started a few weeks earlier, at the beginning of the school year, but she still felt anxious being without her girls in the mornings. Even when she knew exactly where they were—in school, or with Ivy—she worried about their safety. It had been almost two years since the fire, and she still feared that those responsible for her beloved Tony's death would find her in Mill River.

Instead of going home, Josie walked around to the side door of The Bookstop and let herself in. As usual, Ivy was seated at the breakfast table reading the paper. Her aunt looked up as Josie entered.

"Morning," Ivy said. "Coffee's still fresh, and I was waiting 'til you got here to do the pancakes. They're no good once they're cold." Ivy stood up and went to the stove, where she had a bowl of pancake batter already mixed. "Everything go okay with the girls?"

"Yes," Josie said. She went to the cupboard and pulled down a coffee mug. "I think they've pretty much settled into the routine. Rose is still excited about not being a kindergarten baby anymore.

And Emily hasn't cried yet this week. I think she's less anxious now that she knows I'll pick her up at noon."

Ivy nodded. "Yep, and she sees that Rose is a big girl now, going to first grade, so that's a good example for her."

"You know how she's always trying to keep up with Rose." Josie sighed. "Time's flying."

"The older you get, the faster it goes," Ivy said. "How are you doing? With them being in school, I mean?"

"I'm coping. I keep telling myself there's nothing to worry about anymore. It's been almost two years, after all."

"That's true. Just keep sayin' it to yourself. One of these days, it'll sink in and you'll be able to believe it."

Josie watched her aunt ladle batter into a hot frying pan, and she poured herself a cup of coffee. She sat down at the breakfast table, sipping from her mug. After a few minutes, Ivy turned around and looked at her.

"You sure you're all right? You're sorta quiet."

"I was just thinking about what you said. About time going faster . . . about how lots of things seem to be going faster now."

"Such as?"

"Money," Josie said. "I've been so careful over the past couple of years, trying to stretch the life insurance money and what Tony and I had saved. Our expenses haven't been that high, especially with not having rent or a mortgage to worry about." She smiled a little, as she did every time she thought about her miracle house. "But, even so, the money won't last forever. Now that I've got some time with the girls in school, I've got to figure out what I can do for a real job."

"How much longer do you think your savings will last?"

"Maybe another year," Josie said. "But there really aren't any jobs here in town. I figure I'll have to find something in Rutland."

"You've never told me much about what you did before you

were married, other than that you worked in a jewelry store," Ivy said. "I didn't want to bring it up, either, for fear it would upset you, but now, since we need to get you a job . . . did you ever go to college?"

"I wanted to." Josie stared down into her coffee cup. "Mom had no way of helping me, of course. She was lucky to hang on to a job for a few months before getting fired, and when she did get a little bit of money from somewhere, she drank it up. I started working after school during high school just so I wouldn't have to worry about us having enough money for rent or the light bill. We used food stamps for groceries. It wasn't much, but I learned how to stretch it to keep us both fed." She looked up at Ivy with a wry smile. "I make a mean casserole with ramen noodles and govern-ment cheese."

Ivy shook her head as she handed Josie a plate of hot pancakes. "That's a damned shame. No wonder you don't like to talk about her much. I do wish I would've known what was going on with you and your mom all those years. She didn't want anything to do with me or your grandmother after she left, not even a phone call. All those teenage years, when you were supposed to be enjoying growing up . . ."

"I grew up long before I was a teenager," Josie said quietly. "I figured after I finished high school, I'd get a full-time job, save for a while, and then start taking night classes. I found a job as a sales clerk in the jewelry department at Macy's. I'd been working there about a year when a man came in wanting to buy an engagement ring. I spent over an hour with him, talking about the different options. In the end, he didn't buy a ring, but he offered me a job in his own jewelry store in the diamond district."

"That man was Sol?" Ivy laughed. "So, *that's* how you came to know him. He came to Macy's to shop for an employee!"

"Yes," Josie said. "Said the best way to tell how someone would treat a customer was to pose as one. He offered to double my hourly pay plus give me a better commission. I couldn't refuse him."

"Wow. I'll bet that made it easier to save for school, then."

Josie frowned. "It should have. I did save for a time. I was about ready to enroll in my first classes when Mom had a scare." She paused and shook her head, remembering. "I came home from work one night, and the whole apartment was full of smoke. Mom was on the couch, asleep, with a pot on the stove. She's lucky she didn't burn the place down." Josie shuddered. "We really had it out that night. Mom was freaked after learning what had happened, and she agreed to go into rehab. I thought she'd hit bottom and was ready to turn her life around, so I took the money I'd saved for school and used it to pay for her to go into a treatment center."

"Oh, honey," Ivy said. "I can't imagine . . . that must've been so hard for you."

"I was happy to do it," Josie said with a bitter smile. "She'd never agreed to get help before. Never admitted she had a problem. I thought we finally had a chance at a fresh start. I figured I'd save up again and start school when I could."

"How long was Abby in rehab?"

"It was a thirty-day program," Josie said. "She came out sober for the first time in years, talking about getting a good job and paying me back so I could start classes. She went to three Alcoholics Anonymous meetings the first week she was out. It was a good week, one of the best we ever had." Josie paused and smiled, but the smile faded quickly. "I really thought everything was going to be okay. But, when I came home from work the next week, I found her passed out on the couch, plastered, same as always."

Ivy turned to take the last few pancakes out of the pan. Josie could see her jaw clenched tight as she shook her head. "That's exactly how she was while we were growing up. Even before she got into drinking, she never kept with anything for any length of time."

"I'd have done anything for her," Josie said, blinking to stanch her tears. "Anything. And it was so maddening. I loved her so much, and I couldn't help her. Everything I was doing was just pointless."

"Loving someone unconditionally is never pointless. Even when it results in your getting hurt, you can still learn from the experience." Ivy shut off the stove and brought her full plate over to sit across from Josie. "But I still can't imagine how it must've been. Where was your father all this time? After your mother got pregnant with you, she ran off with him. Your grandma tried to stop her, but it was too little, too late. Your mom never came back. We didn't even know where she was for sure or when you were born."

"I never knew my father," Josie said. "Mom didn't like to talk about him much. He left us when I was three months old. I think that's when she really started drinking heavily."

"Have you ever thought about trying to find him?" Ivy asked.

"Mom got a letter from him in 1962, when I was six. He was in Vietnam, and he wrote to apologize for abandoning us and promised to make things right once he was back home. He didn't make it, though."

"I'm so sorry," Ivy said.

"That's all right. I never knew him, so I never felt as if I lost anything, not like Mom did."

"You lost a helluva lot," Ivy said. "No father, no functional mother. It's a wonder you've survived."

"Sol Berman was a godsend," Josie said. "I'm still thankful that he hired me away from Macy's. He was probably the only reason I held it together through the worst of it with Mom. There were so many times I was a total wreck when I showed up at the shop. He used to listen when I needed someone to talk to. He always joked that he was so understanding only because I was the best salesperson he ever had and he couldn't afford to lose me, but I knew it was more than that. Sol was just one of those rare people who are good and kind all the way through."

"So you worked for him for a long while, then, even after Abby died?"

"Yes, right up until I had Rose. I never did go back to school. I meant to, but before Mom died, it was impossible. After that, I needed some time to get myself together, and then I met Tony. Before I knew it, we were married and I was pregnant, so I quit. Sol actually gave me away at my wedding, since I didn't have anyone else to do it, and he passed away suddenly when Rose was about eighteen months old. I miss him."

"I wish I could've met him and Tony, and come to your wedding," Ivy said.

"Why didn't you? I sent you an invitation."

"I know. I didn't get it until a month after, and when it finally showed up here, it was all mangled. The post office really screwed it up. I felt bad and almost called you, but it was so awkward. It was easier not to call than to offer an excuse a month after the fact."

Josie smiled. "Our wedding was small, anyway. You didn't miss much."

Ivy was quiet a moment. She chewed a mouthful of pancakes and stared thoughtfully at Josie. "You know, going back to your job situation . . . you've actually got some decent experience."

"Sol taught me a lot about diamonds and gems," Josie said, unsure of where Ivy was taking the conversation. "There might be some jewelry stores in Rutland, but—"

"No, no," Ivy said. "There's no jewelry store job around here. What I'm thinking about is your *sales* experience. Sol said you were the best salesperson he ever had? What made him think that?"

"Well," Josie said slowly, "he said I had a knack for being able to see whether a buyer was serious and what style suited him. I almost always sold a big engagement ring each shift. Sometimes more than one." Josie looked down at her left hand and lightly traced the wedding band that she still wore. "Tony and I used my commissions to make the last payments on the car and set up a nursery for Rose. We saved what was left for a down payment on a house."

"I think that's exactly what you need to focus on now." Confused, Josie looked across the table at her aunt.

"Houses, I mean," Ivy said. "You've proven you can *sell*. But, the only things that cost as much as diamonds around here are houses. It wouldn't be too hard for you to get your real estate license. You'd probably make enough for you and the girls to live on by selling a few houses a year. Plus, your work hours would be flexible."

Josie sat up a little straighter in her chair and then shook her head.

"I don't think I could risk it. Putting myself out there so publicly, I mean. It would make it so easy for someone to find me and the girls."

"Are you *still* worrying about that?" Ivy asked. Her aunt rolled her eyes. "You've been here almost two years now with no scent of trouble. When are you going to realize that nobody's gonna bother you up here?"

Josie sighed. "Even if you're right, is real estate selling these days?" she asked. "My guess is that real estate agents struggle around here. Houses are small, and interest rates are high."

"Most everybody around here struggles to earn a living, not just real estate agents," Ivy said. "But, don't forget that people always need places to live, whatever the interest rates. And sure, Mill River is full of cute little houses, but the sale of a small house is still a sale. There are plenty of bigger properties outside town—vacation homes of rich people from Boston and New York City, and a whole slew of resorts and condos up near Killington. For someone who knows how to *sell,* I'd say you would do well to get into real estate around here." Ivy glanced at the clock on the kitchen wall and jumped out of her chair. "Lordy, it's nine o'clock! I've got to go open up." She started to clear her place at the table, but Josie waved her off.

"Go on, I'll clean up," Josie said as she reached over and lifted Ivy's plate onto her own.

"Thanks, honey," Ivy said. She pushed open the door that led to the sitting room. "But make sure you think about the real estate thing. I've just got a good feeling about it."

It took Josie only a few minutes to do the breakfast dishes and tidy up Ivy's kitchen. She was headed back to her own home when Larry Endicott reached her block on his daily route.

"Hello, Miss Josie. You've got good timing." With a smile, he held out the day's mail to her.

"Thanks, Larry," she said. He tipped his hat and continued down the sidewalk. When she looked down at the envelopes in her hand, her breath caught in her throat. The letter on top was from the FBI.

Her heart racing, Josie glanced around and ran inside. Her hands were trembling so badly that she had trouble opening the envelope. Finally, she succeeded in removing the letter inside. Josie read it through once, started to sob, and reread it twice more. As she reached the end of the letter the third time, she leaned back against her front door and then slid down to the floor. Relief, grief, love, anger, hope, and relief again ripped through her. She wrapped her hands tightly around herself and waited for the storm to subside.

When she had calmed down and rational thought had returned to her, Josie shoved the letter into her purse and ran back to The Bookstop to borrow a road map from Ivy. A glance at her watch told her that she had two and a half hours before she was due to pick up Emily from nursery school.

She got back into her car and unfolded the map to display all of Rutland County. It was strange—she'd been in Mill River almost two years now, and this was the first time she had looked carefully at a map of the surrounding area. Killington, Proctor, Pittsford, Hubbardton, Castleton, Ira, Tinmouth, Clarendon . . . her eyes swept in a counterclockwise circle, stopping to read the name of each town surrounding the small black dot labeled MILL RIVER. She looked at the map eagerly, with an open mind. The letter from New York had changed everything.

Josie laid the map on the passenger's seat, shifted her car into reverse, and backed out of her driveway. Her aunt was right. Of course she had the potential to do well in real estate. Before, she specialized in finding the right setting and owner, essentially the right home, for a diamond. Now, she would learn how to find the right homes for people. The commonality between them, and her true talent, was her ability to find what *belonged*. Josie smiled, feeling the beginnings of a plan forming in her mind.

To be successful, she would need to know the area as well as the locals. She would need to familiarize herself with the towns and communities, the neighborhoods and school districts. It would take time and effort, but Josie was willing to commit both. Her girls' future, and her own, depended on it.

A FEW WEEKS LATER, JOSIE SAT AT HER KITCHEN TABLE WITH A YEL-low highlighter in her hand. A large pot of pasta sauce and meatballs simmered on the back burner of her stove. The girls were upstairs playing, and the chattering and occasional giggling that drifted downstairs assured her that they weren't getting into too much trouble.

The table was covered with study materials for Vermont's real estate pre-licensing course in which she had enrolled. Forty hours of instruction were required, which she would complete on the mornings when both girls were in school. After she finished the course, she would have to pass the national and state real estate exams. And finally, she would have to find a real estate brokerage willing to take her on as a trainee.

The sound of the doorbell interrupted her train of thought, and she hurried to the door to find Ivy on the front stoop. She had a large typewriter in her arms.

"Here, let me help," Josie said, but her aunt had already pushed her way inside.

"I've got it," Ivy huffed. "Just let me know where to put it."

"The storage room," Josie said. She ran ahead of her aunt and opened a door off the living room. "There's an old card table in here."

"Whew!" Ivy said after she set the typewriter down on the table. "I forgot how clunky this thing is. It's been up in my attic for years."

"Does it still work?" Josie asked. The typewriter was an old IBM electric model. The greenish-gray finish was chipped and worn along the edges, but the keys looked to be in good shape.

"Oh, sure. It's sort of a dinosaur, though," Ivy said. "I've read about the new models they have in offices these days. 'Word processors' they call 'em. They've got a little screen where you can edit what you type before you print it."

"I don't need anything that fancy," Josie said. "This'll be great. I've been working on a cover letter and a résumé to send out to some agencies. Now I'll be able to get them in the mail on Monday."

"The sooner, the better," Ivy agreed. She turned toward the kitchen and sniffed. "It sure does smell good in here. You make Italian food better than any restaurant I ever ate in."

Josie had just followed Ivy back to the kitchen when Rose and Emily thumped down the stairs. The little girls burst into the kitchen wearing a variety of items from their dress-up collection.

"Hi, Aunt Ivy! Mom, we're hungry," Rose said, as Emily trailed behind her, grinning.

Josie took one look at Rose wearing a feather boa, a shimmery blue dress, and a pair of enormous round sunglasses and burst out laughing. Emily's appearance was just as comical. She wore a silk scarf tied over her hair and a pair of too-big overalls. An eye patch was wrapped around her face, but it covered her nose instead of one eye, and a fake mustache was stuck crookedly on her upper lip.

"You girls look like you've been having fun," Ivy said.

"Yeah. I'm a movie star," Rose said, flipping the boa and grinning up at Ivy as the sunglasses slid down her nose.

"And I'm a pirate!" Emily yelled happily.

"Wait," Josie said, squinting at Emily's face. "I don't remember there being any mustaches in your dress-up box. Come here, Em." Josie reached out, pulled her younger daughter closer, and put one hand under Emily's chin to lift it up. The "mustache" Emily wore was a cluster of red hair that was somehow glued onto her face.

"How did you—" Josie started to ask, but Emily's wide eyes immediately prompted her to question Rose. "Rosie, did you cut your sister's hair? And what is this on her face?" Josie grabbed Emily's mustache and tugged. The whole cluster and the clear rubbery blob underneath it stuck to Emily's skin as she tried to peel it away.

"Ow, don't," Emily protested. "That's my mustache, Mom."

"I just cut a little of her hair with my paper-doll scissors," Rose said. "And we used rubber cement to put it on, like we use in school for art. Pirates *always* have mustaches and beards, Mom." Rose's face lit up. "I was going to make her a whole long beard, too, but we got too hungry and decided to come downstairs. Are we going to eat soon?"

For a minute, Josie was speechless. She wanted to laugh and yell at the same time. She turned Emily around and looked to see where Rose had snipped the hair for the mustache. With Emily's hair being curly, the missing bit wasn't too noticeable. It could have been so much worse. As in, *a whole long beard* worse. Josie had a sudden mental image of Emily with long locks of her hair rubber-cemented all around her jawline. Thank goodness they'd come down when they had, or poor Emily would have ended up bald.

"Listen, Rose," Josie said with a sigh, "you are not allowed to cut your sister's hair or your own hair, do you understand? And rubber cement should never go on your face. You could have gotten it in Emily's eyes, and then we would've ended up at the hospital. You will be in *big trouble* if you do this again, got it?"

"Got it," Rose said reluctantly.

"And yes, we're going to eat just as soon as I cook the spaghetti."

"Yay!" Emily said, clapping. "I love sketti and meatballs!"

"Me too!" Rose said. She smiled, already forgetting Josie's scolding.

"Me three," Ivy said, laughing. She winked at Josie. "C'mon, girls, let's go put your dress-up stuff away so you don't get sauce on it when we eat." Ivy herded Rose and Emily back toward the stairs as Josie slid the garlic bread into the oven and put the spaghetti on. With dinner in the homestretch, she meandered back to the little storage room. Other than the ancient typewriter and the rickety card table on which Ivy had placed it, the room contained her vacuum cleaner and a few boxes pushed up against the far wall. *Still, it'll make a cozy place to work, eventually,* she thought. For now, she was tickled to have the beginnings of a home office, albeit one of the makeshift variety.

"Let's set the table," she said when Ivy and the girls came back downstairs. Rose climbed up onto a chair and watched as Josie capped her highlighter and closed her notebook.

"Mom," Rose said, pointing to the still-open study guide, "why are you writing in your book? You always told us we were *never* supposed to write in a book, unless it's a coloring book."

Josie looked at the yellow highlighted passages. "I'm not writing in the book, Rosie. I'm highlighting. It's what you do when you read something that you have to study and that's *really important* for you to remember. See here, how I've made lots of these words yellow? It's because those are the main points in this chapter, and I want to remember them and also to be able to go back and see them quickly when I review them."

"Can I have a highlighter to use?" Rose asked.

"Hmm. What exactly would *you* use a highlighter for?"

Rose screwed up her mouth and was quiet for a minute.

"My spelling words!" Rose said suddenly. She looked up at Josie with a brightened expression. "Mrs. Harp gave us ten words that we have to know by the end of the week. And we have a spelling test on Friday. Don't you think that if I use a highlighter, I'll be able to remember them better?"

"Well," Josie said slowly, "I suppose that would be a good use for a highlighter." *This kid's going to be a lawyer, with the way she can think on her feet.* She looked over at Ivy, who was lifting plates down from the cupboard, trying not to laugh. "All right, I'll let you use one, but only if you promise that you will use it only in your spelling workbook and NOT in any other books or anyplace else. Deal?"

"Deal!" Rose held out her hand and grinned triumphantly as Josie handed her one of the fluorescent yellow markers. "I'm going to go put it up in my room. Be right back!"

"Make sure you cap it after you use it so it doesn't dry out," Josie called as Rose dashed out of the kitchen.

"She got you good," Ivy muttered. She nudged Josie aside to set the plates down on the table. "I call that manipulation through logic, and she's only six! You're in for it, I tell you. You just wait until she gets older."

"You're right," Josie said. She made a mental note to remove Rose's paper-doll scissors from her room. "Rose is diabolical. I'll just have to keep a close eye on her. I shudder to think how she'll turn out if I don't."

CHAPTER 9

Late in the evening, Claudia sat waiting on the sofa in Kyle's apartment, aimlessly flipping through television channels while he said good night to Rowen. She thought back to the afternoon, to the blowup between the DiSanti sisters, and before that, to when Kyle had offered to help unload Emily's things. He was always eager to lend a hand, and it was just one of the things she loved about him. Their relationship had matured during the time they'd been together, and Claudia had no reason to doubt Kyle's feelings for her. But even so, Emily's presence in Mill River made her nervous.

Claudia glanced down at her tummy and thighs, currently covered by her favorite blue jeans. It had taken her so much—months of exercise, strict dieting, willpower, and tears—to be able to fit in those size-ten jeans. Her stomach still wasn't as flat as she would like, and despite her now being at a healthy weight and very fit, she knew she would *never* look like Emily, who was effortlessly lithe with a gorgeous face to match.

Quit being so paranoid, Claudia suddenly chided herself. Of course Kyle had just been his usual polite self. Her own insecurities were trying to get the better of her.

"Well, she's not sleepy yet," Kyle announced as he came back into the living room. "We struck a bargain—she can read for another fifteen minutes and then it'll be lights out."

"She's already sucked into those new books, then?" Claudia asked.

"Yep," Kyle said. "She'll blow through them in a few days, tops. Did I tell you that her last achievement test showed that she reads at the eleventh grade level?"

"Um, you do remember that she was one of my students this past year?" Claudia asked, smiling.

"Oh, yeah." Kyle grinned, and his ears turned pink. "I just can't believe it myself, I guess."

"Nothing wrong with being a proud papa." Claudia snuggled closer to Kyle. He lifted an arm so that she could slide in beneath it and rest her head against his chest. "And it's good for her to read over the summer. Lots of kids don't do anything but watch TV once school's out. When school starts, their brains are still on vacation." She yawned. "I think tomorrow I'll start one of the books I got."

"It sure must be nice being a teacher, not having to work during the summer," Kyle said. "Sleeping late every day, reading novels, eating bonbons—"

"I haven't been eating bonbons!"

Kyle laughed and hugged her closer. "I know, I'm just teasing. And I'm not looking forward to starting my shift in the morning."

"Well, we've got a little time before you need to turn in. Do you want to watch TV? Or, hey, don't you have cable now? Maybe there's something on HBO."

"Oh, so *now* television is good?" Kyle said.

Claudia sat up a little, ready to unleash a witty retort in response to his latest tease, but she never got the chance. Before she could get one word out, he was kissing her. He reached his free hand around to run his fingers through her hair and, after a minute, he slid his hands around her waist and pulled her onto his lap.

"You don't suppose she's asleep yet?" Claudia whispered as Kyle's lips moved down her neck. She shivered and closed her eyes.

"Not a chance," he said softly. "But she can't stay awake all night."

"And you can?"

Kyle laughed and took her face in both of his hands. "Do you remember that night, oh, about five months ago, when we had dinner at the King's Lodge?"

Claudia would never forget that first night they'd spent together. She smiled and kissed him, thrilled that *he* had been the one to bring it up. "Valentine's Day."

"Um-hmm. And do you remember the surprise snowstorm, and how we came back here to watch a movie and couldn't because we lost power?

"Yes," Claudia breathed. Kyle's hands had slipped beneath her shirt, and the feeling of his fingers on her bare skin made it extremely difficult for her to concentrate.

"So you'll probably remember, then, that we were *both* awake for most of that night."

"We were," Claudia admitted. "And sleep is overrated."

Kyle pulled her tight against his chest. She was so focused on his mouth and his wandering hands that she forgot all about Emily DiSanti.

EMILY WAS UP EARLY THE NEXT MORNING. GUS DIDN'T SHARE HER energy, however. He lay across the foot of her bed and lifted his head, watching as she got herself cleaned up and dressed, before lowering it back down with a groan.

"You out of sorts, Gus?" Emily asked him, rubbing his ears. He responded with a whine and a few thumps of his tail. *Poor thing,* she thought. She completely understood his reluctance to get up. For a minute, she toyed with the idea of climbing back under the covers, but she had absolutely no food in the house for herself, and she needed to see about finding some sort of job. Also, as much as she preferred not to think about it after their horrible first exchange the day before, she knew that she would need to have a conversation with Rose at some point to work out how best to move forward.

By the time she had gotten groceries and turned back onto Main Street, the little town was fully awake. There were a few other cars on the street, and people were bustling in and out of the bakery and the other shops. Although she intended to go back to the little house, unload her groceries, and take Gus over to visit Ivy, Emily had a sudden idea as she spotted the hardware store. She pulled into a parking space and went over to the store just as an older man inside turned a sign hanging on the door so that OPEN faced out.

"Good morning, young lady," he said as she entered. "Can I help you with something?"

Emily smiled warmly. "Maybe," she said. "Are you the owner of this store?"

"I am," he said, puffing his chest out a bit. "Name's Henry Turner. And you are?"

"Emily DiSanti," she said, and immediately, Henry's expression changed.

"You're one of Josie's daughters," he said, nodding. "Your mom was my Realtor when I bought this place about ten years ago. You and your sister had already moved away by then, but I got to know your mom pretty well over the years. She was a sweet lady. I'm real sorry for your loss."

"Thank you," Emily replied. "Mom's the reason I'm in town, actually. I'm tying up some issues with her estate, and I expect to be here for some time. I was wondering if you might be in need of any sort of help with the store? I'm pretty handy, and I could be available full time or part time."

"Hmm." Henry's brow furrowed as he looked at her, and

Emily recognized his expression as one she'd seen dozens of times. He was sizing her up, wondering whether someone like her could be helpful to customers looking to buy tools or pipe fittings or paint.

"I have quite a bit of experience in home repair and renovation. For the last several years, I've been supporting myself by restoring old Victorian homes in San Francisco. I can do pretty much everything—plumbing, painting, even a little electrical work," Emily said.

"You don't say?" Henry asked. The wrinkles in his forehead became more pronounced as his eyebrows shot up. "How'd you learn to do all that?"

Emily chuckled. "While I was growing up, I was the one who fixed everything that broke in our house. My mom was always too busy and my older sister was too lazy, to be honest. Later on, I helped Mom spruce up properties she was trying to sell." Emily paused and considered carefully how to describe the next phase of her life. "After I left Mill River, the first job I got was as an assistant to a contractor. He taught me a lot. I started taking some courses at technical schools, too, when I had the time and money. Eventually, I moved further west and began doing jobs on my own. I enjoy it."

Henry looked at her without speaking for a minute. He walked over to one of the shelves, selected a tool from a display, and held it up. "Can you tell me what this is?"

"That's a pipe wrench."

"Yes. What's it used for?"

"You use it to tighten iron plumbing pipes and fittings."

"That's right. Why would you use this kind of wrench for that job?"

Emily smiled a little, amused at Henry's pop quiz. "Well, it's adjustable. Lots of pipes and fittings are made of soft iron. And, they're smooth and rounded, without the angles that a standard wrench needs to get a good grip. A pipe wrench has metal teeth, and the jaws tighten when you apply forward pressure. You need both those things to get a secure grip on a soft iron pipe." Emily's smile grew wider as Henry's mouth dropped open, and she decided to throw in a bit more for good measure. "You wouldn't usually use a pipe wrench on anything made of hardened steel, like a hex nut, because the teeth would ruin it."

"Well, shoot," he said finally. "With what you know, you're just the kind of person I'd hire if I could. The truth is, though, that I really don't have the budget to offer you a decent job. I could maybe give you ten or twelve hours a week at minimum wage, just for the summer. It's not much, but it'd give me some flexibility during our busy season, and it'd be a little change in your pocket."

"I wouldn't turn it down, Mr. Turner," Emily said, "so long as you understand that I'd have to take a second job once I find one."

"Call me Henry," he said. "And sure, I'd expect you need more than a few hours here. In fact, I actually have an idea about that. I'm sure you know Fitz and Ruth, the police chief and his wife?"

Emily nodded. "Ruth was my mom's best friend."

"They own that big white house up on the hill now," Henry continued, pointing over his shoulder in the direction of the McAllister mansion. "They're looking to turn the house into a bed-and-breakfast, and I have a feeling they might need some help getting it ready. I haven't seen the inside, but it's an old place. There's bound to be all sorts of things that need to be fixed or updated, and your experience would be perfect for that."

"It sounds wonderful," Emily said. "Thank you so much for the tip, Henry. I'll speak with Ruth about it as soon as I can."

"Good," Henry said with a smile. "And if you want to come by here around noon tomorrow, we can fill out some paperwork and decide on your schedule."

Emily gave Henry her contact information and left the hardware store with a grin on her face. Once back in her Impreza, she sat quietly for a few minutes before starting the engine. Maybe the good news on the job front was a sign that she had made the right decision in returning to Mill River. Maybe she really was supposed to be here. She couldn't help but wonder, though, whether her dealings with Rose would go equally as well.

ROSE WAS FEELING FRUSTRATED AND SLIGHTLY CLAUSTROPHOBIC. She sat on the sofa in the sweltering living room of her tiny summer house surrounded by half-open boxes, assorted pieces of her own furniture, and heaps of items that she had already unpacked. It didn't help that the house was full of the furnishings her mother had used over the years to stage her listings, as well as countless books and knickknacks and boxes of clothes. Even after he had reloaded some of her things back into the U-Haul, she was still "buried in her own crap," as Sheldon had so helpfully pointed out.

With her son upstairs reading in his room, as usual, Rose looked around at those boxes she had yet to open, trying to figure out which one held what she was looking for. She began hefting them around, restacking and shaking them, until she heard a faint *clink* inside one of them. Her hands trembled as she ripped open the tape across the top and dug through the folded linens inside. Two bottles of gold rum were nestled safely together under the towels.

Rose grabbed the bottles and headed into the kitchen. There were two full ice cube trays in the freezer, thank God, and she still had a few cans of Diet Coke left over from the drive from the city. She opened the kitchen cupboards methodically until she found one that contained drinking glasses. Rose felt giddy and slightly frenzied as she twisted ice cubes out of the tray and opened one of the rum bottles. She could make a rum and Coke in her sleep.

With the first sip of the drink, Rose felt a wave of relaxation roll over her. She downed the rest and poured herself another be-fore returning to the sofa. It was odd, how the temperature in the house seemed to decrease as she savored the sweet burn of the sec-ond drink.

Rose let her head fall back against the sofa. She was finally feel-ing comfortable when the doorbell rang. She ignored it at first, but after the fourth ring, she scowled and hauled herself to her feet.

At the door, Rose peered through the peephole.

Her sister stood on the stoop.

Rose muttered a curse, but she knew that ignoring Emily would only delay the inevitable. She unlocked the dead bolt and opened the door, leaving the screen door in place.

Emily's expression was one of surprise and uncertainty. For a long minute, they stared at each other, but neither of them spoke. Finally, Rose broke the silence.

"Well?"

Emily crossed her arms. "We should put what happened yes-terday behind us and talk about how we're going to do this."

"All right. Talk."

Emily looked pointedly at the screen door that separated them. Rose sighed and rolled her eyes. She stepped out onto the stoop and raised a hand to shield her eyes from the glare of the set-ting sun.

"Look, I don't want this to be any harder than it has to," Emily said. "Do you have a copy of Mom's letter?"

"Yes."

"So do I. I've read it a bazillion times, and I assume you've done the same thing. The letter says we each have a clue hidden, and the clues are different from each other. I think we ought to take inventory of everything in our houses and then compare."

Rose thought about that. It was a reasonable, logical course of action, but the mere thought of trying to make sense of the jumbled mess inside her house—to "take inventory"—gave her a headache. It was annoying, how a conversation of twenty seconds with her sister had completely killed her buzz.

Emily shifted her weight from one foot to the other, waiting for her response. "Do you have a better idea?" she finally asked, with an edge to her voice.

"I don't want to stay here any longer than I have to, but I'll need a few days," Rose said, raising her chin. "This whole place is full of the crap Mom put in here, and I'm not even close to unpacking my own things, much less going through all her stuff."

Emily's jaw tensed. "Fine. Today's Monday. Take the next few days and make a list of everything in there that you didn't bring with you. We can meet Thursday morning, at my house, to go over the lists. With any luck, we'll figure out the clues and find the key quickly. We could be done with this whole thing by the end of the week." She looked Rose full in the eyes before she turned and left.

Rose went back inside and shut the door. She was surprised to find Alex standing in the living room.

"Was that Aunt Emily?" he asked. Alex held a thick book under one arm. He shoved his glasses further up on his nose as he looked at her.

"Yes, sweetie."

"Why did she come over?"

Rose sighed. She walked back to the sofa and picked up her nearly empty glass. There were three tiny pieces of ice left in it, floating in the last diluted bit of her drink. "She wanted to talk about how we're going to find the clues that Grandma left us."

"Oh."

Rose swirled the remaining liquid in her glass before taking it all into her mouth. Alex didn't move from the place where he stood. "What is it, honey?" she asked once she swallowed the mouthful.

"Why don't you and Aunt Emily like each other?"

It was a question she'd expected to have to deal with at some point, and she sighed before responding. "Because of something that happened a long time ago, something you wouldn't understand right now. I'll explain it once you're a little older." Rose watched Alex's face as he thought about her answer, and she was thankful when he didn't try to argue the point.

"Don't you and Aunt Emily have to find the clues to get Grandma's safe-deposit-box key?"

"That's what the letter says."

"How are you going to do that if you don't like each other?"

"Your aunt and I are going to make a list of everything in these two houses. Once that's done, we should be able to see what's different on the lists. Two of those things should be the clues."

"Oh. Well, can I help make the list of stuff that's here?"

Rose felt a little spark of glee at her son's offer. She smiled at him, and the grin that stretched across his face went straight to her heart. For a minute, he was a baby again, smiling at her, toothless and blissfully happy. His nine-year-old smile was bigger and had teeth but was otherwise unchanged. However, she had changed.

"Sure! That'd be great! We've got plenty of time, though. We don't have to show our list to Aunt Emily until Thursday morning."

"That's cool, Mom." Alex said. "I can't wait to figure out what the clues are! Can I start working on it right now?"

"Knock yourself out," Rose said. "Oh, and what do you want for dinner? I haven't gone food shopping yet, but I could call in an order to Pizza Hut."

"Okay," Alex said. He was examining a stack of boxes in the far corner of the living room. "Hey, Mom, this box has Aunt Ivy's name on it," he said. The top of the box was closed with the flaps tucked beneath each other, but it pulled open easily. "It's full of books! They look like they're really old."

Alex brought several of the books from the box to show her. They were paperbacks with faded, worn covers and yellowed pages.

"Huh," she said as she glanced down at the titles. They were all classics—*A Tree Grows in Brooklyn, The Catcher in the Rye, To Kill a Mockingbird,* and *The Count of Monte Cristo.* "Have you read any of these yet?"

"Nope."

"Well, you should. It's been years since I read them, but they're all great. I loved *The Count of Monte Cristo.* It's like, the *ultimate* tale of revenge." She paused and looked over at the opened book box. "You know, every once in a while when your aunt Emily and I were growing up, Aunt Ivy would give Grandma a big box of old books. They were the ones she couldn't sell and that the library didn't want. Sometimes the covers were ripped off, and a lot of them had pages that were falling out. Grandma still read them to us, though. As long as she could see the words on the page, that's all that mattered." Rose smirked. "I'll bet these are all rejects from The Bookstop."

"Can I have them, then?" Alex asked. "I could take the whole box up to my room."

"Sure. Just be careful with the box—it's heavy. You should probably take the books out and make a few trips."

Alex cleared out the books in no time and disappeared back to his room. Rose called in an order to Pizza Hut. She had actually made progress unpacking some of her clothes by the time the doorbell rang again.

That was fast, Rose thought. She pulled her wallet from her purse and hurried to the door.

Instead of the pizza delivery person, Daisy Delaine glanced up at her and nervously fingered a jar that was filled with some sort of bright orange liquid and wrapped with a matching ribbon.

Rose squeezed her eyes shut as she processed the identity of her visitor. It didn't take her long to remember where they had last met.

"Miss Rose," Daisy said with a slight stammer, "I heard you were back in town for the summer, Miss Rose." She swallowed hard, and her voice dropped to a whisper. "I still feel awful about what happened at your mom's house. I decided to come tell you again how sorry I still am for what I did to your mother's ashes. I made this special, for you," she continued, holding up the jar. "It's a forgiveness potion."

Rose kept her hands close to her chest to avoid touching the jar. She could see how the contents left a film on the inside of the glass. There was no telling *what* was actually inside it.

"Uh, thank you, but no," Rose said. All the warm feelings she'd had talking with her son vanished. "I know accidents happen, but you really *are* an idiot if you think that people actually want these potions you make, or that they actually work. Because of that crap you brought to my mother's wake, her remains were ruined. We couldn't even salvage any to have a proper burial for her. So, you can keep whatever the hell is in that jar."

Rose took a last look at Daisy's shocked face and closed the door firmly. She didn't care if she ever saw that weird little woman again.

CHAPTER 10

A FEW WEEKS AFTER SHE HAD SAVED EMILY'S HAIR FROM Rose's scissors, Josie awoke before her alarm clock rang. Her sleep had been fitful, so it was almost a relief to get up. She looked at the new navy suit hanging in plastic on her closet doorknob. She'd bought matching pumps, too, and she was grateful to have gotten the whole outfit at clearance prices. Trying to control the nervous energy that flowed through her, she took a deep breath and went to wake the girls for school. Today, she had an interview at a real estate agency in Rutland.

Josie moved automatically through her morning routine and got the girls off to school. With Rose on the bus and Emily safely at St. John's, she raced back home to get ready. It felt strange, wearing such a formal outfit, along with hose and heels, but she didn't dwell on it. She wanted to get to Rutland with plenty of time to find the Circle Realty office and collect herself before the interview.

Of the many offices to which Josie had written, only one had responded positively to her inquiry about a possible trainee position. Circle Realty was a small agency in the southwest, flood-prone area of Rutland City that locals referred to as "The Gut."

As she drove into Rutland and down the street where the office was located, Josie felt right at home. True, there was nothing fancy about the houses and shops she was passing, and the few people walking outside were dressed plainly. But, there was absolutely nothing wrong with that. *These are just regular, hardworking people.* The Gut reminded her of her old Bronx neighborhood, and it was certainly far nicer than many areas in the Bronx that she used to avoid.

At precisely five minutes before ten, Josie pushed open the door to the Circle Realty office. A small bell rang to signal her entrance. Inside, the front room smelled of old coffee, mildew, and the moist, steamy odor of radiator heat. The gray carpeted floor creaked beneath her feet. An unattended receptionist's desk and a freestanding coatrack were to her left. On her right was a small seating area and a table that held a pot full of coffee, a stack of Styrofoam cups, and a bowl of individual packets of sugar and creamer. A closed door directly before her presumably led to other offices.

For the moment, she was the only one in the room.

Josie hung up her coat. She smoothed her skirt and removed a small piece of lint that was stuck to one of her sleeves. She was wondering whether she should sit down when the door in front of her swung open.

"I thought I heard someone come in," a man said as he entered the room. He seemed to be a few years older than she, maybe in his mid-thirties. He had black hair and dark brown eyes and wore a black and white houndstooth sport coat. "I'm Ned Circle. You must be Josie." Ned held a piece of cold, half-eaten pizza on a napkin in one hand. He wiped his other hand on the side of his pants leg and extended it.

"Yes," Josie said as she shook his hand. "It's very nice to meet you."

"Likewise. Come on back," he said, motioning to the open door with his pizza. "Oh, and I hope you'll pardon my late breakfast. I meant to finish before you got here, but one thing led to another, you know how it goes." He took a bite of pizza and continued talking. "This is from Ted's, by the way, the pizza place up on State Street. Best in Rutland, hands down. I've got a few pieces left, if you're hungry."

"Oh, no thank you," Josie said, as she followed him into an office. She was slightly put off by Ned's casual manner and greasy handshake.

"Here we go," Ned said. They had entered a crowded, disorganized office. Ned sat down behind a desk covered in papers and a paper plate full of hard pizza crusts. He motioned for Josie to sit in a chair facing the desk as he quickly slid the plate into a wastepaper basket. "Sorry about the mess," he said. "My secretary quit three weeks ago, and I've been trying to keep things afloat by myself." He picked up two papers neatly folded together on top of the chaos—Josie's letter and résumé. "Now, Josie . . . wait, is it all right if I call you Josie?"

"Yes. May I call you Ned?"

"Please do. So, Josie, tell me why you want to become a real estate agent." Ned took another bite of his pizza and stared at her while he chewed.

Because my savings are running out and I need a job, something that will let me keep my two babies fed and clothed and warm. Josie looked Ned squarely in the eyes. "Because I would enjoy helping people find the perfect places to live. I also have extensive sales experience."

Ned looked down at her résumé. Josie followed his gaze, watching as his eyes swept across the page.

"You sold jewelry."

"Yes."

"What makes you think your skill in selling jewelry will translate to real estate?"

"If you know the product you're selling and can read people well enough to match them with the product they'll buy, it doesn't matter whether you're trying to sell diamonds or real estate or anything else. You'll be successful."

"Hmm. Your résumé says you're from New York. If you don't mind my asking, what brought you to Vermont?"

"I have family in Mill River. I moved up here with my daughters two years ago, after my husband died."

Ned stopped chewing. "Oh, I'm sorry." Flustered, he paused for a moment, seeming to struggle with what to say next.

"Perhaps you could tell me a little about your agency?" Josie asked. "And also a little about what you're looking for in a trainee? I'm scheduled to take the licensing exam in a few weeks."

Ned jumped at the chance to change the subject. "Of course. Well, I'm a solo broker and have been since I opened Circle Realty about a decade ago. I grew up here in Rutland, in this neighborhood, actually. I've done all right, although the market is tough now with interest rates being what they are. To be completely honest, I wasn't really looking to take on a new agent when I received your letter, but then Marsha quit—she was my secretary—and she really kept things organized. The fact that you're aiming to get your license is a real plus."

Ned took one last bite of pizza and dropped the crust in his wastepaper basket along with a few others. He looked at her with an innocent expression as he waited for her reply.

Josie blinked. *Had she heard this man correctly?* She swallowed, trying to phrase her next question as politely as she could.

"So, Ned, what you're telling me is that you're really looking for a . . . a new secretary?"

"Well," Ned said slowly, "I was thinking that you could start as a secretary, since I've got a lot of things that need sorting and filing." He motioned to the papers that were stacked and strewn about his office. "It's the slow season, anyway, so you could study for your exam once the place is tidied up. After you get your sales license, you could try showing a few houses. And, just to prove I'm a nice guy, I'll even give you a listing to get you started. It'd be a good test to see what you can do. If you can find a buyer for it, well, I'd make you a permanent agent. If you can sell as well as you say, it would work out well for the both of us."

After so much preparation to become a salesperson, Josie had half a mind to tell Ned where he could get off, but a very calm, practical thought emerged through her disgust. If she started as a secretary, she would not be expected to work on commission. Here was a chance at a small, but regular, paycheck, something that would help stretch her savings. She would be able to study for her exams at least part of the time she was at work, and she might be able to hit the ground running with a sale once she was licensed, if Ned really did give her a listing of her own.

"I have a few questions," Josie began.

"Shoot."

"I'd consider starting as a secretary, but my girls are still very young, in first grade and nursery school. Since I'm all they have, I need to be there for them when they're home. Would you still be willing to hire me if I could work only part time for now, during the mornings, when both my girls are in school?"

Ned looked at her with his mouth scrunched up. Josie realized that she had made the right decision in revealing why she had come to Vermont. It was obvious that Ned was trying to balance his sympathy for her situation with the need to have a full-time employee to clean up his mess.

"I suppose that would be all right," he said finally. "But at only part time, I couldn't provide benefits. It would have to be a straight hourly position."

"I understand," Josie said.

Ned nodded and continued. "That's not to say you couldn't work more hours when you're able to. I'm not so worried about phone calls and such as I am getting files and paperwork in order. I trust that you'd be extremely efficient during the hours you're here."

"I assure you I would be," Josie said. "And just so I understand you correctly, if I sell the listing you give me, I'd have a job as only a salesperson, and not a secretary?"

"My word is my bond. In fact, if you sell the listing, I'll even let you keep a hundred percent of the commission from the sale. I'm a pretty nice guy, you know."

Josie stared into Ned's smarmy face and managed a small smile. "I could start as soon as this Friday, around nine o'clock?"

"Excellent," Ned said. He flashed a toothy grin as his dark eyes lit up. "Between now and then I'll get your tax paperwork ready and write out everything we talked about, and the commission structure, too, just so that there are no misunderstandings."

"All right." Josie rose from her chair and extended her hand to Ned. When he clasped it, she noticed that his hand didn't feel quite as greasy as it had earlier. "Thank you, Ned, for giving me this opportunity."

"No thanks necessary, Josie. Hey, I'll see you out."

They exited Ned's messy office and came back into the front room. Josie hesitated at the front door before stepping outside. "I just thought of one more thing," she said.

"Yes?"

"The listing you said you'd give me . . . you already have one in mind?"

Ned smiled again, this time without showing his teeth. "Indeed I do."

"Would you mind . . . well, to be honest, I'm curious. Would you mind if I drove past it to take a look?"

"Ah, no, not at all. Wait just a sec, and I'll get the address for you." He disappeared back through the door and returned quickly with a small piece of paper, which he handed to her. "It's not far from here, and I just put the sign up in the yard last week. Be warned, though, the place is by no means perfect."

Josie looked down at the paper and back at him. "No house is perfect, Ned."

"True, true. But, some are more perfect than others. I was being honest when I said this listing would test you. See you Friday morning." He smirked a little before leaving her alone in the waiting area.

Josie looked at her watch and grabbed her coat. If she hurried, she could get a look at the property that was to be her first, very own listing before she had to pick up Emily.

Once back in her car, she found the street on Ivy's map and started out. Reality was finally hitting her. *She had a job.* It wasn't a great job, and her new boss was . . . well, she didn't even want to start thinking of words to describe Ned lest she ruin her increasingly happy mood . . . but she had a job!

In a few minutes, Josie had driven back through the center of town. The address scribbled on the paper Ned had given her was for a house on Gleason Road, and that street was easy to find. She hadn't gone very far down Gleason when she saw the Rutland City Landfill looming on the right side of the road. She passed City Dump Road, the street that served as the entrance to the landfill, and she slowed the car as a sinking realization developed in the pit of her stomach.

Just beyond the far corner of the boundary of the landfill stood a tiny ranch house with a Circle Realty sign in the yard. Quickly, she turned into the driveway and stared at the little house that faced her.

It was painted an old, dingy brown, and the shingles on the roof were streaked with mildew and tattered. The white Circle Realty sign gleamed by comparison, and Josie couldn't believe that the house had been inhabited anytime recently. The driveway, or what she could see of it, was full of cracks, and a half-rotted wooden fence ringed the yard. Josie got out of her car, but she was afraid to go peek into the darkened windows of the house because of what she might see.

The worst part about the property, though, wasn't even on the property. Perhaps fifty yards and a thin row of trees separated the backyard from the chain-link-fenced perimeter of the Rutland City Landfill. Josie stood, fighting back tears, as she listened to the constant rumbling of trucks and bulldozers working the heaps of trash. A pile of scrap metal was visible in the distance through the leafless trees. When the wind shifted, it carried with it the pungent odor of garbage.

What had started as a day of promise and hope was ending in frustration and despair. Josie leaned against her car, trembling. As she often did when she was worried or upset, she reached up to touch the gold locket around her neck, the gift from Ivy that now held tiny pictures of Rose and Emily. She thought of Tony, too, wondering how she would be able to keep her promise to him. How would she ever manage to build a career and earn enough to support her girls when the first obstacle in her path was literally a mountain of trash?

As she stared at her first listing-to-be, Josie felt her despair turn to anger. She had come too far and had too much at stake to turn back now. She was shocked that Ned could be so cruel as to give her this listing, that he had the audacity to describe it as some sort of gift from "a nice guy." Josie gritted her teeth.

For Rose, Emily, and Tony, she would go forward.

She would launch a successful career in real estate, even if she had to do it by finding a buyer for a dump of a house that also bordered on a dump.

And finally, she would show Ned Circle that he had vastly underestimated her.

CHAPTER 11

On Thursday morning, as agreed, Rose knocked on Emily's front door. Several sheets of paper were folded in her hand. She gripped them tighter as she heard barking and then footsteps approaching.

Emily opened the door and stared at her for a moment, restraining her large dog. She had a pair of safety goggles pushed up on her forehead, and her face was dripping with sweat.

"I brought my list," Rose said, holding up the papers. "Shall we get it over with?"

Emily nodded. "Back up, Gus," she said as she held the door open.

Rose stepped inside the house. It was a little larger than the one she and Alex were sharing, but more sparsely furnished and very tidy. "You're unpacked already?" she asked. Emily's dog came up and began sniffing at her, and she raised her hands to avoid coming into contact with his cold wet nose.

"I didn't bring much," Emily replied, "and there wasn't a lot in here to begin with." She grabbed the dog's collar and pulled it toward the back of the house. Rose followed at a distance.

"What's with the goggles?"

"I do stained glass," Emily said, pointing into a room off to the side as they passed. "I was just cutting pieces for a new design." Rose caught a glimpse of a large worktable covered in small tools and bits of glass in various sizes and shapes.

Emily picked up a small stack of papers in the kitchen and continued out the door onto a small deck. As Gus rushed past them, Emily took a seat at an old aluminum patio set and looked up expectantly.

"So . . . I didn't find anything over here that jumped out at me," Emily began after Rose had sat down. She spread the list out on the table. "I went through every room and even the garage, but nothing's out of the ordinary. It's all just basic house stuff—furniture, dishes, books, tools, and a few drawers and boxes of assorted junk."

Rose nodded. "My house is the same way, although I got more of Mom's old staging furniture than you did. There's a bunch of boxes from Ivy's, too."

"Well, maybe that's something important. You having more furniture, I mean. Maybe one of the clues is—"

"What, a chair? Or a lamp, maybe?" Rose interrupted. "No way. Mom would've picked clues that had some sort of special meaning for her and for us. I was trying to think of stuff that happened while we were growing up."

"How about something having to do with the kitchen?" Emily said. "It's where we all hung out most of the time. Mom loved to cook, even though she was usually too busy to do it. And, do you remember what happened that one time with the dishwasher?"

"Yeah," Rose said. Despite her feeling so uncomfortable and awkward at having to interact with Emily, she felt the corners of her mouth curve up into a smile. She hadn't thought about the dishwasher incident in years, but for one fleeting moment, her mind skipped over all of the guilt, the blurred hangovers, and the painful, gaping hole in her life that had been left when Emily cut off all communication with her. She was her nearly eleven-year-old self again, clutching her sister and squealing with laughter as they both tried to keep from falling on the slippery kitchen floor.

In that one instant, Rose had an overpowering urge to reach over and grab Emily's hand. She would squeeze it and beg for forgiveness. Or maybe words would be unnecessary, and she would somehow convey through their connected hands the love that she tried to forget. Maybe, somehow, she could find a way to repair Emily's heart and restore their relationship.

Then, just as quickly, the moment passed, and her usual guilt and shame returned.

Rose blinked hard and began sorting through her papers until she found a copy of the letter their mother had written to them. "We're supposed to be looking for two different objects," she said as she scanned it again. "I didn't pay much attention to the plates and things in the cupboards, but maybe one of the clues is an old coffee mug or something?"

Emily sat very still, with a wistful expression. "It could be," she said finally. "We should both go through our kitchens again. And I think we should look at the books in our houses, too. Mom almost always read to us at bedtime. And the letter says that one of the clues 'will reveal the location of the key.' It makes sense that that one would be a book. Something in it could reveal a location, right? So, how many books are on your list?" Emily peered over at her papers.

Rose sighed. "I didn't actually count them or list them all out. There are tons of them everywhere, on shelves, in boxes. Some are so old they're falling apart." She was beginning to get a headache, and she could feel herself becoming irritable.

"Well, I've got lots, too, and I *did* list them individually," Emily said. "You need to go back and write down all your titles so we can compare."

Annoyed at her sister's bossy tone, Rose rolled her eyes. "And then what? If she chose a book as a clue, how are we supposed to know? Especially if it's one we haven't read?"

"Mom wouldn't have expected us to read hundreds of books in only two months," Emily said. "If one of the clues is a book, it'll be one we've already read."

"Maybe," Rose said. "But even if it is, we'll still have to figure out what the second clue is to find the key."

"The second clue, 'something that will help you obtain it,' could be a book, too, just a different one," Emily pointed out.

What I wouldn't give for a drink, Rose thought. She closed her eyes and leaned her forehead on her hand.

"Look, at least we've started," Emily said. "Let's just go back, list out every detail of what's in our kitchens. You should list which books you have and which you've already read. It shouldn't take that long, just a few more days. Maybe we can meet again this Sunday."

"Fine," Rose said as she stood up to leave. She had truly expected to be done with their mother's stupid directive within a few days. She'd even stopped unpacking in the hope that they'd be leaving soon, but now it looked as if they might be stuck in Mill River all summer. *It figures,* she thought. If their mother had wanted to force them to interact, wouldn't she have wanted them to live next door to each other for as long as possible?

ONCE ROSE HAD GONE, EMILY TOOK GUS BACK INSIDE AND RUBBED his ears. "I'll be back soon, boy, and then we'll go for a nice walk." Even though Gus whined in protest, she slipped out the front door. She had a meeting scheduled with Ruth and Fitz.

"Emily! Come sit. I just made some coffee," Ruth said as she arrived at the bakery. "Or, would you rather have tea?"

"Coffee's fine, Ruth," Emily said. "Thanks."

"I don't know how much you've heard about Mary McAllister," Fitz said once they were all seated. "She was the lady who lived in that big white house on the hill. No one ever saw her much or even knew anything about her. Turns out she suffered from a mental illness all her life and never went out much. But, she did a lot for folks here in town without them knowing it."

"I did her grocery shopping for years," Ruth chimed in. "I only saw her in person once, though."

"And she's still magically gifting people things. After she died in February, she left the house to Ruthie and me," Fitz said. "We've always dreamed of running a bed-and-breakfast, and we figure now that the bakery's been restored to what it was before the fire this past March, we're ready to start working on that."

Emily nodded. "It looks beautiful from the outside. Is the place in good shape?"

"It seems to be," Ruth said. "It's well built, and Mrs. McAllister hired contractors for any necessary maintenance and repairs while she lived there."

"It has seven bedrooms, all but one with a private bath, but most of them were never used," Fitz said. "Some of the bedrooms aren't even furnished. They've just sat, closed and empty, for more than seventy years."

"Wow," Emily said. "It sounds amazing. But, what would you need to do to convert it to a bed-and-breakfast?"

"To be honest, we haven't decided everything yet," Ruth said with a smile. "I think we should freshen up the place. New paint, certainly, and maybe we could get new carpets and refinish the hardwood floors."

"I think we'd need to swap out the bathroom fixtures for new, modern ones," Fitz said, "and we should also check the plumbing to see if anything's worn out."

"And the kitchen, of course," Ruth said. "I'll need new appliances and better work space. The kitchen might need the most work of anything."

"You ought to think about the basic systems in the house, too," Emily said. "Heating and cooling, and a hot water supply that would be enough to accommodate a houseful of guests. You might need an upgraded electricity supply, too."

"You're right," Fitz said.

"When would you want to be ready to open?" Emily asked.

"We haven't set a date," Ruth said. "Certainly, there's no rush. We figured we'd do the work a little at a time and see how it goes. We're so busy with our jobs, though, we don't have much time to devote to our little retirement project." Ruth reached over and grabbed Fitz's hand as she smiled.

"It sounds wonderful," Emily said. "I'll be honest, though. What you've described is a lot of work for one person. I'm not even sure I'm qualified to do some of the more complex repairs. Everything will have to be brought up to code if you're going to operate it as a motel. I'm sure you'll need to install smoke detectors and maybe make other changes to protect against fire. And, since it's an older house, you might have some lead-based paint problems to deal with. Which brings me to my next question—what kind of budget do you have for the improvements?"

"We've got enough to do pretty much everything," Fitz said. "Mrs. McAllister left us a generous amount to be used for renovations. Before we start, we'll have to submit a formal estimate for the work to Jim Gasaway, who's overseeing the distribution of her estate. I don't think it'll be a problem, though. It's just a matter of finding the right person, or people, to do the job."

"We know you've worked miracles with old houses," Ruth said. "Your mom used to tell me all about your projects. I think we'd be happy to have you do as much with the house as you can, and we'd pay whatever fee you typically charge. If there are things you need help with, we'll hire whatever other contractors you need."

"Well, okay then," Emily said. "I'm working at Turner's a few hours a week, but I still have lots of time. When should I start?"

"It might be a few weeks. I'll call Jim tomorrow and get the ball rolling on the release of funds," Fitz said. "I'm sure he'll want to see a proposal and an estimate for what we want to do."

"But, if you wanted to, you could go up and take a look around the place," Ruth said. "Maybe you could spend a little time at the house and plan out what might be good to do first."

"I'd love to," Emily said. "In fact, I could work up a proposal and prepare an initial estimate of everything for you, if you'd like."

"That would be perfect," Fitz said.

"I've got keys upstairs," Ruth said. "Just wait while I run and get one." She disappeared through the back room of the bakery, where a staircase led to the two upstairs apartments. In only a few minutes, she was back, breathless and holding out a large key to Emily.

"Thank you," Emily said to the Fitzgeralds. "I really appreciate your giving me this job."

"Oh, pish. We're grateful you came to town when you did and are willing to help us out," Ruth said, and Fitz nodded in agreement. "There's no one else we'd rather have."

As Ruth rushed to tend to waiting customers, Emily left the bakery to get Gus. It took only a few minutes of driving to reach the edge of town and the entrance to the winding driveway of the big white mansion. It would be best to see the place with the mid-day sun shining brightly overhead, and she felt giddy with antici-pation as she reached the top of the driveway and parked her car.

She inserted the key in the lock and let herself in the back door. A rush of cool, stale air met her face as she stepped inside a small mudroom. Gus whined behind her, and she took him gently by his leash and led him forward into the kitchen.

The large room was quiet and dim. Emily walked to the window above the sink and raised the blinds. She noticed that the appliances and fixtures on the sink were relatively modern, but everything else in the kitchen—the floor, countertops, and cabinets—looked to be the original versions. All were worn and in need of replacement. Still, Emily could see that there was plenty of space to update and modernize, and she could envision Ruth standing in the finished room sliding pies into a new professional oven.

"Stay here, boy," Emily said, as Gus flopped down on the old kitchen floor. "I'm just going to let some light in."

She walked slowly from the kitchen. The large gathering room she entered had a vaulted ceiling, and a grand staircase led to the second floor. To her left, there was a dining room with a dusty chandelier hanging from the ceiling. To her right was another, smaller room that might have been used as a parlor or a library. What furniture remained in the rooms was covered by white sheets.

Emily headed straight across the room toward a wall of heavy drapes. She gripped the thick fabric and pulled, squinting as the sunlight streamed through the uncovered picture windows. When her eyes adjusted, she looked from the dust particles floating in the light back into the room. Only then did the splendor of the mansion—the sheer size of the house, the fine woodwork and moldings, the exquisite paintings of horses and Vermont countryside that still hung on the walls—come into view. Emily smiled. She couldn't wait to see the beautiful home spruced up and open for all to see.

She turned to peer out the window at the little town below. From where she stood, the view of Main Street was absolutely perfect. In fact, almost all of Mill River was clearly visible from her unique vantage point. She looked down at The Bookstop and next to it, her mother's house, where she'd grown up. It was strange to think that she now stood in the former home of the person who had given her mother that little house in her time of greatest need.

After a moment, Emily's line of sight drifted from her childhood residence to the two little houses across the street from it where she and her sister were stuck for the summer.

Emily sighed as she thought about her initial meeting with Rose. It had gone well, but it would be a miracle if they actually managed to figure out what their mother had hidden for them without killing each other. In fact, she could barely stand the sight of her sister. The thought of them reconciling, as their mother had so desperately wanted, was such a joke.

She turned to look again at the beautiful room in which she stood. She could patch walls and refinish woodwork. She knew how to replace rotted floorboards and fix leaky faucets, and even how to coax a shine out of the most tarnished metal. She was absolutely confident in her ability to return the old mansion to its full glory.

And she was just as confident that her relationship with Rose was beyond repair.

CHAPTER 12

ON THE FIRST MONDAY MORNING AFTER THE NEW YEAR, Josie arrived at Circle Realty a few minutes early to prepare for a meeting. She stood at the door, fumbling for the key, when the bracing test blasts of the loud air horn atop the fire station—what locals called the "ten-of-nine whistle"—startled her so badly that she nearly dropped her purse. Since the fire, she'd become so sensitive to sudden loud noises, and the damned air horn nearly gave her a heart attack every morning.

In the warmth and quiet of the Circle Realty office, Josie hung up her coat and waited for her heart to stop pounding. She was pleased to see that the office was almost as tidy as she'd left it on Friday. Since she'd accepted Ned's offer of employment, she'd completely organized and de-cluttered everything. All of the office files were now properly placed in drawers for open listings, pending sales, or closed deals. The surfaces of all the tables, counters, and storage cabinets were bare and dusted, and even the dark wooden top of Ned's awful desk was visible in places.

Above her own neat workstation, her newly issued real estate license was already framed and hanging on the wall. Now, finally, she was permitted to show houses. Unfortunately, Josie had arrived at the conclusion that it would be useless to show the listing Ned had given her. The dilapidated house bordering on Rutland's municipal landfill would be virtually impossible to sell—a fact that was not lost on Ned. Clearly, he had set her up to fail. But, she was determined to deny him the satisfaction of seeing her struggle. Never would she give Ned any indication of the shock and despair she'd felt upon seeing the property that he had tasked her with selling.

And, she had already come up with a plan.

The property bordering the dump would require an unorthodox buyer, and she had scheduled a meeting for later in the morning that was, in her opinion, her best shot at finding that buyer.

Josie took an old vacuum cleaner in a storage closet and gave the front office carpet a once-over. It was beginning to feel as if her job title should also include "custodian," but now was not the time to get worked up over that. After she put away the vacuum cleaner and started the coffeepot, she returned to her desk to look over the file for the property.

At twenty past nine, Ned strolled through the front door, late as usual. He was midway through eating what looked like a large bran muffin, and he didn't seem to notice the trail of crumbs he left as he came inside.

"Morning," he said as he chewed. "Sorry I'm late, just one of those days. Good, you made coffee. Any calls yet?" He was shifting the muffin from one hand to the other as he removed his coat, which scattered more crumbs and some larger pieces on the floor.

"No, nothing yet," Josie replied. "I figured it would be slow today, so soon after the holidays, so I was planning to do a walk-through of my listing this morning. It'd be good to see if there's anything useful to know about it that's not in the file."

It was a small lie, because she'd done the walk-through just before Christmas. The inside of the house had been even worse than the outside. Leaks in the roof and plumbing, soiled carpet, and peeling, hideously patterned wallpaper marred the interior.

She suspected that the house had many more problems that weren't so obvious. She raised her gaze to meet Ned's and smiled calmly, confidently, as though she hadn't any worries.

"That's a good idea," Ned said. "The owner's name is Al Celebrezze. Little Italian guy, works down at the Ford lot. His father refused to sell it when the city first opened the landfill and offered to take it off his hands. Al said he was holding out for more, but the city never came up on its lowball offer. Pretty dumb decision in hindsight. His father passed back in October, and now Al's stuck with the property. He'll be thrilled if you can help him unload it." Ned returned her smile as he poured himself a cup of coffee, but Josie saw a hint of a smirk appear on his face before he headed back to his own office.

Once he was gone, Josie quickly bent down and picked up the larger pieces of muffin on the floor. Her hand shook with suppressed anger as she deposited them in the trash. She had learned very quickly that Ned had a talent for trampling all over her last nerve. *Breathe,* she told herself. *Focus.* With great effort, Josie went back to reading the file on her pathetic listing.

She was still engrossed in the file when Ned came back into the front office to refill his coffee mug.

"I have a question," she said as she looked up just in time to see Ned spill powdered creamer onto the carpet. "There's a note in here that three Realtors turned down Al's house before you took it on. I was wondering if you would ever refuse a listing if it's one you thought you couldn't sell."

"That's an easy one," Ned said. He took a sip of his coffee and added more sugar. "I've never turned down a listing."

"Really? Have all of your listings sold?"

"Of course not. But they don't have to."

Josie looked at him quizzically.

"Obviously, you've got to sell *some* houses to get by. But, even if I don't think I can sell a house, it's worth trying. I might surprise myself and make a sale. Another agent might bring me a buyer for it. If neither of those things happens, it still might bring me some good business connections or referrals. The networking's important, even if you can't move a property, and you never know. A situation you might think is hopeless could lead to great things." His eyebrows shot up as he smiled. Ned seemed to be pleased with the advice he'd given her.

"That makes sense," Josie said. She offered him a perky smile. "Thanks."

"Don't mention it." Ned raised his mug to her, took another drink, and headed back to his office.

When he was gone, Josie muttered a few curses, retrieved the vacuum from the storage closet, and cleaned up the spilled creamer. Then she put on her coat and headed out.

Her situation was far from hopeless.

At ten-thirty sharp, Josie arrived at the redbrick city hall building. The holiday wreaths were still up on either side of the front door, and the twin lampposts were encircled with festive red and green garlands. She asked directions and found her way to the mayor's office, where a clerk greeted her and showed her in.

"Ms. DiSanti? Phil Lawson." A blond, youngish fellow dressed in khakis and a rugby shirt sat behind the desk. He rose to shake her hand.

"Nice to meet you, Mr. Lawson."

"Oh, please call me Phil. 'Mister' is too fancy for this office." He grinned as he sat down and invited her to do the same. "I understand you're here with some questions about a certain property?"

"Yes," she replied. "I'm the listing agent for a residential property along Gleason Road. To get right to the point, I'm wondering if the city might be interested in purchasing the property, rezoning it, and using it to expand the landfill?"

"Hmm." Phil opened a storage closet and removed a large,

rolled-up piece of paper. "I've got a map of the city here," he said as he unrolled it on top of his desk. "Can you show me exactly where the property is?"

Josie looked at the map and pointed to the location of the sorry little house.

"It's pretty small," he said, shaking his head. "Probably too small to use for any significant expansion. It might work for a transfer station, though."

"Transfer station?"

"Yep. The landfill opened officially back in 1970," Phil said. "It's almost full now, and folks are starting to think about what we're going to do with all the garbage once the landfill is closed in a few years."

"What *will* you do?" Josie asked.

Phil shrugged. "Trash'll have to be shipped out to other places. And, we'll need a transfer facility where waste and recyclables can be sorted and loaded onto trucks and sent out. The city's already planning to construct one at the landfill once it's closed, but state regulations prevent anything from being built on top of the actual garbage, even after it's covered and sealed. It'll shift and settle over the years, so it'll be too unstable to support buildings or roads. Our problem is that most of the property is already filled up with garbage, so there's not enough land left to build on. This parcel might solve our problem. What's the asking price?"

"Thirty thousand," Josie replied. "There is a residence on the property, but it's in poor shape. The asking price pretty much reflects only the fair market value of the lot."

"Hmm." Phil paused for a moment. "That seems a bit high, especially if the property's not good for much," Phil said. "I think twenty thousand would be reasonable, and I expect the board would approve that amount without a problem."

"Board?" Josie asked.

"The Board of Aldermen," Phil explained. "The board runs the city and has to authorize all expenditures and transactions."

"Ah. I thought that as mayor, you'd have the authority to make a decision like this."

"I wish I did," Phil said with a chuckle. "It'd sure make my life easier."

Josie thought about the twenty-thousand-dollar offer. It was an offer, yes, but it was definitely on the low side. She owed it to her client to try for more.

"I don't know that my client would go that low," she told Phil. "Seeing as how the property *would* be very useful to the city, what would you say to splitting the difference at twenty-five thousand?"

Phil squinted at her and scrunched up his mouth. "All right, here's what I'll do," he said. "I'll ask the board to authorize an offer for the property in the amount of twenty-five thousand. I can't guarantee they'll agree to that amount, but I'll ask for it. If the board approves the purchase and appropriates the funding, and your client agrees to the offer, we'll have the city attorney draw up a formal contract to purchase. There's a board meeting this coming Monday, so I'll ask the clerk to get it on the agenda."

"You mean, a decision could be made within a week?" Josie asked.

"Yep," Phil said. "We can do things pretty quickly and informally around here."

"That's amazing," Josie said. "I grew up in New York, in the Bronx, and let me tell you, I've waited longer in the line at the post office than it took to meet with you today."

Phil laughed and smiled good-naturedly. "That doesn't surprise me at all. I'll be sure and give you a call after the board meets—you said you're with Circle Realty?"

"Yes, and I'm in the office most mornings," Josie said as she extended a stiff, new business card to Phil. "Feel free to call me before then if there's anything else I can do to help the process along. It's been a pleasure meeting you, Phil. Maybe we'll have other chances to work together in the future."

"This is a small community," Phil said. "I'm sure our paths will cross again."

Josie was quivering with excitement as she drove back to the office. Never in her wildest dreams did she imagine that she would leave city hall with such potential for an offer on her listing. *Don't get your hopes up,* she kept telling herself. And by no means would she say anything to Ned unless and until the board extended a firm offer.

When she arrived home for the day, she parked in her driveway and hurried next door to The Bookstop. The front door was locked and Ivy's AT LUNCH sign was in the window, so she went back around and through the side door.

"Hello?" she called. She could hear Ivy's low voice and Emily's squeaky one coming from the kitchen.

"We're in here," Ivy replied. Josie entered the kitchen to find her aunt and her daughter having lunch.

"Hi, Mommy," Emily said from her seat at the table. "I really like chicken salad." She had half a sandwich in one of her little hands, and she was swinging her feet merrily as she chewed.

Just the sight of her younger daughter made her feel better. She was still nervous anytime the girls weren't with her, even though she trusted Ivy completely to care for them.

"You do? Well, that sounds like a yummy lunch. If Aunt Ivy made it, I'm sure it's good."

"Actually, I didn't make it," Ivy said. "I got it from Ruth's. I don't bother trying to make anything she sells there, 'cause there's no way my version will be as good as hers." With an exaggerated pout, Ivy picked up her own sandwich. "Josie, there's plenty. Come make yourself something to eat."

"That's okay," Josie said. "I'm not really hungry."

Ivy turned around to look at her. "You ate already?"

"No, I've just not got much of an appetite right now."

"Are you sick?"

At Ivy's question, Emily perked up in her chair. "Mommy, are you going to throw up?"

"No, Mommy's not sick," Josie answered, and then she looked at Ivy. "I'm going to get a cup of tea, and I'll eat something in a little while."

Ivy eyed her suspiciously. "Something's going on," she said. "It was that Ned again, wasn't it? Got your dander up, did he? What'd he do this time?"

Josie smiled. "No, it's not Ned." She took a glass from the cupboard. Out of the corner of her eye, she saw Ivy waiting for an explanation, but she didn't offer anything more. The quiet in the room expanded until it was punctured by Ivy's exasperated sigh.

"Fess up, girlie," she said with her mouth full. "I've only got a few more minutes until I've got to be back out front."

Josie filled her glass at the faucet and turned around to face her aunt. "I may have a buyer for the house."

Ivy's mouth fell open for a second before she spoke. "Really? Who? Wait, I've got to unlock the front door and flip the sign. Come out there with me and tell me all about it. Emily, honey, let me grab your plate and cup and you come, too." Ivy was a blur as she picked up Emily's lunch and rushed them out into the front room.

Josie settled Emily onto one of the beanbags as Ivy reopened the little bookstore. "Now start talking before we get a customer in here," her aunt said once she had seated herself at her desk. Josie proceeded to tell Ivy of the city's interest in the listing and the upcoming meeting of the Board of Aldermen.

"Mommy, did you sell a house?" Emily asked.

"Not yet, but she will," Ivy said. "And then, you'll get to blind-side that idiot Ned with the good news." Ivy grinned. "What I wouldn't give to be there and see his face when you tell him."

"Aunt Ivy, what does 'blindside' mean?"

"It means to surprise somebody with something really big."

"I'm afraid to let myself think about it or get my hopes up," Josie admitted. "And I'm not sure how I'm going to get through the next week. I'm already a nervous wreck."

"Try not to dwell on it," Ivy said. "The time'll pass faster than you think."

"And if the board says yes, it won't just be a matter of telling Ned. He's my broker, so he'll have to sign off on it before things can be finalized."

"Oh, he'll approve it," Ivy said. "He might be as dense as a cabbage, but even he wouldn't refuse an offer on that place, if you get it."

Despite her anxious mood, Josie felt her mouth twitch up into a smile. Her aunt was usually right about things, and she had a week to wait until she would know whether Ivy's latest prediction would come true.

CHAPTER 13

Late on Sunday afternoon, Alex was up in his room wishing there was Wi-Fi when he saw his aunt Emily outside. He crept closer to the window. Emily had her dog on a leash beside her, and they were heading toward his house. He jumped up and quietly made his way downstairs. His mother was still snoring on the sofa, and he tiptoed past her to open the front door just as Emily was coming up onto the stoop.

"Um, hi, Aunt Emily," he whispered, sticking his face out the partially opened door. Before his grandmother's wake, he had never met his aunt in person. It was a little strange, talking to someone he knew mostly from the many pictures of her that had been displayed in his grandmother's house.

"Hey, Alex," Emily said with a smile. "Wow, it's great to finally talk to you."

She grinned, and he smiled in return. He could still hear his mother's snoring, so he came out of the house and closed the door quietly behind him.

"You have a dog?" he asked. "Can I pet him?"

"Sure," she replied, "just let him smell your hand first. I guess you didn't see him that day we moved in. His name's Gus, and he loves kids. Actually, he likes pretty much everyone."

Alex extended his hand to Gus's nose. The dog sniffed it and wagged his tail. Alex gently stroked Gus's head and, as he grew more comfortable, began rubbing his floppy, velvety ears. "I wish we could get a dog. Lots of my friends in the city have them, but Mom hates them. She says they're dirty and smell bad."

Emily sighed. "Well, dogs don't smell if they get regular baths and live inside most of the time. But I can't imagine your mom having one. She never did like pets much, and they do take some work."

"Did you come over to see her? Because she's not feeling good today. She's been sleeping on the couch all afternoon."

"Oh," Emily said. "Well, we were supposed to . . . I don't know how much she told you about what's going on, but we were supposed to make lists of what's in our houses and compare them today."

"Alex?" a voice screeched from inside the house. "Alex, where are you? Is someone here?" Alex cringed as the door swung open and Rose, wearing huge, dark sunglasses, appeared behind it. Her blonde hair was disheveled, and the red lipstick she wore was smudged all over her mouth.

"Sorry, Mom," Alex said, jerking his hand away from Gus. "I came out here to tell Aunt Emily you were sick. I didn't want to wake you up."

"I'm up," Rose said. "Alex, did you touch that dog? You know dogs are filthy. Come in here and wash your hands right now." She held open the screen door. As soon as he'd darted inside, his mother stepped out onto the stoop and closed the front door.

He knew he should do as his mother had instructed, but instead of heading for the nearest sink, he stood against the wall beside the door, where he could overhear the conversation.

"Why are you here?" his mother asked.

"It's been a week. We were supposed to meet up today, after we looked through the kitchen stuff again and you listed out the titles of all the books in your house. I got tired of waiting for you to come over."

"That was today? Well, we're not done, not with the books, at least. I don't even know how much Alex has gotten done."

"What do you mean, 'how much *Alex* has gotten done'?"

"He's doing the book inventory. He's even making a spreadsheet of all the titles," Rose continued. "He offered, and I thought it would be a good project for him. He spends so much time reading as it is, and Lord knows there's nothing else for him to do around here."

"This is *important,* Rose," his aunt said. "Alex is what, nine? You put a nine-year-old in charge of this project?"

"My son is *brilliant.* He's in accelerated classes, and he has an incredible gift of being able to remember everything he reads in perfect detail. He is quite capable of making a simple list of the books in this house."

Alex smiled to himself, pleased at his mother's praise and words of confidence.

"He's still only nine," Emily said. "And, this is something *you* should be doing. Alex has no way of knowing which book, if any, Mom might have chosen as a clue, and Mom wanted *us* to be the ones to figure it out."

"You know, right now, I don't give a rat's ass what Mom wanted. Alex is perfectly capable of helping me, and it won't kill you to wait a few more days. Hell, we have until the end of August."

"Oh, so now you're in no rush to finish up Mom's business? I don't get it. A few days ago, all you wanted was to get out of here."

"I still want that," Rose said. "But it's clear now that it won't happen as quickly as either of us would like."

Alex chanced a look out the window beside the front door just in time to see his aunt reach out and pull his mother close.

"What are you doing?" Rose yelled, quickly breaking Emily's grasp. "Get the hell away from me."

"Well, that explains it," Emily said. "You reek of booze and cheap mouthwash, just like you always did. Mom believed you when you told her you'd given up drinking, but I can't say I'm surprised. After all this time and everything that happened—"

"I'm not *drinking excessively*. I have a drink every once in a while. It's no big deal," Rose said.

"That's bullshit, Rose, and it *is* a big deal. You're up here by yourself, with important stuff to do and a kid you're responsible for. And you're hungover, passed out, whatever, on the sofa all afternoon? Nothing has changed with you, that's for sure."

"Nothing has changed, you got that right. I don't need any lectures from you. Alex is fine. I'm fine. We'll finish the goddamned list when we're good and ready, and until then, you and your filthy dog just stay the hell away from here." Alex heard the squeak of the screen door as his mother prepared to come back inside.

He turned and quickly walked away, but not before he heard his aunt's parting shot.

"You're not fine, Rose. You're an ugly drunk and a poor excuse for a mother."

AS SHE APPROACHED THE BOOKSTOP, DAISY DELAINE SAW IVY sitting with Emily in the front porch swing. The little gray dog at her side pricked up his ears and yipped.

"Good idea, Smudgie! Before we go see Miss Rose, we'll go visit with Miss Emily first. I haven't apologized to her yet. Yoohoo," Daisy called. Emily and Ivy stopped talking and looked at her.

"Well, hi, Daisy-lady," Ivy said as Emily wiped at her eyes. "Haven't seen you in a few days. You doing all right?"

"Yes," Daisy said as she and Smudgie walked toward the porch. "I've been pretty busy with my garden recently. Lots of my herbs are ready for picking and drying now, so that's what I've been doing. That way, I'll have plenty to use for my potions the rest of the year. Except today was so nice, I thought I'd take Smudgie for a long walk."

"You're right, today was just perfect," Ivy said as she lifted a bare foot to wiggle her toes in the summer breeze.

Daisy nodded and looked at Emily. "Miss Emily, I've been meaning to come see you to apologize again for the accident at your mom's house. You know, with the ashes." Daisy bowed her head and spoke more quietly. "I still feel so bad about that. I tried to apologize to Miss Rose again, too, but she wasn't too happy to see me."

"What?" Emily said, sitting up straighter. "You went to see Rose?"

"Um-hmm, last week," Daisy said. "I even made a special batch of forgiveness potion for her. She was still pretty angry, though. Miss Emily, do you think you could help me think of a way to get Miss Rose to forgive me?

"Daisy, you best stay away from Rose right now," Ivy said from the porch swing. "She's got some problems of her own to deal with, and she needs some space. Maybe later in the summer you could talk to her, but now's not a good time."

"Ivy's right," Emily said. "Look, Daisy, what happened was an accident. There's nothing to forgive. Plus, Rose hates dogs, so going over there with that cute little fella is a really bad idea."

"Oh," Daisy said. "I guess I'll wait, then, as long as Miss Rose will be here for a while." She looked up for reassurance and was surprised to see Ivy scowling and Emily's mouth pressed into a hard, thin line.

"She will be," Emily said. "I'm sure of it."

———

IN THE KITCHEN OF HER LITTLE HOUSE NEXT TO ST. JOHN'S, Claudia was working on dinner. Kyle was coming over after he dropped Rowen off at a friend's house, and she was looking forward to a nice, private evening together.

She had a pan of chicken tenders sizzling on the stove. Thanks to an herb marinade and cooking spray, the recipe was low in fat but still very tasty. She'd already made a tossed salad and a fresh fruit salad, and both were chilling in the refrigerator. In another pot on the stove was a colorful mixture of green and wax beans, which she would season with sea salt, extra virgin olive oil, and a dash of garlic powder. For dessert, she'd picked up an angel food cake, some fresh strawberries, and some light Cool Whip to make a healthier version of strawberry shortcake.

Over the past five months, she'd learned that Kyle was definitely a "meat and potatoes" sort of man, but he was willing to try almost anything she made. Claudia smiled to herself, remembering how he'd eaten three helpings of her Greek stuffed eggplant.

Her thoughts were interrupted by a soft knock at the front door, followed by the sound of a key opening it.

"I'm in the kitchen," she called. She was turning the chicken and listening for Kyle's footsteps when she felt his arms slide around her waist from behind.

"Hey," he said in her ear as she leaned back and looked around at him.

"Right on time," she said, before he leaned to kiss her quickly on the mouth. "There's fresh tea in the fridge. And I think there's cold beer in there, too. How was your shift?"

"Quiet," Kyle replied. He opened the door to the refrigerator and removed a pitcher. "But Fitz told me when he came in that the DiSanti sisters had a bit of a blowup this afternoon."

"A blowup?"

"Yeah, apparently they got into it and started yelling at each other in front of their houses, right out in the open. Upset Emily pretty bad, or at least that's what Ruth said. She was over at The Bookstop when it happened."

"That's the small-town gossip chain for you," Claudia said with a half-smile. She felt a twinge of insecurity as Kyle mentioned Emily's name, but she quickly brushed it off.

"I know, it's tough to keep anything private in Mill River," Kyle said. "But if you go and scream at someone in public, well, I can't imagine you'd care about privacy."

"Almost everyone in town knows about Josie's will now, anyway. I went walking with a couple of the teachers yesterday—Jan the science teacher and Brenda from special ed—and they were telling me that people in town are starting to think of the situation as Mill River's own little reality show." Claudia looked at Kyle and did her best impersonation of a dramatic television announcer. "Will the DiSanti sisters find the clues hidden on their properties and discover the key to their inheritance? Will they start to rebuild their relationship and honor their mother's memory? Or, will they lose out on another chance to change their lives? Find out on this week's episode of *The Treasure Next Door*."

"A little melodramatic, but not bad," Kyle said, grinning at her.

Claudia rolled her eyes. "I have no idea how it's going to turn out, not that it's any of my business. The only thing that worries me is that Josie DiSanti was my landlady, and I've been paying my rent to her attorney since she died. If her estate sells this place, I'll have to find somewhere else to live. It sure would be easier to move during the summer, before school starts again."

"Yeah, that's true. The sisters have until the end of August to do what they're supposed to, but it might not take them that long. And you might find out about your house situation a little sooner."

Claudia nodded. "That would be good. They could just finish

what they need to and get on with their lives, without any more shouting matches."

"Fitz says they've been feuding for years, and there's no telling how bad it'll get. Back when I was in Boston, we had two women in my district who were neighbors and bitter enemies. I swear, we were out there every other day breaking up arguments. We finally ended up arresting both of them after they got into a fistfight." Kyle chuckled and shook his head. "I'd hate for calls to start coming into the station here if they get into it again."

Claudia felt another jab of insecurity as she envisioned Kyle, in his attractive police uniform, potentially making repeated visits to the beautiful DiSanti sisters to mediate their disputes. *What if the sisters began to have physical altercations? Wasn't watching a "chick fight" supposed to be a huge turn-on for men?*

"Claudia? Earth to Claudia, please come in, over." Kyle's voice jarred her back to their conversation.

"Sorry," she said. "I zoned out a little. What did you say?"

"Just wondered what we're having. I'm starving."

Claudia ran down the menu for him as she dipped a finger into the tub of whipped topping thawing on the kitchen counter. "Everything's pretty much ready, other than the strawberries for dessert. Here, come grab a plate."

"Awesome," Kyle said. As she served him some chicken, he balanced a dish on one hand and slipped his other arm around her waist. "I was just thinking," he said in her ear, "how I've fallen in love with the perfect woman. Smart, drop-dead gorgeous, and a good cook to boot. But, I think I'd like something other than strawberries for dessert."

Claudia leaned back against him and smiled coyly. "Oh, really? That's a shame." Secretly, she was delighted that he'd reassured her of his feelings for her at exactly the moment she'd needed him to. She held up her serving tongs and turned to face him. "I splurged, you know," she said, batting her eyelashes. "I got an angel food cake and whipped cream and everything to make strawberry short-cake."

"Whipped cream is good," he said as she giggled. He put his plate on the counter and pulled her closer. "But, I'm not sure we'll be needing anything else."

CHAPTER 14

"Mommy, you're *pacing* again," Rose pointed out as her mother casually walked laps in their small kitchen. She emphasized the new word she'd learned from watching her mother deal with uncertainty over the potential sale of her first house.

"Am I? Oh. I guess I am. Nervous energy has to go somewhere. Finish up your dinner, girls. I want you in bed a little early tonight."

At this, Rose sat up straighter in her chair and looked with wide eyes at her sister across the table.

"Why? Today's Saturday, so it's not a school night." Her mother didn't reply, so she guessed at the answer. "Is there going to be a fire drill?"

"Maybe."

"Why do we have to have another one? We've already had lots of drills."

"Because it's important to practice often, in case there's ever a real fire. I want you girls to know how to get out of the house by yourselves if you have to."

Rose sighed. It was the same explanation every time, and she knew by now that there was no use arguing.

Sure enough, late in the night, she and Emily were awakened by the high-pitched screeching of the smoke alarm.

"Oh, no," Emily said. She sat up in bed and peered around. "I don't want to go outside. It'll be cold."

"Come on," Rose said. She was already up, stepping into her shoes and pulling on a jacket over her nightgown. "It'll just take a minute, and then we'll be back inside. We've got to hurry, though. Mom's waiting."

When Emily had put on her shoes and coat, Rose grabbed her little sister by the hand and led her to the bedroom door. They paused there, both of them reaching to press a palm flat against the door.

"It doesn't feel hot," Emily said.

Rose nodded in agreement. "The important thing is to check. We're just pretending now, so we can go out."

They opened the bedroom door and went to the top of the stairs.

"Remember to hold the rail, and walk bent over so you're close to the ground," Rose said. Still holding Emily's hand, she led the way downstairs, through the darkness pierced by the wail of the smoke detector. As they felt their way down, Rose had strange rec-ollections of walking down a different set of stairs. In one, a much larger hand held on to her own. "Not too fast, Rosie," her father's voice said in her memory. "One step at a time." She remembered looking up at him. It wasn't a face that appeared in her mind's eye, though, but a tanned, muscular forearm and a shiny wristwatch.

She also remembered being carried down those same stairs, crying and struggling to breathe in thick smoke.

As Rose's foot stepped onto the floor, the loud reality of her situation drove the memories away. She waited a moment for Emily to join her, and together they headed toward the front door. It was the closest exit to them, but when they reached it they real-ized that a small balloon had been tied to the doorknob.

"Uh-oh," Emily said.

"Yeah, it's a no-exit balloon. That means the fire is near here, and we have to find another way out. Let's go to the kitchen." With one arm stretched out in front of her, Rose pulled Emily into the dark kitchen toward the sliding glass door. There was no balloon tied to the handle, so she unlocked the door and pulled it open.

The frigid January air surged against their faces and nearly froze the goose bumps on their bare legs. Rose stepped outside, but Emily hesitated.

"Rosie, I have to go pee."

"Come on," Rose said, tugging on Emily's hand. "Just hold it a few minutes until we meet Mom. We're almost done."

They walked across the back deck, down onto the path that had been cleared of snow, to the gate. Once they were through it, they could go around to the front of the house and meet their mother at the usual rendezvous point in the far left corner of the yard.

Rose reached up to raise the wooden bar holding the gate closed, but the metal hinge was stiff. It didn't move when she pushed upward on it.

"Rosie, hurry!" Emily pleaded beside her.

"It's stuck," Rose said. Her teeth chattered, and her nightgown blew against her legs in the cold wind. She tried hitting the bar from beneath with her hand, but it was still immovable. When she placed her hand against the hinge, she felt a cold liquid materialize on her palm.

"I think there's ice on it," she said. Rose brushed away the snow on top of the bar and pressed her hands against the hinge, first one, then the other, trying to warm it. When she could no longer bear the cold of the metal against her skin, she cupped her hands together and breathed into them.

"Rosie, I, oh, no," Emily said beside her. It was the last thing her little sister said before she started to cry.

Rose blinked back tears of her own and placed her hands back over the hinge. After another minute, she grabbed the wooden bar and heaved upward with all her strength. The bar raised slowly, stiffly, until it finally cleared the latch. Quickly, she pushed open the gate.

"Come on," she said. She held out a hand to Emily, and feeling the warmth of her sister's smaller one as she clasped it was exquisite relief. They trudged through the snow around the corner of the house. Rose spotted their mother standing in the usual meeting place. "There's Mom."

"She's going to be mad at me. I peed in my pants," Emily said between sobs. "I hate fire drills."

Rose put her arm around Emily's shoulders and pulled her sister close as they both shivered. "Don't worry, she won't be mad. She'll just be glad we got out." The horrible sound of the smoke alarm was still audible, even outside the house. "It's okay if you pee your pants, as long as the fire doesn't get you."

On Tuesday morning, Josie arrived at work on time and had scarcely taken off her coat when her phone rang. When Ned arrived a few minutes later, she was bundled up again and heading back outside.

"I've got a meeting on the listing," she said as they passed each other at the front door. "I won't be long." She rushed out and didn't look back or give Ned a chance to ask questions.

When she emerged from Phil Lawson's office a half hour later, her trembling hands carried a large manila envelope. A huge grin was plastered across her face. Still, Josie waited until she was securely inside her car with the doors closed before she allowed her barely controlled excitement to escape. For a good long minute, she whooped and hollered at the top of her lungs. When the rush was over, she leaned forward, smiling, laughing to herself, with her eyes closed and her forehead resting on the steering wheel.

A knock on her car window startled her.

She looked up to see a stooped, well-dressed elderly man with a cane peering in at her. She rolled down her window.

"I'm sorry, ma'am," the man said. "I overheard you yelling . . . I just wanted to make sure you were all right." He cocked his head and waited for her reply.

"I'm fine," she said, wiping her eyes. She glanced around, but no one else appeared to have been within earshot of her private celebration. "I just got some very good news, and I guess I got carried away. It was kind of you to ask, though."

"Um-hmm," the man said, nodding, although he didn't appear entirely convinced that she was mentally stable. "Happy tears are the good kind. You take care now." He smiled at her and continued on his way.

Josie couldn't help but giggle as she started her car.

Once she'd returned to Circle Realty, she took a deep breath and headed to Ned's office. He sat tilted back in his chair with his feet up on his desk, immersed in some sort of real estate newsletter. He held a large, half-eaten bagel.

"Hi, Ned," she said. "Do you have a minute?"

"Hey, Josie, sure. How'd your meeting go?" His tone was polite but superficial, and he slowly, reluctantly uncrossed his feet and put them under his desk. "Wait, don't tell me," he continued as he used his thumb to wipe a bit of cream cheese from the corner of his mouth. "You sold Al's dump by the dump." Ned's dark eyes lit up as he smirked at her and took another bite. Clearly, he thought himself amusing, and he hadn't a clue that she'd actually done it. Josie rolled her eyes and smiled, playing along.

"No, I haven't sold it . . . *yet*," she told him as she handed him the contract drawn up by the city. "At least not technically, until you've signed off on this offer and Al gives me the okay." She waited, stifling a smug grin as he wordlessly took the offer letter and began reading it. After a moment, he put down his bagel, causing a blob of cream cheese to drop from it onto his desk, but he didn't look up. Josie watched his eyes flick back and forth as he continued to read.

When he finally did meet her gaze, his typical smart-aleck expression was gone and replaced by a hint of astonishment. It was as if he were seeing her for the first time.

"You got an offer from the city. For twenty-five thousand."

"Yes. The landfill is due to close in a few years. The city needs the property to build a transfer station to ship out garbage and recyclables."

"So, they'd raze Al's house and rezone the lot, I suppose."

"I'm sure. It would never sell as a residential property, anyway. The city was the only potential buyer that I could think of. Luckily, the mayor thought the purchase would be a good idea and got approval for it from the Board of Aldermen."

"You met with Phil Lawson?" Ned asked.

Josie nodded. "About a week ago. The board authorized the offer last night." She was beginning to get impatient. "Given the undesirability of the place, I think the offer from the city is more than fair. If it's all right with you, I'd like to present it to Al today. I told Phil I'd have an answer for him soon."

"Well, yeah, sure," Ned said with a sigh. "It is a fair offer, and it's always a good thing to have the mayor's support on a deal." Josie nodded, wondering whether Ned had really ever closed a deal in which the mayor was personally involved. It didn't matter, though.

"Great," she said. "I'll call Al right away." She held out her hand for the contract, and Ned returned it to her without hesitation. "Oh, and going back to our original agreement . . . since I've sold this listing, I assume I'll be promoted to a full-time sales position?"

Ned's shoulders slumped forward, but he managed a wan smile. "That was our agreement. Congratulations." He extended his hand to her.

"Thanks, Ned," Josie said as she shook it and smiled sweetly in return. Although she normally found it revolting to watch Ned consume anything, she had *thoroughly* enjoyed seeing him eat humble pie.

Al Celebrezze was ecstatic when she reached him at the Ford dealership to let him know she had an offer. He arrived at the office during his lunch hour, breathless and smiling. "I can't believe it," he said as he sat down with her to go over the details.

Josie laughed. "I just got lucky when I found out the city was interested in buying your property."

"You didn't get lucky, you worked a miracle is what you did," Al said.

"You give me more credit than I deserve," Josie said. "But, the offer is a good one, I think. After my commission and closing costs, you should end up with more than twenty thousand dollars on the sale."

"Twenty thousand dollars," Al repeated. "I don't think I ever had that much at one time in my life. And we need it, we really do. My oldest boy is a senior in high school this year, and my wife and I have been worrying how we'll pay for college. Rachel and I have saved what we could, but it's still not enough. This money'll be a lifesaver."

"I'm so glad," Josie said. "I'll tell you something, Al. This was my very first listing and my very first sale as a real estate agent, and the fact that it means so much to you and your family makes it even more special."

"Your first one?" Al asked. "Well, you hit a homer on your first time at bat, and with a real stinker of a listing." Josie smiled, feeling her cheeks turn pink as Al looked at her thoughtfully. "I'll tell you what, I'm going to make sure everybody knows about you and what you did for me. If I can send some more business your way, I'll be happy to do it."

Once Josie was back in Mill River, she picked up Emily at St. John's and headed home. It was hard not to tell her younger daughter the good news, but she wanted to wait until Rose was home from school to tell them both, and Ivy, all at the same time.

She and Emily met Rose as the school bus dropped her off in front of The Bookstop. "Hi, baby," Josie said as she hugged her six-year-old. "C'mon, let's go in and see Ivy. Mommy has a surprise for all of you." She took one of her girls' hands in each of her own and walked with them toward the front door.

"A surprise!" shrieked Emily, jumping alongside her.

"What is it?" Rose demanded to know, tugging on her arm. "Tell us!"

"Hold your horses," Josie said. "I want Aunt Ivy to hear, too."

Ivy was just finishing up with a customer as the three of them entered the front room. She looked up as the lady she'd been help- ing made her way out of the store.

"Okay, Mom, now tell us!" Rose said.

"Well?" Ivy asked, looking expectantly at Josie.

Josie smiled and stooped down to gather her girls in her arms. "I sold a house," she said in a choking voice as tears unexpectedly filled her eyes. "Mommy sold a house, so she's a real estate agent now."

"Hot diggity!" Ivy exclaimed. She jumped up and nearly tack- led Josie. "I knew you could do it," her aunt said in her ear as she squeezed her tight.

"Mommy, did you blindside the idiot?" Emily asked. While Rose looked up at them with a confused smile, she and Ivy laughed until their sides ached. Finally, while Ivy caught her breath, Josie looked down at her girls and smiled.

"I can't believe you remembered that, Em, but yes, I guess I did."

"This calls for a happy dance!" Ivy said, holding out her hands to the girls.

"Happy dance!" Rose yelled. She and Emily joined hands with Josie and Ivy, and the four of them formed a circle, laughing and pulling each other around and around on the worn multicolored rug.

That evening, Josie treated them all to a rare dinner out in Rutland. She would receive a nice commission from the sale, so she was comfortable with a small splurge. She felt a tremendous sense of accomplishment, too, and she'd delighted in Ivy's cackles as she told her aunt of her conversation with Ned. Despite the day's happy events, though, she still felt a certain absence, as if someone important had been left out of her celebrations. After Ivy and the girls were asleep, Josie sat down on the edge of her bed, opened her nightstand drawer, and carefully lifted out a rectangular metal box.

In the two years since she'd fled to Mill River, since the horrible fire that devastated her life, she hadn't been able to part with Tony's ashes, to commit them to a final resting place, despite Father O'Brien's encouraging her to do so. It was morbid, she knew, but the box was her last tangible connection to him.

The fire had claimed everything in their house—including every photo of her husband, every image of their life together. She hadn't had a photo of Tony in her purse, which, aside from the clothes she had been wearing, was her only possession to have survived the flames. What she wouldn't give now for a single picture of her husband, a picture to show the girls and to see with her own eyes. Instead, all she had left of her husband were her memories, her daughters, and the metal box.

"I'm doing it, Tony," she whispered to the box, almost too quietly for her own ears to hear. "I'm taking care of the girls, just as I promised. I'm just starting now, but I'm going to provide well for them. Wherever you are, you don't have to worry about them, or me. Rose and Emily are growing and happy. I'm . . . happy." The admission brought knives of guilt into her chest and triggered a fresh round of tears. It did not seem fair that she could feel happiness again when her beloved Tony had suffered so much. She wiped her cheek and placed her moistened hand atop the box. "Almost," she added softly.

Deep down, she knew Tony would want her to be happy, that he would hate for the pain of his death to taint what remained of her life. She remembered the few minutes she'd spent hollering in her car in downtown Rutland and the startled little man who'd stopped to check on her. "Happy tears are the good kind," he'd said. The elderly gentleman was right, of course, and she knew in her heart that Tony would have rejoiced had he been the one to see them rolling down her cheeks.

After another moment of silence, she sighed and gently placed the metal box back in her nightstand drawer. "Good night," she whispered. "Love you, always."

CHAPTER 15

As HE WALKED SLOWLY ALONG THE SIDEWALK AWAY FROM St. John's, Father O'Brien took a deep breath. The late-evening air was still warm and laden with the sweet scents of fresh-cut grass and honeysuckle, and he noticed that yellow evening-primrose blooms were beginning to open in the flower bed around the church's sign. A bit of breeze danced over his balding head, playing with the few hairs left on top. He could hear crickets and tree frogs singing, and their steady chorus was occasionally punctuated by a dog barking or the low hum of a car driving through town. It was a calm, peaceful evening, typical of midsummer in Mill River.

Father O'Brien liked to walk when the weather was good. Walking helped ease the stiffness in his hips and knees, and it also provided him some time for relaxation and reflection. Summer was the nicest time to be outside, when the deep chill of the Vermont winter was long forgotten and the sunlight lingered for hours after suppertime.

For months, since early in the spring, he'd used his daily walks to deal with his grief. It had been almost six months since he'd lost his closest friend and confidante, the reclusive widow Mary McAllister. For seventy years, they'd had an entirely platonic and yet incredibly close relationship, until she had taken her own life in the final stage of her battle with pancreatic cancer. He had never had a better friend; indeed, Mary had helped him overcome his greatest sin, and she had been his soul mate in every way permitted by his vows.

He looked up toward the white marble mansion on the hill overlooking the town, which had been Mary's home. Even though Mary had left her house to Fitz and Ruth, he half expected to see her form silhouetted in one of the windows, peering down at Mill River. He could still hear her quiet voice, and sometimes, in his mind's eye, he saw her face reflect various expressions—happiness, worry, empathy, disapproval—in response to his own thoughts and decisions. His sadness over Mary's death was manageable now, partly because time had begun to temper the rawness of his emotions, but mostly because he had come to understand that she was still a part of him and always would be.

Father O'Brien took another deep breath and tried to focus on the present. Tonight, he strolled purposefully toward The Bookstop, where he would meet Ivy Collard for tea. He'd wondered how it was going with her great-nieces, and when he'd called to offer his assistance, Ivy had invited him to come by.

As he approached Ivy's house on the corner, he saw that her porch light was on, as were the lights in the front room. Through the open front door, he could see Ivy organizing books on one of the shelves.

"Is that you, Father?" she called through the screen door as his footsteps sounded on the porch stairs. "Come on in, I'm just straightening up."

"Thank you," he said as he pulled open the screen door and stepped inside. "You're working late."

"Only catching up on things I procrastinated," Ivy said. "During the summer, I get sucked into my porch swing and can't seem to make myself get out of it, even when I've got things to do. Just shows it's true what they say about getting too comfortable, I guess."

"Comfortable is good. And summer is short," Father O'Brien said.

"Agreed. Come on back to the kitchen." Ivy stepped away from a bookshelf and opened the door that led back into her living quarters. "I'll put the kettle on, and we can chat."

Father O'Brien followed her through the small house and settled himself at the kitchen table. Ivy put some water on to boil and brought over a small plate of cookies. "They're oatmeal butterscotch, made 'em this morning."

He reached for a cookie as Ivy bustled around at the counter, pulling things from cupboards and drawers. Finally, she came over with two mugs and two spoons, as well as a small bowl holding an assortment of tea bags. "I've got lemon, sugar, and milk, whatever you like," Ivy said as she sat down opposite him. "It'll be a few minutes before the water's ready, though."

"Just a bit of sugar would be fine," Father O'Brien said. He tried very hard not to stare at the shiny silver teaspoon she had placed before him, focusing instead on the soft, chewy cookie he held in his hands. "These are very good," he added after he took another bite.

"Thanks," Ivy said. "These were actually Josie's favorite. I haven't made 'em since . . . well." She paused, and he looked up to find her staring at him sadly.

"I miss Josie, too," Father O'Brien said. "It's always horrible to lose someone dear to you, but when it happens suddenly, without time to prepare or say a proper goodbye, it's a terrible shock. Of course, facing the death of a loved one when you know it's coming . . ." He lightly traced a finger around the edge of his cookie and saw Mary's face in his mind. "I'm not sure whether you feel this way, but it seems that the older I get, the more difficult it is to lose someone. Maybe it's because, at my age, the few people I'm close to who are still left I've known for a long time, so the bonds are stronger. Or, maybe, getting old has made me a little less sturdy emotionally. I'm not sure."

"I know what you mean," Ivy said. "I'm not exactly a spring chicken myself, you know." Her voice grew a little quieter. "I imagine you've had a rough time of Mary McAllister's passing."

"It's been much harder than I anticipated," he replied, "and I'm no stranger to grief or loss. It's just that, this time, *I've* been the one going through the grieving process. I had a younger sister who died when she was a baby. My one surviving sibling, a brother, passed on many years ago. He was seven years older than me, and we weren't all that close to begin with.

"Mary was like the sister I never had. When we first met, we had no way of knowing our lives would become intertwined for decades afterward. She became the closest thing I had to actual family." Father O'Brien felt tears threaten to spill out of his eyes. He rarely allowed himself to remember Mary in the presence of another person, and he seldom spoke of her to anyone. He glanced up at Ivy and found that her eyes, too, were watery with emotion.

"Josie had been in my life for such a long time. Ever since she came to Mill River, she was like a daughter to me. She filled a void in my life, that's for sure. After Thomas and I split, I pretty much resigned myself to being alone. Never expected to have a family and never realized how much I was missing until Josie showed up. It was a blessing having her here, and her girls, too, until they grew up and moved away."

Father O'Brien nodded and was quiet a moment. He was surprised to hear Ivy mention Thomas Dearborn, her former fiancé, with whom she had first opened The Bookstop. He'd always been curious about the reason for their parting, but it was none of his business, and Ivy had never sought his counsel on the situation. Now, as they sat together sharing their grief, he considered asking her more about Thomas before he decided against it. It was still none of his business, and it had nothing to do with the reason for his visit.

"Well, you know I've been wondering about Rose and Emily," he said. "Daisy stopped by my place earlier. She's still set on getting Rose to forgive her, and this afternoon, she almost gave it another try. I heard that you and Emily talked her out of it. That's a good thing, if you did."

"Yes, she doesn't understand that it'd be best for her to steer clear of Rose right now. It's funny, though, how Daisy always seems to be in the know about what's going on. She has a knack for being in the right place at the right time," Ivy said with a little smile that gave way to a heavy sigh. "Emily was with me when Daisy came by. The girls got into it this afternoon, and Emily came over to see me afterward. She and I have always been pretty close. Rose, on the other hand . . . we started out close, too, but once she got to be a teenager . . ." Ivy paused and shook her head. "She's mostly kept to herself since she got here. I've only seen her on the day they arrived and again a few days later, when she came over here with Alex to get him a few books.

"But, as I was saying, Emily came right over after they got into it. She thinks Rose is drinking again, or that maybe she never stopped. I know Rose had Josie convinced she didn't have a drinking problem anymore. But, maybe she wasn't being truthful. Or maybe it's just something that's too easy to fall back into."

Father O'Brien shook his head sadly, noticing how the movement was mirrored as a tiny, blurred image in the teaspoon in front of him. "Addiction is a powerful and terrible thing."

"It is," Ivy agreed. "And drinking seems to bring out the worst in people. Emily's actually more worried about Rose's son. Alex is only nine, and he's alone over there with her."

"Do you think the boy's in danger?"

"No, not at the moment," Ivy said. "But Emily and I are trying to keep close tabs on the situation. Emily said Rose gave Alex the chore of listing some of the stuff in the house, but I tell you, it's poor judgment, leaving that job to a nine-year-old."

The teakettle on the stove began to whistle, and Ivy jumped up to turn off the burner and pour hot water into their empty mugs.

"I've been wondering how I might help those girls," Father O'Brien said. He selected a tea bag and began to dunk it up and down in his cup. "Maybe I should go over and try to talk with Rose."

"I'm grateful for the offer, Father, but I don't know that it'd help, at least, not yet. I think we need to give her and Emily a chance to make a go of things. I'm still hoping the girls will do what their mother wanted on their own. Let's give them some time. We'll monitor things as best we can. If the girls don't make any headway or things continue to deteriorate, I'll take you up on your offer."

"I'm happy to do whatever I can. This wouldn't be the first time I've dealt with problems brought about by addiction. I've seen all kinds." Father O'Brien stole another glance at his teaspoon.

"I'm sure you have. You might be able to counsel Emily, too. She's frustrated and upset, and if things go downhill, I think it would make her feel better if she knew you were trying to move things along. Emily was so close to Josie, and she knew you helped her mother through some difficult times. Emily's just trying to do what her mother wanted. I think she also came back here this summer to move past what happened between her and Rose once and for all, even if she hasn't quite admitted that to herself."

"What if they end up staying estranged?"

Ivy shrugged. "Emily needs closure. I know she's never been able to escape the accident. It still haunts her. Losing Andy like that was bad enough, but not a lot of people realize that, for all intents and purposes, she lost her sister that day, too. Those girls used to be so close."

"I remember," Father O'Brien said.

"Emily's been running ever since, but maybe she's come home to Mill River to make peace with the past, regardless of whether things work out with Rose. I think she knows that's her only way forward."

Tea with Father O'Brien ended up lasting far longer than Ivy anticipated, but she was glad it had turned out that way. They lingered in the kitchen, talking and laughing, and occasionally dabbing at tears, for close to two hours. She chuckled to herself as she remembered how they'd both risen slowly from the table, stiff with arthritis after sitting for so long. The soreness from the hard wooden chairs aside, it had felt wonderful to visit with an old friend, and she was glad he'd opened up to her about his grief. She imagined that, despite his role in the community and having constant contact with people, dealing with a profound loss of his own might have brought a certain loneliness to his life.

Father O'Brien had left the same way he'd arrived, through the front door of The Bookstop. After she relocked the door behind him, even though it was late, Ivy decided to finish shelving her new inventory. For some reason, she wasn't sleepy yet, and she was still ruminating over her visit with the priest. Using her cane to steady herself, Ivy pushed a box of books across the carpet with her foot until it was positioned near the children's bookshelves.

Ivy sat on one of the small, brightly colored beanbags, humming to herself as she labeled the new books and found room for them on the shelves. She loved browsing through the titles already there, especially those that were perennial favorites. So many of the folks in Mill River had grown up coming to her little shop. She could still recall which children had loved certain books, children who were now grown up with kids of their own.

Memories of Rose and Emily also came back to her as she sat in the Kids' Corner. How many times over the years had she looked over to see the girls sitting here? Some weeks, especially right after Josie had started working in that god-awful real estate office and the girls needed a supervised place to go until she got home, it seemed as if Rose and Emily had practically lived at The Bookstop. She remembered all those times the girls had done homework at the kitchen table, sat among the books in the front room, played or napped in the attic, and raced downstairs, eager to see Josie when she arrived from work to take them home.

Ivy sighed and hoped that, if she did have to call upon him, Father O'Brien would somehow find a way to help Rose and Emily. She still loved both girls fiercely. It pained her to see them so cold and hateful toward each other and suffering from their own problems on top of that, when she knew how strong their bond had been all those years ago.

Several hours after Father O'Brien had made his way from The Bookstop back to the parish house, Rose DiSanti woke from a fitful slumber on the sofa. It was dark in the living room, and she groped around until she felt the base of the lamp on the end table. The dim light from its fluorescent bulb revealed a haphazard collection of empty glasses and bottles. Beyond that, there were still many unpacked boxes scattered around the room, resting on the floor and the seats and surfaces of unmatched furniture.

Rose pushed herself up into a sitting position and rubbed her eyes. Slowly, she remembered that Emily had come by earlier. While most of the exchange was a blurry memory, her sister's stinging words surged back into her mind. Rose felt enraged all over again as she remembered Emily's expression of disbelief at her explanation for not having completed her list. She saw absolutely no problem with having Alex complete the book inventory.

She looked around her chaotic living room and realized that perhaps she had underestimated the length of time Alex would need to sort through the books and other things in the house. Maybe it would take him longer than what Emily would consider reasonable. Just for reassurance, though, or maybe to prove to herself that Emily was dead wrong about his ability to handle the project, Rose decided go upstairs to check on Alex's progress.

As Rose neared the top of the stairs, she heard slow, steady breathing coming from Alex's open door. She nudged the door farther open and peeked inside. The light in his tidy room emanated from a small lamp on his nightstand. Alex was on his bed, sound asleep. He was wearing his pajamas, but he was stretched out on top of his covers. An open book was smashed between his cheek and his pillow, and his thick glasses were pushed up crookedly over one side of his face. Rose did her best to tiptoe quietly across the room to examine the laptop on the desk.

She touched the keyboard to end the screensaver, and an Excel spreadsheet appeared on the screen. Alex appeared to be making good headway with the list. She saw columns for the titles, as well as for plot summaries, and spaces to indicate whether she or her sister had read the title. Many of the plot summary slots had been filled. In fact, she was surprised that Alex had already read so many of the titles he'd listed.

Rose felt a sudden wave of pride and triumph. Emily was an *idiot*. Trusting Alex to compile the list had been perfectly reasonable. With a smug smile, she turned around and looked again at her sleeping son, but after a moment, her smile disappeared and was replaced by a calm, wistful gaze.

No matter how grown-up he acted when he was awake, no

matter the wise-beyond-his-years expressions he so often wore or the ways he demonstrated his powerful intellect, sleep always revealed how young and innocent Alex was. Many times, she had reminded herself that he was only nine, but tonight, as she looked down upon him in his slumber, she smiled with wonder that he was *already* nine. Where had the time gone? It seemed that only a few days ago, she was cradling him as a tiny infant, kissing the wrinkled, velvety skin of his newborn forehead, marveling at how quickly he had become the one bright star in her life.

As quietly as she could, Rose left Alex's room and retrieved a blanket from her own bedroom across the hall. Once she returned, she carefully, gently pulled the open book from beneath his cheek, removed his glasses, and placed them both on his nightstand. He stirred a bit, turning his head slightly as if he were relieved to finally feel the soft pillow against his face. Rose unfolded the blanket and spread it over Alex. She watched him for another moment, reaching down to smooth his soft blond hair before turning off his lamp.

Back downstairs, Rose made her way into the kitchen. She couldn't remember when she'd last eaten, and she felt slightly panicked as she wondered what Alex had been doing for meals. The refrigerator contained a six-pack of beer, a half-gallon of milk, a few slices of pizza, and a nearly empty jar of peanut butter. The pantry wasn't much better, and there wasn't a stitch of fresh produce anywhere. She hadn't been to the supermarket since a few days after they'd arrived. When she saw an empty cereal box and several empty soup cans in the trash, Emily's words crept back into her mind. *"You're an ugly drunk and a poor excuse for a mother."* She felt a wave of guilt and the truth in her sister's insult reverberate in the pit of her growling stomach.

She's an idiot, Rose reminded herself, and another flash of rage shot through her. With her eyes squeezed shut, she resolved not to waste any more time or energy thinking about Emily. Instead, she heated up a piece of the leftover pizza and grabbed a few beers from the fridge. It was already after ten o'clock, so she couldn't go shopping right now, but she would make a grocery list and head out first thing in the morning. Better yet, she'd take Alex out for breakfast beforehand, and then they could go stock up on things together. After all the time he spent up in his room, the poor kid probably needed some fresh air.

She opened a beer and thought about where they might go. In her neighborhood on Manhattan's Upper East Side, anything from a fresh, hot bagel to a fancy omelet with gourmet coffee was readily available. Here in Mill River, it was very different. It had been a long time since she'd been to Ruth Fitzgerald's bakery-café, but she remembered that it was a decent place to have breakfast. Hell, it was probably the *only* place in town to have breakfast.

Rose was surprised how much better she felt with some food in her stomach. The cold beer helped, too, and for a minute after she finished eating, she sat with her elbows on the table and her chin resting in her hands. She wondered what Sheldon was doing. They hadn't spoken in three days, and their last conversation had ended on a sour note. Was he even temping? Or was he sitting at home in their gorgeous apartment, moping around until she secured her inheritance and their financial future?

Rose opened the second beer and took a long swig. As much as she wanted to leave Mill River, to get away from her sister and the prying eyes of the locals, she didn't look forward to facing her dejected, unemployed husband and precarious personal finances back in New York. So much about her life was such a mess.

"You're a poor excuse for a mother." The words kept ringing in her ears, even though she was doing her best to forget them. Emily really didn't know anything about Alex. She'd never seen what Rose and Sheldon had invested in his care. He'd had the best

schools, the best nannies, and the best healthcare his entire life. He wanted for nothing, other than the latest game console that all his friends had. She and Sheldon didn't approve of videogames. They were proud that books were still their son's most prized possessions.

Alex went to marine biology summer camp and routinely sang solos in the school choir. His achievement-test scores were off the charts. Yes, he was a gifted child, partly because of his own innate intellect, but partly because she and Sheldon had recognized and nurtured his brilliance. *I'm not a bad mother.*

And yet . . . Rose turned to look at the beer bottles on the table. They were evidence of the truth in her sister's words. When she began to cry, she realized that she had let Emily get to her. Angrily, she wiped her eyes with the heel of her hand. Sheldon was right. She would have to lay off the booze, and she'd do it just to prove her sister wrong. She was not about to give Emily any reason to further criticize her parenting or, even worse, start spewing lies to Ivy and the rest of the town.

Despite her efforts to squelch it, the ugly anger that was fueled by her sister's comment continued to spread through her. Tonight, she'd teach Emily a lesson. Rose pulled open a drawer and pawed through the utensils until she found a sturdy knife. After a defiant look at her unfinished second beer, she slipped out the front door.

Most of the homes along the street, like Emily's, were dark and quiet. Unexpectedly, Rose was overcome by a strange sense of déjà vu. The sleeping houses, the gentle night breeze rustling the trees, the background hum of crickets and tree frogs, the delicious anticipation of the unknown . . . it was all unchanged from the Mill River of her youth. She felt like her teenaged self all over again, sneaking out into the night for reasons that were anything but good.

Rose stopped alongside her own car to make sure no one was

watching and then squatted down next to one of the front tires on Emily's beat-up Subaru. The sight of the still-misshapen front bumper caused her fury to rise further, reinforcing her resolve, and she rammed the blade of the knife into the black rubber sidewall.

At first, she enjoyed the angry satisfaction of hearing the faint hiss of air escaping from the tire. She had acted in defense of her son and her own self-respect, after all. As she walked back to her house, she fought the urge to return to the tire, to stab the tough rubber again and again to release years of hurt and hostility. At the same time, though, it troubled her to envision how the air inside the tire was disappearing into the darkness, invisible and lost forever.

CHAPTER 16

1986

Iᴛ ᴡᴀs ᴡᴇʟʟ ᴀꜰᴛᴇʀ ɴɪɴᴇ ᴏ'ᴄʟᴏᴄᴋ ᴏɴ ᴀ Fʀɪᴅᴀʏ ᴇᴠᴇɴɪɴɢ in May when Josie finally began the short drive home to Mill River. She was grateful for the length of the late spring days because the evening sunlight made working long hours a bit more bearable.

Word had spread quickly after she'd sold the house bordering on the Rutland City Landfill. She'd been inundated with clients. Al had made sure to tell every customer who came to his dealership, and everyone else he knew, how she'd made the miracle sale for him. One man had bluntly told her that he "didn't think it was possible that anyone could sell Al's shithole," before asking her to be the listing agent for his own home. Before she knew it, she had five new listings and had already sold three. She'd also closed deals on three more listings of Ned's.

As she sped down the highway, she couldn't help but laugh when she remembered Ned telling her how "a situation you might think is hopeless could lead to great things." He'd been absolutely right, although in a way she was sure he hadn't expected to be.

The trade-off was that the demands of her job had started to cut into her time with Rose and Emily. Ivy was a godsend for having offered to keep the girls with her at The Bookstop when she'd had to work, but Josie knew it was unreasonable to expect the arrangement to continue long-term. She would have to find a few good babysitters soon.

Having to rely on anyone else to help take care of her girls made her feel so guilty, even if the caregiver was her dear aunt. *I'm their mother, and their only parent. I should be the one with them.* While she was at work, Josie reached for her locket often, comforted by the feel of her girls' photos resting above her heart. The hard truth was that if she was to earn a living, there would be lots of times when she couldn't be with her babies.

She stepped on the accelerator, determined to make it home before the girls were asleep. Once there, she followed the sound of voices into the kitchen. The heavy back door was open, and Josie paused before the screen door. Ivy and the girls were sitting three-across on the steps facing the yard. The air was crisp, and light from the full moon cast a glow over everything.

"You see, the North Star is the brightest star in the sky," Ivy was saying as she pointed upward. "And, once you find the North Star, you can find the Little Dipper."

"What's a dipper?" Emily asked. Josie stifled a laugh to avoid calling attention to her presence for a moment longer.

"A dipper is a ladle, or a scoop with a handle," Ivy said, chuckling. "The Little Dipper is a group of stars—a constellation—that makes the shape of a dipper in the sky." Her aunt pointed again and motioned with her hand. "If you look carefully, you can see a line of stars with the North Star on the end. That's the handle part. At the other end, three more stars make a little rectangle. That's the scoop part. Together, they make up the Little Dipper."

"I see it!" Rose yelled as she jumped off the steps and into the grass. "I see it, Aunt Ivy!"

"Where?" Emily asked. She went to stand beside her sister as she turned slowly and continued to squint upward. "Where? I don't see the dipper."

Rose put her arm around Emily's shoulders and directed her

sister's gaze. "Look right there, Em. The stars are like dots. You have to pretend you're connecting them together." Silently, Josie watched her girls standing together, their upturned faces illuminated by moonlight and filled with wonder.

"Star light, star bright, first star I see tonight," she finally said quietly. At the sound of her voice, both girls startled and looked toward the door.

"Mom! Aunt Ivy's showing us *con-stel-la-tions*!" Rose said, taking care in pronouncing the big new word she had learned. She pointed proudly. "Look, there's the Little Dipper!"

"Yes, I see it," Josie said as she stepped outside.

"*I* can't see it," Emily complained. "I want to see the dipper, Mom."

"Sometimes it takes practice to spot it," she said to Emily. "We can look again another night. Right now, it's late, and you girls need to be going to bed."

"They begged to wait up for you, so I let 'em stay up a few minutes more, as a treat," Ivy said. "Figured I'd teach them something in the meantime."

Josie smiled and nodded. "Girls, go on upstairs. I'll be up in just a minute." As Rose and Emily pushed past her into the house, she bent down to speak in Ivy's ear. "I've got something exciting to tell you, but I just want to say good night first." Before Ivy could say anything, she hurried inside.

The second floor was dark, although the small lamp in the girls' room glowed weakly through their open door. She paused at the top of the stairs, listening to them talk as they climbed into bed.

"Maybe we can go to the playground tomorrow," Emily said.

"Tomorrow's Saturday," Rose said. "Mom'll probably have to work. She always has to take people to see houses on the weekends."

Josie felt a surge of guilt rise up through her exhaustion from working a week of twelve-hour days, and she nearly started to cry. Instead, she bit down hard on her lower lip and went into the room.

"Mommy, we wanted to stay awake until you got home," Rose explained in her most authoritative seven-year-old voice. "Aunt Ivy said we could. Are you mad?"

"No, honey. Even though it's way past your bedtime, I'm glad I got a chance to say good night. What did you girls do with Aunt Ivy today? Before the stars, I mean."

"We had fun," Emily said. "We got to help her unpack the new books for kids."

"And she taught me how to make change with real money," Rose added.

"That's great," Josie said. "I don't have to work tomorrow morning. How would you girls like to go to the playground and then out to lunch on the way home?"

"Can we?" Emily screamed, clapping her hands.

"I want to get a Happy Meal!" Rose said as she bounced in her bed.

"All right," Josie said, laughing. She grabbed one of her girls in each arm and kissed them on their foreheads in turn. "Now, go to sleep so you're not tired tomorrow!" Josie tucked Emily and Rose back under their covers and kissed them both again before leaving their room.

When Josie came back downstairs, Ivy was fidgeting on the sofa. "Kid, if it had been for any reason other than to see the girls, I'd have scolded you for dropping that hint on me and leaving," she said. "You know better than to tease me like that."

Josie laughed. "Yes, I know you were a town crier in your previous life. Well, I got a referral today from Phil Lawson. You remember I worked with him on the landfill property? He gave my name to a couple he knows who are looking to buy a resort chalet up in Killington, and the woman called me this afternoon. She and her husband are coming up from New York on Sunday so I can take them around."

Ivy sat up a little straighter. "New York? Oooh! Maybe they'll go for something expensive. You might get your biggest commission yet."

"True, but I'd get more than that," Josie said. "If I can sell them a property, the deal would be my eighth." Josie's eyes sparkled, and Ivy nodded with understanding.

"After eight transactions, you can get a broker's license," she said. "The fault, dear Josie, is not in our stars, but in ourselves." She stood up and stretched.

Josie's tired brain tried and failed to make sense of Ivy's last comment. "What? Are you talking about constellations again?"

"It's from *Julius Caesar*," her aunt said. Josie rolled her eyes, but Ivy ignored her expression. "Basically, it means that we, and not the stars or whatever powers that be, control our own destinies. And you've done just that, Josie. You've outworked and outsmarted Ned at every turn. One more sale, and you'll be able to ditch him and open your own office."

"I've fantasized about doing that since day one, but I never thought I'd be able to do it so soon. If I'm able to leave when my year's up, it'll be just as well. Ned makes money from my sales, of course, but it chews him up when people call wanting me as a listing agent and not him."

"Anybody with half a brain can see that he's the nitwit and you're the star," Ivy said as she walked to the front door to leave. "I couldn't be prouder of you."

"Thanks, Ivy," Josie said, kissing Ivy on the cheek before her aunt stepped outside. "And thanks for looking after the girls today." She stood on her front porch, waiting until Ivy was safely inside her own home before quietly closing the door.

Saturday passed in a blur of laughter, monkey bars, work, and the usual weekend errands, and Sunday arrived before Josie had even caught her breath. She arrived in the shabby Circle Realty office, running mostly on adrenaline and hope, to straighten up and brew fresh coffee for her clients.

Edward and Elizabeth Stanfield arrived promptly at two o'clock, and Josie spent the rest of the afternoon showing them resort properties in the area. Edward's Rolex watch and Gucci loafers and the fabulous diamond in Elizabeth's wedding band set told her immediately that they were serious buyers with significant financial resources.

As was her usual practice, Josie saved the best property for last. Everything about the chalet-style home in Killington was spectacular. As she escorted the couple into the great room of the house, with its floor-to-ceiling windows and views of pristine pine forests and Killington Resort, she stepped back to hear their reactions.

"Stunning," Edward said.

Elizabeth remained silent, but as she gazed out the enormous windows, her bright eyes reflecting the view of forest and mountain and her hand reaching out to touch Edward's arm, Josie knew that she had sold the chalet.

Certainly, she had expected the Stanfields to fall in love with the house. What she hadn't expected, though, was the tidal wave of emotions she experienced as she watched the couple tour the home. How many times had she dreamed about going house-hunting with Tony? About strolling through rooms, talking about square footage and furniture placement? How often had she imagined the moment when, together, they would find the perfect home? When, years later, they would have their little family tucked warmly and safely beneath the roof?

And although she had already helped several couples find new homes, what was it about *this* particular couple that had set in motion such an avalanche of sadness?

Even if Tony had survived, they never would have had the designer clothing and luxury accessories of the Stanfields. They never would have been able to afford a home like the chalet in which she now stood, fighting back tears and keeping an artificial smile plastered across her face. But something about the Stanfields reminded her of exactly how it had been with Tony.

Edward and Elizabeth were completely in tune with each other. They strolled through room after room, often communicating through facial expressions alone. They moved in sync, separately and yet strangely in rhythm. The couple never drifted too far apart, and one of them often reached out casually to touch the other. Certainly, their physical attraction to one another was palpable. And, when they looked at each other, their gaze conveyed an unending, quiet affection. The Stanfields were soul mates— perfectly matched and hopelessly in love.

Just as she and Tony had been.

It was late by the time she had finished drawing up a contract for the Stanfields to sign. Once the couple had left her office, she deposited the finished offer on Ned's desk and went to her car. Finally alone and hidden from view in the darkness, she sobbed as she drove home, happy to have effectively freed herself from Ned's leash but overwhelmed by a renewed grief and deeper awareness of how alone she really was.

When she slipped into her house, Ivy was up reading on the sofa, as usual. Her aunt took one look at her and immediately jumped up. "Please tell me those are happy tears," she said. Josie forced a smile and nodded as Ivy rushed to hug her. "I knew it! Oh, you did it! The girls and I knew you would."

"I've just got to focus on studying for the broker's exam now, and once my first year with Ned is over, I'll be able to—"

Josie caught sight of the table in her kitchen. There were balloons of every color taped around it and a lone plate covered in aluminum foil. Next to the plate stood an empty wineglass and a bottle of sparkling grape juice. There was a card, too, a piece of folded yellow construction paper with "MOM" written in crayon on the front.

"What's this?" Josie asked.

Ivy came up beside her and shook her head. "The girls wanted to fix you a special dinner for getting your eighth deal," she said. "They made it themselves. Well, I supervised and helped a little, but it was mostly them. Have a look."

Josie opened the card and read, "You can be a brokur now. Love, Rose and Emily." Blinking back tears as she smiled, she then uncurled the foil from around the plate to reveal a large, stiff glob of macaroni and cheese, an apple cut into slices that were beginning to turn brown, and a pile of overcooked peas.

"We didn't know you'd be home so late," Ivy said. "I even let 'em stay up a while to wait for you, but Emily was falling asleep sitting up, so you'd better be sure and visit with 'em in the morning."

Josie nodded, but she barely heard Ivy's words. She reached up and touched her locket. Her babies had fixed her supper for the first time ever, and she hadn't even been home to eat it. She gathered the pieces of apple in her hand and took the rest of the food to the microwave to heat it.

Ivy watched her with sympathetic eyes as she came back to the table with the plate, sat down, and poured herself a glass of the grape juice. Her aunt quickly took another glass from the cupboard and held it out to her, and Josie filled it as well.

"To Rose and Emily," Josie said, holding up her glass. "The treasures of my heart."

CHAPTER 17

Emily was in a fabulous mood when she and Gus left her house and stepped into the morning air. It was just after seven o'clock, and she knew Ruth's bakery-café would already be open and serving up rich, dark coffee. When they reached the sidewalk, though, Emily noticed that her car seemed to be resting at an odd angle along the curb.

The front right tire was completely flat.

In an instant, her buoyant mood was gone. She rolled her eyes and cursed under her breath. Gus whined and pulled on his leash, but she stood rooted to the sidewalk, reworking her morning plans. Since it was Monday, the hardware store was open, and she was scheduled to work all afternoon. She had been planning to go over her list of possible clues again beforehand, and she wanted to start cutting glass for a new design she had in mind. But now, she would have to deal with the tire before anything else.

Emily put her hair into a ponytail and let Gus out into the backyard. It took some time to move things around in the back cargo area of her car so she could access the spare tire compartment.

The wheel cover was easy to remove, but the lug nuts proved to be difficult. They were rusted solidly in place, and pulling on the tire iron with all her strength did nothing to budge them. Her next move was to give each nut a good shot of WD-40. After waiting a few minutes for the substance to work its way through the rust and grime, she repositioned the tire iron and tried again, heaving backwards as hard as she could until she lost her footing and fell onto her rump. Frustrated and out of breath, Emily jumped up and stormed into her house. When she reemerged, she carried a Hot-Head torch, safety goggles, and a can of MAPP gas.

The damned lug nuts had met their match.

She put on the safety goggles and screwed the torch into place atop the gas canister. Rather than throw away the bits of glass left over from her projects, she'd learned how to use the torch to melt them down and form beautiful glass beads, which she could sell to bead shops or on eBay. But, a torch was useful for many things other than beadmaking.

Emily ignited the flame and positioned it on the head of one of the lug nuts. The WD-40 she'd sprayed earlier immediately started smoking, but it didn't take long for the lubricant to burn off. After the first lug nut had been under the flame for several seconds, she turned off the torch and picked up the tire iron. This time, a gentle tug on the wrench was all she needed to spin the heated lug nut from the bolt.

She had jacked up the car and was positioning the spare on the newly exposed bolts when she heard the front door of Rose's house open and close. Her nephew walked toward her, looking over his shoulder every few steps.

"Hey there," she called as Alex reached Rose's black BMW and stopped. He glanced around again and came over to where she was working.

"Hi," he said. "Mom's coming soon. We're going out for breakfast, and food shopping, after that."

"Oh." Her first thought was to wonder whether Rose was sober and could safely drive Alex anywhere. She noticed that Alex's posture was tense, and he seemed preoccupied with watching the front door of his house.

"That sounds like fun. Hey, are you okay?" she asked. "You look worried about something."

Alex frowned, and she could barely hear his muttered reply. "I heard you and Mom talking yesterday. She's not a bad mother." His big blue eyes were filled with hurt and anger.

A lump of regret formed in Emily's middle. "I'm sorry you overheard that," she told him. She just looked at her nephew, trying to decide what more she should say. "As angry as I was, I shouldn't have said that. The truth is, though, your mom does drink, and it's not good for her, or you, that she does."

Alex was quiet for a minute. "Dad says that drinking too much is a disease, and she can't help it."

"Your dad's right about it being a disease," Emily said. "She *can* help it, though. She just has to want to change badly enough, but that's a tough thing for anyone to do." She sat down in the grass and looked squarely into Alex's eyes. "Listen, I know we don't know each other, and you overhearing me and your mom talking probably didn't give you a good impression of me. I'm sorry things started out with us that way." Emily waited a moment before turning back to the spare tire. "But, Alex, if anything happens with your mom and you feel like you need help, or if you think *she* needs help, I'm here for you."

Alex seemed to mull over her reply. "She won't tell me why you don't like each other," he said next, "but she says it's better if I stay away from you."

Emily was disgusted with Rose and sad for Alex all at the same time. She also felt a strong instinct to do everything she could to make sure he was being cared for properly. "If your mom doesn't want to explain it yet, it's probably not my place to do it," she told him. "But, we're family. You're my only nephew, and I think it would be really cool if you and I could get to know each other a little."

Alex didn't reply, but his expression was pensive as his eyes searched her own. After a moment, he looked back over his shoulder again.

"Hey, if you think your mom will be ticked if she sees you over here with me, just go up and stand by her car. We can still talk." She encouraged him with a mischievous grin.

Alex smiled back at her, although his eyes conveyed more relief than anything else, and he hurried up toward Rose's car and leaned against the front passenger's door. "What happened to your tire?"

"I have no idea." Now that the spare was in position, Emily lifted the tire iron and began to spin the lug nuts loosely back onto the bolts. "It was flat when I came out here this morning. Might've been a nail or something. I'm going to take a closer look at it once I finish with the spare. How're things going for you today? I wondered if you were okay after you went inside yesterday."

"Oh," he said, shrugging. "Mom always yells. I try to stay out of her way when she does, until she calms down."

"She yelled all the time growing up, too," Emily said. "It about drove me crazy."

Alex didn't respond to that comment, and she quickly changed the subject.

"Your mom told me you're in charge of going through the books in your house, so we can figure out whether one of them is a clue Grandma left us."

"Yeah," Alex said. His face brightened. "I'm pretty much done. I've been meticulous about it."

"Meticulous, huh? That's great!" Emily said. She sat back on her heels beside the wheel of her car. "My list is done, too, so I guess now your mom and I need to compare them. We know our two clues are different, so we need to be able to see which you have in your house that I don't have in mine. I think it's the only way we can narrow down what the clues might be."

She started to say something else, but Alex suddenly crossed the sidewalk and bent over to examine the lawn between their houses. He reached out and grabbed a feather that had been sticking out in the grass. It was long and blue, with black stripes and a white patch at the end. Alex held it up and twisted it back and forth, watching the sunshine play off the surface.

"Looks like a blue jay lost a tail feather," Emily said. "There's lots of them around here. I hear them squabbling in the morning. They bully most of the other birds."

"I love birds," Alex said, still staring at the feather. "There are quite a few kinds in the city, but they're hard to spot, other than pigeons."

"There's everything here," Emily said. "Cardinals, blue jays, grackles, sparrows, woodpeckers. What about in Central Park? I'll bet you can see tons there. I think I read a while back that falcons had moved into Manhattan, too."

"Yes," Alex said. "There are sixteen nesting pairs right now. They eat pigeons and other birds. Did you know they can fly more than two hundred miles an hour when they're hunting?"

"No, I didn't. That's amazing," Emily said. "I feel sorry for the pigeons, though."

"Well, yeah," Alex agreed. "I wish I could go to the park more, but Mom says all the trees and plants bother her allergies. Plus, she doesn't like birds much."

"Or dogs," Emily added. "But, hey, now that you're here for the summer, you can see all sorts of birds in the yard." She frowned as she watched her nephew and his fascination with the feather. It was obvious that, despite having been born into a world of privilege, Alex had lived an incredibly sheltered life. "A little sunshine would do you good. You should kick off those shoes and go barefoot, at least on the grass. That's not something you get to do much in the city, is it?"

"I've never walked on grass barefoot." Alex was staring at his new-looking sneakers.

From the look of those shoes, he doesn't walk outside much at all, Emily thought.

"Alex?" Rose yelled. She emerged a moment later wearing a miniskirt, heels, and the usual large, round sunglasses. A shiny leather handbag was looped over her shoulder.

"I'm over here, Mom," he said, backpedaling to her car. "I'm all ready to go, just waiting for you." Emily noticed that the blue feather he had been holding lay in the middle of the sidewalk.

"All right," Rose said as she came down the front steps. Emily watched her every movement, searching for any indication that she might be intoxicated. Her sister unlocked the doors so Alex could climb in, but instead of going to the driver's side door herself, Rose came around to the back of the BMW and leaned against the trunk.

Emily couldn't see her sister's eyes through the sunglasses, but there was no missing the curl of Rose's upper lip or the haughty, raised chin. Emily focused on lowering her car back down so that she could tighten the lug nuts.

"Alex told me this morning that he's almost finished going through the books. I could meet tomorrow to go over our lists again, if you'd like."

Emily glanced up at her sister. "Sure." She stood up under the pretense of repositioning the wrench, but as she moved slightly closer to Rose, she took in several deep breaths through her nose. With Alex already in the backseat of the BMW, it reassured her that the only scent emanating from her sister was a heavy perfume. She knelt down again and tried to concentrate on the tire.

Still hesitating before getting in her car, Rose gave an exaggerated sigh. "Now, that flat's just a shame. I guess you never know what sorts of problems an older car might have," she said in a light, taunting voice. Emily glanced up in time to see Rose run a perfectly manicured finger over the gleaming surface of the black BMW and check it for dust.

"Even a new car is only as good as its driver," Emily blurted out.

Rose turned and glared at her. "I'm a perfectly good driver—"

"—when you're sober." Emily finished for her, with her gaze focused on the spare tire.

"I would *never* drive if I'd had anything to drink, especially with my son in the car." Rose's voice was little more than a hiss. Emily looked up and saw Rose's nostrils flaring.

"Well, then, maybe I was wrong about what I said. About how nothing's changed." Emily looked evenly at Rose's dark sunglasses. Her sister stood silently for a few seconds, working her jaw as if she were thinking of what she could say, before getting into her car and slamming the door.

Even after the BMW had pulled away and turned the corner, Emily was still so angry she was shaking. She grabbed the tire she'd removed from her car and hurled it as hard as she could onto her lawn. The rubber made a muted *thwup* as it hit the grass. Emily wiped the sweat from her forehead with the back of her arm and leaned against the hood of her car.

"You okay, honey?" a voice called to her from across the street. Emily stood up straight and turned to see Ivy leaning on her cane on the porch of The Bookstop. She exhaled slowly and waved.

"I'm fine," she said when she'd reached her great-aunt. Ivy held out her free arm for a hug, but Emily only took her hand and pecked her on the cheek. "You don't want to squeeze me right now. I'm sweaty and gross."

"Fair enough. What were you doing over there with that tire?" Ivy asked.

"Changing it," she said. "It was flat when I got up this morning."

"So, you threw the tire to punish it for going flat?"

"No, I was just blowing off steam," Emily said. "Rose saw me and offered some helpful comments as I was finishing up."

"Oh."

"She and Alex were headed out. She didn't look like she'd been drinking," Emily said, easily anticipating Ivy's next questions. She hoped that her tone made it clear she didn't want to go into what happened.

"Well, that's good, at least," Ivy said as she sat down in the porch swing. "I guess you two didn't make any more progress on your mother's clues?"

"No, but I think we'll meet again soon, and I was able to talk with Alex alone before Rose came outside. The poor kid's doing what she should be doing, and he's so eager to help. Rose doesn't want him interacting with me, but I'm going to try to figure out ways around that."

Ivy nodded. "Might be a good way for you to keep tabs on him, and Rose."

"Exactly." She sighed and looked across the street at her car. "Where should I go to have a flat repaired? I've got to work this afternoon, so I need to see if it can be patched this morning."

"Take it over to Russell's, just off Route 103. It's about the only place to go outside Rutland, but they do honest work. They could probably help with your bumper and anything else you wanted fixed, too. Ask for Bob Russell, the owner. I've known him a long time. He'll treat you right."

"Okay. Thanks, Aunt Ivy."

"Don't mention it, honey," Ivy said. She kicked off her sandals to reveal hot-pink polish on her toenails as Emily turned to go back across the street.

When she was upset or angry, talking with Ivy, or even just being around her for a few minutes, always made Emily feel better. After she retrieved the tire from her yard and loaded it into the back of her car, Emily picked up the blue feather from the sidewalk and put it in her back pocket. She would give it to Alex when they met later.

Russell's Auto Repair was easy to find. Emily pulled into the parking lot carefully and rolled the flat tire up to the door of the office. An older man wearing greasy coveralls and a faded baseball cap leaned on the counter reading a wrinkled copy of the *Rutland Herald*. He looked up as she entered.

"Howdy, miss," he said. "Can I help you?"

"Yes, I've got a flat tire, unfortunately," Emily said. "I'm not sure what caused it. Are you Bob Russell?"

"I am."

"Oh, good. My name's Emily DiSanti. My aunt Ivy Collard recommended I come see you about it."

"Ivy's your aunt, is she? How's she doing? I haven't talked with her in quite a while."

"She's my great-aunt, actually, but she's doing fine. Same as always," Emily said as he followed her back outside and grabbed the tire. It was a relief that Bob didn't mention anything about her mother's death. She followed him as he rolled the tire along, leading her from the door of the office around to an adjoining work bay. He gave a loud grunt as he hoisted the flat onto a low workbench next to a large tub of water.

"Let's see if we can spot the problem," he said, switching on a bright floodlight over the tire. "If we can't, I'll blow it up and give 'er a dunk in the tub." Bob moved the tire around carefully under the light for a few minutes and then looked up at her. "Bad news, I'm afraid," he said. He pointed to the edge of the sidewall of the tire, near where it joined the shoulder. "Your tire was slashed. See here?" Emily squinted down and saw a thin, clean cut a little under an inch long.

"You're sure?" she asked.

"Positive," Bob said. "If it'd been in the tread, I wouldn't be able to say for sure, but there's no way anything you ran over would've punctured it there, on the side. No, it was probably some teenaged hooligan and his trusty pocketknife."

Or a thirty-something hooligan with a taste for designer clothes and Bacardi Gold, Emily thought. Struggling to hide her rage, she muttered, "And since the cut's in the sidewall, it can't be repaired."

Bob looked at her with surprise. "That's right. The pressure's so high there that you'd be risking a blowout if the patch didn't hold. It's interesting that you know that already, though. Most ladies don't."

"I know just enough to be dangerous," Emily said with a resigned smile. "I guess I'll have to replace it, along with the other front one. How much would that be?"

"Come back to the office with me, and I'll check for you. Just need to look up the different brands that'll fit, and you can decide which kind you want." They returned to the office, where Bob began typing on an old computer that sat on the far end of the counter.

"By the way," Emily said, "I'd like to keep one of my old tires. I was thinking I'd make a swing out of it for my nephew."

"Um-hmm. You know, I wouldn't use a radial for a swing," Bob said as he continued to type. "The steel wires could come loose and hurt a kid. But, I've got some old nylon tires in the back. You're welcome to swap one of yours for one of those, and if you do, you'd have to pay the disposal fee for only one tire."

"That'd be great," Emily said. "And thanks for the tip about the wires."

She leaned against the counter. Bob's hands were large and dirty, and his fingers with black grease caked under the nails seemed out of place as they slowly negotiated the keyboard. She was struck by how they contrasted with her sister's perfect red manicured nails. The contrast highlighted exactly what was wrong with Rose, what had always been her biggest problem.

Her sister was obsessed with appearances—how she looked, what she wore, what she drove—to the detriment of internal qualities that were truly important. She'd never been able to acknowledge her faults, and from what little Emily had seen this summer, Rose had gotten worse as time had passed. She was like a helium balloon that had been released into the sky. At some point, her shiny exterior would be stretched to a point at which she would no longer be able to contain what was inside.

Emily couldn't prove Rose had been the one who slashed her tire, but she could think of no other person who would do such a thing, especially since Rose's own car, parked just ahead of hers, hadn't been touched. She remembered her sister's smirk as she'd been working on the tire and decided to file a police report about the incident. As she shifted her position against the counter, she slid a hand into her pocket and felt the sharp tip of the blue-jay feather there. It gave her an idea, one that prompted a small, wicked smile.

Weren't balloons meant to be popped?

CHAPTER 18

1987

On her one-year anniversary of selling the chalet, Josie resigned her position with Ned's office and began working for herself out of her home office. By October, she had enough saved to lease a small commercial space along Center Street in Rutland. It was a good location, surrounded by other businesses on one of the most picturesque streets in the city.

One gorgeous Sunday afternoon, Josie, Ivy, and the girls went to take a look at the new office. The phone lines were hooked up. All of the furniture and files were moved in and ready for the opening of business the next day. The sign above the entry read Home at Last Realty, and under that, in smaller letters, "Proudly helping buyers and sellers find happiness."

Driving back to Mill River, past the preternatural reds and oranges that filled the landscape, she silently acknowledged the passage of time. She was thankful that she could finally think about Tony without being completely crushed by her sadness, thankful for being able to keep him in her heart and help her beautiful girls grow and thrive. Time was slowly helping transform her from a grieving widow into a strong, self-sufficient single parent.

Ivy was quiet as she sat in the passenger seat, but Josie knew her aunt had been thinking about time recently, too. More than once over the past few months, she'd commented about Josie's relationship status.

"You know, you've been up here a while now. You're smart and good-looking, and you're still so young," her aunt had remarked one evening. "Have you ever thought about trying to meet someone?"

"Aunt Ivy," she'd replied with an exasperated sigh, "even if I had the interest, even if I were to find someone I wanted to date, where would I find the time to do it? I'm home less and less now, and what time I have is left for the girls."

"You've got to take care of yourself, too," Ivy replied. "I know you still love Tony, but I think you might be able love someone else now, too, if the right person came along. You could be lonely for that kind of a relationship and not even realize it. And the right somebody could offer you a lot . . . the girls, too."

Josie knew her aunt was right, at least in some respects, but it still bothered her to imagine any man other than Tony as her husband or as a father figure for Rose and Emily. Yes, it was partly because she still loved Tony. She would always love Tony. But, she was also terrified of investing in a relationship. She feared what would happen if the relationship didn't work or, even worse, there was a repeat of that awful day of the fire when she had lost the love of her life unexpectedly.

No, she figured that if she was meant to meet someone else, it would happen in its own good time. If it didn't, well, that would be all right, too. She wouldn't have to worry about being hurt, or her girls being hurt, again.

When they arrived back home, the Johnson and Weider kids were running and laughing in the yard across the street.

"Mom, can we go over and play?" Rose asked.

"Please, Mom?" Emily chimed in.

"Fine," Josie said. "But, wait, so I can watch you cross the street. You and Emily hold hands and look both ways, and I don't want any dillydallying when I call you for dinner."

Rose and Emily scrambled out of the car. The neighbor kids called to them and waved, and it was only a few seconds before the girls were integrated into the group.

Josie said goodbye to Ivy and unloaded a few things from the car before going inside. It didn't take her long to straighten up the kitchen and fix supper, and she soon went back to the front door to call the girls. She shielded her eyes from the early evening sun as she watched the children playing across the street.

The girls were on the tire swing, Rose on the top and Emily in the hole below, as other kids stood on either side, taking turns pushing them. Instead of yelling to catch their attention, Josie just leaned against her front door and watched. The girls were squealing and laughing, hanging on to the swing for dear life as they were pushed and spun in different directions. She touched her locket. The girls were so much older now than they had been when the tiny pictures she kept inside it had been taken. It was time at work again. *Before long, they won't play like that anymore,* she thought.

Josie watched and listened with greedy eyes and ears, trying to capture and commit to memory every detail of what she was seeing. The deep orange leaves of the oak tree glowed in the sunlight, forming a brilliant awning over her swinging girls. She saw Rose's ponytail and Emily's curls swept back and forth by the motion of the swing and their heads thrown back in delight. Their laughter, so familiar and easily distinguishable to her from that of the other children, carried across the street. Finally, one of the Weider boys grabbed the swing to stop it, and Rose and Emily climbed off, teetering with dizziness and still giggling. The girls clutched each other as they regained their balance and caught their breaths. Overcome with love and gratitude, Josie felt a little dizzy as well.

Time was passing faster and faster now, and before she knew it, Rose and Emily would be grown up. That knowledge only reinforced the fact that the precious scene Josie had just witnessed would stay with her for the rest of her life.

1990

"So, Mom, since I'm going to be *eleven* next week, can I please have a sleepover party with pizza?" Rose said one evening at dinner. She used her sweetest voice and her usual wide-eyed, pleading expression.

"I suppose we could do that, Rose, if we scheduled it for Friday night. I could be home early that night, and you wouldn't have to go to school the next morning."

"Thanks, Mom!" Rose squealed. "I want to invite Jill, Becky, and Sherri from my class, and Jennifer Johnson from across the street. And maybe I'll ask—"

"You know, four sounds like plenty," Josie interrupted. "I know you'd like to have every girl from your class over here, but the house really isn't big enough to hold them all."

Rose crumpled her face into a pout.

"Can I have a friend over, too?" Emily asked from her place at the table. "Otherwise, I'll have nothing to do while Rose has her party."

"It's *my* birthday," Rose said before their mother could answer. "And you just said there's not enough room for more than four people."

"I said we don't have room for your whole class," her mother answered. "And, yes, it's your birthday, but if your sister has a friend over as well, you won't have to worry about her bugging you and your friends." Rose glared at her and then turned to look at Emily, who flashed a smug, taunting smile.

Rose started to grumble, but the phone rang, and her mother jumped up to answer it before she heard the complaint.

"Hello?" Josie listened for a moment and then carried the

phone into her office. She bustled out a few minutes later with her pocketbook. "Girls, I'm so sorry, but I've got to run back to the office for a little while. I shouldn't be too long, hopefully no later than eight. Make sure you take care of the dishes after you finish supper, all right?"

"Sure, Mom," Emily said.

"You're my angels," her mother said as she headed out. "Ivy's next door, and my office number's on the fridge, if there's an emergency."

As soon as their mother had gone, Rose jumped up from the table. She left her place setting behind without saying a word.

"Hey," Emily called, "Mom said we're supposed to do the dishes."

"You're the one who said you'd do them," Rose replied. She bounded upstairs, ignoring her sister's look of disgust.

Rose was giggling on the phone with Becky McIntyre when a huge crash sounded from the kitchen. She rushed back downstairs to find Emily and an overturned chair on the floor, surrounded by bits of a shattered coffee mug. The dishwasher and several cupboards were open.

"What happened?" Rose asked. "Are you okay?" She bent down and helped Emily up.

"I think so. I was trying to put the clean dishes away, but I couldn't reach the shelf where the cups go," she said. Tears filled Emily's eyes when she saw the sharp pieces of ceramic on the floor. "That was Mom's favorite mug."

"The one we gave her last Mother's Day?" Rose said, and Emily nodded. Rose reached out and picked up the two largest fragments of the mug. Held together, the writing on the pieces read "#1 Mom."

"I'm so sorry," Emily sobbed. "I didn't mean to break it. Mom's going to be so upset."

Rose stared at her younger sister, but instead of feeling angry, she was only ashamed that she'd left Emily to clean up the kitchen alone and relieved that she hadn't been hurt. She reached out and squeezed Emily in a big hug, which only made her cry harder.

"Don't worry, I'm not upset, and Mom won't be, either," Rose said. "Let's gather up all the pieces. After we get the dishes done, I'll try to superglue it back together."

Together, they collected all the bigger chunks of the mug and then swept the floor to get all of the tiny ones. Rose took the bag of mug pieces up to their room, where she could keep it hidden until she had the glue and the time to reassemble it. Then, she helped Emily put away the rest of the clean dishes and load the dirty ones into the dishwasher.

"I don't think we have enough Cascade left," Emily said as she took a green, rectangular box from the cupboard beneath the sink. She turned the box upside down and aimed the pour spout toward the dishwasher's soap reservoir, but only a few particles of powder came out.

"Mom forgot to get more when we went shopping," Rose said. "But, no biggie. We've got plenty of the liquid kind." She grabbed the bottle of Dawn by the kitchen faucet and filled the soap reservoir with it. It took her only a moment longer to close the dishwasher and turn the dial to start the wash cycle. "There. Now, all we have to do is wipe the counters and we'll be done. Do you know whether Mom has any superglue?"

"No, but we could check her office," Emily said. She had picked up the bottle of Dawn and was reading the back label. "Hey, Rose, are you sure we can use this in the dishwasher?"

"Don't worry, it'll work fi—" Rose started to say, but at that moment, the sound of the dishwasher motor took on a strange, muffled quality. She turned just in time to see a thick stream of white suds spill from the crack where the door of the dishwasher attached to the unit. It was like a white, fluffy waterfall, gushing in a steady veil all over the floor.

"Oh, my gosh, what do we do? What do we do?" her sister yelled. "It's flooding everywhere!" Emily was frozen in place, watching with a horrified expression as the suds approached her feet.

"Turn off the dishwasher!" Rose ordered.

Emily gasped. "We can't do that. It's already running. If we break the dishwasher, Mom will kill us."

Rose sprinted out of the kitchen to the bathroom, where she grabbed as many towels from the linen closet as she could carry. By the time she got back, suds had covered nearly the entire floor, and they were still being churned out of the dishwasher at breakneck speed.

She ran back into the kitchen with the towels, took two steps on the soapy floor, and felt her feet slide up and out in front of her. With a great *splat,* she landed on her rear end.

"Rose!" Emily said. "You're not hurt, are you?"

As she gasped, trying to catch the breath that had been knocked out of her, Rose shook her head. She was buried in towels, and the warm suds and water on the floor had soaked through the entire backside of her jeans.

Emily giggled. "I guess we're even now, right?"

Her sister's good humor helped soothe her. Rose slowly, slowly moved her hand under one of the towels to scoop up a handful of suds. "Almost," she said as she flung the bubbles at her sister.

Emily's mouth dropped open as she inspected the globs of bubbles stuck on her shirt. Then she was bending down, trying to keep from slipping as she used her hands to launch a return assault. It didn't take long before they were both sopping wet and soapy, continuing to attack each other with the suds and shrieking with laughter as the dishwasher kept up a steady supply.

"Mom's gonna be so mad," Emily said, gripping the breakfast table for support.

"Hey, at least the floor's really clean now," Rose said. "Maybe we can get it all mopped up before she gets home."

"Too late."

Rose startled at their mother's voice and looked toward the kitchen doorway, where she and Aunt Ivy stood looking in at them.

"What in the hell happened here?" Josie demanded. "For God's sake, what did you put in that dishwasher? Why didn't you turn it off?"

Rose watched her mother step out of her dress shoes and into the suds.

"Be careful," Ivy called from the doorway. "It must be slicker than owl snot in there."

Rose tried unsuccessfully to suppress a giggle.

Josie slid and sloshed her way to the dishwasher, turned the dial sharply to OFF, and opened the door. A wall of suds made it impossible to see any of the dishes inside, and more suds and quite a bit of hot water poured out onto the floor.

The expression on Emily's face was pure panic, so Rose gave her a quick wink before turning to her mother. "It's all my fault, Mom," she said. "We were out of the powder for the dishwasher, and I thought it would be okay to use Dawn even though Em wasn't sure. And, we didn't know you could turn off a dishwasher once it was started. We thought about doing it, but we were afraid of breaking it." She glanced again at her sister, who shot back a quick, grateful smile.

"Lordy, Lordy," Ivy said under her breath.

"Well, I suppose you didn't mean any harm," Josie said after a long pause. She stared down at the bubbly mess that came well up above her ankles.

"You'd better get that water up, before it seeps down into the floor," Ivy said.

"Yes. I'll get the push broom from the garage," Josie said. "You girls pick up those towels—whoa!"

Her mother had taken only two steps forward before her feet slipped out from under her, just as Rose's had. She landed in the middle of the kitchen floor.

"Mom! Are you all right?" Rose leaned over, trying to grab her hand.

"Ow. Yes, I'm fine," Josie said. She smiled and laughed a little as she carefully got to her feet. The back and side of her suit were soaked and sudsy.

"Rose slipped, too, Mom. That's how the bubble fight started," Emily said.

"It's a good thing nobody got hurt," Josie said.

"It could've been worse," Ivy said, still standing safely in the doorway. "At least this mess is just soap and dirty dishwater."

"Yeah," Rose chimed in. "It's way better than owl snot!"

CHAPTER 19

Claudia woke up alone. She opened her eyes slowly and stretched, enjoying the feeling of having slept late and being fully rested.

The feather pillow next to hers had an indentation in the middle from Kyle's head. He'd managed to get up and leave for his early shift without waking her. Maybe it was because their time together before falling asleep had involved enough physical exertion to result in her sleeping more soundly than usual. She smiled at the memory of it and wondered whether she'd gotten enough exercise last night to justify skipping the treadmill. It was tempting, but she also remembered the delicious feeling of having watched Kyle's gaze slowly travel the length of her naked body, of seeing his attraction to her reflected in his expression.

Being physically attractive to anyone was still new for her, and she understood that physical attraction was not love. But, her journey from obesity to a healthy weight had been long and difficult. She had no desire to regain the pounds she had lost or return to the world of dateless Saturday nights and cheesecake all to herself.

What she felt for Kyle was an intense mixture of love, admiration, and a physical attraction that often left her breathless. Of course, she was still incredibly inexperienced in the relationship department, but even so, she knew a good thing when she saw it. Kyle was strong, honest, and kind, and a wonderful father. He was handsome, too, and his good looks were enhanced by his inner qualities. She had realized over the last several months, as her feelings for him had deepened, that he was everything she had dreamed of in a partner.

The thought of losing him, after all she had been through, after all the dieting and workouts and the struggle to overcome her insecurities, was more than she could bear. Although he insisted that he loved her for the person that she was on the inside, she *needed* to stay attractive to him on the outside.

She would maintain her healthy weight.

She would put in her time on the treadmill, and she would reward herself by surprising Kyle with lunch at work. He was, after all, her ultimate guilty pleasure.

It took her a couple of hours to work out, shower, and prepare a lunch-to-go for two. With a little chuckle to herself, she included the strawberries left over from their dinner the night before.

The police station was on Main Street several blocks up from her house, and the weather was perfect for the walk. Besides, strolling through the little town always left her with a cheery, friendly feeling. She would almost always pass a person or two who would smile at her as they went about their business, and this time of year, the window boxes on many of the homes and businesses were overflowing with blooms. She approached the front door of the station humming, her skin warmed by the sunshine, and feeling a bit of a rush as she looked forward to seeing Kyle again. A small bell atop the door announced her arrival.

There was a tall counter in the main office of the station, in front of the desk where the receptionist and the officer on duty typically sat. She couldn't see Kyle seated below the counter, but she could hear his voice. The woman with whom he was speaking was standing in front of the counter with her arms resting lightly upon it.

"I'd love to have you come by—" the woman was saying, but

she stopped talking suddenly as she became aware of Claudia's presence. "Oh, hey, Claudia," Emily DiSanti said with an awkward smile.

Kyle's head popped up above the counter, and he stood up. "Claudia! Hi! What are you doing here?" He, too, gave her an odd smile before glancing back at Emily.

"Um, I just decided to bring you lunch. As a surprise," Claudia said. "Hey there, Emily." As they all stood silently for a few seconds, Claudia had to make a conscious effort not to gape at Emily's exceptional beauty. The younger DiSanti sister wore a sleeveless shirt and Daisy Duke shorts, both of which accentuated her toned limbs. Her long red hair was pulled up into some sort of a messy bun, and tendrils of it had fallen down around her face. Even without makeup, her perfect skin was dewy and flushed, as if she had just finished some strenuous activity. *She looks like a sweaty pinup girl,* Claudia thought.

Emily looked down at the bag in Claudia's hand and then back at Kyle. "Wow, you're a lucky guy."

"The luckiest," Kyle agreed with a smile, and Claudia felt a satisfied grin spread across her face. "Judy's on phones today, but she's out running an errand on her lunch break. I'm just finishing up something here. Do you want to go back to the break room and wait for me?"

"Oh, sure," Claudia said. She'd been in the break room before and knew where it was.

"Nice seeing you again," Emily said.

"You, too," Claudia said, still beaming. As she walked past the counter and down a hallway, she looked back over her shoulder at the two of them before they were out of view. Even though she was tickled by Kyle's reaction to her surprise lunch, she couldn't shake the feeling that she had walked in on a conversation she wasn't meant to hear.

As Claudia unpacked the lunch she'd brought, the sound of

Kyle and Emily speaking in muted tones drifted down the hall. "Take care," she finally heard Kyle say in a louder voice, followed by the sound of the bell that rang when the front door opened. It seemed that the door didn't close right away, though, and soon enough, she heard the bell again and realized that someone else had entered the police station.

"Hello there, Officer," Claudia heard a distinctive, singsong voice say to Kyle. "I came over to ask about something. You know I specialize in potions of all kinds, right?" Daisy continued. "Well, I had a great idea. Since it's pretty hot outside, I wondered if I could set up a potion stand in town to sell my famous cooling potion. Sort of like a lemonade stand is how I picture it."

Oh, dear, Claudia thought. She had to stifle a laugh, and she listened closely to see how Kyle would respond.

"I see," Kyle said. "Well, where exactly were you looking to set up the stand, Miss Delaine?"

"Someplace near all the businesses on Main Street would be best," she replied. "The more people who see it, the better."

"Well, I don't know that we could allow a stand in the business district," Kyle said gently. "The town code requires sidewalks to be kept open and free of obstructions. That's why the shops are required to shovel their walks after snowstorms, and it's also why we couldn't let you put a potion stand there."

"Oh," Daisy said. "Well, could I put up a stand in my yard?"

"Of course," Kyle said. "That would be fine, since it's your own property. I'm curious, Miss Delaine . . . what exactly is in your 'cooling potion'?"

"I'm sorry, Officer. I wish I could tell you, but all my potion recipes are *top secret.* I brought along a sample, though, to show you what I plan to offer at my stand." Claudia heard a soft clunk as a hard object was set on the counter. "Go ahead, Officer. Try it while it's nice and frosty."

Claudia bit her lip to keep from giggling out loud.

"You know, I was just getting ready to take my lunch break, so I'll have it in just a few minutes," Kyle told her. "But, thank you. It does look refreshing."

"You're welcome, Officer. If you like it, there's plenty more where that came from!"

Claudia tiptoed to the door of the break room and peeked out just in time to see Daisy, wearing a bright blue sundress, leaving the station. *Finally.* She was about ready to sit down at the table when she heard the rolling chair behind the counter out front pushed backwards and footsteps running down the hall toward the break room. Kyle flew into the room holding a Mason jar filled with a bright pink substance. Before she could say a word, he'd set the jar on the table and pulled her into his arms.

Although Daisy's request had temporarily helped distract her from thinking about Emily's visit to the station, Kyle's mouth against hers, moving along her jawline and down her neck, banished whatever negative feelings remained.

"I didn't want to leave you this morning," he said in her ear, which caused the familiar weakening in her knees, the rush of heat that colored her face and left her breathless. She eased herself backwards a few steps, pulling Kyle along by the large buckle on his duty belt, until she felt the reassuring support of the break-room table against her backside. Kyle lifted her onto the table and stepped forward, drawing her thighs up around him. He kissed her forehead and brushed a still-damp strand of her hair from her face. "I've been thinking about you . . . and last night . . . all morning."

"Me, too. I didn't want to be apart from you the whole day," she said, which prompted him to tighten his arms around her and move his mouth back to hers. "It's too bad you have to work," she added when she could speak. She moved her hands from his waist to a lower location, delighting in his sharp intake of breath. "I don't suppose . . ." She glanced around at the table and then looked back at him with a naughty question in her eyes.

"Claudia . . ." She knew he was tempted, but he closed his hands over hers and pulled them back up around his waist. "We can't. I don't dare, as much as I want to," he said, reading her expression. "Judy could be back any time. Besides, it wouldn't be that comfortable."

"Hmm. How about in the Jeep, then? We could wait 'til Judy's back and go out on patrol."

"Oh, God, no," Kyle said, laughing a little. "That's crazy. In the department's vehicle? Can you imagine what would happen if somebody saw us? Especially Fitz or Ron?"

"All right," Claudia said with a mild pout. "I was just thinking that its windows are tinted, and the seats in there might be nice and soft."

"They are," Kyle admitted. "Buttery-soft leather, and heated, too. But I can't risk it." He kissed her again and stroked her cheek with the back of his hand. "Tonight, okay? Can you come over after Rowen's asleep?" When she nodded, he took a deep breath and turned his attention to the lunch she'd unpacked. "So, what did you bring me?"

"Nothing fancy, just sandwiches and fruit . . . the strawberries we didn't eat last night." Kyle smiled as he sat down. "So, are you really going to drink Daisy's potion?" Claudia eyed the Mason jar.

"Of course not," Kyle said. "I just took it to be polite." He picked up a sandwich Claudia had unpacked and took a bite.

"It doesn't look that bad, actually," Claudia said. The outside of the cold jar was covered in small droplets, which had begun to run down the sides and pool on the table. "Go on, try it. I dare you."

Kyle hesitated. "I will if you will."

Claudia looked at the jar and back at Kyle. "Okay," she said, raising her chin. "But you first." She pushed the jar toward Kyle and sat down in a chair opposite him. He took it in his hands and carefully twisted off the lid.

"Smells fruity," he said after he sniffed at the pink liquid inside. "A little minty, too." He raised the jar to his mouth and took a small sip, then a bigger one. "You know, it's pretty good. See for yourself." He pushed the jar across the table to her.

Somewhat reassured and wanting to appear brave, Claudia took a swig of the potion. It was basically a runny, watermelon-and-mint-flavored sorbet, but it was so tart. Her face puckered and her eyes started to water. Kyle laughed as she whirled around and rushed to the sink in the corner of the break room.

"Ugh, what is in this? And how did you manage to swallow it without letting on it was so sour?" Claudia filled a cup of water and rinsed her mouth out.

"I just kept thinking about how funny it'd be to see your reaction."

"Uh-huh." Claudia shot a nasty look at Kyle as she rejoined him at the table. "I just lost my appetite."

Kyle laughed again. "Well, I still have mine. And I should hurry so I can get back out front." He resumed eating.

"So, why did Emily DiSanti stop by earlier?" Claudia asked, trying to keep her tone casually curious.

"Somebody slashed her tire, and she wanted to report it."

"Really? That sort of stuff doesn't happen much around here. Did she see who did it?"

"Nope, but she thinks it was her sister." Claudia remembered what Kyle had said about the possibility of the sisters' dispute taking a turn for the worse. "Regardless of who was behind it, Emily asked if we'd drive by the house while we're on patrol, just to deter any more vandalism."

Claudia focused on keeping her expression neutral to hide her annoyance. No matter how secure her relationship, she didn't think any woman in town would be happy to have her partner doing the bidding of Mill River's resident supermodel. Apparently, though, Kyle would have to deal with the DiSanti sisters, and she would have to deal with her stupid insecurities. Thankfully, she completely trusted him with her heart.

EMILY RETURNED HOME FROM WORK AT THE HARDWARE STORE IN the early evening. Normally, she would have walked the few blocks to Turner's. Today, though, even with the puny spare tire still on her car, she'd driven to work so that she would have a way to transport home a few things she'd purchased for herself. In addition to the tire swing, Emily had another surprise in store for her nephew, and she couldn't wait to show him. She had a little something for her sister as well, but she would have to wait until nightfall to deliver it.

Back at her house, Emily let Gus outside and grabbed the list of things that she'd compiled. She also took her drill and a utility knife from her toolbox before going back to her front porch. After her visit to Russell's, she'd returned home with one of his old tires and scrubbed it all over with a mild bleach solution. It had dried nicely on the front porch while she'd been at work. Now she quickly drilled several holes along one side of the tire and rolled it over to the large oak tree that stood between her house and Rose's.

It was an enormous tree, sturdy and strong, and it had one lower limb that stretched out almost horizontally. The Weider kids had had a tire swing on that limb years ago, and she and Rose had spent countless hours playing on it. She doubted that Alex had ever been on a tire swing, and she wanted him to be able to experience the fun of something that many kids took for granted.

While Gus sunned himself in the grass, Emily went to her

garage. She found an old garden hose among the junk there, and she used the utility knife to cut a short piece from it. It would serve as a protective sleeve for the rope, to keep it from fraying against the limb. The folded stepladder leaning against the wall would also be useful. She was carrying the length of hose and the ladder toward the oak tree when Alex came outside. He had a notebook tucked under one arm.

"Hey there," she said to him. "I didn't expect to see you again today."

"What are you doing?" he asked her as she laid the ladder on the grass. He stood next to it, shifting his weight from side to side.

"You'll see." She jogged over to her car and removed another of the shopping bags. "I got you something to help you do some bird-watching." She reached in and removed a pair of binoculars. "These are pretty powerful. You should be able to spot birds from quite a distance."

Alex's eyes opened wide. "Wow," he said. He set his notebook on the lawn and accepted the binoculars gingerly, as though they were a rare treasure. "I don't have anything like this, but . . . wow. Thanks, Aunt Emily." He smiled at her and looped the carrying strap attached to the binoculars over his head. His growing delight was plain on his face.

"They're adjustable, and they have a special wide-angle view. The box and instruction manual are in this bag for you. Oh, and here." She reached into her pocket and gave him back the blue-jay feather. "I picked this up for you. You dropped it earlier."

Alex accepted the feather as well. "Yeah. I was afraid Mom would see me with it and yell about how birds carry diseases or something."

"Ah. What's your mom up to, anyway?"

"Taking a nap on the couch."

"Hmmm." Emily's brow furrowed, but she did her best to

hide her worry. "Well, she's right—birds do carry diseases. But, it's not like you're going to eat that feather, and I'm sure you'll wash your hands well after touching it, right?"

"Right," Alex said. "I'll even give the feather a shampoo, so it'll be clean, too."

Emily laughed. "That's a good idea."

"So, what are you doing with the tire? And this ladder?"

"My flat tire couldn't be fixed, so I traded it for another old one without steel wires to make a tire swing for you."

"Cool!" Alex said. "I've never been on a tire swing."

"I suspected," Emily said. "What's with the notebook?"

Alex picked up his notebook and removed some papers from a folder inside. "I made a copy of my spreadsheet for you, the one of all the books in our house. He held the sheets out to her.

"You did this all yourself?" Emily asked. She was shocked at the number of entries in the chart. "My gosh, there's a lot of them."

"I know. That's sort of why I wanted to give you a copy now. I thought that maybe you could get a head start on comparing our list to yours."

"Well, yeah. This will definitely help." Emily smiled up at Alex, and he was beaming back at her. She leaned back against the trunk of the oak tree as she took a moment to study the spreadsheet. It went on for pages. If one, or both, of the clues was a book, how would she and Rose know? It would take forever to go through them all.

She had to admit that if her mother's goal had been to force her and Rose to interact, to work together, she had devised a brilliant plan to achieve it. Then again, she wasn't technically interacting with Rose herself, which was just as well. Alex was endearing, and she was grateful for the opportunity to build a relationship with her only nephew.

"This is just great, Alex," she said. "I'll go over it tonight, as soon as I'm done out here. And when you show this to your mom, ask her to mark which books she's read and which she hasn't. I think she and I should focus on those we've read first."

Alex nodded. "I'll talk to her about it as soon as she wakes up."

"All right," Emily said. She folded the papers and slipped them into her back pocket. "I should get working on the swing while it's still light."

"I can't wait until you're done," Alex said. He grasped the binoculars around his neck and traced a finger around the circular lenses. "Aunt Emily, is it okay if I don't tell Mom you gave these to me? She wouldn't like it if she knew."

"Sure," Emily said, "but what will you tell her about how you got them?"

Alex thought a minute. "I can always say I found them in the house somewhere. I can even have her put them on the list." He gave her a sly grin, much like her earlier one, and she smiled.

I'm really starting to like this kid, Emily thought.

"I suppose there's no harm in that," Emily said. She didn't exactly want to encourage her nephew to start lying, but she didn't want Rose to take away the binoculars, either.

"I should get home in case Mom wakes up," he said. Alex stood up, but instead of leaving, he stood next to Gus, patting the dog's head. He didn't look at her as he spoke. "You know, I really want to help Mom find her clue. She's been worried about it . . . she and Dad argue about it on the phone, and it upsets her."

"I'm sure it does," Emily said, and her nephew's words made her heart ache. "It's frustrating for me, too, and I know how flustered your mom can get. It can't be easy for you to deal with that, either. I was always the one keeping her in line and trying to make her feel better about things while we were growing up, just like you are now." It occurred to her that this sheltered, loving little boy had unwittingly assumed her still-too-familiar role as Rose's keeper.

"They're having money problems," Alex continued. He made eye contact with her, and she tried her best not to tear up at the sad expression on his face. "Dad lost his job a long time ago, and he hasn't been able to get another one. I hear them on the phone when they think I'm sleeping. They're going to lose our apartment in New York unless they get money from Grandma's lawyer."

Although it was difficult to feel sorry for her sister and Sheldon potentially losing what was most likely a multi-million-dollar apartment, she realized that it was probably the only home Alex had ever known. She was increasingly concerned about her little nephew, and she would do her best to serve as a compassionate outlet—one that wouldn't ignore him in favor of sleeping on the sofa.

"Money problems can be really stressful for parents," Emily said, "but I know they wouldn't want for you to worry or be upset about it. Your mom and dad love you, and your mom will do whatever she has to to take care of you. She's super-protective of people she loves. She always stuck up for me when we were little." Emily was surprised to hear herself say such positive things about her sister. She hadn't thought about her childhood relationship with Rose in years.

"Mom *is* stubborn," Alex said with a sheepish grin. "Dad sometimes calls her a mule to tease her."

Emily couldn't help but chuckle. "Even if they have to find another place for all of you to live," she continued, "your mom and dad'll work it out. You should just focus on enjoying your summer, your books, your binoculars. You've got the rest of your life to worry about grown-up problems." She gave him a reassuring smile. "And, I'd love your help in sorting out this mess Grandma got us into. Maybe together, we can figure out what the clues are and find out where she hid her key."

"That would be cool," Alex said.

"All right. I've got a few jobs lined up—one at Turner's Hardware, and another that'll be starting soon, remodeling that big white house on the hill," Emily said, pointing in the direction of the McAllister mansion. "But, let's try to meet toward the end of the week, so I'll have a few days to study the lists and you have time to go over yours with your mom."

"Okay." Alex half smiled, turned as if to walk back to Rose's house, and suddenly rushed forward and threw his arms around her. "Thanks, Aunt Emily, for the binoculars and, uh, everything."

"You're welcome." She returned his hug and grinned as he detached himself. "You know where to find me if you need me," she added. "And Aunt Ivy's here for you, too, don't forget."

"Yeah, I know," Alex said. "She's offered to loan me some new books if I don't like the ones in our house, and she said I can come over to The Bookstop anytime." He grinned and patted Gus one last time before he left. "See you, boy."

The sun was beginning to go down when Emily finally stood back and looked at the finished tire swing. "Here goes nothing," she said to Gus, who had been dozing while she worked. She grasped the rope of the swing, pulled it back, and stepped up and onto the tire as she pushed it forward. In that instant, as she gripped the rope with both hands, her feet tucked down inside the center hole and the tire spinning and swaying in the warm evening air, she forgot her sad, lonely, nomadic life, her problems with Rose, her mother's death.

She was a child again, and there was only joy.

CHAPTER 20

1992

Time continued its inevitable march, seemingly faster and faster, as Josie became more successful with her brokerage and the girls started middle school. Even though she added a receptionist, several new agents, and an assistant broker to her staff, she rarely had a free moment. Those that she did have were almost always spent with or for Rose and Emily. The girls were good students and well liked at school, and there were more and more school functions and after-school activities in which they became involved. Despite Josie's best efforts, though, her attendance at spelling bees, school plays, and softball games was never a sure thing. That first time she had failed to arrive home in time to enjoy the supper her girls had prepared became the start of an inevitable parade of missed events. Her schedule was often at the mercy of her clients, and she felt compelled to give deference to a professional obligation if a conflict couldn't be avoided.

She had to make sure she could pay the bills, so her job had to take priority.

Things were especially difficult on weekends and during the spring and summer, when the real estate market was most active. During those busy periods, she resorted to scheduling her day in thirty-minute increments, trying to make time for the girls in the mornings and evenings and between appointments. Their tradition of reading aloud together at bedtime was almost sacred, and Josie was pleased that she managed to be there most of the time.

Still, she worried it wasn't enough.

Josie kept a running mental list of everything she'd missed. The most recent entries were Rose's first starring role in the school musical and Emily's winning exhibit at the school's art show. Every time the list grew longer and she had to face the dejected face of one of her daughters, she felt as if a small piece of her heart was sliced away. Her hugs and the apologies she murmured into the girls' ears were hardly enough to make up for her absences. She wondered how other single parents managed.

One night, when the girls were thirteen and eleven, she arrived home late and went up to their room. They were still awake. Rose was sitting in her bed reading from a book in her lap while Emily lay on her own bed, her head propped up on one elbow, listening. Josie knocked softly on the open door and smiled as she came in and sat down at Emily's feet.

"Keep going, don't stop," she said when the girls looked up and saw her. "You're getting to one of the really good parts."

The book on Rose's lap was *To Kill a Mockingbird,* and she had almost reached the part in the story where Atticus Finch guns down a rabid dog. As she listened to Rose's voice, Josie mused over how much she and the fictional father in the story had in common. They'd both lost their spouses and were single, working parents of two children. They were both determined to protect and raise their children well.

"Mom?" Rose's question jarred her from her thoughts.

"Hmmm?"

"Will you tell us . . . well, Em and I were wondering if you would tell us about Dad."

"About how he died," Emily added.

The question took Josie by surprise. Her girls knew, and had known from the time they were old enough to understand, that their father had passed away when they were very young. She had never talked much about it, though, and the girls didn't know the details.

"Where did this question come from, out of the blue?" she asked them.

"I was asking Rose about it before you got home," Emily replied. "You've never told us."

"Don't you think we're old enough to know?" Rose asked. It was clear from her tone that *she* felt she was plenty old enough to hear what had happened.

Josie exhaled slowly, trying to decide how to answer. The girls *were* older now, but they still weren't adults, and there was no way she would tell them the whole truth. Not yet, anyway. "He died in a fire," she said. "I was out running errands and came home to find the house burning. Your father was in the kitchen when I found him. He was already gone. You girls were upstairs in your room, and I managed to get you out."

"What started the fire?" Rose asked.

"It was ruled an arson," Josie said. "The police finally made an arrest about two years after we moved here." It had been a long time since she had remembered the sheer terror of seeing the flames, of struggling to breathe as thick smoke twisted down her throat and seared her lungs while her babies cried out for her.

"Is that why we left New York and came to live with Aunt Ivy?" Emily asked.

"Yes. The authorities told me our house had probably been targeted for some reason, and it wasn't safe for us to stay in New York."

"I remember that night, when Aunt Ivy came and we all got in the car," Rose whispered.

"Is the man still in jail?" Rose asked.

"Yes, honey. He'll be in jail for the rest of his life."

"Tell us about Dad," Emily said quietly, after they had all sat in silence for a minute. Josie saw the longing expression on her younger daughter's face, whose blue eyes matched those of a father she didn't remember at all. "What was he like? Where did you meet each other?"

"He was a wonderful person, in every way, and he loved you girls so much."

"Tall, dark, and handsome, right, Mom?" Emily asked, and Josie laughed and nodded. She wished again that she had a photo of Tony that they could see, especially now that his features and expressions were showing up more and more on their adolescent faces.

"We met on a blind date," she began, relieved that Emily's questions had changed the subject to one that was somewhat easier for her to remember and talk about. "My old roommate, Darlene Giordano, set us up. She was constantly trying to find dates for me, but the guys she wanted me to meet were always sleazy or smelly, and sometimes both." Rose and Emily giggled together and wrinkled their noses.

"I told Darlene I was through with her blind dates, but she said she'd finally met a guy who was perfect for me. Someone polite and good-looking, and smart, too."

"Was it Dad?" Emily asked, and Josie nodded.

"I met him for coffee at a little hole-in-the-wall diner. At the time, your dad was in college, studying to be an accountant. He was working part time at a diamond import company in New York City, and I was working in a jewelry store back then, so we had something in common."

"Did you think he was cute?" Rose asked.

"Of course. Your father was very handsome," Josie said, feeling a little color come to her cheeks. "But the longer we talked, the more I realized that I'd never met a kinder, more compassionate person. That's what really attracted me to him.

"On that first date, we stayed at the restaurant until it closed, and then he walked me home. I'd had so much coffee by then that I couldn't sleep, so I was still up when Darlene got home from work. She could tell right away that we'd hit it off."

"I'll bet she was happy," Rose said.

"Yes, Darlene bragged for years afterward how she matched us up," Josie said to the girls. "I wonder what happened to her. I haven't thought about her in a long time." She was quiet for a few seconds. "Your dad has been gone for years now, but I still see him every day, in you girls. When you furrow your brow and concentrate on something, Rose, you look exactly like he used to. You have his stubbornness, and his determination, too. And Em, I've told you before that your eyes are just like his, but I think your strong sense of justice also came from him. Your father always insisted on doing the fair thing, the right thing, even when there was an easier way out."

"I'm glad you ended up with Dad," Emily said.

"Me too," Rose said.

"I'm grateful every day that I took a chance on one more of Darlene's blind dates and met your father," Josie said. She reached out to smooth a strand of Rose's hair away from her face. "Otherwise, you girls wouldn't be here, and we wouldn't all have each other. In the end, that's the only thing that matters."

1994

EMILY AWOKE WITH A START. THE BEDROOM SHE SHARED WITH Rose was dark and quiet, but something had disturbed her sleep. The clock on the nightstand read 1:46 a.m. She thought perhaps Rose had had a nightmare and called out, but the lump in Rose's twin bed was silent and unmoving. Emily was ready to close her eyes again when she heard the floor creak on the other side of the room. She turned to see Rose, fully clothed, standing at the open window.

"What are you doing?" Emily asked, sitting up. She glanced over at her sister's bed again, confused as to what was under the covers if Rose herself wasn't there.

"Shhhh. I'm going out."

"What?" Emily was wide-awake now. "What do you mean, going out?" Only then did she notice trailing out the window the portable fire-escape ladder that their mother insisted they keep in the bedroom. "You're going *down the ladder*?"

"Duh," Rose said. "Tyler and Jason are coming by to pick me up. Tyler Crowe's the most popular guy in school. He's a *senior*! And he just got his own car. Crystal's coming, too. They should be here any minute." Rose craned her neck out the window, obviously watching for someone.

"Where are you going to go?"

"I'm not sure, just riding around, probably. But it doesn't matter," Rose said. "We're just going to have a little fun."

"You're crazy. What if Mom finds out?" Emily asked. "She'll kill you."

"Look, Mom's hardly home anymore unless she's sleeping. If she really cared about what you and I were doing, she wouldn't be like that. So, I figure I'll just hang out with my friends. *They* want to spend time with me."

At that moment, they both heard a hushed voice calling from the lawn below. Rose stuck her head out the window and waved.

"Rose, what if Mom wakes up and finds out you're gone?"

"She won't. The only way Mom'll find out about tonight is if you tell her," Rose hissed. "But I know you wouldn't do that, right? 'Cause we really need to look out for each other."

"I don't think this is a good idea," Emily said, but she knew nothing she said or did would prevent her sister from leaving.

"It'll be fine," Rose said, clambering out onto the ladder. "I'll be back before morning. Go back to sleep." When she finally uprooted herself from her mattress, Emily made it to the window just in time to see Rose and a boy she didn't recognize run together around the side of the house.

Emily sighed. Of course, there was no way she could go back to sleep now. She was torn between risking her sister's wrath by going to wake their mother and just waiting for Rose to return, hopefully unscathed and unnoticed. She climbed back into bed and pulled the covers up over her head. Everything having to do with Rose was difficult these days, and it was getting worse.

Her sister was a sophomore in high school. So much had changed since the beginning of the school year. Rose was blonde, beautiful, and gregarious. She was easily the most popular girl in her class. In fact, she was one of the most popular girls in the whole high school, and she'd recently begun to hang out with a couple of the seniors.

Maybe that's why she's wearing so much makeup, Emily thought. Heavy eye makeup and lipstick were now the norm on Rose's face even though their mother disapproved. On the first day Rose had tried to leave for school wearing bright red lipstick and blue eye shadow up to her eyebrows, a huge fight between Rose and their mother had ensued.

"Go wash that off your face, every bit of it. No teenage daughter of mine is going to leave this house looking like that," their mother had insisted before confiscating Rose's cosmetics. It hadn't done any good. The next day, Rose had left the house with a freshly scrubbed face and returned after school looking like she'd stepped out of a cosmetic advertisement in a fashion magazine. With her vast circle of friends, Rose could get her hands on new makeup, or nearly anything else she wanted, almost immediately. Their mother's continued seizure of beauty products, scolding, and grounding hadn't worked. Eventually, she'd given up trying to enforce the cosmetics rule, and Rose now wore as much as she liked.

The makeup was only one of the ways Rose was changing. In eighth grade and even during her freshman year, Rose had been a straight-A student. Last semester, though, Rose hadn't had a single A on her report card. She'd become more and more preoccupied with her appearance and her social life, and Emily rarely saw her do homework. Even worse, Rose had developed a blasé attitude toward school.

"Oh, Em, it's just a stupid book report," her sister had said when she'd asked whether she'd finished the assignment for her English class. "Mrs. Wilson is a pushover. She'll let me turn it in late." Rose had turned to her and pointed to her bangs, which she had curled and teased into a puffy ball. "How does this look? Hurry, 'cause I need to spray it before it moves."

"Fine," Emily had responded. Talking to her sister about school was useless when Rose's main concern these days was spending time with her friends.

Emily couldn't imagine herself ever sneaking out like her sister just had, even if she'd been offered the opportunity. She was quiet and shy, and she had none of the easy popularity Rose possessed. "Boring" was how Rose teasingly referred to her, but it wasn't anything she could change about herself even if she wanted to.

The question now was whether to tell on Rose. Part of her was worried that something would happen to her sister while she was out joyriding and doing whatever else. But another part of her looked forward to hearing about Rose's middle-of-the-night adventures and experiencing the excitement vicariously. This was her big sister, after all. As far back as she could remember, Rose had always been there, watching out for her, and Emily loved her fiercely. As different as they were, and as comfortable as she was in her own skin, she still looked up to Rose and basked in any sort of praise from her bold, funny, adventurous sibling.

Emily uncovered her head and looked toward the open window. Of course she would remain loyal to her sister. She wouldn't alert their mother, but would stay in their room and wait for Rose to return.

CHAPTER 21

A<small>N HOUR AFTER SHE AND</small> A<small>LEX HAD FINISHED SUPPER,</small> Rose was still seated at the kitchen table, nursing a bottle of white wine and staring at the empty Stouffer's packages that had contained their meals. Although Alex had dutifully cleared his place after he'd finished eating, she hadn't gotten around to doing the same. When her phone rang, she glanced at the number and rolled her eyes before answering it.

"Rose?" Sheldon spoke before she had a chance to say anything. "Rose, what in the hell is wrong with you? How many times have I told you to be careful about what you post on my wall? You know I'm keeping my profile totally public while I'm looking for work."

"Hi, honey, so nice to hear your voice, too," she said in an overtly genteel tone before continuing in her normal voice. "I called you earlier, several times, actually, and you didn't answer. Sometimes I think Facebook is the only way to get in touch with you."

"I was out running errands. Actually buying a new toner cartridge, if you must know, and my phone battery went dead. And then I come back and find your little post for God and everyone to see."

Rose tried to remember exactly what she'd written on Sheldon's Facebook page earlier in the afternoon, but it was a bit of a blur. All she could remember was crying over her laptop and typing the words "bald," "unemployed," and "George Costanza."

"It wasn't a big deal, Sheldon. I was just pissed because you didn't pick up."

"It *was* a big deal, Rose. A potential employer might've seen what you wrote and decided against considering me for an opening. Why would you do something like that? Were you 'drunk Facebooking' again?"

Rose remained silent. She didn't have a rational answer for him. In fact, although she truly didn't remember what she'd typed, she now felt ashamed to have done anything that might jeopardize Sheldon's finding a job.

"Rose, are you there? Rose?"

"Yes." Overwhelmed by emotions, Rose felt her face crumple.

"Rose, how much are you drinking?"

That question, and especially Sheldon's tone in asking it, sparked enough anger to stanch her despair and allow her to regain her composure. She had every intention of cutting back, as she had resolved to do the previous evening. Tonight, though, she'd really needed something to take the edge off.

"I'm not drinking," she said. She swigged the last of the wine in her glass. "But I *am* miserable. Isolated, stuck up here in a matchbox of a house with no air-conditioning. Did I mention that the house is full of junk, and I can't stand being around my sister? Neither of us has any idea what my mother meant for us to find, and there's so much crap to go through that we may never figure it out. I just want to come home."

"Well, I'm not exactly a happy camper, either. I had a consulting job fall through today, and your little stunt didn't improve my prospects at finding more. You can't come home yet, and if you want a home to come back to, you'd better suck it up and do what you need to do to get your inheritance. And, stay off my Facebook page. That's all I have to say to you, but I want to talk with Alex. I'm starting to think that maybe he should spend the summer here with me after all. When you're drinking, you're in no shape to take care of him."

"I'm *not* drinking," she snapped. "And Alex is fine. You can hear for yourself." Rose pulled the phone away from her face and yelled for Alex to come downstairs. "Here," she said, thrusting the phone at him when he appeared in the kitchen. "It's your father."

Alex smiled as he took the phone from her. "Hi, Dad," he said. Rose couldn't hear exactly what Sheldon was saying, but listening to Alex's replies made it possible to follow the conversation.

"Yeah, I'm okay. She's fine, too," Alex was saying. "No, not too much . . . She just doesn't like it here, that's all. We went out this morning, to breakfast and to go shopping . . . I've been reading books, mostly. I was going to ask Mom if I could go see Aunt Ivy and get a few new ones when I've finished the ones I have . . . uh-huh, I love you, too, Dad. Bye." He pressed the END button and returned the phone to her.

"Thanks," she said, leaning back in her chair. She was thinking that she would be far more comfortable in her usual spot on the sofa when she realized that Alex was still standing in the kitchen watching her.

"Mom, are you okay?"

Rose looked at her son. She smiled, fully intending to offer him all manner of reassurances, but she couldn't seem to articulate anything. Alex's eyes were large and round behind his glasses. He stood, waiting for her to say something. Her lower lip began to tremble, and she turned her face away so that he would not see the tears that had appeared.

"Mom, please don't cry." Alex came closer and patted her arm, as if he were trying to comfort her but didn't know quite what to do.

"Come here," she said, turning in her chair and revealing her tear-streaked face. When she opened her arms, he embraced her eagerly, putting his arms around her neck and his head on her shoulder in the same way he had when he was a toddler.

She pressed her cheek against his head, breathing in the familiar sweet and slightly sweaty smell of his hair. "Everything is going to be fine," she managed to say. "I'm just frustrated right now, with your dad, with everything. Except you."

Alex didn't say anything for a few seconds. Then, he pulled away so that he could look into her face. "Mom, I've been working really hard on the list of books. I'm almost done with it. I know you said you didn't want me to be around Aunt Emily, but I really want to help figure out Grandma's clues. Since I read fast, I could skim the books for you. I've already read a lot of them, and if you told me which ones you've read, I could talk to her about them so you won't have to. Please, can I do it? I don't want you to be sad anymore."

Rose smiled through her tears. Alex was so earnest and innocent. He had no idea what had happened to drive her and Emily apart all those years ago, no idea how difficult it was to live with the knowledge of what she had done, and now, to be forced to live next door to the most obvious reminder of it. Most days, she was able to keep it bottled up, pushed to a dark corner of her mind, away from the regular flow of thought required to navigate each day. Recently, though, it was increasingly difficult to ignore the dark episode that she had long tried to forget.

"I know, baby," Rose said. "I'm so glad you're with me." She took both his hands. "I wish I could turn over this whole project to you, but I'm afraid that your aunt and I are the only ones who knew your grandma well enough to figure out the clues. But, why don't you finish up our list of books and let me see it? I'll give you the list I made of the rest of the stuff in the house, too, and you can take everything over for Aunt Emily to see. I already have a copy of her list, so we could each look over everything separately. That way, your aunt and I wouldn't have to meet again unless one of us has an idea about the clues."

Alex smiled. "Okay. I'll have the book list done by tomorrow morning, promise." He glanced at her wineglass and tugged at her hand. "Why don't you go upstairs and take a bubble bath? It might make you feel better. I can clean up the rest of the kitchen."

Rose sighed and slowly got to her feet. "Maybe I will," she said. She leaned down and kissed Alex's hair. "I know I don't say it often enough, but I love you, Alex. I don't know what I'd do without you."

ALEX WAITED UNTIL HE HEARD HIS MOTHER'S FOOTSTEPS REACH the top of the stairs before he dared move. *Don't cry, only girls cry,* he told himself as he stood in the kitchen. Despite his best effort, a few tears squeezed out the corners of his eyes, and he wiped them away angrily, not even bothering to remove his glasses.

With his vision watery and distorted, it was easier to just close his eyes for a moment. It helped ease his worry, too. In his mind, he could go anywhere, to any happy place he wished. He decided to revisit his last birthday, when his mother had awakened him in the morning with a huge smile on her face.

"Happy birthday, baby!" she'd said, hugging him. "You're nine! I can't believe it, can you? I love you so much! Hurry and get dressed. Clara's got your breakfast ready, and I've got something special planned for today. A surprise!"

Even though it had been a school day in early May, she'd taken him on his very first visit to Coney Island. It was extra-special, just the two of them spending all day in a kid's paradise. Better yet, his mother had been so happy and carefree. She hadn't made any snide comments about the filthy sidewalks. She hadn't said a word about his father or complained about how the sun gave her a headache.

She bought cotton candy and funnel cakes and laughed when he pointed out that mustard from her hot dog had fallen in a yellow glob on the front of her shirt.

He'd ridden everything in the kiddie park. Next, on the bumper cars, he'd held on for dear life, alternately giggling and screaming, as his mother steered around the ring. They careened into walls and bashed other cars. After their third ride, with their sides aching and their heads spinning, they'd linked arms and walked to the Wonder Wheel.

They had definitely saved the best for last. In the soaring outer car of the famous Ferris wheel, a hundred and fifty feet up, he'd been able to see for miles—the waves rolling in across the vast ocean, the city stretched out on the other three sides, the sun starting to sink down behind the skyscrapers in the distance. The fresh, salty air skimmed their faces and whipped through their hair. He felt buoyant, almost overcome by the exhilaration of it.

"It feels like we're birds. Like we're flying!" he'd said to his mother.

"It does," she'd agreed, her voice calm and wistful. "Like we're flying away." He wondered after the fact why his mother hadn't grimaced at his comment, since she disliked birds. But, she'd only touched his cheek, smiled a little, and gazed out at the view.

The memory of salt water and sunshine faded, replaced by the lingering odor of microwave dinners. Through the ceiling, Alex listened to the squeaks of his mother's steps heading toward the bathroom and then heard the muffled roar of water rushing into the bathtub. Only then did he seize the half-empty bottle of wine that still sat on the table and pour it down the kitchen sink.

CARRYING A PLASTIC GROCERY SACK, EMILY STEPPED OUT ONTO her front porch. The moon had risen, and the street was quiet. She looked over at Rose's house and was pleased to see that even the upstairs lights were out. Quietly, she went to her car to retrieve the last shopping bag she'd brought home from work. That bag was heavier than the one she had brought from her house because it contained birdseed.

Using one of her car keys, she punctured the plastic birdseed bag and then slipped her fingers into the hole, pulling the plastic apart to widen the opening. A couple of times, she scooped up a handful and then let the tiny round grains run through her fingers. At first, it was a pleasant sensation, one that brought back child-hood memories of reaching into the bag her mother had always kept to refill the feeder in their yard. One memory led to another, though, and soon she was a fourth-grader again, waiting for the bus on a dreary, rainy morning just a few feet from where she currently stood.

It had been her turn to bring in something for show-and-tell. Aunt Ivy had helped her make a bird feeder out of Popsicle sticks, and her mother had allowed her to take some of their birdseed to school with it, in case her teacher allowed her to fill and place it outside the window of her classroom.

As she had stood holding the feeder and birdseed carefully in a shoe box, an older boy she didn't recognize approached her.

"What's in the box?" he'd demanded to know.

Emily hadn't answered him immediately. She'd been so shy back then. Instead, she'd taken a step backward, moving further under the large umbrella Rose held over both of them.

"I said, *what's in the box?*"

"A bird feeder, for show-and-tell," she'd whispered.

"Well, if it's for showing, let's see it, then," the boy had said, grabbing the box roughly from her. He'd opened the shoe box and removed the bird feeder.

"Please, give it back," Emily had said. She'd glanced across the street, at her own house, but her mother had already left for work. The Bookstop next door wasn't open yet, and its front windows were still dark. She also noticed how, by that point, the other children clustered at the bus stop were staring at what was going on.

Apparently seeking to make the most of his audience, the new boy had smirked and dropped her bird feeder onto the sidewalk.

"Oops," the boy had said.

Emily remembered her face getting hot as she'd stared at chunks of glued Popsicle sticks on the wet concrete.

"That was my sister's project for school," Rose had yelled, stepping in front of her. "She didn't do anything to you. Why would you be so mean?"

"Aw, it was just an accident," the boy had said. "But, since it's broken, I guess she won't be needing this anymore." The bully had opened the small container of birdseed in the box. With another smirk, he'd lunged at them, hurling the contents forward. Rose's attempt to shield them with the umbrella came a second too late. Emily could still feel the tiny seeds spraying against her face, lodging in her curly red hair.

She remembered the look on Rose's face then. With her eyes squinted and her nostrils flaring, Rose had brushed the birdseed from her long, blonde ponytail. "You'd better apologize," she'd said to him through gritted teeth.

"Or what?" he'd laughed, looking down at Rose. "You're just a *girl*. You know, though, I wouldn't mind having a nice umbrella like that."

Rose had stared at him for a moment before she closed the umbrella and held it out to him. "All right," she said. "Here."

Apparently thinking he'd scored another win, the boy had stepped forward for the umbrella. When he was within range, before he or anyone else realized what she was doing, Rose lowered the pointed end to the ground and then snapped it upward. The firm center pole struck squarely between the bully's legs, and he cursed and dropped to his knees. Emily remembered staring at Rose, at once horrified, awestruck, and proud, as the boy groaned with his hands clasped over his crotch.

"You owe *my sister* an apology," Rose had said, smacking him on the backside with the umbrella. "And yes, I *am* a girl. Don't you forget it."

Still standing on her front porch, Emily could see Rose's freshly washed BMW gleaming in the moonlight. Part of her, the shy fourth-grader cowering before the bully from her youth, argued against doing what she had planned. It went against her character. It just wasn't nice. And yet . . . her gaze traveled back to her own car, where the tiny spare tire was still mounted on the front right wheel. So much had changed. She didn't know or understand the Rose of today, the once-protective sister who couldn't face reality and who had ruined her future.

Emily glanced around again and then carried the birdseed and the smaller grocery sack a few steps up the sidewalk to Rose's car. Carefully, because she didn't know whether the BMW had a touch-sensitive alarm, she lifted a handful of birdseed and sprinkled it across the black trunk. She worked her way around the car, dribbling the birdseed on the hood, the roof, and anyplace else that was flat enough to keep it from rolling onto the ground. When she was satisfied with her application, she took the lighter grocery sack and dumped the contents, which were courtesy of Gus, on the ground right outside the driver's side door.

If her dog-and-bird-hating sister wanted to play the vandalism game, she was more than happy to give Rose an *au naturel* taste of her own medicine.

CHAPTER 22

1995

"C'MON, EM, PLEASE? MOM'S GOT A LATE MEETING, AND she's being stubborn. She won't let me take the car unless you go, too. Now that I've got my license, I'll look like a total loser if Mom drops me off."

Emily rolled her eyes. Unlike Rose, she rarely went to football games and never went to school dances afterward. The music was always so loud, and even if she had known how to dance, she didn't have a boyfriend to dance with.

"Why can't you get a ride with one of the other cheerleaders? They'll all be going, too."

"I'm always bumming rides," Rose complained. She was adjusting her red, white, and blue uniform with the school's Minutemen logo. "It gets old after a while. Can you just come with me, this once? You can bring a book or your sketchpad or something and hang out in an empty classroom. You don't have to dance. We can meet up when it's over."

Emily sighed. Trying to deny her sister was always a losing battle.

She ended up bringing her homework for English class. After the football game, as Rose disappeared into the darkened gymnasium, Emily slipped into an unlocked classroom. To her surprise, she was able to block out most of the pulsing rock music coming from the gym and focus on her reading.

When the music stopped, Emily looked at the clock on the wall and gathered up her things. It was almost eleven. Sure enough, the other students were filing out of the gym. She watched for Rose, waiting until the last of the kids cleared out, but her sister wasn't among them.

She joined the other students walking toward the parking lot. Her mother's old station wagon was in the same space where they'd left it before the game. Emily leaned against the back end, assuming that Rose would soon show up, but after another fifteen minutes had passed, the wagon was the only car left in the lot.

Emily placed her books on the hood of the car and walked back to the school. Already, the lights inside were turned off and the outer doors were locked. The chaperones at the dance must have made sure before they'd gone home that nobody was left in the school. But, if Rose wasn't inside, where was she?

A fluttering, panicky feeling started to build in her stomach.

Maybe she left with some friends. Of course, after Rose had made such a big deal about driving to the game herself, that was unlikely. *Maybe she really did get locked inside the building.* Trying to ignore the chilly autumn air, Emily started to walk the perimeter of the high school, looking in through the main glass doors and tugging on the handles in the hope of finding one that was still open.

The back of the school faced the football field. As she rounded the building's corner, a movement near the bleachers in the distance caught her eye. Someone had stepped out from behind them just for a moment. At about that time, she heard an angry female voice, followed by a scream that was cut short.

Rose.

Emily ran toward the bleachers. The sounds of struggle became audible—the scraping of shoes on the ground intermingled with deep laughter and muffled screams.

There were two tall, well-built young men. One of them was trying to keep Rose's arms pinned behind her and a hand over her mouth, but she was twisting and kicking with all her strength to break free from his grasp. The other man was reaching under her cheerleading uniform as he laughed. Neither one of them heard Emily approach.

"That's my sister! Get your hands off her!" Emily screamed as loud as she could. The men whirled around in surprise. For a moment, no one spoke.

"Well, would you look at that," one of the men finally said. "Now we don't have to share."

"And she's a *redhead*," the other man replied. He leered at Emily and started toward her.

I'll never outrun him, Emily thought, and even if she ran, there was no one around. Besides, she wouldn't, couldn't leave Rose. She felt her legs start to shake. For a split second, her eyes locked with her sister's, but it was long enough. A great wave of energy seemed to flow from Rose's green eyes into her blue ones, infusing her with newfound courage. Her trembling subsided.

"You get your hands off my sister!" she screamed again. She didn't run or even flinch. She glowered at the man advancing on her and pointed in the direction of the school parking lot. "Our mother is waiting in the car over there, and her best friend is married to the chief of police. If we're not down there in thirty seconds, and maybe even if we are, you're gonna have every cop in Rutland County after you. I'd start running now, if I were you."

The man advancing on her stopped cold and looked over his shoulder at his companion. At exactly that moment, Rose managed to bite down on her captor's hand.

"Ow! Goddamnit, she bit me," he said. He released Rose roughly, shoving her to the ground, so that he could cradle his bleeding hand.

"Aw, fuck this," the other one said. Together, the men took off into the trees behind the athletic field.

"Rose!" Emily rushed to her sister and helped her up. "Are you hurt? Did they—"

"No, they didn't. I'm fine," Rose said.

"We've got to get to the car, in case they come back. Where's your purse?" Her sister seemed rooted to one spot, so Emily searched around the bleachers until she found Rose's purse on the ground. Quickly, she returned to her sister. "C'mon."

"Oh, God, Em." Rose took a step forward and stumbled as she started to cry uncontrollably. Emily wrapped her arm around her sister's waist for support. Rose smelled like sweat, their mother's expensive perfume, and booze.

When they reached the car, Emily pulled the keys out of the purse and helped Rose into the passenger's seat.

"You're fourteen. You can't drive," Rose objected when she realized what Emily was doing.

"I can tell that you've been drinking, and you're still messed up from what those guys did," she replied. "And I *can* drive. I've practiced on the back roads with Mom. Better to drive sober without a license than drive drunk and kill someone. Unless you'd prefer to call Mom to come get us."

Rose sat back in the seat. Emily took her silence for acquiescence and started the engine.

"I thought you were going to the dance. How did you end up outside, behind the bleachers?" Emily asked. "Did you know those guys?"

Rose rubbed her eyes and fished around in her purse for a tissue. "One of them, the one I bit, I met at the game. He came up and flirted a little afterward, and I snuck him into the dance. We went outside to hang for a little while 'cause he had some stuff to drink. I didn't know he had someone else waiting up at the field."

Emily gritted her teeth. Now was not the time to criticize Rose's lack of good judgment. "You need to report this. Those guys need to go to jail."

"Are you kidding? Mom'll never let me out of the house again if she finds out about this. Or you, either. You've gotta swear, Em. You can't say anything about tonight to anyone."

Emily sighed. She had a viselike grip on the steering wheel as she drove out of the school parking lot. The terror she had suppressed earlier finally began to ripple through her body, and she focused on her sister to keep from losing it before they got home. "Rosie, are you sure you're okay? Do you need to go to the hospital?"

"I'm fine," Rose said again, although she sounded as if she was trying to convince herself of that. "Another five minutes, if you hadn't come . . ." She turned to Emily. Her heavy eye makeup was smudged and running down her face. "Th-thank you."

"I guess we're even now," Emily said in a shaky voice. She half smiled at Rose even as her lip trembled. "And I didn't even have an umbrella."

CHAPTER 23

Rose unfolded and refolded the several sheets of paper in her hand. There was a printout of Alex's spreadsheet, her own handwritten list of objects in their house, and a copy of Emily's list, which Alex had gotten from her sister. Many items in each column were highlighted in yellow. She'd tried to indicate the books and objects that might have a greater probability of being clues, but now, looking at the number of yellow marks, she realized that she really hadn't made much progress at all. The headache she had from staring at the pages for so long wasn't helping, either.

It was incredibly frustrating, not being able to discern what her mother might have left as her clue. And, even though Alex was eager to help, he lacked the in-depth understanding of his late grandmother, and knowledge of Rose's own time growing up in Mill River, that would certainly be needed to figure out her mother's idiotic scheme. She hated to admit it, but her sister was right. Their only option, if they wanted to get out of Mill River anytime soon, was to sit down to discuss and think through the lists together.

Rose took a deep breath. She would have given almost anything for some vodka in her orange juice at breakfast, but the wine she'd had the previous night had been the last of the alcohol in her house. A trip to the liquor store was definitely in order. It was just as well for now, though. If she had to interact with Emily, she would make sure she was stone-cold sober. The last thing she wanted to do was give her sister's criticism any validity.

Rose grabbed her purse and keys. "Alex, I'm going out for a bit. Stay in the house," she called up the stairs.

"Sure, Mom," he answered from his room. "I'm just reading, anyway."

Typical, she thought. She stepped outside and saw Emily's junk car parked down the street, which meant that her sister was home.

Rose was already on the sidewalk before she noticed that there was something different about her own vehicle. Yesterday, her black BMW had been spotless. Now, the finish was mottled, covered in small, black-and-white lumps and splotches. She rushed over to get a closer look. *There must be hundreds of them,* she thought. Her beautiful, newly washed car was covered in bird crap. It was as if a whole flock had roosted on it.

She was thinking about how to get back to the car wash without being seen driving such a horrendous mess when she noticed the birdseed. There wasn't much of it, just some sunflower-seed shells and a few smaller, uneaten kernels remaining among the droppings on the hood. Rose backed up, feeling an ugly rage beginning to work its way up her body. She ran to Emily's front door and pounded on it.

Emily's dog started barking immediately. By the time her sister had restrained the beast and come to the door, Rose was trembling so much that she had difficulty articulating her words.

"I left my house intending to come over here and ask you whether you'd like to work through these," Rose said as she held up the stack of papers. "But now, I'm here to tell you to stay the hell away from my car."

Emily's eyes opened wide, but Rose knew her well enough to see that it was an expression of mock surprise. "Good morning to you, too," Emily said, meeting her angry stare calmly. She held a cup of tea in one hand, and she casually sipped from it before continuing. "And I have no idea what you're talking about with your car. What, did someone slash a tire or something?"

Rose felt her nostrils flare. "You covered it in bird shit. Don't you know that chemicals in bird shit can damage the finish on a car?"

Emily shushed the dog, who was whining and trying to get past her out the door. "Oh please, Rose, no one can force birds to poop in any particular place." Emily smiled. "If you're serious about going over the lists, though, you're welcome to come in."

"You can play Little Miss Innocent all you want, but I *know* your face and I *know* when you're lying. I'm going to have my car washed—AGAIN—and if there's any damage to the clear coat, you're going to pay to have it redone."

"Like hell I am."

"And I may just file a police report while I'm out," Rose said.

"Go ahead," Emily said. "You have no way of proving anything."

Rose clenched her teeth and nearly raised her hand. Even though she knew her sister was right, it was all she could do to keep herself from slapping the smug expression off Emily's face.

"As for the lists," Emily went on, "none of the books or other stuff in your house or mine jump out at me as being things Mom would've left as clues. I assume you haven't recognized anything obvious, either. Since Mom's letter said that her safe-deposit-box key is also hidden somewhere on our properties, I'm going to forget about finding her clues and focus on searching for the key itself. If you want a quick end to our situation, I suggest you do the same." With that, Emily grabbed her dog by the collar, pulled him backward into the house, and slammed the door.

Rose screamed in frustration at the closed door before she got herself under control. She turned around and marched down the steps to the sidewalk, where Daisy Delaine was walking along the edge of the street on the other side of Emily's car, staring at her. A little gray dog strained at the end of the leash in Daisy's hand.

"G-good morning, Miss Rose," Daisy stammered with a shy smile.

"The hell it is," Rose snapped. With one hand in her purse fishing for her keys, she nearly ran to her car. She paused at the driver's side door and had just pulled her keys from her purse to unlock it when she realized she'd stepped on something. Expecting to find that she'd tread on a big wad of chewing gum, she looked down and gasped. What was beneath her left foot and smeared up over the edge of her beautiful new Jimmy Choo cork sandal was far more disgusting.

"You should clean up after your dog, do you hear me?" Rose yelled at Daisy's back. She saw the short little woman startle at her words, but she didn't bother to watch the rest of Daisy's reaction. Fighting a worsening headache and a strong urge to vomit, she carefully slipped her left foot out of the sandal and, holding it out-stretched in front of her, walked with one bare foot back into her house.

EMILY, WHO WAS SPYING ON ROSE THROUGH THE WINDOW, BURST out laughing when she saw her remove one of her sandals and carry it inside.

"All right, Puppy-G, let's get to work," she said to Gus, who was sitting at the window beside her. While Emily had already searched through every closet, drawer, and cupboard without find-ing any sort of key, there were still many other places where it could be hidden. With Gus trailing behind her, she went from room to room, feeling along the top of each window frame and doorjamb. She got a flashlight and peered behind and under every piece of furniture. She even felt around inside heating vents and along the pipes under the sinks.

Still without success after hours of searching, Emily's next step was to scour the garage in the same meticulous manner. That was a far dirtier and more unpleasant task but yielded the same results. When she finished in the garage, she went inside to the kitchen, wiped her grimy, sweaty face with a paper towel, and poured herself a glass of iced tea.

Emily took the copy of her mother's letter from its usual place on the dining room table and went out to the front porch to reread it for what seemed like the millionth time. Once seated in a folding chair, though, she found herself staring across to her mother's barren house. Her gaze fixed on the concrete stoop at the end of the walkway. She had sat there once, with Andy. They'd brought a blanket out of the house and wrapped themselves in it, intending to watch a late-night meteor shower. The shooting stars had gone unnoticed, though. All she could remember was Andy sitting next to her, kissing her passionately . . .

"Hi, Aunt Emily."

Her nephew's voice startled her, and she looked up to see Alex standing at the base of her porch steps.

"Hey!" She folded the letter and stuffed it into her pocket. "I was wondering when I'd see you again. You been all right?"

"Yeah," he said. He looked back at his house. "Mom's sleeping again, so I thought I'd come out for a while."

"I'm glad you did." Alex's dejected expression turned into a smile. "Your book list was a huge help," she continued. "It was so detailed and complete, and it convinced your mom and me that we don't have time to look for the clues. It'll be better to just focus on the key itself, and maybe now, with both of us looking for it, we'll find it faster."

"I can help look, too, can't I?"

"Of course!" she said, and Alex's face brightened further. "In fact, I think your mom would appreciate your help. It's a lot of work searching a house for something so small. It took me all day."

"You already searched your whole house?"

"Yep. I looked in the house and the garage, but I didn't find any key. I guess now I'll have to check the roof and the yard."

"It might not be in either of those places," Alex said. "It could be somewhere in *our* house."

"That's true," Emily said. "But, I've got to be thorough. If I check the last places over here without finding it, we'll know it's over at your house."

Alex nodded. "What was that paper you were holding a few minutes ago?"

"The letter your grandma left me and your mom," Emily said. "I was going to read it again in case there's something in it, maybe a hint of some kind that I didn't catch earlier. Your grandma was always extremely careful about everything she did and said."

"Mom let me read her copy of the letter, so I know it by heart," Alex said.

"Really? The whole thing?"

"Yes," Alex said. "I have an eidetic memory. After I read something, it just sticks in my brain."

"Are you serious?" Emily was surprised by her nephew's admission, and she was curious as to what he really could do. She pulled the letter out of her pocket and unfolded it. "Okay, let's see," she challenged him with a playful smile. "Tell me what it says."

Alex smiled in return, but then his expression became solemn. He recited her mother's letter word for word.

Rose had been telling the truth about Alex's brilliance.

"Wow, Alex," she said. "That's . . . you're . . . just amazing. I've never met anyone who can remember things like that. Can you do that with everything you read?"

"Pretty much," he said. "That's why I don't have to read anything more than once. And, if I want to reread something I really like, I don't have to pick up the book again. I can just do it in my head."

"So, it's sort of like you have a built-in library in there," Emily said, tapping her temple with one finger.

"Yeah, sort of," he said. "You know, I have an idea about where the key might be."

"Really?"

"Yes. Grandma's letter said that you and Mom would be '*partners in a sort of treasure hunt,*' right? Well, every time you hear about treasure, isn't it always buried somewhere?"

"Well . . . yes. Geez, that totally makes sense. And, you know, the letter doesn't say that the key is in one of our houses. It says that it's somewhere on the *properties.* So, it could very well be in one of our yards!"

Emily was jubilant. That *had* to be it. The answer was so obvious, and it would be just like her mother to use such precise wording in the letter to convey that kind of information. And growing up, how many times had she and Rose made their way outside during one of her crazy, middle-of-the-night fire drills to meet her *in the front yard*? She stared at the lawn before her, a vast expanse of possibility.

"But how would we know where to dig to find it?" Alex asked.

"Easy. We get a metal detector, the kind people use to find stuff on the beach," Emily said. "I work at the hardware store on Main Street, and my boss would probably order one for me at cost." Emily's thoughts were coming faster and faster. "Why don't we do this . . . you go home and search your house as quickly and thoroughly as you can. In the meantime, I'll check into getting a metal detector that we can both use."

"Okay," Alex said. "I'll tell Mom about it, too. Maybe she'll let me search our yard, once you get it. But, what if the key is on your roof? Or on the roof of our house?"

"I can always go up and look," Emily said. "If we don't find anything buried, I'll do it. But, somehow, I don't think it's on one of our roofs, because I can't see how your grandma would've gotten up there to hide it. She was always terrified of heights."

"Okay," Alex said. "I'm going to go start looking right now! It's like we're on a real treasure hunt!"

Emily chuckled. "I guess so." At least her poor nephew would get some enjoyment out of looking. "Let me know if you find something."

A WEEK AFTER SHE HAD SPOKEN WITH ALEX, EMILY RUSHED HOME from work and removed a large metal detector from her car. She had her arm in the rigid support cuff and was about ready to activate the detector when Ivy called to her from across the street.

"I'm a little afraid to ask what you're doing with that contraption."

"Come on over, and I'll show you," Emily replied. She waited as Ivy grabbed her cane and slowly made her way across the street. "This is a metal detector," she said once her aunt was standing beside her. "It can sense things the size of coins and keys that are buried up to eight inches deep, and bigger metal objects up to three feet deep."

"And you're using it to look for—"

"—Mom's safe-deposit-box key," Emily said. "Rose and I can't make any sense out of what's in our houses and what the clues are supposed to be. Frankly, I don't think I could stand to be in the same room with her at this point. We're just going to search for the key itself."

"Hmmm." Emily took advantage of her great-aunt's silence and turned on the metal detector. Slowly, she walked forward, methodically moving the disc at the end of the detector back and forth in front of her.

"You're sure this is the best way to go?" Ivy asked as Emily completed her first run and moved past in the opposite direction. "Not looking for the clues, I mean?"

"I'm not sure of anything, but it seemed as good an idea as any. Finding the key is the only thing that matters. We've already searched inside—" She stopped speaking as the metal detector emitted a loud beep.

"What's that? Did you find something?" Ivy asked as she hurried over to stare at the ground under the machine.

"Maybe," Emily said. Standing in one place, she moved the disc in a small area to confirm that there was actually something metal in the ground. "Hang on," she told her aunt. Then, she carefully removed her arm from the cuff on the handle, laid the detector on the ground, and sprinted into her house.

Emily returned quickly carrying a small garden trowel. There was nothing metal visible on the surface of the lawn, so she dropped to her knees and used the trowel to loosen and turn over several clumps of grass and soil. In the third trowel full of material, something metal glinted up at them. Emily plucked the object from the dirt.

It was a small gold key.

"Holy smokes!" Ivy said.

Emily's breath caught in her throat. Her heart was hammering, driven by a shot of adrenaline that left her limbs tingling. "I don't believe it," she said.

"Quick, let me see it," Ivy said. With a trembling hand, Emily gave her the key. Ivy held it up, looked closely at it, and groaned. "I'm sorry, kid, but this isn't it. Your mother's key is smaller than this, and it's silver. There's a number engraved on it, too. I think it was 338, to match the box number."

"Well, shoot. I knew it couldn't be that easy," Emily said. She was in the strange, quivery state of coming back to earth after her hopes had shot sky high. "But hey, at least we know the metal detector works, right?" She stood up, grabbed the machine, and repositioned her arm in the cuff.

"I feel for you," Ivy said as she wiped her brow and looked up at the thick gray clouds. "You're gonna be out here for a while, and it's getting muggier by the minute."

"I know," Emily said with a resigned sigh. "The whole yard is a lot to cover. I didn't expect to finish this evening, though."

"Well, if you find any other keys or interesting stuff, bring it over. These houses have been here forever, so there's no telling what's found its way into the ground."

"Yeah, thanks, Aunt Ivy." Emily smiled at her great-aunt and then refocused her attention on the lawn. Every so often, the alarm would sound, and she would stop and dig. She found a beer-bottle cap, several coins, and an old men's watch with a flexible metal band. Several times, Emily told herself that the pass she was completing would be her last for the evening, but then the alarm would sound again, and she would be on her knees, scooping up dirt with the trowel. It was amazingly addictive.

Emily was in the middle of the lawn, digging in response to yet another blast from the metal detector, when she found a second key. This one was smaller than the first and silver in color, and her heart leaped as she frantically pulled it from the soil. She turned it over and held it up, searching for any sign of an engraved number. There was none. Dejected, Emily slipped the key into her pocket with the other things she'd found. She was grateful that Ivy had already described the key she was looking for, since it saved her hopes from rising and crashing as hard as they had with the first key.

She crossed the walkway and continued in a straight line. Not thirty seconds after she'd resumed her path, the detector sounded again. She bent over and looked at the grass. This time, she didn't even need to dig, as she could see the shiny silver top of something protruding slightly from the ground. Emily grabbed it and yanked.

It was another key.

Was it a joke? Emily wondered how she could have found three keys so quickly in such a small portion of the yard.

Emily was beginning to realize that something just wasn't right. She resumed scanning, but now she was moving much faster, covering ground as rapidly as she could. The alarm sounded again, and she moved like clockwork. Set down the detector. Kneel down. Dig.

Within seconds, she was holding a fourth key in her hand. Again, it was silver, but it wasn't her mother's.

In the next fifteen minutes, she found three more keys. One was gold, one was silver, and the third looked like a child's house key. The shank of the third key was silver, but the bow, the part that would be grasped to insert the key in a lock, had "Looney Tunes" printed on one side. On the other side was a color image of Tweety Bird.

Emily's chin snapped up.

She whirled around to face Rose's house and then looked down at the small jumble of keys in her hand. Propped up against her fingers, Tweety's big blue eyes stared back.

Her gaze drifted to Rose's black BMW as she reached into her pocket and withdrew the other keys she had found. The finish on each of them was shiny and new-looking, not weathered and dull as would be expected for a key that had been buried for any significant length of time. In fact, they looked like they had been cut from the same modern kinds of blanks she routinely used to copy keys down at the hardware store. One by one, she held up the keys, comparing the teeth cut into the shanks against each other.

As far as Emily could tell, they were identical. All seven of the keys were made to open the same lock.

It took her only seconds to reach Rose's front door. The house was dark and quiet. She raised a hand to knock on the door and then stopped. On a whim, she took one of the keys and inserted it into the keyhole. When she turned it, the dead bolt slid back with a quiet *click*. She really didn't need proof of what her sister had done, but here it was—absolute and incontrovertible.

Emily took a deep breath and walked into Rose's house. The living room was just off the foyer, and she didn't have to go far to find Rose sprawled out on the sofa. Not wanting to involve or alarm Alex, Emily tiptoed onto the carpet and leaned over her sleeping sister. The all-too-familiar smell of rum wafted up into her face.

"Rose," Emily said. She waited a moment as her sister stirred and mumbled something. "ROSE!"

Rose's eyes, then her mouth, flew open.

"Get your ass outside, right now," Emily said, then turned on her heel and went back out the front door and down the sidewalk a ways, away from the house. Rose emerged a few seconds later, unsteady and disheveled and fighting mad.

"How *dare* you? How dare you break into *my house*?" she screeched as she walked down the stairs from her front stoop.

"I didn't break in, you idiot," Emily said. She pulled a fistful of keys from each of her pockets and let them rain down on the sidewalk between them. "I *let* myself in, with one of the many keys you so kindly planted in my yard. What in the hell were you thinking? If Mom's key is buried over there, it'll take a lot longer to find now. Or maybe, you're having such a good time boozing it up that you really don't care about that anymore?"

"What I do in my own house is none of your business," Rose said. "And I care *plenty* about finding Mom's key. Alex and I have already searched inside our house for it. It's not there, so I guess now we'll start looking, I don't know, outside here." She waved her hand haphazardly in the air. "Alex is all excited about the metal detector. You're probably pretty good at using it by now." Rose swayed and teetered off balance as she laughed.

"Look at you," Emily said. "You're so drunk you can hardly stand up. And where's Alex? Up in his room? Or do you even know? I swear, Rose, I'm tempted to call Sheldon and tell him what a wreck you are. Or maybe I should just call the police and let them bring in child protective services. It's obvious you're barely capable of taking care of yourself, much less Alex. You need to get it together. This is your last warning." She turned on her heel and walked up onto her lawn, but her sister stormed after her.

"My last warning? Oooh, I'm afraid," Rose said. "My son is fine, anyone can see that. I just had a drink to relax after Alex and I turned the house upside down looking for Mom's key. Sheldon would totally understand that, too. Anybody would, except maybe someone who's so unhappy with her own life that she has to stir up trouble in other people's."

Emily tried to ignore Rose, to keep her back to her sister and dismiss her comments as the ravings of a drunkard. She almost succeeded.

"In fact," Rose continued, her words slurring slightly, "you have no business telling me or anyone else to 'get it together.' It's been, what, fourteen years since you left Mill River? What have you got to show for it? No house, no husband, and no children. No material possessions to speak of, other than a few boxes of junk that fit in your crappy car. You still don't get that bad things, even terrible things, happen to people all the time. Normal people get over them. But you, you just go from place to place, with your shit car and your filthy dog, wallowing in self-pity. *You're* the one who needs to get it together."

Emily whirled around and slapped Rose hard across the face. "I would have all of the things that I don't if it weren't for you!" she screamed. Before Rose could recover, Emily lunged at her, throwing all her weight forward and knocking her sister to the ground. Despite being intoxicated, Rose put up a pretty good defense, but Emily was wild, fuming with years of pent-up anger, and completely determined to give her a good thrashing.

She didn't know how long they had been rolling around with their fists flailing, but a loud, authoritative voice finally caught their attention.

"What in the hell is going on?" Ivy thundered. "You girls had better quit this nonsense before I take this cane and wallop you both. For shame! Fighting like two schoolyard brats, and in public! You're lucky nobody called the police. What would your poor mother say if she were here?"

Emily was sitting astride Rose, and she looked up to see Ivy glowering down at them. With one last shove at her sister, she jumped up. Rose got to her feet, too, but she didn't say anything before she turned and ran for her house.

"What was all that about?" Ivy demanded.

"She doesn't know when to keep her mouth shut," Emily said. "And I'll tell you something else, Aunt Ivy. I'm done with her. I've tried, I've really tried. I know what Mom wanted, but Rose is impossible. I don't care what happens to Mom's estate. If I can't find the key by myself, then screw it. Rose can have it all.

"And I swear, I'm going to make damn sure that people in town can see for themselves what kind of person she is."

CHAPTER 24

1997

As she worked on disconnecting the pipes beneath the bathroom sink, Emily could hear her mother crying in the living room. If it had been a new situation, or even an infrequent one, she would have gotten up and gone to console her as best she could. But Rose storming out of the house and leaving their mother sobbing was anything but new.

After a few minutes, Emily heard the front door opening and the low, soothing tones of her aunt Ivy's voice. It took a while until her mother stopped crying enough to speak coherently and she began to make out snippets of their conversation.

". . . don't know what I'm going to do with her," Josie said. "She's running with older kids . . . don't like that boy she's been seeing . . ."

". . . out of control, just like your mother was at her age," Ivy said. Emily could just imagine how her great-aunt was shaking her head as she spoke.

". . . threatening to leave after high school. I blame myself for not being there. I should have seen what was happening . . ."

". . . can't blame yourself, now. You've tried everything . . ."

Today's argument was pretty bad, Emily thought as the U-bend under the sink came loose. She stuffed the end of a rag into the open pipe jutting out of the wall and tried to pour the contents of the trap into the bucket she'd placed beneath it. Unclogging sink drains was a skill she'd learned out of necessity. How many times had Rose borrowed some piece of jewelry from their mother without her permission and managed to drop it down the drain? Or thrown up in the sink when she hadn't quite been able to get to the toilet in time after a night of partying? Whatever the reason, Emily had been subject to her sister's pleas to help fix the problem more times than she could count. The first time she'd disconnected the plumbing had been a disaster—she hadn't thought to place a bucket under the pipes to catch the backed-up mess before disconnecting the plumbing—but now, the job was almost routine.

When nothing but water came out of the U-bend, Emily steeled herself and stuck her finger into the pipe. She was able to scoop out a clump of slimy, foul-smelling hair in which her mother's gold earring was entangled. Emily breathed a sigh of relief. Although it was a disgusting job, which would have been easier had the outdated trap had some sort of a clean-out plug, at least she'd managed to retrieve the earring successfully. She placed it in the medicine cabinet for safekeeping and went to rinse out the U-bend in the kitchen sink before she reassembled the plumbing.

Emily was worried about her sister, who was now a senior. Rose's grades were so bad that she was in danger of failing the year, and she took little interest in anything but her looks and hanging out with her friends. She had a boyfriend, too, a bad-news guy named Linx who looked to be in his twenties. Emily had met him one time in the middle of the night when he'd climbed up the portable fire-escape ladder to tell Rose to hurry up and come down.

It had taken their mother a long time to figure out that the ladder was enabling Rose to come and go as she pleased in the wee hours of the morning. Her sister had finally been busted after rumors started spreading in town that Rose had been among a group of teens spotted loitering in a parking lot in Rutland. On a night soon afterward, their mother had found Rose's bed stuffed with pillows and the ladder hanging out the window. Emily recalled how Rose had climbed back through the window, tipsy and giggling, only to find their mother sitting on her bed in the dark, waiting for her.

Of course, their mother realized that Emily must have known what Rose was up to, and Emily had had some explaining to do. It wasn't an easy position, being caught in the middle, having to choose between lying to her mother or ratting out her sister when she loved them both. In the end, she admitted to knowing about Rose leaving the house a few times, but she managed to feign ignorance about the length of time that Rose had been putting the escape ladder to use.

Emily sighed and returned to the bathroom. Out in the living room, her mother's cries had quieted, but she and Ivy were still talking.

". . . don't know what I can do at this point other than let her go," her mother was saying. "She's technically an adult now."

"Well, maybe a taste of the real world will knock some sense into her," Ivy said. "Tough love, I tell you, that's what she needs now . . ."

Sometimes, Emily wondered how she'd managed to emerge unscathed and relatively normal from the last few years of tension between her mother and Rose. The constant conflict weighed heavily on her, and she'd tried her best to talk some sense into her sister, to convince her that sneaking out, drinking, and not caring about school would only hurt her in the long run.

"Em, I get enough lectures from Mom," Rose had told her just after she'd turned eighteen. "I don't need them from you, too. God, I can't wait until I can figure out a way to get the hell out of here for good."

"You know it's just because I care about you," Emily had said. "I still don't understand why you hate it here so much."

Rose had rolled her eyes. "Don't you ever feel like *nothing* happens here? You see the same old people day after day, nothing new or exciting, and it never changes. I feel . . . *stifled.* Like every day I spend here is a day of my life that's wasted."

"I don't think Mill River's so bad," she'd said. "I like the fact that it's quiet and safe. Plus, Mom's here, and Aunt Ivy, and me."

"Yeah, but Aunt Ivy's got her store to keep her busy, and Mom's never around, same as always, not that I really care about that anymore. You and I will always be close, but we're getting older now. We won't always be in the same place, doing the same thing."

"I know," Emily had said. "I guess you could always leave after high school, if you want. I'm just worried that, at the rate you're going, you're going to get into a lot of trouble. If you'd just focus on your grades and finish the semester, you could probably still get into a college somewhere and *bam,* you could move out and be free."

Rose had laughed. "You can be the good girl and go to college if you want to. I'm done being stuck anywhere—in a classroom, in this house, anywhere. I'm an adult now. I'm leaving, and Mom won't be able to stop me."

"Where will you go?" Emily had asked.

"I don't know. Boston, maybe. Or New York. Linx has family in Brooklyn. We could get jobs and then get a little place together eventually. Maybe I could even do some auditions. I've always wanted to be an actress. You never know unless you try, right?"

It might have been because she was younger than Rose and not as confident, but Emily couldn't imagine leaving her family and her hometown so easily. She was happy in Mill River. Someday, after she finished school, she could even see herself returning to live in the town, so long as she could find a job nearby. At this point, of course, she couldn't be sure where she would end up, but at least she knew that her path would be steady, well thought out, and probably the complete opposite of Rose's.

Several hours after their most recent shouting match, Josie sat on the sofa in the living room, waiting for Rose to come home. She hoped her older daughter would return during the night at some point, but after the huge argument they'd had earlier, she didn't know whether Rose would come home at all. The last thing she wanted was for Rose to disappear, to cease all contact with her family like her own mother had done. Her eyes were red and swollen from crying, and after her talk with Ivy, she'd realized that if she wanted to preserve any sort of relationship at all with Rose, she would have to let her go. No, she would have to *encourage* her to go, and hope that her daughter didn't ruin her life with more bad choices.

It was nearly four in the morning when Josie was startled awake by the sound of a key being inserted in the front door lock. She sat up and rubbed at one of her eyes as Rose let herself in. They made brief eye contact before Rose raised her chin and walked briskly toward the stairs.

"Rosie, please, just give me a minute," Josie said. She stood up and took a step toward her daughter. "I'm through yelling and lecturing. Please just listen to what I need to tell you. You don't have to say anything."

Rose stopped at the foot of the stairs and, after a second or two, she turned and looked warily at her.

"If you want to move out, to go live someplace else and do whatever it is you feel you can't do here, in Mill River, I won't stop you. I need you to know that I'm sorry for not being there for you when I needed to be. Maybe, if I hadn't worked so much, or if I'd been more in tune with what was going on in your life, we wouldn't be standing here right now." Josie's voice cracked as she continued. "I need you to know that I love you with everything in me. Everything I've ever done has been for you and Emily. You girls are my life. I'm just asking you, please, please don't cut me out of yours. You're an adult now, and you want your freedom . . . you're entitled to it . . . so, that's fine. I won't stand in your way anymore. Just please promise me that if you leave my house, I'll not lose you completely. I couldn't survive it if I did."

Rose worked her jaw from side to side with her eyes gleaming. "All right," she said quietly, triumphantly, before bolting up the stairs.

For the rest of the week, the house was eerily silent. Rose came and went at will while Emily kept mostly to herself. Josie buried herself in her work. She ran sales meetings with her brokers and showed several houses each day, all while struggling to maintain a professional façade. Her smiling, cheerful demeanor belied the emotional turmoil inside her.

When she returned home after work on Sunday afternoon, Rose was on her way downstairs carrying a suitcase and a large duffel bag. Emily, with a pale, tear-streaked face and panicked eyes, was close behind her.

"What's going on?" Josie asked.

"I'm leaving," Rose said as she reached the bottom of the stairs. "I'm going with Linx to New York. His uncle owns a restaurant and can give us both jobs, and we'll stay with him until we can get our own apartment."

Josie fought hard to keep her voice under control. "Rose, I . . . I don't know what to say." She was still so shocked at the sight of Rose on her way out that she could barely speak. *What if I'd come home fifteen minutes later? Would she really have left without saying goodbye?*

Rose set down her luggage. For the first time in months, the expression on her face as she spoke was serene and devoid of hostility.

"I thought a lot about what you said, Mom. I don't want to lose you. I never did. I only want space to live my life." Josie remained speechless as Rose approached her and hugged her tightly. She wrapped her arms around her daughter, her first child, whose gold-encased picture she still wore next to her heart.

Rose pulled away after a moment, and Josie was shocked to see that her older daughter was also crying. "I'll write to you, both of you, and I'll try to call every week so that you know I'm okay," she said, looking from Josie to Emily. "And I *will* be okay, Mom. I'll be *fine.*"

Rose went to Emily and embraced her as well. "Remember what I told you," she said quietly to her younger sister. A car horn sounded outside. Rose picked up the suitcase and duffel bag and hurried to the door. "I'll be fine," she said again, and then she was gone.

CHAPTER 25

Still not quite believing what he had just seen, Alex backed away from the window in his room. He didn't know what had started the fight between his mother and his aunt, but by the time he'd heard their raised voices and gotten up from his desk to look outside, they were wrestling on the lawn.

He went downstairs to the kitchen. "Mom?" he called. His mother was standing in front of the freezer, popping ice cubes out of a tray and crying. "Mom? Are you okay? I saw you and Aunt Emily—"

"Baby, can you hand me the dish towel over there?" his mother asked. He grabbed the towel on the counter and gave it to her, then watched silently as she wrapped the ice in it and held it to her eye.

"Mom, why were you guys fighting?"

"I don't want to get into it, Alex. But look, will you do me a favor? Can you wait a day or two and then talk to Aunt Emily about borrowing her metal detector, once she's done with it? We've got to search our yard for your grandma's key, but I just can't handle dealing with your aunt anymore."

"Okay," Alex said. He was thrilled that his mother wanted to get the metal detector. In fact, he secretly imagined himself operating the machine, finding the elusive safe-deposit-box key in an obscure corner of their yard, and presenting it to his mother. *She would be so proud of me, and she'd be smiling then, instead of crying like she is now,* he thought. With her being so upset, though, he wasn't sure what else to say to his mother, so he simply took her hand and squeezed it.

"Thank you, baby," she said. Unexpectedly, she set down the towel and pulled him into a stifling embrace. "I'm so thankful you're here," she whispered into his hair. "I don't know how I'd get through this without you."

At lunchtime on the Saturday after her altercation with Rose, Emily sat on her front porch, feeding bits of her sandwich to Gus and looking at a morning's worth of metal-hunting loot lined up on the porch rail. There were objects of all kinds—more coins, someone's 1982 high school class ring, and a fork that was bent nearly in half. *Probably tore up someone's lawn mower,* she thought. She'd also found another seven keys, including two more of the "Tweety" variety. Obviously, Rose had thought using the bird-themed keys to be an especially clever touch.

Emily glanced over at her sister's lawn and smiled. In another day or two, Rose would find herself the recipient of an equally clever gift.

She was ready to start sweeping the remaining section of the yard when Alex emerged from his house. Thinking quickly, she pocketed the fake keys she'd found as he walked across the grass toward her.

"Hi," he said, but he didn't look her in the eye right away. "I saw you and Mom, out in the yard."

"Oh, Alex," she said, and she was filled with regret at her nephew's having witnessed the latest encounter with Rose. "I'm so sorry. That wasn't right of us. In fact, it's inexcusable that we came to blows, and I'm so embarrassed about it. Your mom and I are just . . . we're just very different people, with very strong opinions about things. And, she'd been drinking again, before we started arguing."

Alex shifted his weight from foot to foot. "You're not really going to call the police, are you? Because I'm doing okay, you know. I'm fine. Dad's been calling every night to check on me, and Mom's been like this a long time. I'm used to it."

Emily sighed. Her heart was heavy with sympathy for her nephew. "I don't want to call anybody, Alex. I just want your mom to get her act together and do what your grandma wanted. I think everything will get better once you and she can go home to New York."

"Yeah, I do, too. And so does Dad." Alex was quiet for a moment. "Did you find the key yet?"

Lots of them, Emily thought.

"Nope, nothing but junk so far. Come see." She motioned him onto the porch, where he examined the objects sitting on the porch rail. "The metal detector's working really great, though, and I've still got a little to finish up, so we still might get lucky. Besides, we can always check your yard if we don't find the key over here."

"Mom was hoping you'd let me use the metal detector after you're done with it." Gus got up from his nap on the doormat to sniff at Alex, and her nephew reached out to rub the dog's ears.

"Sure. The machine's not too heavy, and it's easy to use. If we end up having to search your lawn, I'll teach you what to do and let you have at it."

"Cool," Alex said. His grin slowly faded. "I think us finding the key is the only way I'll be able to make Mom happy again."

ON SUNDAY MORNING, ROSE AWOKE, BLINKED, AND TURNED toward the window. The first thing she noticed was that the soreness in her eye was finally diminishing. And, to her surprise and delight, the sky was a crisp, deep blue, a welcome change from the clouds and uncomfortable humidity that had been the summer norm so far.

"Alex, sweetie, are you up? I think a cold front came through last night," she said as she went into his room. Alex was still in bed, and he stretched as she came in and sat down. Two paperback books lay facedown and open at the end of his bed.

"It feels a lot better in here," he said. "Almost like there's air-conditioning." Alex sat up and reached for his glasses on the nightstand. "I think I stayed up too late reading."

"That's nothing new," Rose said. Thinking how wonderful it was to be comfortable instead of sticky and perspiring, she reached over and rumpled his hair. "I think we should put fans near the windows to air out the place."

"Can I sleep a little more?" Alex asked as he lay down again. "I'm still tired."

"Sure," Rose said. "There's nothing we need to do today. I'll make some breakfast and leave it on the table for you." She leaned over and kissed Alex on the forehead before she left his room.

Downstairs, Rose opened all the windows as far as they would go. She also unlocked and propped open the heavy front door, reveling in the fresh breeze that blew through the screen door against her face. When she looked down at her front lawn, though, her jubilant mood vanished.

On each side of the stairs and sidewalk leading down from her front door, large swaths of her lawn were yellow and wilted. She came down from the stoop to get a better look. As she stood facing her house, she realized with a sick feeling that the large, dead areas of grass were in fact letters that had somehow been burned into the lawn:

LUSH

Rose gasped and immediately looked over at Emily's house.

She started toward it, then backtracked. With a final glare at her lawn, she ran up the stairs into her house and grabbed her cell phone.

Her hand was shaking so much that it was difficult for her to hold her cell phone as she was connected to the Mill River Police Department.

"Mill River Police, Officer Hansen speaking."

"Hello, my name is Rose DiSanti Frye. My yard has been vandalized, and I'd like for someone to come out and file a report on it."

"I'm sorry to hear that, Ms. Frye. You're over on Maple Street, right? Across from The Bookstop?"

"Yes, right across from it, number 130."

"All right. I'll be down in a few minutes to take a look."

Rose hung up the phone. She was standing at the front door, staring straight ahead and trying not to look at the grass, when Alex came up behind her.

"Mom? Were you going to fix breakfast? I can always have cereal if you decided not to."

"That would be good, baby."

"Mom?" Alex came closer. "Mom, are you okay? Is something wrong?"

"I'm fine, Alex. Someone messed up our front lawn, and I'm waiting for the police to come."

"You called the *police*? Really?" He stood on his tiptoes as he peered out the front storm door, trying to get a look at the lawn. "What did they do?"

"There's a word etched into the grass. Whoever did it must've poured something on it to make it die off in the shapes of the letters."

"Is it a dirty word?"

Rose hesitated a moment before answering. "No."

"Well, can I see, then?"

She held open the door. "Go look and then come right back." Alex ran out the door and stood staring at the lawn for a few minutes before returning.

"Who do you think did it? Do you think it was Aunt Emily?"

Of course it was, Rose thought.

"We don't really have any way of knowing."

"Whoever did it, it wasn't very nice, but at least they picked a word that describes our lawn. I mean, it is *lush.* Maybe whoever did it was jealous of how nice it looks? You think so, Mom?"

Despite everything he'd read and could instantly recall, her brilliant, sweet, naïve son hadn't yet come to understand the double meaning of the word or the insult it delivered so openly for all to see. She wasn't about to explain that to him, either. It was a relief when a Jeep with the Mill River Police Department logo pulled up alongside the curb.

"Stay inside, Alex." She put on her sunglasses and stepped outside as an officer got out of the vehicle and waited on the sidewalk for her.

"Hi, Ms. Frye?" he said. "Hi, I'm Officer Hansen. We spoke on the phone, and I think we actually met earlier this summer."

"Yes. Well, you can see what's been done," she said. She lowered her voice, so that Alex wouldn't hear what she said next. "And I'm sure it was my sister, Emily, who did this, but there's no way I can prove it."

"Your sister?"

"You probably know she lives next door there." Rose jerked her chin in the direction of Emily's house.

"Could I ask what makes you think it was your sister?"

Rose rolled her eyes. "We've not been getting along. This is just the latest."

"Let me take down your contact information first," the officer said as he held up a clipboard. Rose gave him her cell phone number and her permanent address in New York.

"And do you own this property?"

"No, my mother owned it, and now it's part of her estate. Her attorney is managing the property. I'm just . . . staying here for a few months to tie up some loose ends."

The officer nodded. "You should probably inform your mother's attorney about this," he said. "Did you see your sister do anything to your lawn?"

"No."

"Did you see anyone else around your home? Anyone you didn't recognize?"

"No."

"And, is today the first time you noticed this? Was there any other damage done to your property today or at any time recently?"

She thought back to her bird-shit-covered car and felt a fresh wave of anger. "No, no other damage that I know of. I first noticed it right before I called you."

"All right." The officer looked down at her lawn and half smiled. "Not to diminish the seriousness of this, but you got lucky in a way. It could've been an obscenity instead of a . . . compliment of sorts."

Behind her dark sunglasses, Rose rolled her eyes. *First her son, now the cop, and there was no way she could explain that the word in her lawn was no damned compliment.*

"You know, Ms. Frye," he continued, "your sister filed a vandalism report with us not long ago. One of the tires on her car was slashed. Would you happen to know anything about that?"

Even though she was an expert liar, she could see when she looked the officer square in the eyes that he would not be taken for a fool. The fact that they hid her black eye nicely wasn't the only reason Rose was glad she was wearing the sunglasses.

"No. I saw her changing a flat tire a while ago, but I have no idea how she got it."

He stared at her without speaking for a few seconds and then nodded. "Okay, Ms. Frye. I'll go see your sister and see if she has anything to say about this, but there's really not much for us to go on here. At least now you'll have this incident on file, in case you have any further trouble."

"Fine," Rose said. "You wouldn't know what causes grass to do this, would you?"

The officer looked down at the yellow, wilted letters and shrugged. "I'm no lawn care expert, but I'd guess that somebody sprayed it with Roundup. It's a fast-acting herbicide, and you can buy it pretty much anywhere. If you want to hide the letters, you could probably spray the whole area so everything turns yellow like that within a day or two. Then, you can just turn the soil over and replant." He ripped one of the pages from his clipboard and handed it to her. "Here's a copy of the report. Give us a call right away if anything else happens."

"Thank you," Rose said as she accepted the piece of paper. She watched the officer walk toward Emily's house, and then she went back through her own front door to get her purse. It took a lot of willpower to ignore her growing need for a double-strength rum and Coke, but that would have to wait until the afternoon. Right now, she had to get to the Home Depot, and fast.

Alex was still standing in the entryway. "Get your shoes on," she said as she passed by him. "We're going out."

ONCE FATHER O'BRIEN HAD SAID GOODBYE TO THE LAST OF HIS parishioners after Sunday Mass, he tidied up the sanctuary and changed into more casual attire. While he ate lunch in the parish house, he looked over some paperwork relating to the town's new

Hayes Memorial Park and Recreation Area. The plans for the land that had been Samuel Hayes's horse farm and Mary's childhood home were coming along beautifully. It was a stunning piece of property, tucked away down a country lane just outside of town. The perimeter had been fenced, and the playground equipment and basketball court would be installed soon. There would be other sports facilities, too—a baseball diamond and two tennis courts. A purchase order had also been submitted for two picnic tables.

Most special of all, he had arranged for a monument to be crafted for Mary's grave site, a marble embodiment of his memory of her as a young woman. His memory of the funeral service he had conducted for her was far more bittersweet. Mary had been laid to rest on top of the hill where her father's old farmhouse had once stood. It was a fitting location, beneath a cluster of sugar maples and with an expansive view of the whole property. He took comfort in the fact that Mary herself had helped shape the plans for the new park, which would soon be open for everyone to see and enjoy.

Slowly, on account of his arthritis, Father O'Brien rose from the table, put his few dishes in the sink. There were two wrapped packages on the kitchen counter, courtesy of Ivy. He made sure to take one of them with him as he left the parish house.

Outside, the warmth of the sun soaked into his shoulders and soothed his knees, and he knew his joints would limber up as he walked. There was only one other thing on his schedule for the afternoon—a counseling session of sorts—but the person he intended to counsel was not aware of his impending visit.

As he crossed Main Street, he thought of the phone call he'd received from Ivy Collard two nights ago. "I'm thinking that it's time I take you up on your offer to talk with the girls," she'd told him. "Emily says that they're not working together or talking much, and it's almost August. I'm afraid they're going to run out of time. And I have something for you to give each of them, from Josie. She prepared a little message to each of the girls, just in case they needed it."

He rounded the corner onto Maple Avenue just in time to see Kyle Hansen exit Emily's house. He was in uniform, and the police department's Jeep was parked alongside the curb. Kyle smiled as he approached.

"Father, how are you?" he asked. "You picked a good day for a walk."

"Hi, Kyle. It is beautiful today," he agreed. "I'm actually here in my official capacity, and I suppose you are as well. I hope everything is okay."

"Ah." Kyle's smile disappeared and he shook his head. "I don't quite know what to think, Father. These two . . ."

"The two DiSanti girls, you mean?"

"Yep. They're like oil and water, and living next to each other isn't helping. Rose thinks Emily's the one who's vandalized her lawn," he said as he motioned toward Rose's house.

Father O'Brien turned and saw the wilted yellow letters in the grass. "Oh, dear," he said.

"I know. Emily denies any involvement. Of course, there's no way to prove anything."

Father O'Brien sighed and shook his head.

"I think each of them has serious issues," Kyle continued. "Maybe you can talk some sense into them."

"Maybe," Father O'Brien said as he patted Kyle on the shoulder. "I'll do my best."

Emily's surprise at seeing him on her porch was readily apparent. "Father O'Brien! Come in," she said when she opened the door. "Gus, back up, boy, and let the father through." As she held the door open, she glanced past him and down the street, as if she had expected someone else had rung her doorbell. "What brings you by?"

"Good afternoon, Emily. It occurred to me that I was long overdue in welcoming you back to town, and I wondered if you might have time to chat for a few minutes?"

"Sure," she said with a smile. "Come on in. I was just about to indulge in a little ice cream. Could I interest you in some?"

"Well, that depends," he said as he followed her. "What flavors have you got?"

"Butter pecan and chocolate mint," she said.

"Oh, my," he said. "I don't think there's any way I could refuse a little butter pecan."

"You got it," she said. They passed a small room off the center hallway that looked like a den, and Father O'Brien couldn't help but stop and stare. The room had been spectacularly transformed into a glasswork studio. There was a table in the center of the room covered in sheets of glass and spools of a copper-colored metal foil. Smaller pieces of glass that had been cut into shapes lay on the table as well, along with a torch and various hand tools.

What had first caught his attention, though, were the large windows in the room. The center window was clear and open, letting in fresh air. But, the windows on the side were almost completely hidden by various framed, finished stained glass pieces that had been propped against the window panes and hung from the ceiling. The sun shining through the windows passed through all of them, sending colored beams of light in every direction.

"My goodness," he said. "That is beautiful."

"Oh," Emily said as she backtracked to him. "It's my little hobby."

"I didn't know you did stained glass work."

She shrugged. "Just something I picked up over the years. I got into it when I started renovating houses for a living. I really enjoy it. In fact, I'm starting a new project for the McAllister mansion. I'm helping Ruth and Fitz convert it to a bed-and-breakfast."

"Ruth mentioned that to me when I last saw her," Father O'Brien said. He was still mesmerized by the beauty of the pieces in the windows.

"Father, would you like to see what I'm planning?" Emily pointed to a side table, where a pattern was positioned on a light box and beneath a large sheet of glass. When she turned on the lights, he could see that the illuminated pattern formed a scene of horses grazing in a field, surrounded by hills and trees.

"Ruth told me that Mary McAllister used to keep horses on the property, in the stable down behind the house, and that her father raised Morgans. I thought that would be a nice image to have in the house—something involving horses and the Vermont scenery, I mean."

"It's a splendid idea," he agreed. "I used to go riding with Mary. She had a black mare named Ebony who was very gentle . . . and very patient with inexperienced riders like me." He smiled, and Emily saw his eyes glaze over just for a moment as he reminisced. "She had a copper chestnut mare named Penny, too, and a red bay gelding named Monarch. They were all beautiful animals. I'll look forward to seeing this when it's finished."

In the kitchen, Emily prepared a generous serving of ice cream and handed it to him. "Here you go. Spoons are right in that drawer next to the stove."

"Thank you." He set the wrapped package on the table so that he could accept the ice cream and, with some trepidation, he pulled open the drawer she mentioned. For a few seconds, he stared down into the silverware tray, admiring the sturdy tablespoons and the smaller, delicate teaspoons that were stacked there. A few mismatched serving spoons of various sizes were tucked in outside the silverware tray, too, and even these were attractive.

So lovely, and such an opportunity, he thought, but since Mary's death, he had kept his promise and found the strength to battle his addiction. As he tentatively picked up one of the tablespoons, he could see Mary's face in his mind, nodding her approval and smiling with encouragement.

"Have a seat, Father," Emily said as she sat down at the kitchen table. "I hope you don't mind my saying so, but I'm getting the feeling you're here to talk about more than my arrival in Mill River."

"Well, there are a couple reasons, actually," he said. He pulled out a chair and joined her. Quickly, he took a bite of the ice cream and smiled at her. "This hits the spot, by the way. Thank you."

Emily smiled and nodded in return, waiting for him to continue.

"I suppose the first thing I wanted to ask you was whether you and your sister have discussed any sort of burial for your mother."

"Oh, no," Emily said. "No, we haven't talked about that at all. In fact, we really haven't talked all that much about anything. I feel bad about it. I know Ivy still has Mom's ashes, which puts her in an awkward spot, but we're no closer to deciding anything about her burial than we were at her wake."

Father O'Brien nodded. "It's important that her remains be placed in consecrated ground. Just know that I'm happy to help whenever you and your sister are ready. I'm sure Ivy doesn't mind keeping the ashes until then, seeing as how she loved your mom so much. Ivy did mention that she was concerned about Rose and Alex because she suspects Rose is drinking again."

"Oh, I'm sure of that," Emily said with a bitter edge to her voice. "I don't think she ever stopped."

"Addiction is a terrible thing," Father O'Brien said. He swallowed another mouthful of ice cream as he ran his thumb up the smooth, polished handle of the spoon in his hand. "I'm convinced that the only way anyone can overcome it is if the decision to stop drinking, or smoking, or whatever, comes from within. It's troubling, though, to think that Rose has her young son with her if she's still struggling with alcohol."

"I know," Emily said. "But, I've been sort of keeping tabs on Alex, and he and I have gotten to know each other a little. Rose has been letting him do a lot of what Mom asked of us, and he's actually done a good job so far. He's an amazing little boy, smart and kind and loving, despite his mother. I get the feeling that he takes care of himself most of the time, and I think he takes care of Rose quite a bit, too. I can totally sympathize with that."

"How do you mean?" Father O'Brien asked.

Emily snorted. "The whole time we were growing up, I was the one covering for Rose, lying to Mom about where she was, taking care of her when she came home drunk after sneaking out or was sick with a hangover in the morning. I did the cooking and the dishes when Mom always had to work long hours. Rose did whatever she wanted, and I don't see how that's changed. Alex seems starved for his mother's attention and approval, but based on what he tells me, she's passed out on the sofa a good part of the time."

"Do you think a call to the authorities would be in order?"

"I actually threatened her with it already," Emily said, "but I don't see how it would change anything. Rose is good at hiding her drinking and putting her best foot forward when she has to. Alex doesn't show any outward signs of abuse or neglect. He's well fed, has nice clothes and a nice place to live, and is so smart and loves her so much that he wouldn't say anything to implicate her. I think a social worker would be hard-pressed to find anything wrong."

Father O'Brien was quiet for a moment before he spoke. "I know Ivy's worried about him, too. If what you say is true, even if Alex seems fine, the whole situation just strikes me as one where a child slips through the cracks and where something awful could happen when we least expect it. But you're probably right that an official visit from the county would probably be pointless right now. I do intend to talk with Rose myself, though, and soon."

"Good luck with that," Emily said. "If you've got a suit of armor, you might put it on, just in case."

"My armor is a spiritual one, and it's always with me," he replied with a smile. "I'm still alive and kicking, so I think it's protected me very well so far."

"Father, could I ask . . . well, it's a little awkward, but I wonder how it is that you've stayed here, in Mill River, for so long? I thought priests were moved around quite a bit?"

"Yes, that's true," he replied. "Most priests are moved every five years or so, and most Catholic clergy are required to retire at age seventy. I was granted an exception to those rules long ago by a bishop who obtained a papal dispensation on my behalf. To make a long story short, my presence was needed here to help care for someone who could not survive on her own, and I agreed to stay to keep a promise I made to provide that care."

"You're talking about the Widow McAllister, aren't you? After the last town meeting, Mom called me up and told me all about it. She was so touched by what Mary did for everyone here for so many years."

"Yes. Her husband's grandfather, Conor McAllister, was a man of considerable influence. When Mary's husband died suddenly and the rest of the family turned against her, he was the only one who remained committed to her well-being. He was also on very good terms with the Catholic leadership in Burlington, and Bishop Ross was able to secure the dispensation for me at Conor's request. I've been lucky and thankful that the church hierarchy since then has continued to honor it."

"I hope that Mrs. McAllister's death won't jeopardize your staying here now," Emily said.

"I don't think it will," Father O'Brien said. "Mill River is a small parish, and priests are harder and harder to come by. Even though I'm far past the normal retirement age, I expect the current bishop of Burlington will let me serve this community until I no longer can."

"It sounds like you're safe, then," Emily said with a smile. "I'm glad. I think my mom would've been glad, too."

He smiled at her and worked on his ice cream for a moment, which was melting faster than he was eating it, as he debated with himself how to broach the next subject. "Could I ask *you* a somewhat awkward question?" he finally said. "Your aunt Ivy mentioned that you and Rose have basically given up on working together on your mother's directive, and she's worried that you won't come up with the hidden safe-deposit-box key before the deadline."

"Ah," Emily interrupted with a wry smile. "Now I see what's going on. Ivy sent you over here to talk some sense into me."

"Ivy is very concerned," he admitted. "In fact," he said as he pushed the wrapped package across the table toward her, "she asked me to give this to you. Said it was something your mom wanted you to have when the time was right, and Ivy feels that time is now."

Emily slowly reached out for the package with her brow furrowed, but she didn't open it.

"I know very well myself how much it hurt your mother that you and Rose have been estranged for so long," Father O'Brien continued. "I've also known both of you since you were little girls. There was a time when you were inseparable, when you loved each other very much. Your mother believed with all her heart that that kind of love never disappears, and I believe that, too. It can be compressed and overrun by negative feelings and horrible deeds, but it can't be broken. I wonder if there isn't some way you can discover within yourself a spark of that love for your sister, enough to find a way to carry out your mother's final wishes?"

"I'm doing the best I can, Father," Emily said evenly. "I came here for the summer because of what my mother said she wanted us to do in that letter. I thought being here would be hard, that I would constantly be thinking about what happened between Rose and me. I was right about that, but there've been good things, too. I finally feel as if I'm back where I belong. I feel close to Mom here, too, even though she's gone. But as for Rose . . . I'm not sure what I feel for her, Father. For a long time, it's been anger and resentment and disgust all intertwined, and recently it's been getting worse. I'm pretty sure I don't love her anymore, and I don't think I could even if I wanted to."

"If you still love her at all, you may not recognize it right now. But, I think you do, and that love is the key to forgiving her for what she did. I know it's not an easy thing to do, but forgiveness is what will help you resolve all of those negative feelings you have. If there's any hope of you two rebuilding your relationship as your mother hoped you would, you must forgive Rose first."

"Rose has never taken responsibility for what she did to me," Emily said. "For what she took from me. My life would have been so different if it hadn't been for that one night. I don't think I could ever forgive her unless she admits what she did and that her drinking was the reason it happened. And she needs to truly understand what I lost."

AFTER FATHER O'BRIEN HAD GONE, EMILY SLOWLY OPENED THE package he'd left her. It was a book of Shakespeare's complete works, very much like the one her mother had kept on her nightstand as long as she could remember.

There was an old Polaroid wedged into the pages. It was a

yellow-edged image of her and Rose from years ago, taken during a visit to the marble museum in Proctor. They were standing together, in front of a block of white marble, making funny faces. She vaguely remembered posing for that photo while her mother had begged her and Rose to smile nicely instead of crossing their eyes and letting their tongues hang out like drooling monsters.

Emily looked at the page bookmarked by the photo. A passage from *The Merchant of Venice* was highlighted in yellow.

> The quality of mercy is not strained,
> It droppeth as gentle rain from heaven
> Upon the place beneath. It is twice blest:
> It blesseth him that gives, and him that takes:

She gazed again at the photo, taking care not to let her tears moisten the image. When she turned it over, her mother's cursive writing jumped out at her.

Emily, sometimes you have to look far into the past to find the strength and grace to forgive and move forward. I know what your heart is capable of. I believe in you, and I love you. Mom

CHAPTER 26

Aᴌᴍᴏsᴛ ꜰᴏᴜʀ ʏᴇᴀʀs ᴀꜰᴛᴇʀ sʜᴇ ʜᴀᴅ ᴡᴀᴛᴄʜᴇᴅ ʜᴇʀ sɪsᴛᴇʀ leave home, Emily stood beside the Christmas tree in her mother's house staring out the front window. She was nervous and excited, so much so that the sound of Ivy humming in the kitchen and the feeling of Andy's arm around her shoulders did little to help.

"I can't wait for you to meet my sister," she told him.

Andy laughed and squeezed her closer. "You've said that at least a hundred times this past week."

"I know. I'm just anxious to see her."

Rose had been living in New York since that terrible day when she'd packed her bags and left. During her sporadic calls home, their mother had always gotten on the line first, and when she'd been satisfied that Rose was alive and well, she'd handed the phone to Emily. Her older sister tended to monopolize the conversations, chattering away about Linx or her latest audition. To Emily, though, it sounded as if Rose's life in New York was a little too perfect.

Once the letters had started to come, Emily's suspicion had been confirmed. There were those addressed to their mother, which sounded like written versions of Rose's happy phone calls. Then, there were those addressed only to Emily. They were written in stream-of-consciousness fashion, some over several days with

various dates scrawled across the pages to indicate the correspond-
ing day's passages. Those letters revealed just how miserable Rose
really was.

Her relationship with Linx had started to deteriorate about a
year after they'd arrived in New York. She'd recently ended things
completely. Despite the nasty breakup, she still had a job working
for Linx's uncle at the restaurant. As a hostess and now the new
bartender, Rose learned that her good looks were so helpful at
bringing in business that his uncle considered her too valuable to
fire. He'd told her as much himself, right before he'd grabbed her
ass and offered her a chance to make a little extra money on the
side.

Without Linx to foot some of the bills, money was tight. Rose
had moved into a cramped studio in an old building. It was a
fourth-floor walk-up and not much bigger than a closet, but it was
better than nothing. She spent what little free time she had trying
to break into acting, but after dozens of auditions for parts in plays
and commercials, Rose had yet to land an acting gig.

It was so upsetting for Emily to read her sister's letters. Of
course, their mother would have been frantic with worry had she
read about the true state of Rose's life, but neither she nor Emily
could force Rose to come home. Emily was careful to keep her own
letters from Rose hidden from their mother, all the while being
thankful every time she received a new one. She sent prompt replies pleading for Rose to come home, get her GED, and make a
fresh start, but her sister was stubborn and proud. Rose wasn't at all
ready to admit that she'd made a huge mistake by running off. The
letters just kept coming, and Emily did the only thing she could by
continuing to offer advice and support.

Once she had enrolled at Middlebury College and moved into
the dormitory, keeping their correspondence hidden from their
mother had no longer been difficult. Now, Emily was a sopho-

more. She and Rose were both out of the house, but they lived in completely different worlds. Rose endured long hours at work, the lonely aftermath of a bad relationship, and increasing disappointment with her choices. Emily's life, though, was happy and exciting, filled with interesting classes, new friends, and her first serious relationship.

She'd first met Andrew Coulter in her freshman studio art class. While Emily was taking the course because it was required for an eventual degree that would allow her to become an art teacher, Andy was a premed junior who needed to fulfill one of the college's distribution requirements for courses outside his biology major. Their easels happened to be situated next to each other, and Emily was surprised at how quickly they'd gotten to know one another while they practiced drawing with pencil and charcoal. Andy had light brown hair, and she couldn't decide whether his eyes were blue or green. She was often grateful that she could stare at her easel as he spoke to her, because she found that looking into those eyes often resulted in her losing her train of thought.

It was a good thing that Andy intended to become a pediatrician and not an artist, because even by the end of the semester, despite hours and hours of practice, the only things he could draw well were stick figures. He always approached the easel with good humor, though, and Emily found his goofy attempts at art to be endearing. She had kept several of the drawings that he'd made and given to her, including a still life depicting a lopsided wine bottle and a misshapen bowl of fruit under which he'd printed "Dinner with me?" That first-date invitation had led to a dizzying, exhilarating relationship, the kind of intense first love that left Emily longing for Andy even before they'd said their goodbyes for the evening.

She was eager to tell Rose all about Andy, about the wonderful times they'd had, but the time had never seemed right. As much as she wanted to share her happiness with Rose, she couldn't bear to gush about Andy after her sister complained about how horrible everything was. Emily had settled for telling Rose that she'd met a nice guy and had been dating him for almost a year. Rose would be able to meet Andy in person, and learn more about their relationship, when she came home for the holidays.

Rose was calling more frequently now, often in tears and slurring her words so much that Emily had trouble understanding her. Even more worrisome was that Rose often couldn't remember past conversations or things she'd mentioned in her letters. It was obvious that she was drinking more, and Emily was concerned that she was in far worse shape than she had been when she used to sneak back home through their bedroom window. It would be good to see Rose in person, to be able to talk with her, really talk, and maybe get through to her. More than anything, Emily just missed her big sister.

Her mother's car turned into the driveway and interrupted her thoughts. "Oh, they're here!" she said as she bounced on her toes and grinned up at Andy.

"It's about time," Ivy said as she came out of the kitchen. "Gravy's been made for a good twenty minutes, and my arm's tired from stirring it."

Emily threw open the front door and grabbed Rose in a huge hug the moment she was through it. When they separated and Ivy had had a turn to embrace Rose, Emily turned to Andy and pulled him forward. "Andy, this is my big sister, Rose. Rose, this is Andy Coulter."

"Hi, Andy," Rose said as she shook Andy's hand. "It's nice to finally meet you." Although Rose grinned at him, Emily couldn't help but notice the bags under her eyes and a certain sadness that seemed to dim their expressiveness.

"And you as well," Andy replied, although he glanced at Emily nervously as he spoke.

"Andy wanted to meet everyone, so I invited him to spend the holidays with us," Emily said.

"Actually, she took pity on me, being alone for the holidays," Andy said. "My mom and dad are off on a cruise for their second honeymoon, so I really didn't have anywhere to go."

"We're so happy to have you with us, Andy. And Ivy, it smells fabulous in here," Josie said. "Is there anything left to get ready?"

"Nope. You ought to wash up and come sit down," she said to Rose and Josie. "And," Ivy continued as she hugged Rose close again, "I can't wait to hear all about your latest big-city adventures."

IVY'S COMMENT REINFORCED FOR ROSE JUST HOW AWKWARD IT WAS when she came home for a visit. Everyone was always so curious about what she was doing in New York. Was she still working at the restaurant? Had she met anyone new? What were her plans for the future? Was she ever going to do anything else with her life? Her aunt Ivy was the worst with the questions and her incessant need to be "in the know." It felt horrible to have nothing exciting to tell her family, nothing that would make them sit up a little straighter and regard her with pride and respect.

Except this time, there *was* something she'd been waiting to tell them, something she was holding on to with every ounce of hope she still possessed. Midway through the dinner, after everyone had been served and the questions started in earnest, she put down her fork and smiled.

"I have a little announcement," she said. "Something I'm pretty excited about." Once everyone's eyes were focused on her, she let them in on her news. "I got a part in a small play." She waited and watched as her mother stopped chewing and Emily's face lit up. Her aunt Ivy actually let out a whoop.

"Really?" her sister asked. "That's fabulous!"

"Tell us about it," Ivy said. "What's the show? Is it something on Broadway?"

"Um, well, no. It's a play that'll be put on at a small experimental theater that just opened. It's called *The Journey of Me,* and it's about a man who suffers a stroke and falls into a coma. While he's unconscious, he's given a second chance to travel back through his life and atone for his mistakes."

"That sounds really cool!" Emily said. "What part will you be playing?"

"The former girlfriend—you know, the proverbial 'One Who Got Away.' It's not the biggest part, but it's a start, right? I've heard that casting agents sometimes come to these kinds of shows, so maybe it'll lead to something bigger."

"Hmm. That's true," her mother said. "You never know. My old boss told me once that even a situation you might think is hopeless could lead to great things, and he was right."

"Although *this* doesn't sound hopeless," her sister said quickly, and Rose flashed Emily a grateful smile. "Acting is hard. It takes a while to get your foot in the door and get a break, and this does sound like it could be the beginning of something good."

"That's right," Ivy chimed in. "You gotta start somewhere."

"I think this calls for a toast," Andy said, and they all raised their glasses to wish Rose success.

The moment was wonderful, but it turned out to be just that—a moment. Within a few minutes of the toast, Emily and Andy became the focus of the conversation. Rose rearranged what remained of her roast beef and mashed potatoes on her plate as she listened quietly. A part of her was thrilled to have her shy sister sitting beside Andy with happiness radiating from her face. Emily's eyes sparkled just a bit every time she looked at Andy, and judging by the similar expressions that were starting to appear on the faces of her mother and Aunt Ivy, he seemed to have won the approval of both of them.

But, why shouldn't he? Rose thought. Everything about him seemed to have come straight off a good-boyfriend parental checklist. Polite? Check. Smart and ambitious? Check. Good-looking, funny, and most of all, caring and respectful toward Emily? Check, check, and check. Andy was the teddy bear sort of guy a person could picture with little kids on his lap, the kind with a goofy grin who would pull off awesome practical jokes and give amazing hugs. And yet, Rose could see the intelligence and a glimmer of seriousness in his blue-green eyes, which coupled with the firm set of his jaw told her that Andy was no spineless wimp.

She couldn't help but think how different he was from Linx, the good-for-nothing thug she'd followed to New York. Linx had always been the bad boy, the tough guy. To her teenaged self, he'd been excitement and rebellion personified. Unfortunately, though, she'd learned the hard way that on the inside, Linx was a quivering mass of insecurity. How many times had he forbade her from going out without him or insisted on choosing what she wore? How many welts and bruises had she had to conceal throughout their time together? It was hard to believe that only a few years ago she'd have gone anywhere and done anything for such a foul-mouthed, heavy-handed control freak. Even now that they were no longer together, Linx still made it a point to stop in at the restaurant from time to time to harass her. She was worried that he might do something crazy to get back at her for ending their relationship.

No, Andy is definitely not like Linx, and that's a good thing, Rose thought. He was just another example of the things that seemed to come easily to Emily—a harmonious relationship with their mother, a certain self-confidence about who she was and what she wanted from her life, a quiet satisfaction with what she had, and now, a Mr. Perfect to build a future with.

Everything in her own life, on the other hand, was always so difficult. Nothing seemed to work out the way she wanted. Even with her success at landing her first acting job, a little voice inside her already cautioned against getting her hopes up. It was only experimental theater, after all, with a flimsy stage and a cast of nobodies.

Later that evening, Rose sat on her old bed in the second-floor bedroom that she used to share with Emily, listening to her sister and Andy talking softly downstairs in the living room. The lovebirds were supposed to be saying good night, but they were curled up together on the sofa bed, which their mother had made up for Andy. Their voices carried up the stairs, punctuated by periods of silence and the occasional loud creak from the springs supporting the pullout sofa mattress.

It boggled her mind that her younger sister was romantically involved with someone. She still pictured Emily as a little girl with curly red pigtails, or as the quiet high school student who never seemed to be able to pick out a stylish outfit. Even though she was happy that Emily was happy, seeing her involved with anyone was going to take some getting used to.

Emily's soft laugh came from downstairs. Rose didn't know how much longer her sister would be down there, but she was tired of waiting. She went to her suitcase and removed a small bottle of amber-colored rum. The first swallow was always a relief, a sweet, familiar burn that almost immediately muted her despair. *Thank God for this one constant,* she thought. Once she had a few drinks, everything would be okay.

2001

ON A BLUSTERY DAY IN MARCH, NEARLY THREE MONTHS AFTER Emily had brought Andrew Coulter home to meet everyone, Josie hung up the phone in her office, squelched a squeal of delight, and took a quick look around to make sure everything was in order. The house was spotless, as usual, including the kitchen, which showed no sign of having recently been used to prepare the lasagna baking in the oven. Her girls were home—Emily on her spring break from college and Rose because Josie had begged her to come to Mill River for a few days to be there for what she promised would be a momentous occasion.

The late afternoon phone call had been from Andy. He was waiting to be picked up at the Amtrak station in Rutland. Everyone except Emily knew that he was coming for a visit, but the bigger surprise for her younger daughter would be the reason for his return to Mill River.

Josie got misty-eyed as she remembered the call she'd received from Andy about a month before. It had been during the last week in February, and she'd been working in her home office, going over the paperwork for some new listings. Andy's call was unexpected, and at first, she was afraid something awful had happened.

"No, no, Mrs. DiSanti, nothing's wrong at all," he'd reassured her, but his voice had trembled slightly as he'd continued. "I was wondering . . . would you have a few minutes to talk with me? I'd be happy to call back if this isn't a good time."

"Well, yes. Of course, now is fine."

"Okay." He'd taken a deep breath before plunging into the conversation. "Well, I wanted to speak with you because I know that Emily's father died when she was very young and that you raised her and Rose by yourself. You've been her only parent, her mother and her father. You know that Emily and I have been together for quite a while now. She is the most amazing person and the most important thing in my life. I've never met anyone like her, and I couldn't imagine living the rest of my life without her. I love her . . ." Andy's voice had cracked a bit, and Josie's heart melted as he'd steadied himself and continued. "I love her with everything in me, and I would like very much to ask her to become my wife. I'm calling you today to ask for your blessing for me to propose to her."

"Oh, Andy, you've made me cry," Josie had said as she wiped at her eyes. "I know Emily loves you just as much as you love her, and I think you are a wonderful person. Of *course* you have my blessing. I couldn't wish for a more wonderful husband for my daughter, or a nicer son-in-law."

"Thank you, thank you so much," Andy said with great relief. "I think I totally lucked out in the future mother-in-law department, and I promise you that I'll do everything I can to make Emily happy." He paused a moment before continuing. "The second thing I wanted to talk to you about is how I'm thinking of popping the question."

"You already have something in mind? And you're willing to tell *me* about it? Oh, this is so exciting!"

Andy laughed. "Yes, well, I was wondering if we could arrange a surprise for Em over our spring break in about a month, during the last week in March. Right now, she thinks we're spending the vacation separately. I'm supposedly going to visit my folks in Providence, and she's coming down to see you and her aunt Ivy. But, what if I were to show up in Mill River midweek and ask here there, in front of all her family?"

"Oh, Andy, that would be wonderful! I'll do whatever you need to set it up. I don't dare tell her aunt Ivy just yet—she can't keep anything secret for long—but, goodness, I've got goose bumps just thinking about it!"

Now, the day of Andy's surprise proposal had finally come, and it was time to pull everything together.

"Em?" Josie stepped into the living room where Emily was sitting on the sofa reading. "That was Ivy calling. She's got some new books to stock, and she wondered if you could go over and give her a hand? She can't heft those boxes around like she used to."

"Sure, I'll go," Emily said as she closed her book.

"Thanks, hon. I'm going to finish up making dinner. I'll call you when it's ready, and you should ask Ivy to come over, too. Is Rose still asleep?"

"Yeah, I think so," Emily replied as she opened the front door. "She had to work late and then get up at the crack of dawn to catch her bus up here. She'll be in a better mood at dinner if we let her sleep a little longer."

Once Emily was safely out of the house, Josie called upstairs to Rose.

"Rose, it's time. Can you come down?" When she heard Rose's mumbled reply, she went into the kitchen and began removing dishes and glasses to set the table. She'd purchased new champagne flutes especially for the occasion, and there was a bottle of bubbly chilling inside the refrigerator.

"Everything's ready?" Rose asked in a sleepy voice as she came into the kitchen.

"Yes, Andy's at the train station in Rutland. Can you take my car and go pick him up? I'm going to set the table and arrange everything so it's perfect for when everyone gets here. Emily's over helping Ivy unpack some boxes, and Ivy knows she's supposed to keep her busy until I call."

"Okay." Rose giggled. "I haven't driven for a long time, you know."

"You'll be fine," Josie said. "This is Vermont, not New York City. My keys are in my purse."

"And your purse is—?"

"On my desk in the office," Josie said. "And, hey, if Andy wants to stop somewhere to pick up some flowers, take him over to Hawley's on Center Street. They always have such nice arrangements. But try to get back here as soon as you can."

Josie vaguely heard the door opening and closing as Rose left, followed by the sound of the car engine starting. She flew around the table, positioning plates and napkins, silverware and delicate stemware, until everything was perfect. By that time, the lasagna had filled the house with its spicy aroma, and she removed it from the oven and set it on the stove to cool. She prepared a green salad and mixed a cruet of balsamic vinaigrette. When she finally glanced at her watch, she was surprised to see that more than an hour had passed since Rose had left.

They'll be here any minute, she thought. She wondered whether she should call over to Ivy's and then decided against it. Her impatience was driven by giddy anticipation, and it would be better to call after Rose had returned with Andy. Josie sat down in a kitchen chair to wait.

Another thirty minutes dragged by before she heard the front door open. She hurried around to the foyer to see Emily coming through the door. Ivy followed her with an apologetic look on her face.

"We finished up everything, and we figured you had dinner about ready," Emily said with a smile. "Smells great in here."

"Yes, we're about ready. Just waiting for Rose. I sent her out to fetch a last-minute something, but she should be back any minute." Josie glanced out the window. It was almost seven o'clock and nearly dark.

"Wow, Mom, you went all out," Emily said as she lifted one of the champagne flutes. "What's the occasion?"

"Oh, I just thought it would be nice to have a fancy dinner, since we're all together."

"You know you've got an extra place setting here," Emily said as she examined the table. "With Rose, there's only four of us."

"I wonder what's keeping Rose?" her mother asked, completely ignoring her comment about the place setting. "Em, do you know whether she has a cell phone? She said something about wanting one a while back, but the only number I have is for her apartment."

"I don't think she has one yet," Emily said. "What did you send her to get?"

Josie didn't reply. Instead, she looked at Ivy, who shook her head and shrugged.

"What?" Emily asked, looking back and forth between them. "Something's going on. What is it?"

Ivy pursed her lips for a moment, as if she was struggling to keep from speaking, but Josie could see her aunt's resolve slipping away. *Here she goes,* Josie thought as Ivy started to blab.

"It's just a little surprise we have for you. We didn't want to say anything, but Andy decided to come for a quick visit. Rose went to Rutland to pick him up."

"Really? He's coming here?" Emily asked as a smile stretched across her face.

Josie glanced at Ivy and nodded, thankful that her aunt hadn't revealed the whole reason for Andy's visit. "I guess a week apart from you was too much for him to handle," she said to Emily.

"I guess," Emily replied.

"But, you should act surprised when he gets here, okay?" Ivy asked. "Andy didn't want you to know he was coming, and if he hears that we told you—"

"You mean, that *you* told her—" Josie interrupted, with a playfully stern look at Ivy.

"—yes, well, there'll be hell to pay," Ivy finished.

"Don't worry," Emily said as she smiled and reached over to grab Ivy's hand. "He'll never know."

CHAPTER 27

LATE SUNDAY AFTERNOON, CLAUDIA SMILED AS KYLE'S pickup truck pulled into her driveway. Rowen grinned and waved from the small backseat as Claudia opened the passenger's side door.

"Hey, Claudia! What are you bringing to the cookout?" The little girl looked with curiosity at the foil-covered dishes Claudia was holding.

"Hey yourself," she said. "I've got deviled eggs and fruit salad. Nothing fancy, but I hope Jean doesn't have either one already."

"Even if she does, there'll be plenty of people at the cookout," Kyle said. "Just those two boys of hers could probably clean up half the food themselves."

"I can't wait to see Jimmy and Johnny again. They have a lot of cool stuff," Rowen said.

"I'm sure they miss having you around," Claudia said. "I know you had a good time staying with them while the bakery was being rebuilt."

"Yeah," Rowen said. "It would be nice to have a brother. Or a sister." She looked at her father and raised her eyebrows meaningfully.

"Uh-huh." Kyle's ears turned pink as he rolled his eyes at Claudia, and she smiled in return. Rowen had been dropping hints like that for a while now.

As Kyle pulled into the Wykowskis' driveway, the smell of charcoal smoke and grilled meat was in the air. The Fitzgeralds' SUV was there, along with the police department's Jeep. Rowen spotted the Wykowski boys playing with a Frisbee and was out of the pickup and running before Claudia's feet had hit the ground.

"Stay in the yard, now," Kyle called to his daughter. Rowen turned back and waved briefly to show that she'd heard him.

"I love cookouts," Kyle said. He took a grocery sack of hamburger- and hot-dog buns from the truck, and together they walked around back. The Wykowskis had a large deck that spanned the width of their house. A table was set up on one end and covered with condiments and all sorts of wonderful-looking but very fattening side dishes. *Maybe I'll splurge on a little potato salad,* Claudia thought as she examined the spread. She noticed two beautiful pies at the far end of the table, almost certainly Ruth's contribution. *On second thought, maybe I'll save the calories for dessert.*

"Hey Kyle, Claudia," Ron called. He was flipping burgers on a grill at the opposite end of the deck. Fitz stood next to him, along with another man Claudia didn't know who was wearing a police uniform. "There's drinks on ice over there. Help yourselves to some and come on over."

Kyle reached toward a tub of ice at the end of the food table. "You want the usual?"

"Sure, that'd be great." He handed her a Diet Coke and took a beer from the ice for himself.

"You haven't met Matt yet, have you?" Kyle asked her. "Fitz hired him a few weeks ago to replace Leroy. He's on duty right now—took over for me when my shift ended earlier—but I think Fitz let him leave the station to come out here and get to know everyone a little better. C'mon, I'll introduce you." He put his hand at the small of her back as they approached the grill.

"Hullo, you two," Fitz said.

"Glad you could make it," Ron said as he turned to greet

them. "Haven't seen you in a while, Claudia. How's your summer been so far?"

"Great," Claudia said. "When you're a teacher, the summer's always great."

"Well, you look rested and happy," Fitz said.

"Actually, I don't think she's met Matt yet," Kyle said. "Claudia, this is Matt Campbell, our new officer. Matt, meet Claudia Simon."

"Hi," Claudia said. She smiled at Matt, who had dark hair and eyes and a friendly face, and shook his hand. "Nice to meet you."

"Likewise, ma'am," Matt said. Claudia felt her surprise register on her face. It had been a long time since someone had called her "ma'am."

"You'll have to excuse him," Fitz said as he clapped Matt on the shoulder. "Matt here just got out of the service—the Marines— but the formality hasn't gotten outta him yet."

"The Marines? Wow," she said. "Where were you stationed?"

"The Middle East, mostly," Matt said. "Two tours in Iraq and another in Afghanistan. When it came time to re-up, though, I felt like I was ready for a change. That, and I realized that I really didn't want to spend another couple years in the desert."

"After going through one of our winters, you might reconsider that decision," Claudia said, and they all chuckled. She was pleased to feel Kyle's hand move around her waist and gently pull her against him.

"Don't worry, I know what's coming," Matt said. "I grew up in Maine, and I'm really looking forward to the cold and snow."

"He flew through his certification training at the police academy," Fitz said. "I think we got ourselves a good one here."

"Agreed," Kyle said. "And a massive improvement over the prior occupant of the job. Speaking of which, have you heard anything about what's going on with Leroy's trial?"

Claudia shuddered. Just hearing the name of the former police officer who had stalked her gave her the heebie-jeebies. It was Leroy Underwood who had set fire to the bakery in the misguided belief that he would be able to rescue her from Kyle's apartment above it and win her affection.

"As a matter of fact, I just spoke with the D.A. on Friday," Fitz said. "Looks like Leroy's about to accept a plea deal. They're working out the final terms, but he'll definitely be doing some hard time."

"That's wonderful news," Claudia said. She had no desire to hear anything more about Leroy. "I think I'm going to go see if Jean needs any last-minute help," she said to the men. She squeezed Kyle's hand before she slipped through the sliding door that led into the kitchen.

"Hey ladies," she said to Jean and Ruth as she entered. "Kyle and I just got here. I set a few dishes on the table outside. Can I help with anything?" Ruth was standing at the sink juicing lemons for a pitcher of lemonade, while Jean was removing a casserole dish of baked beans from the oven.

"We're about ready," Jean said. "But, could you be a dear and set these beans out on the table? I'll start slicing up some fixings for the burgers."

"Of course," Claudia said. She took the oven mitts and trivet Jean handed her and carefully carried the casserole dish outside. The rich, brown sauce was still puckering at the sides of the dish, and the smell of bacon and brown sugar wafting from it made her stomach growl.

It took her a few seconds to rearrange the food already on the table to make room for the beans. As she shifted the bowls and platters, she could hear Kyle and the other officers talking at the far end of the deck.

"Now that you've got yourself a job, you oughta start looking for a nice girl to settle down with," Fitz was saying.

"Yep, a nice girl would warm up your winter," Ron added. "You should check out that younger DiSanti sister, what's her name? Emily? I hear she's single."

Claudia's back stiffened at the mention of Emily's name. Immediately, she slowed her movements so that she could linger at the table.

"She is a pretty girl," Fitz agreed. "Weren't you out at her place today, Kyle?"

"Yeah," Kyle said. "Her older sister actually called the station to report some vandalism on her property. Somebody used herbicide to write the word 'lush' in her lawn. Rose was all jacked up about it and adamant that Emily was responsible, although there's no way to prove that. I just took a report from Rose and then went over to talk with Emily. Of course, Emily denied knowing anything about it."

Lovely, Claudia thought.

"Ruth says their mother's plan to get them to reconcile isn't working too well," Fitz said.

"I'd say that's accurate," Kyle said. "The two of them are hardly speaking, and Emily had a tire slashed on her car a while ago."

"Now, Matt, you should know that stuff like that rarely happens around here," Fitz said.

"So, you think Rose did the slashing?" Ron asked.

"That'd be my guess. I could've sworn she was lying today when I asked her about it, but again, no one saw anything," Kyle replied. "As for Emily, well, I feel sorry for her. She's been through a lot, and she strikes me as being a nicer person than Rose. Still, I think Rose is right that Emily's the one behind the lawn vandalism. And now that they're damaging each other's property, there's no telling how bad things'll get."

"Just what I need, a vengeful woman who's into weed killer," Matt joked, and the men laughed.

"Aw, c'mon," Ron teased. "I think you just might be able to overlook those things once you see her. Besides, you're a former Marine who survived three tours in hell. I'm sure you could handle her."

The sliding door to the deck opened, and Jean and Ruth stepped outside with a pitcher of lemonade and a plate of sliced tomatoes and onions.

"Hon, are the burgers about done?" Jean called to her husband.

Claudia didn't hear Ron's reply. She was still thinking about the men's conversation and trying not to let Kyle's visit to the DiSanti sisters bother her. Of course, he'd just been doing his job. And, on the plus side, while Fitz had commented favorably on Emily's appearance, Kyle hadn't said a word about it. That made her *very* happy.

The rest of the evening passed in a blur. Claudia helped herself to a slice of Ruth's pie—a *small* slice—but the to-die-for blueberry filling and flaky crust were worth the splurge. The only problem was that the dessert was far richer than anything she was used to eating, and her stomach had begun to feel a little queasy.

"Are you all right?" Kyle finally leaned over and whispered to her. "You're quiet."

"I'm just not feeling great all of a sudden," she said. "Upset stomach."

"Do you want to get going? I've got the early shift tomorrow again, so I wouldn't mind leaving now." She nodded gratefully.

After they said their goodbyes to the Wykowskis and the other guests, Kyle dropped her off at home, kissing her tenderly in the foyer while Rowen waited in the pickup. "Have a good night," he said. "I'll call you tomorrow to see how you're feeling."

When he was gone, she paced around her house. She had no desire to exercise or watch TV or read, and she wasn't sleepy yet.

Finally, she headed into the bathroom. It had been a long time since she'd treated herself to a long, hot bath, and she decided that a good soak was exactly what she needed.

Claudia turned on the faucet. Her favorite pink bath gel sat on the side of the tub, and she added a good squirt to the water before she undressed and lowered herself into the rising bubbles. As her anxiety drained out of her body, she picked up the bottle of bath gel again and reread the "love sweet love" description printed on the label. She had to smile at how those words rang true. Every one of her days with Kyle, every memory she made with him, was sweeter and more precious than the one before. And, if the past few months were any indication of what was to come, she certainly had wonderful things to look forward to.

IT WAS NEARLY NINE O'CLOCK WHEN IVY WAS FINALLY DONE straightening up The Bookstop for Monday's opening. As usual when she worked late, she used the time to think. She wondered whether Father O'Brien had had a chance to speak with the girls, and how they might have reacted. Soon, it would be August, and Rose and Emily seemed no closer to finding Josie's key than they had been on their first day back in Mill River. The fact that they had recently come to blows was especially worrisome.

A soft knock at her locked front door startled her. When she turned on the porch light and looked out, she saw Alex standing there with a pile of books balanced carefully in his arms.

"Well, here's a surprise," she said as she let him in. "I was almost ready to turn off the lights."

"Hi, Aunt Ivy," he told her as he handed her the stack. "Mom said I could bring these to you if I didn't stay too long."

"You know you're always welcome to stay as long as you like," Ivy said. "Where'd you get these? They look pretty old."

"There are some boxes in our house with your name on them. They're all full of old books. Mom says they're your rejects. I've been going through them anyway, and these are the ones I'm finished with. I didn't know whether you wanted them back."

"Well, I'll be," Ivy said. "I don't even remember when I packed up those boxes. It must've been years ago. I used to give your grandma worn-out copies to read to your mom and your aunt. Maybe I'll see if I can donate these somewhere. You say you read these already?"

"Yep. I read pretty fast." Alex was looking at the packed shelves in the Kids' Corner. "You sure have a lot of books for kids."

"Always have," she said. "Reading's so important, especially for young kids, and I've always thought that the younger you learn, the better. I love seeing 'em light up when they come in here and pull a new book off the shelf."

"Why didn't you ever get married and have any kids of your own?"

"Oh." Alex's question caught her off guard. "Well, I guess . . . the truth is, I almost got married. I had a fiancé once. His name was Tom. He was the one who came here with me, to Mill River, and helped me open this place. We were going to settle down and start a family, live happily ever after, you know? But at some point, I realized I didn't love him. I'd fallen in love with someone else . . . someone who loved me in return but wasn't in a position to marry me."

"Who were you in love with?"

"Oh, it was so long ago, it doesn't matter anymore. I never stopped wanting kids, though. It just wasn't meant to work out for me."

"I think you would've been a great mom."

"You know, in a way, I feel like I had a second chance at it when your grandma came here with your mom and aunt Emily. I think . . . thought . . . of your grandma as my own daughter. I loved her like that, and your mom and your aunt Emily have always been like my own grandchildren. And you—you're like a great-grandson to me, even though you're technically my great-great-nephew."

She could see Alex was pleased with her reply, as a blush spread across his pale cheeks and he smiled down at his shoes. "Thanks," he said. He turned toward the door but then hesitated. "Aunt Ivy?"

"Hmm?"

"If I ask you something else, would you promise to answer it without telling me that it's something I shouldn't hear until I'm older?"

Ivy looked into Alex's huge blue eyes and wondered what question he would possibly want to ask now. "Well, I can't say for sure unless I knew what the question was. You don't mean to ask . . . um, well, I mean, you already know how babies are made, don't you?

Alex giggled. "Yes, I already know that. Mom told me about that a loooong time ago."

Ivy relaxed and laughed with him. "Well, that's really the only question I was worried about. So, shoot."

"Okay. Why do Mom and Aunt Emily hate each other?"

Ivy felt the smile disappear from her face as she realized that what Alex had just asked would be far more difficult to handle than even the birds and the bees.

"Something happened a long time ago, but neither one of them will tell me what," Alex added in a soft voice. "I'm not a baby, Aunt Ivy. I'm old enough to know."

She sat down on one of the larger beanbags, struggling with what and how much she should say. She remembered the advice she'd given Josie years before when her niece had been trying to help Rose and Emily understand their father's death. "Tell 'em the truth in terms that they can understand," she'd said to Josie. Now, as she looked down at the precious little boy before her, she realized that the advice was still sound. "Oh, honey," she said to him, "it was just the most heartbreaking thing."

CHAPTER 28

2001

In the front seat of her mother's car, Rose came to. Her head was throbbing, and she could feel cold air meeting wetness along the side of her face. The only sources of light were the headlights shining into a thicket of trees and the dim glowing of a few of the gauges in the dashboard. Most of the windshield was gone, as was the window on her side, except for a few pieces of glass that clung haphazardly to the frame.

Rose realized that her body was positioned at a strange angle, almost sideways, actually, and that the passenger's side of the car was slightly lower than the driver's side. The ceiling was lower, too—she could feel the hair atop her head brushing against it as she moved. She tried to reach up and touch her face, but the pain that shot through her left arm when she moved was excruciating.

It was all coming back now—Andy's surprise visit to Mill River, picking him up outside the train station, stopping for roses before they left Rutland. Rose turned her head toward the passenger's seat.

"Andy?" She squinted, but she could only make out the silhouette of the back of Andy's head resting against the passenger's side door. His face was obscured by the large bouquet of flowers he'd been holding.

"Andy?" Rose asked again. She turned slightly in her seat,

which brought a new stab of pain in her midsection. Carefully, she stretched out her right hand to touch Andy's arm. Using what little strength she had, she grabbed his shoulder and tried to rouse him, but he didn't respond.

"Oh, my God. Oh, my God." Rose fought against a rising panic. Flashes of memory began to invade her mind—the fleeting image of a deer jumping out in front of the car, a desperate jerk of the steering wheel, the sensation of being airborne, of crashing and rolling down, down, and then nothing. She leaned her shoulder against her door and reached her right arm across her body to pull on the handle as best she could, but it wouldn't open.

"Help," she whispered as tears slid down her face. Her voice was raspy and barely audible. "Help me, help us, please," she managed to say a little louder. She could hear the occasional car drive past on the highway, but the drone of the engine always faded away as quickly as it approached.

Andy was still and silent beside her.

"Andy!" Rose said. Ignoring the pain, she reached out again. "Andy, can you hear me? Please wake up." Her fingers found Andy's forearm, then his wrist. There was no pulse, only quiet, unmoving warmth.

Rose struggled to keep her eyes open. She didn't know what time it was or how long she had been in the car, but the pain in her abdomen was worsening, and it hurt to breathe. At some point, she opened her eyes and stared at the trees through the broken windshield. They had begun to give off alternating bursts of red and blue light. *How strange,* she thought before her eyes closed again.

EMILY SAT AT HER MOTHER'S DINING ROOM TABLE. HER AUNT IVY sat beside her, while her mother paced nervously in the kitchen.

The lasagna for their dinner remained on the stovetop, cooled and uneaten. It was after nine o'clock, and Rose still hadn't returned with Andy.

"Something's wrong. They must've had car trouble, a flat tire or something," Josie said as she swept back into the dining room. "Ivy, do you think we should go for a drive to see if we—"

She was interrupted by the doorbell.

"Oh, finally!" Josie said, and Emily breathed a sigh of relief. She turned toward the door as her mother rushed to open it, but she was surprised to see Ruth Fitzgerald step into the foyer, followed by her husband, who was wearing his police uniform.

"What is it? What happened?" Josie asked immediately, and Emily and Ivy both came to stand with her.

"Jo, there's been an accident," Ruth said. "Fitz was out on patrol and found your car down an embankment off Route 103."

"Rose—" her mother said, but Ruth immediately grabbed her hands and interrupted her.

"Now, you listen. Rose has been hurt, but she's alive and already on her way to the emergency room. We came to drive you to the hospital. Get your coat."

"What about Andy?" Emily asked. "Rose went to pick him up. Was there someone in the car with her?" She looked back and forth between Ruth and Fitz's faces as she started to tremble. "Was there?"

Emily shuddered as Ruth's face crumpled and Fitz cleared his throat. "He was there, Emily," Fitz said in a quiet, gruff voice. "I'm so sorry to have to tell you this, but he didn't make it. The paramedics tried to revive him at the scene, but he was already gone by the time we found the car."

Emily felt her legs give way as hands reached out to steady her.

The rest of the night became a surreal jumble of tears and hugs and hushed conversations. They gathered in the hospital waiting room, praying and hoping that Rose would pull through. A surgeon finally appeared to give them an update shortly after two in the morning.

"Your daughter is out of surgery," he said as he looked her mother in the eye. "She had a ruptured spleen, which caused quite a bit of internal bleeding, but we were able to get it under control. She also has a concussion, a broken arm, and three broken ribs, as well as some superficial cuts and bruises. It'll take her a while to heal, but we think she'll pull through. She was very lucky the police found her when they did."

"Oh, thank God, and thank you, Doctor," Josie said. "When can we see her?"

"She's in the recovery room now, and she'll be moved to the ICU as soon as she's fully awake from the anesthesia, probably within an hour or two. You'll be able to visit her there, but only for a few minutes at a time. I'll have a nurse alert you as soon as she's been moved."

Exhausted, Emily sank into a chair. The relief she felt at hearing Rose would survive was overpowered by the raw grief of knowing that Andy was gone. She didn't know what to do. She couldn't imagine her life without him.

"Emily?" A familiar voice startled her, and she looked up to see that an older couple with tear-streaked faces had entered the waiting room. Her brain slowly processed their identities. They were Mike and Melissa Coulter—Andy's father and mother. She'd met them before, over the New Year's holiday right after Andy had come to Mill River to meet her own family. Emily stood up and fell into a joint embrace with both of them.

"We've just come from the morgue," Mike whispered. "We got in the car and drove up here as soon as we got a call about the accident, but he . . . we had to identify him for the authorities."

"They told us about your sister, that she was here," Melissa said, "and we wanted to come see if she was all right."

"She's had surgery," Emily managed to say, "but the doctor thinks she'll be okay."

"Thank goodness for that," Melissa said. "That's wonderful news, a real blessing," and Andy's father nodded in agreement.

"I'm so sorry. I don't know how this happened," Emily said. "I didn't even know Andy was coming up here to see me."

Melissa looked up at her husband as tears fell freely from her eyes. Mike nodded again and lifted a small paper bag. With an unsteady hand, Andy's mother reached into the bag and removed a small, velvet box.

Emily felt an arm slide around her waist, and she turned to see her own mother standing beside her. Ivy came up on her other side, but neither said anything as they waited for Andy's mother to speak.

"They gave us . . . his personal things," she told them as she looked at the bag and choked back a sob. "His wallet and keys and such. This was in his coat pocket . . . the reason he was coming to surprise you. We think you should have it. Andy would have wanted you to have it."

Melissa pressed the box into her hand.

Emily looked down, afraid to lift the lid and already suspecting what it contained, but Andy's parents were still standing before her, waiting. She grasped the top of the box and gently pried it open. Before new tears completely obscured her vision, she caught a glimpse of a stunning diamond engagement ring shining against the velvet.

EMILY STOOD ON THE SECOND-FLOOR LANDING, WATCHING AS Rose leaned on their mother's arm as they made their way slowly up the stairs. It had been two weeks since the accident and a week since she'd traveled to Rhode Island for Andy's funeral, and now her sister had finally been discharged from the hospital.

Rose walked with halting steps into the bedroom they'd once shared and exhaled as she lowered herself onto her old bed. There was a cast on her left arm and a healing gash that ran from her eyebrow down the left side of her face. She looked thin and pale, and she still couldn't stand, sit, or lie down without wincing.

"Do you want anything to eat?" Josie asked. "I could make you a sandwich or some soup."

"No, nothing right now, Mom," Rose said. "I just want to rest."

"How about a soda or just some ice water? You need to keep your fluid levels up," Josie said.

Rose sighed. "Fine, you could bring me a Coke."

"Good. I'll be right back," she said. "Em, why don't you help her get changed into something more comfortable?"

"Sure, Mom," Emily said. As Rose reclined against a wall of pillows their mother had arranged on the bed, Emily went to Rose's suitcase and unzipped it.

"There should be a clean set of pajamas in there, gray, with pink flowers," Rose said with her eyes closed.

Emily spotted the pajamas folded under a few other pieces of clothing. As she pulled them out, she saw a small glass bottle protruding from the clothes stacked beneath the pajamas, and she removed it as well.

"What's this?" Emily asked, holding up the half-empty bottle of rum.

As Rose ignored her question and lay against the pillows, Emily couldn't help but remember the image of Andy's body resting in his satin-lined coffin. It was the thing about going to his funeral that she had dreaded most—although the shock of being introduced to other mourners by Andy's parents as his fiancée had been equally difficult—because she knew it would be her last time seeing him. That memory would be seared into her mind forever.

The funeral home staff had managed to make him look presentable, but there had still been subtle clues to the massive head trauma Andy had suffered during the crash. His hair hadn't quite looked right, as it had been styled to hide the swelling. And, the pancake makeup on his face had been applied in a thick layer, no doubt to hide bruising. Being restrained by his seat belt hadn't protected Andy when the car had rolled and crushed the roof.

For days while Rose had been in the hospital, she had drifted through the hours, crying, sleeping when she could, waking suddenly from nightmares and unrelenting anxiety. It hadn't helped to hear her sister's semiconscious vocalizations, most of which alternated between screams of "No! No!" and pleas for forgiveness. When her condition had stabilized, Rose had explained to all of them what had happened, or at least, what she claimed to remember, but Emily was still left with a desperate craving to know more about Andy's last moments on earth.

She also had one question in particular for her sister. It was a question that she had asked herself and dreaded asking her sister, a question to which she knew the answer even as she tried to convince herself that she was wrong. She'd been hesitant to have any sort of lengthy conversation with Rose while she'd been in the hospital, but now that Rose was home and on the mend, she had time and opportunity.

"Rose?" Emily asked. She sat down on the edge of Rose's bed, and her sister opened her eyes and looked at her. "I know you told us what happened earlier, but . . . I'm having a really hard time." Emily's voice became raspy with emotion. "Is there anything else, about the accident . . . or Andy . . . ?"

Rose sighed. "I told you everything," she said. "We stopped at Hawley's before leaving Rutland, and we were on 103 heading down to Mill River. We were just making small talk. I didn't really know him that well, you know, but he was super-excited about what he had planned. A deer ran out in front us, and it was there before I could slow down or anything. I swerved to try to avoid hitting it, and the last thing I remember was the car going over the guardrail." Rose's voice was trembling as she finished the summary. "Em, I don't know what else to say. I'm so sorry. So sorry." She was crying now, and her gaze shifted to the rum bottle that Emily still held in her hands.

Emily squinted at Rose through her own tears. "I need to ask you something else, and I need you to tell me the truth," Emily said. "You were taking a nap that day, before Mom asked you to go get Andy. Had you been drinking?"

"*No,* I wasn't driving drunk that day. They tested my blood alcohol level in the hospital, you know. It was perfectly normal."

"Alcohol clears from the bloodstream over time. You weren't found right away, not for a couple hours after you left here. What I asked you was whether you'd been drinking before you left the house."

Rose opened her mouth and closed it, and Emily cut her off before she could utter the lie that her expression foretold.

"Do you realize that if you'd been sober, you might have handled the car differently, maybe kept control of it, and that Andy might still be here with me?" Emily wrapped her arms around herself. She could feel her emotions slipping and spiraling out of control.

"My blood alcohol was *normal,*" Rose argued. "It's proof that I was *fine* to drive. It was just a fucking horrible accident, all right?"

Emily put her hands on her forehead and slid them up over her hair. "You're lying. To *me,* your *sister.* Can't you even tell *me* the truth? God, I don't know how I didn't see it before, what you really are," she said, shaking her head. "I've always been there for you, always. Covered for you while you were out running wild, read your sorry letters, listened to you slobber on the phone, and tried to support you while you made one stupid decision after the next. Would you have done the same for me? I can't imagine it. And now, you don't even have the decency to admit what really happened. I'm the one you're supposed to be closer to than anyone, but you can't even be honest with *me*." She wiped her eyes. "Do you remember what you told me that day you left home? I do. You said that even though we'd be living apart, nothing would come between us. Well, you know what? That was complete bullshit." Sobbing, she threw the half-empty rum bottle against the wall.

"Em—" Rose said, but Emily kept going.

"How many more are there?" Emily returned to the suitcase and began throwing clothes out onto the floor. She found two more bottles of liquor and held them out toward her sister.

"You have a drinking problem, Rose. You do, don't try to deny it. I know, even though you're good at hiding it."

"I *don't* have a drinking problem." Her voice was defensive, haughty. "Sure, I have a few drinks now and then to take the edge off, but that's no big deal. I'm a bartender, for God's sake. I know exactly what people with real drinking problems are like."

"Do you see these?" Emily screamed at Rose. She thrust the liquor bottles in her sister's face. "Do you see? Because of these, *you killed somebody.*" Then, with all her strength, Emily hurled the bottles just as she had the first.

Rose flinched as the glass shattered and the whiskey they had contained began to form dark rivulets down the ivory-colored wall, but she didn't speak. Emily was shaking so violently that she could barely get her words out.

"Have you ever loved anybody more than yourself? Anybody at all? *I* have. Mom, and Aunt Ivy, and you. And *Andy.*" Her voice broke as she said his name. "He was the most wonderful thing that ever happened to me. I've never loved anyone like that before, and I know he felt the same about me. He was my future. And you took his life and mine in your hands and threw them away, just like you do your empty booze bottles. You know something, Rose? It should've been *you* that died in that car. It should've been you, and I wish now that it had been. So, you can just go to hell. It's where you belong."

Emily lunged for the door. Her mother was midway up the stairs when she rushed past.

"Emily? I heard glass breaking. What's going on? Where are you going?"

"To get some air. And I'm going back up to school tonight, if Ivy'll drive me."

"What? Why do you want to leave? Is your sister all right?"

"Ask her yourself," Emily said. "But she's not my sister any-more."

CHAPTER 29

CLAUDIA WAS DRESSED AND READY TO LEAVE HER HOUSE when her phone rang.

Her bubble bath the night before, followed by a good night's sleep and an intense run on the treadmill, had done wonders. She felt buoyant and energetic, and her mood was boosted even further by the sound of Kyle's voice on the phone.

"Hey, beautiful, are you feeling any better than you were last night?"

"Yeah, I am," she said, smiling into the receiver. "I felt fine when I woke up this morning, and I was just heading out for a bit. I thought I'd grab some coffee at Ruth's and then head into Rutland to see if I could find a few new things to wear for work. The summer clothes are going on clearance."

"Sounds like fun," he said. "Well, as fun as shopping can be, I guess. Better than sitting in an office or a patrol car."

"True," she said. "I'll give you a call this evening, okay?"

"Okay," he said. "Love you."

"Love you, too," she said as she smiled again. "Bye."

She walked out the door, but it felt more like she was floating on cloud nine.

WITH HER LITTLE GRAY DOG WATCHING FROM HIS USUAL POSITION on a kitchen chair, Daisy Delaine put the final touches on a gift basket of produce and sweets. Vegetables from her garden, chocolate chip cookies made from scratch, and homemade strawberry preserves were nestled in the basket's cloth lining.

"How does it look, Smudgie?" she asked the little dog as she positioned the items in the basket. "Won't Miss Rose be surprised by our basket? The veggies are perfect and the cookies are oh-so-delicious, even if I do say so myself!" Smudgie barked and wagged his tail.

The two unpleasant encounters she'd had with Miss Rose might have deterred others from any further attempts at smoothing things over, but Daisy had decided to try one last time. She ripped a blank page from an old notebook and scribbled a simple apology. Then, she folded the note and tucked it into the center of the basket between two large tomatoes.

"We can only do our best, can't we, Smudgie? That's what Father O'Brien always says." Daisy picked up the little dog and hugged him close. "I hope Miss Rose believes me. I really am so sorry," she whispered in his ear.

CARRYING A WRAPPED PACKAGE IDENTICAL TO THE ONE HE HAD given Emily, Father O'Brien found himself walking more and more slowly as he approached Rose DiSanti's house. True, he wasn't looking forward to the conversation he was about to attempt, but he slowed his gait more because he was contemplating exactly how he should explain the reason for his unexpected visit. As he neared the corner and the side of her house came into view, he decided that the best approach would be his usual one—simple, gentle, and straightforward, with unflinching honesty.

The door opened quickly after he knocked, but he was surprised to be greeted by Alex.

"Hi, Father," the boy said.

"Good morning, Alex. Is your mother home? I wondered if I might visit with her for a few minutes."

"Who is it, Alex?" Rose's voice called from inside the house, and before the child could answer, Father O'Brien heard footsteps and the door opened wider.

"Oh, hello, Father," Rose said. "What a surprise. I didn't know you'd be coming by."

"I realize that, and I apologize for not calling ahead," he told her. "Ivy invited me for lunch today, but I'm running a few minutes early, so I thought I'd swing by to say hello while I was in the neighborhood."

"Oh, well, come in, then," she said, but it was obvious by the tone of her voice that she wasn't thrilled to have company.

Alex looked up at him and then at his mother. "I'm going back up to my room, okay, Mom?"

Rose nodded, and Alex cleared out in a hurry.

"Please sit down," Rose said, motioning to an armchair. "I just poured myself a Coke. Can I get you something to drink?"

"Thank you, no," he said. Father O'Brien lowered himself carefully into the chair and placed the wrapped package on his lap. Rose sat down on the end of the couch farthest from him. He saw that she had a bruise around one of her eyes, and she noticed that he noticed.

"I tripped in the night and fell against my bed," she said, touching her eye lightly.

"I wondered about that," he admitted. "But, it's good that it's healing up." He looked away from her and glanced around. There were stacks of boxes and extra pieces of furniture in the room, arranged in such a way as to leave paths where people could walk or reach those furnishings that were actually being used. It was, he imagined, almost like being inside an ant farm.

"So, how've things been at the church, Father?" Rose asked.

She took a sip of her drink, staring at him over the top of her glass.

"Fine, fine," he said. "It's still a small, friendly congregation. I sure do miss seeing your mother there, though, and you girls, too, even after all these years."

"I know Mom enjoyed the services there," Rose said. "She liked everything about Mill River, especially how close the people are."

"Yes. I expect it's a very different place from New York in that way. It's easy to get lost in such a big city."

"Mmm." Rose pursed her lips and raised her eyebrows, and he couldn't tell whether she was agreeing with him or merely trying to avoid saying something unpleasant. He decided to push onward.

"Your mother was always worried about you being there," he told Rose. "She knew how it was in the city, you know."

"I know. She grew up in the Bronx," Rose said. "Father, I don't mean to be rude, but I keep getting the feeling that you're not just here to make polite conversation."

Father O'Brien drew a deep breath. "Well, that's true. I'm here partly because I'm wondering how you and your sister are doing with your mother's last directive. From what I've heard, things don't seem to be going too well."

"Ivy obviously put you up to visiting me. I should've known."

"Actually, I offered to speak with you, and she accepted my offer. That you and Emily haven't been following your mother's instructions is only one of the things she's worried about."

Rose sighed. "We're doing the best we can, Father. At least, I am. What my sister is doing is really not something I waste time worrying about. In fact, I can't stand the sight of her, so I try to avoid her as much as I can. There's still more than a month before Mom's deadline for finding her key, and these houses are hardly mansions. We *will* find it. You and Ivy needn't worry."

Father O'Brien nodded. "All right." He took the wrapped package from his lap and held it out to her. "I also told Ivy that I'd bring this to you. It's from your mother, something she wanted Ivy to give to you at the appropriate time."

"From my mother?" Rose reached forward to accept the package, her expression wary, almost disbelieving. "What is it?"

Father O'Brien shrugged. "I couldn't say, but I'm sure you'll want to open it in private."

Rose looked down at the package in her hand and chewed on her bottom lip.

"There's one last thing I wanted to talk with you about," Father O'Brien said. "It's a sensitive subject, but I'm going to be completely open with you. Your aunt Ivy is convinced that you're drinking quite a bit, Rose. She's afraid for you, and Alex, that it's spiraling out of control."

Rose's face snapped up and her eyes flashed. "I do NOT have a drinking problem, Father, and I take excellent care of my son. I always have."

"Your son seems very well cared for," he countered evenly, "but you do have a drinking problem, Rose, just as sure as Coke isn't the only thing in that glass you've got there. I know you've struggled with alcohol for a long time, ever since the accident." He watched as Rose rolled her eyes and looked away. "There are people who are ready and willing to help you, but you have to admit you have a problem and ask for help first."

"Father, I do not need help, and I'm not about to sit here and listen to this," Rose said, jumping up off the couch. "Maybe you've known my family since I was young, and maybe you were good friends with my mother, but you really don't know me. Not at all. You can't just come into my home and accuse me of being a . . . an alcoholic . . . and neglecting my child."

"No one has said you neglect your child." Father O'Brien

worked hard to keep his voice low and soothing. "And as for the drinking, I'm just stating a fact, as difficult as it is for you to hear. Any kind of addiction is hard to admit, I know."

"You know?" Rose asked. "*You* know *how*? Through your excellent armchair diagnosis?"

"Of course I'm not a physician, Rose," he said. "But I do have a very good idea of what you're dealing with. I've counseled many, many people with addictions . . . and I'm an addict myself." Father O'Brien paused after his last statement. He hadn't planned on openly stating that truth; indeed, it was the first time he had done so in decades. It had just slipped out, and now he waited to see Rose's reaction.

She raised her eyebrows. "*You're* an addict?"

He nodded solemnly. Rose's eyes narrowed, and he couldn't tell whether she was genuinely confused or trying to suppress a smile.

"Well, what's your poison, Father? Or is it a drug of some kind? Or maybe caffeine?"

"None of those, actually. I'm addicted to . . . stealing. Spoons, in particular. Although I'm currently in recovery."

Rose's mouth fell open. She stared at him for a few moments and then burst into laughter. "You're a priest and a . . . recovering spoon addict? That's hysterical, Father, really. Maybe the funniest thing I've ever heard. I'll be sure and lock up my flatware the next time you stop by." She continued to chuckle until she realized that he wasn't laughing or even smiling.

"It's not at all funny to me, Rose," he said. "Stealing anything compulsively is a very serious problem, just like yours is. You may not be prepared to acknowledge it yet, but I want you to think about what I've told you, and I want you to know that I face a similar struggle every day. So many times, an addict, particularly someone who is addicted to alcohol or drugs, doesn't ask for help until something awful happens. He or she ends up getting hurt or hurts someone else." Father O'Brien softened the tone of his voice even further, until he was almost pleading. "The accident all those years ago was enough tragedy for a lifetime, don't you think? I came here this afternoon because I don't want anything else, any other horrible thing, to happen to you, Rose, and neither does Ivy. But we can't help you unless you're willing to help yourself."

Rose clenched her jaw and remained silent.

Father O'Brien rose from his chair. "I'll see myself out." As he reached the front door, he turned back to look at Rose. She was still standing there, biting her lip again, with a pensive expression on her face. "Please think about what I've told you, and know that I'm one of those people who are ready to help you," he said to her. "You are in my prayers."

WITH FATHER O'BRIEN SAFELY OUT OF HER LIVING ROOM AND HER glass refilled, Rose sat down on the sofa and ripped the paper from the package he'd brought. The book of Shakespeare's plays inside was stiff and new, unlike the old copy her mother had used to induce sleep over the years.

Why would Mom want me to have this? Rose wondered. She flipped it open and removed a small photo that had been tucked within the pages. It was a picture of her and Emily as very young children nestled together on a beanbag in The Bookstop. They had a large picture book spread open across both their laps, and Emily was leaning against her shoulder with a pacifier in her mouth. She realized that the photo must have been taken soon after their arrival in Mill River.

A bright yellow caught her eye, and Rose turned her attention to the pages marked by the photo. A short passage from *Hamlet* had been highlighted.

To thine own self be true,
And it must follow, as the night the day,
Thou canst not then be false to any man.

"Really, Mom?" Rose said aloud. Angry tears began to dribble out of her eyes, and she glanced wildly up at the ceiling and around the room, trying to decide where to direct her voice. "Do you really think I don't try to do that? Do you not know that I wake up every day, *every fucking day,* and think about what I am, and what I've done, and how I can never go back and change things, even though I'd give anything for that chance?"

She slammed the book shut and threw it across the room. The photo that she had removed from it slipped from her fingers and fell, landing on the carpet facedown. Only then did she notice the familiar, elegant handwriting on the back of it. She plucked the picture off the floor and held it up to read.

Rose, it is never too late for a fresh start. It takes strength, bravery, humility, and a real desire to change, but it is never too late. You are and have always been capable of great things. I believe in you, and I love you. Mom

CHAPTER 30

"MOM, I NEED SOME MORE HANGERS," EMILY SAID. "ARE there extras in your closet? The shirts in the dryer are almost done, and I don't want them to get wrinkled."

"Goodness, Em, you didn't come all the way from San Francisco to do my laundry!"

"I know, but it was piled up in your room. I figured I'd help out, since you've had a rough week."

Josie sighed and turned from the living room window. "I did, and I appreciate it, sweetie. Old habits die hard, I guess."

"Me doing laundry, you mean? Or you working too much?"

"Both." Josie smiled as Emily rolled her eyes. "There are plenty of hangers in the closet. Help yourself."

Emily had just gone back upstairs when a car door slammed outside. Josie jumped up, took a deep breath, and slipped out the front door.

"Hey, Mom," Rose said as she climbed out of a shiny maroon BMW parked along the curb. She pushed her sunglasses back onto her head and smiled.

"Oh, Rosie, I'm so glad you're here. I've missed you." Josie walked to her older daughter and caught her up in a long embrace. "You're a little late. Was traffic bad?"

"It always sucks getting out of the city, but once I got into Westchester, it was a breeze."

"Well, you're here now. Let's go in. I've got some cold lemon-ade in the fridge." Josie was tempted to pull Rose by the arm, but her hands were so cold and clammy that she decided against it. Instead, she held the door open as her daughter maneuvered a small suitcase inside.

"Come sit down, honey," she said as she motioned Rose into the kitchen.

"Just let me stand a minute or two, Mom. I've been cramped up in the car for hours. I was going to hit a rest stop along the way, but since I was running late—"

Rose stopped speaking as the rapid thumping of someone de-scending the stairs sounded through the house. Her mouth opened slightly as she turned and saw Emily approaching the entrance to the kitchen.

"What is *she* doing here?" Rose whirled around and made eye contact with her before turning back to Emily.

"Mom? What's going on?" Emily held a cluster of clothes hangers in each hand. She stopped and started to backpedal as she stared at Rose.

"Girls, please, please, listen to me for a minute," Josie said. "Now that you're both here, I just want—"

"You want what?" Rose said. "For us to kiss and make up? God, I don't believe this."

"Is that why you begged me to come for a visit? For this little rendezvous?" Emily snorted. "I'm in the middle of a huge renova-tion. I had subcontractors and supplies scheduled to show up every day, and leaving totally put me behind schedule. You promised you'd never have us visit at the same time."

"Honey, I know, but it has been ten years," Josie said. "*Ten years* since the accident and since you've seen each other. I know it was a terrible thing, but this *separation* of yours has gone on too long."

"You've got to be kidding," Emily said. "I can't believe you would do this to me."

"You're sisters. You need each other," Josie said in a pleading voice. "I know you don't see it, but you do, and you will."

"Like hell we do," Rose said. "And I've said everything I intend to say about that night a long time ago. Now, if you'll excuse me, I'm leaving while I can still make it home before rush hour." She went back to the front door and snatched up the suitcase she'd brought inside.

"Rosie, please wait," Josie said, but Emily blocked her path. Her younger daughter shoved the clothes hangers into her arms before returning upstairs.

Josie fumbled around, clutching at the curved hooks as several of the wire hangers fell around her feet. By the time she got out the front door, Rose was back in her car with the engine running.

"Rose, please Rose!" she called, but her older daughter stepped on the gas and peeled down the street without looking at her. A few moments later, Emily came out the front door carrying a bulging backpack.

"I'm going to Ivy's. I'll be leaving in the morning, if the airline will let me change my ticket." Emily wiped at her eyes and started toward The Bookstop before Josie grabbed her arm.

"Em, please. I'm sorry I upset you. Won't you stay with me?"

Emily looked into her eyes for a long while. "You don't get it, Mom," she finally said. "Rose and me . . . it's not going to happen. It's not something you can fix, and it's about damn time you stopped trying."

Josie watched her run over to Ivy's and through the side door. She made it back inside her own home and had collapsed on the sofa when Ivy knocked softly and let herself in.

"It was a crazy, desperate idea, and you knew it probably

wouldn't work to bring them together like that, but at least you tried," Ivy said.

"I can't have them hate each other for the rest of their lives. It'll be the death of me, and they'll be so alone," Josie said. "I'll never give up on them. I can't. But I don't know what else I can do."

Ivy bent over to hug her and kiss her cheek. "Kid, you need to realize that you've done all you can."

2013

AS TIME PASSED AFTER HER FAILED ATTEMPT TO BRING THE GIRLS together, Josie found comfort in her little home in Mill River. Every room in the house held happy memories of the girls and their growing up. She could close her eyes and remember sitting with them at the kitchen table, sharing a meal or helping with homework. How many movies and holiday specials had they gathered to watch in front of the television in the living room? In the bathroom, she'd given them bubble baths when they were well, sponge baths when they'd had fevers, and lessons on how to apply makeup when they'd become teenagers. And their bedroom had always been her last stop before she herself had retired for the night.

Even during the hard early years, when the girls were young and she was always exhausted, and later, after her relationship with Rose had started to become more confrontational, she had never grown tired of watching their beautiful faces as they slept. She still sometimes paused at their old room on her way to bed. She could almost hear the giggles and whispers of two sisters sharing their dreams.

In the years that she'd been an empty-nester, Josie had continued to build her already successful real estate business. She now employed a dozen salespeople at her brokerage and still handled listings herself. It was a rare treat for her to have any time off, but today, the first Wednesday in March and the day after Mill River's annual town meeting, Josie stayed home from work. Still wearing her pajamas and robe, she poured a fresh cup of coffee and settled herself on the sofa.

Today, however, she was not staying home to relax or to catch up on sleep or errands. She was expecting an important phone call, and it was not the type of call she wished to receive at work, or anywhere in public for that matter.

She focused her gaze on the phone sitting on the end table closest to her. At the same time, her hand moved to softly, gingerly touch the small lump in her left breast. It had been exactly a week since she'd discovered it in the shower, and beneath her pajamas, the area was now bruised and sore from the needle biopsy she'd endured two days ago.

For those two days, she'd experienced wildly vacillating emotions. Fear and worry dominated, of course, and not only for herself, but also for Rose and Emily. She knew very well that a cancer diagnosis for her would mean that her girls would be at much higher risk of developing it themselves. For that reason, even though her preference would have been to keep any diagnosis of cancer and subsequent treatment to herself, she would have to tell Rose and Emily about it, if the biopsy was positive.

If.

In her mind, she had already rehearsed a thousand times how she would tell them.

There was also the fear of what treatment she might have to endure, and whether it would ultimately be successful. What would happen to her girls if cancer took her life? After watching her suffer through a terrible illness, they would be alone. Permanently alone. Without her being there, goading and encouraging them, the tiny chance of Rose and Emily reconciling at some point would surely drop to zero.

The phone suddenly shrieked on the table next to her. Josie

flinched so severely that some of the coffee in her mug sloshed onto her lap.

"Hello?" she said, even though she recognized her doctor's number in the caller ID window. When she began speaking, Josie just listened, trying to focus on the doctor's words over the pounding of her heart. When she heard the words "benign" and "fibroadenoma," she gasped with relief. It seemed that she had been holding her breath, because for several minutes after she hung up the phone, she remained on the sofa, trembling, breathing deeply, and wiping away tears of relief.

The nightmare scenarios and the painful conversations she had envisioned during the past few days slowly, slowly began to fade from the center of her thoughts.

Eager to encourage this, Josie actively sought something else to think about. She began to reflect on the town meeting that had taken place during the prior evening. At the time, with her mind clouded with worry, it had been impossible to feel fully the extraordinary warmth of what had happened. Now, though, bathed in relief, Josie could fully appreciate the love and kindness that had been shown to so many.

The town meeting had started the same as any other she could remember, with Fitz calling the meeting to order, working his way through the votes on town business and the other items on the agenda. But then, Father O'Brien had stepped forward to read a note from Mary McAllister, the old woman who had lived for some seventy years in the big white house overlooking the town. Josie had heard all the rumors about Mary over the years, of course— that she was a witch, or perhaps suffering from some sort of serious illness. Like almost everyone else in attendance, Josie had been moved to tears to hear Mary's tragic story, to learn about her great generosity. She knew now that her own home, the little house that had miraculously dropped into her lap all those years ago, had in fact been given to her by Mary. The old widow had loved Mill River and its people, and she'd done what she could to help them despite the agoraphobia and severe social anxiety disorder that had kept her isolated in her home.

At the town meeting, Mary had managed to find a way to speak directly to the townspeople from beyond the grave, to express her love for the neighbors she'd cared about for years but had never been able to meet in person. Josie found Mary's determination and success at achieving such a lifelong goal incredibly inspiring. She likened Mary's longtime struggle to her own lengthy effort to get Rose and Emily to end their estrangement from each other.

Josie blamed herself that something so terrible had happened to ruin her daughters' once-close relationship. For a few years, after she'd gotten them all settled in Mill River, it had seemed as if everything would be fine, but now, in hindsight, with her family splintered and no reconciliation in sight, she could see that she'd been foolish to believe that. Even worse, Josie realized, was the fact that she was getting older. The same years that etched lines more deeply into her face also widened the chasm between her girls. And, even though it had turned out that she didn't have breast cancer, she had a new appreciation of her own mortality. She now feared that her life would end without her daughters finding a way back to each other.

Josie thought again of Mary McAllister and how the old woman had set in motion a plan triggered by her death, a plan to achieve her goal to finally communicate with her fellow townspeople. Could she follow Mary's example to help Rose and Emily?

With her hand covering the gold locket around her neck, Josie rose from the sofa. She would wait a few days before calling Jim Gasaway, just to make sure she had thought through everything, but deep down, she knew what she had to do. Long ago, she had saved her children from a fire. Now, she would make good on her promise to Tony by doing whatever it took to save them again. If, upon her death, the girls hadn't realized the importance of their relationship, this last-ditch effort to bring about their reconciliation would remind them of the treasure they still had in each other.

"THANK YOU, FRED. I APPRECIATE YOUR BRINGING THE CERTIFIcate by in person," Ivy said. "You've always been there for me."

Dr. Richardson nodded and hugged her before opening the front door of The Bookstop. "I know you've got a rough time ahead of you, my dear, so you call me if you need anything else."

After the doctor left, Ivy leaned on her cane and looked again at the document she held in her other hand. It was still a shock to see an official death certificate with Josie's name written at the top and Fred's signature as the regional medical examiner at the bottom. Her niece's house next door was dark and quiet, but it still felt as if she could pop through the kitchen door for an impromptu visit any minute. In the coming days, though, as Josie's wake was planned, as Rose and Emily arrived to pay their final respects to their mother, the fact that she was gone would sink in and become real for all of them.

CHAPTER 31

From his room, Alex had heard bits of his mother's conversation with Father O'Brien. He lay on the bed on his stomach with a book open under his chin, but he hadn't read a word. He'd been surprised by how much the priest had known about how his mother acted, and by Father O'Brien's complete honesty. The priest had told his mother exactly what he himself longed to be able to say to her, and he'd done it without raising his voice or being intimidated.

Alex was impressed.

He'd thought a lot about his mother and her drinking, especially since the fistfight between his mother and his aunt, and since Aunt Ivy had told him why they didn't get along. He was still struggling with his own feelings about it. Mostly, he felt sad and sorry for both his mother and his aunt.

As much as it made him feel like a traitor to his mother, he sympathized with his aunt Emily. His grandmother's death was the first he'd ever faced, and it had been awful. He couldn't be sure, but he guessed that it had been just as bad for Aunt Emily, or worse, when her boyfriend had been killed. Plus, he was willing to bet Aunt Emily understood exactly how his mother was with alcohol and how awful he felt every time he watched his mother pour a drink.

And yet, his love for his mother was stronger than everything else. Alex knew in his bones that his mother loved him just as much, and he longed for a way to help her stop drinking. If it were only possible to help her separate out the part that needed alcohol so badly, everything would be so much better. But, he didn't know how to help her. He wasn't brave enough to confront her, not like Father O'Brien had been, and he was terrified of telling anyone about the situation for fear that he would be taken away from her. Alex sighed and rested his chin on his open book.

I wish she could get out of here, Alex thought, but he knew his mother was effectively trapped either until the end of August or until she and his aunt found his grandmother's safe-deposit-box key. He scrunched his eyes shut and wished again that he could figure out where the key was. His aunt Emily hadn't said anything to him about finding it in her own yard, so maybe she was ready to lend him the metal detector.

For a few minutes, Alex lost himself in his fantasy of discovering the key, of presenting it to his mother. The sound of his mother yelling interrupted his daydream. He listened more intently, heard the yelling become crying, and wondered whether he should go try to comfort her, but then the sound of his mother's phone ringing pierced his thought. He knew by the ringtone—the familiar theme song from *Seinfeld*—that the caller was his father.

He crept to the doorway of his room, where his mother's voice carried up the stairs and was most easily heard.

"Things are fine, Sheldon, really. No, we haven't found— *what?*"

There was a pause, and Alex knew his mother was trying to keep from crying on the phone.

"You do *not* need to come up here. He's *fine, and I'm not drinking.*"

Another pause.

"And what will *you* do with Alex in New York? How will you

look for jobs with him there? You said yourself—I told you, I'm *fine,* and so is he. I don't care if you don't believe me. Alex going back with you won't work. I need him here. I *need*—Sheldon? *Sheldon?"*

He heard his mother curse, followed by what sounded like her phone hitting the wall.

Alex knew then what was going to happen. His father was coming for him. He didn't know when, and he didn't particularly want to ask his mother right now. But, it was clear that his remaining time in Mill River, and his opportunity to find his grandmother's key, was slipping away.

The familiar *thunk* of a cork being pried from a wine bottle triggered a fresh wave of frustration. It was only just after noon, but his mother seemed to be preparing to take to the sofa already. His suspicion was confirmed when he heard the floor squeak as she walked from the kitchen into the living room.

Think about the metal detector, Alex told himself as he closed his eyes. *Maybe there's still time.* He would read for a little while, until his mother had fallen asleep, and then he'd go next door to see his aunt.

For the first time that day, he focused his attention on his book. It was *To Kill a Mockingbird,* one of the old books his mother had let him have when they'd first moved in. He'd been reading the books in the house as quickly as he could, and he was halfway done going through the tattered copies in the box from The Bookstop.

Alex found the place in the text where he'd left off. When he turned the page to begin the next chapter, though, he was surprised to see that a number of the passages were highlighted in neon yellow. At first, he ignored the markings. As he devoured the words, though, Alex realized that all of the marked passages had to do with gifts and trinkets that were left for the young protagonist and her brother by the town's resident recluse. All of the presents had appeared in a knothole in an oak tree on the edge of the recluse's yard.

An oak tree.

Alex raised his head and looked toward his desk, where the copies of his aunt's list and the one he had prepared were neatly stacked. He didn't need to pick them up or read them again to realize that he had somehow forgotten to include the old books from the box in his own inventory or to recall that his mother had highlighted more than half of the items on his spreadsheet and the list he'd gotten from his aunt Emily before she'd given up trying to eliminate certain items as clues. Alex's hands broke out in a cold sweat, and he began to feel jittery. His mother had a habit of high-lighting *everything,* and here was a book that had been placed in her house, with passages marked in a way that would catch her attention. Maybe he was onto something.

Alex climbed off the bed and walked to his bedroom window, which faced his aunt Emily's house. He couldn't see much of his aunt's house, though, because the large oak tree, the one from which his aunt had hung the tire swing, rose up past his window, obscuring his view.

He reached over to pick up the book and then closed his eyes, concentrating on recalling certain passages in his grandmother's letter. *"The clues are two different objects. One will reveal the location of the key to my safe-deposit box . . . and the other is something that will help you obtain it . . ."*

Alex opened his eyes and looked again out the window, into the thick leaves of the oak.

The key was hidden in the tree. The book revealed the location, he was sure of it. Now he needed only to figure out the *"object"* that his grandmother had promised would help him *"obtain it."*

Alex stole downstairs as quietly as he could. He peeked around the corner into the living room, where his mother was stretched out and snoring. Part of him wanted to shake her awake and shout out his revelation, but the other part of him was still enmeshed in the fantasy of finding his grandmother's key all on his own. Maybe he could have it both ways, by waking her without telling her exactly why, so that she could come watch him find the key.

"Mom?" he said, gently rubbing her arm. "Mom, could you come outside and help me with something? Mom?"

His mother squeezed her eyes tighter closed without opening them. ". . . so tired, Alex." Her voice was faint, her words slurred. "Can it wait 'til later?"

"It's really important, Mom, and I think it'll make you really happy." Alex rubbed his mother's arm again, but the only reply he received was a deep sigh and a soft snore as she turned her face toward the back of the sofa.

Despite his sense of urgency, he knew from experience that any further attempt to rouse her would be useless. So often since his father had lost his job, his mother had collapsed on the sofa, sluggish and heavily intoxicated. He still remembered the first time he saw her do that—the day after his father had arrived home from work early with a box of his belongings. They'd had a huge argument that night, and he'd never heard his parents scream at each other for so long.

Before that, his mother had been more normal. She'd usually been up and cheerful when he arrived home from school, eagerly asking him about his day. Back then, she cracked jokes and hosted a ladies' book club and sometimes even cooked him dinner herself.

What if I find the key? It would fix everything, he thought. *We could all go back to New York together when Dad gets here, and Mom would become her old self again.*

As he stood looking down at her, wishing that she would suddenly wake up and come outside with him, another, more unpleasant, thought found its way through his disappointment. *What if I'm wrong?* If he succeeded in getting her up and the key wasn't in the tree, she'd be angry and disappointed. *No,* he decided, *it's better to look for it by myself.* Quickly, he slipped out the back door and over to the large oak. His aunt's car wasn't parked along the curb, so he really was on his own.

For a few minutes, he circled the trunk, looking it up and down as far as he could see, but there was no knothole in view. He thought for a moment and then went back inside his house. When he came out, he carried the binoculars his aunt had given him. Again, he walked around the base of the tree, this time stepping back so that he could inspect the higher parts of the trunk through his binoculars. He stopped just before he walked into the tire swing, but avoiding a collision wasn't the reason for his sudden halt.

He had spotted a small, dark knothole perhaps five feet above the branch supporting the swing.

"Help you obtain it," Alex mused.

What did he need to obtain the key, if it was in the knothole? Alex lowered the binoculars and looked past the tree toward his aunt Emily's garage. There was a ladder in there, the one she'd used to put up the tire swing. And, a ladder was something that he and his mother hadn't found in their own house. He walked over to his aunt's garage. The overhead door was down and closed, but there was a small door into the garage on the side. He reached for the doorknob and turned it.

The door opened.

The aluminum ladder was resting against a wall. It was heavier than he thought it would be, but he was able to tip it sideways against his body and drag it through the door. Once he had it beneath the oak, he laid it in the grass and tried to pull the rails apart. The joints in the spreaders were stiff, though, and only by pushing against them with his foot was he able to straighten them.

With the ladder now opened all the way, he grabbed one side of it and pulled it upright. Next, he dragged the ladder so that it was positioned under the limb supporting the tire swing and far enough from the tree's trunk and roots to be on even ground. Alex leaned some of his weight against the ladder to test its steadiness, and he smiled when it remained firmly in place. Finally, he removed the binoculars from around his neck, left them propped against the base of the tree trunk, and began to climb.

Alex had never been up on a ladder before, and he found his heart beating faster and faster with each step he left behind. The limb was a few feet above the cap of the ladder. He would have to step on the top step, and then on the cap, the very top of the ladder, to climb onto it, but from his current height, he could already touch the limb and use it to steady himself as he ascended. Carefully, he stretched his hands out to the limb and placed one foot on the top step. On the count of three, he stepped up, on the top step and then cap, before quickly swinging a leg up and over the limb.

Once astride it, Alex paused to catch his breath and think through his next move. He would have to stand up on the limb in order to reach the knothole. Facing the tree trunk, he scooted forward until it was less than an arm's length from his body. With his hands gripping the limb and trying not to look down, he brought one knee up onto the limb and then the other. Slowly, he reached out to the trunk for balance, put one leg in front of him with his foot flat on the limb, and raised himself into a standing position.

It was an amazing feeling, balancing untethered on his perch. He had never been up so high without being inside a building or a structure of some kind. His senses were heightened. He could see clear up and down the street. His ears could pinpoint the location of cicadas in the branches above him, and with the energy coursing through his body, it seemed as if he could almost leap onto the rooftops of the houses in the neighborhood. But, he reminded himself, he had gotten up here to do something much more important.

Now, the knothole was just above his head. He couldn't quite see into it, but he could easily get a hand in. Alex took a deep breath and reached into the hole.

His fingertips felt the hard, prickly tips of twigs, the brittle edges of dried leaves, and then something softer. He closed his hand around the softness and pulled out a small tuft of fur. He startled and fell against the trunk, thinking at first that he'd grabbed some living thing, and the fur slipped from his hand and landed silently on the grass below. *Did I stick my hand in a squirrel's nest?*

Alex stood still for a few minutes to calm himself. Hoping whatever had made its home in the hole wasn't still in there, he reached in again. This time, he felt something smooth with a distinct edge. *A Ziploc bag,* he thought, as he carefully grasped it and lifted it from the knothole.

It *was* a sandwich-size plastic bag. As he held it up before his eyes, he was almost afraid to believe what he was seeing. Inside the clear plastic was a gold locket—the one he remembered his grandmother always wearing—with a small silver key also strung on the chain.

"Yeeeaaaah!" he yelled, but the sound of his joy was muted by the rush of oak leaves building to a crescendo in a burst of summer wind. For just a moment, he was on the Wonder Wheel again, flying with his mother on top of the world.

Although he was giddy with excitement and eager to show her what he'd found, Alex realized that he had to be careful about climbing down. He would need both hands to get back on the ladder, but he was wearing a T-shirt and knit shorts, neither of which had a pocket. He thought about dropping the locket and key down to the lawn, but he couldn't bring himself to let go of them. Carefully, he sat back down to straddle the limb and removed the necklace from the Baggie. The chain was just long enough that he could slip it over his head.

Now that the key was safe, he released the plastic bag into the breeze and scooted backward on the limb until he could see the top of the ladder. For some reason, it seemed to be much further below the limb than it had on the way up. Alex leaned forward until the front of his shirt touched bark. Slowly, keeping most of his weight on his stomach, he slid his left leg back over the limb and allowed his right leg to drop down until he felt his toe make contact with the ladder.

With the ball of his foot squarely on the cap of the ladder, he raised himself from the limb and transferred his weight to it. *So far, so good,* he thought. Next, he tried to bring his left leg back over the limb and down, but the rubber-soled heel of his tennis shoe caught on the bark. That slight hitch was enough to throw him off balance. He lurched backward and felt the ladder tip, felt himself falling backward. He clutched at the limb, scratching the bark with his fingernails. The hands that sought something, anything to grab on to closed around nothing at all.

CARRYING THE BASKET SHE'D ASSEMBLED FOR ROSE, DAISY trudged along toward Maple Street. It had turned out to be heavier than she'd expected, especially now that she'd been lugging it for several blocks. When she reached the corner outside the bakery-café, she stopped, setting down the basket and thinking how thankful she was for the occasional breeze that cooled her face and tousled her hair.

"Daisy? Do you need help?"

Claudia Simon came up beside her and pointed down at the basket. "That looks heavy. Let me give you a hand."

"Oh, Miss Claudia, would you? I'm just taking it around the block, up to Miss Rose's house, but it's harder than I thought it'd be."

"No problem. I was just on my way to Ruth's to get coffee, but I can easily swing by after we drop this off." Claudia took one side of the basket's handle, and Daisy grabbed the other. "So, what's this for? Is it a gift?"

"Sort of. It's to apologize, for what happened at her mother's wake. I . . . I spilled her mother's ashes." She looked down at her shoes, watching as her feet moved over the concrete squares of the sidewalk.

"Oh, right. I heard what happened. But Daisy, it was an accident. Surely Rose understands that. And, I've also heard that Rose has a terrible temper. Maybe it's not such a good idea for you to approach her again."

Daisy shook her head. "I know Miss Rose is still pretty angry with me, but what happened *is* my fault. To tell you the truth, Miss Claudia, I don't think she wants to forgive me. I don't think she likes me very much. But, I feel bad about what happened, and I'm going to try one more time to make up for it. If this doesn't work, I'll at least be happy that I tried my best, and I won't worry anymore about what she thinks of me."

"That's very wise, Daisy." Daisy looked at Claudia and was surprised to see the corners of her mouth turned up in a wistful smile. "I wish I didn't worry so much about what people think about *me*. Certain people, anyway."

"You just have to learn to be happy with yourself, Miss Claudia. I'm a little different than most people. You know, with the way I can make potions and such. It took me a long time to accept that, and to realize that if you love yourself just the way you are, what other people think of you doesn't matter much. And now, I'm happy most of the time." Daisy grinned as they rounded the corner onto Rose's block.

When she and Claudia first spotted an overturned ladder beneath the oak tree in front of the DiSanti sisters' houses, Daisy thought nothing of it. As they came closer, though, she saw the form of a boy splayed out along one side of it. He was lying on his back with a leg bent beneath his body. His face was turned away from her, but she could see a pair of glasses resting on his cheek, still hooked behind one of his ears.

It was Miss Rose's son, Alex.

Daisy and Claudia dropped the basket on the sidewalk and ran to him. While Claudia felt for a pulse and checked to see whether he was breathing, Daisy touched the little boy's cheek, then his shoulder, but she didn't know whether they were strong enough to move him or if they should even try.

"Alex?" Daisy said as a feeling of panic rose up into her throat, but the boy remained motionless.

"He's alive," Claudia said, "but we need to get help, and I don't have my phone with me."

Daisy stood up and looked around. Emily's house was quiet and her car was gone, but Rose's black BMW was parked along the curb. She raced to her front door.

"Miss Rose! Miss Rose!" she screamed. She rang the doorbell and pounded on the front door as hard as she could. "Miss Rose, come quick, it's Alex! He's hurt, Miss Rose!"

When the door finally opened, Rose looked as if she had been sound asleep. "What?" she snapped. "What do you mean, Alex is hurt?"

"He's on the ground over there," Daisy said as she pointed. "There, under the tree. Miss Claudia and I found him lying there—" she started to say, but Rose pushed past her and ran toward the oak.

"Alex? Oh, God, Alex!" She knelt down by her son, touching his face, his hair. "Baby, wake up. Wake up, Alex." Suddenly, her head snapped up. "Call an ambulance!" she yelled. "Get over to Ivy's and call 9-1-1!"

Daisy nodded and took off again. She reached the front porch of The Bookstop just as Ivy and Father O'Brien were coming outside.

"We need . . . ambulance," she gasped, breathing heavily. "Miss Rose's little boy . . . under the tree."

Father O'Brien took one look at her and then glanced across the street to where Claudia and Rose were on their knees in the grass. "Go to them," he said to her and Ivy. "I'll call for help."

IN THE HUGE CENTRAL ROOM OF THE MCALLISTER MANSION, Emily was working on refinishing the wood floors. All the furniture and carpets had been moved into the adjacent rooms, leaving only a vast open space. She'd rented a power sander and was just about done with a first pass over the floor. She still had to finish the edges of the room and buff and vacuum the bare wood, but she planned to start on those steps in the morning.

Emily switched off the sander and was surprised to hear a siren. She went to the window and looked down just in time to see an ambulance coming up Main Street. Sirens were rare in Mill River. Her heart rose into her throat as she watched the ambulance turn from Main Street and drive a few blocks before turning again, this time onto Maple Street. She gathered up her things and ran outside. The ambulance had slowed by The Bookstop, and she was terrified it had been called for Ivy.

As her own hatchback was finally out at Russell's for much-needed repairs, she had been using Ruth's car to get to and from the marble mansion. Now, she drove the borrowed car back into town as quickly as she dared. When she turned onto Maple Street herself, she was shocked to see the ambulance, with lights still flashing, parked not outside The Bookstop, but in front of her own house. Her aunt Ivy, Father O'Brien, Claudia Simon, and Daisy, along with a few other people, were clustered on the sidewalk watching a stretcher being loaded into the back. She couldn't see who was on the stretcher, but her mouth opened in shock as she watched her sister climb in after it. There would be only one reason Rose would voluntarily get into an ambulance.

Alex.

Emily parked the car and jumped out, but the ambulance pulled away before she reached the bystanders. "I saw it coming over here while I was working at the McAllister house. What happened?" she asked as she came up beside her great-aunt.

"Nobody's sure, but we think Alex fell out of that tree." Ivy rubbed her eyes, and Emily saw that tears were working their way down the crevices on her face. "Daisy and Claudia happened to be coming by and found him in the grass, unconscious. He still wasn't awake when they left with him."

"They're taking him to Rutland Regional?"

"Probably," Ivy said. "I know things have been difficult between you and Rose, but she's totally alone right now. Given the situation, I think we should all go to the hospital, too."

Father O'Brien nodded his agreement.

Claudia seemed to take this suggestion as her cue to leave. She embraced Emily and Ivy and urged them to call her if there was anything she could do to help.

As Claudia made her way down the sidewalk, Emily watched Ivy talking quietly with Father O'Brien. She was anxious and afraid. Of course she understood that her great-aunt would find his company comforting at a time like this, but she didn't at all like thinking about a priest in a hospital. Too often, it was an image of last rites and imminent death, and she couldn't bear the thought of losing her nephew. Still, neither her fear nor her discomfort would stop her from going with them.

"All right," she said finally. "My car's in the shop, but if we can take your car, Aunt Ivy, I'll drive."

"Actually, if you can drop me by the parish house on the way, I'll drive separately in my truck," Father O'Brien said. "It might be better to have more than one vehicle."

On any other day, Emily might have tried to discourage the elderly priest from getting behind the wheel, but today she only nodded.

"Let me get my keys and purse," Ivy said. "It'll just take a minute." She hurried back across the street.

Daisy was standing, listening to the plans being made and holding a large basket of vegetables and preserves. "I was bringing this to Miss Rose," she explained as she caught sight of Emily's curious look. "Miss Claudia was helping me carry it. I wanted to try to apologize one last time."

"That's so kind of you, Daisy. Your being here just at the right time probably saved Alex, you know." Daisy blushed, causing the reddish birthmark that curled up onto her cheek to become a little less noticeable. "I wonder if you'd be willing to do me a huge favor? I haven't fed Gus or taken him for his evening walk yet, and I have no idea how long I'll be at the hospital. Could you take care of Gus for me until I'm back?"

"Oh, Miss Emily, I'd be happy to." Daisy's teary eyes lit up. "He could even stay with me. I just know Smudgie would love to have company, too!"

Emily ran into her house. She threw a few cans of dog food into a plastic grocery sack, put Gus on his leash, and hurried back outside. "Here he is," she said as she handed the food and leash to Daisy. Gus wagged his tail and whined, eager for attention.

"Don't you worry, Miss Emily. I'll take good care of him for as long as you need me to. It'll be like a doggie daycare!" Daisy reached out to stroke his head. "I hope little Alex is okay," she added.

"Me too, Daisy, and thank you again, so much," Emily said, just as Ivy came huffing across the street with her purse on her arm. "After we drop off Father O'Brien, we'll give you and Gus a ride to your place so you don't have to lug that basket all the way back."

On the short drive to Rutland, she didn't say much, preferring to remain silent while Ivy wondered aloud what had possessed Alex to climb up into the oak tree. Emily was terrified for her nephew and plagued by a sense of déjà vu as they approached the hospital. It was the same feeling of dread she'd had when Andy had died and Rose had been the one who was hurt. Just as it did back then, the drive seemed to take forever, as if time were moving backward in an attempt to shield them from the agony ahead.

At the hospital, they walked together into the emergency entrance and then the waiting room, the place where her world had fallen apart so long ago. As she looked at the rows of identical chairs, the dull industrial carpeting, and the stacks of worn magazines, Emily struggled to push away the memories that came flooding back. *Now isn't the time,* she told herself. *We're here for Alex. You need to stay positive for him.*

There were only a few people in the waiting area. Rose was among them, sitting hunched forward and tense in a chair off to the side.

"Rose?" Ivy said, and they started toward her, but almost at the same time, a man wearing scrubs came into the waiting room and called out, "Ms. Frye?"

Rose immediately jumped up and went to him, and Emily and Ivy moved closer. Still with her back to them, Rose was listening to the doctor and nodding, but Emily was able to hear what he was saying.

". . . results of the CT scan. Your son has an epidural hematoma. What that means is that he has bleeding inside his skull that's causing pressure to build up on his brain. Alex needs to have surgery to relieve that pressure as soon as possible. We've alerted neurosurgery at Fletcher Allen in Burlington, and we have a DHART helicopter en route to transport him there. It should be arriving here in a few minutes."

"Will I . . . can I ride with him? Please let me go with him," Rose asked in a shaky voice.

"That shouldn't be a problem," the doctor said. "Stay here, in the waiting area. A nurse will be down in a few minutes to escort you to the helipad."

Rose nodded again as the doctor hurried off, but she didn't move from where she was standing.

"Rosie, honey?" Ivy said. Emily watched as her great-aunt went to put an arm around her sister. "We heard what the doctor said just now. Have you seen Alex since you got here?"

Rose shook her head and glanced back over her shoulder to where Emily was standing. Her face was splotchy and red, and she was still crying uncontrollably.

"Have you gotten hold of Sheldon?" Ivy asked.

Rose nodded. "Not yet, but I've left messages," she managed to say between sobs. "Oh, Aunt Ivy, this is all my fault." She fell into Ivy's arms, and Emily watched as her great-aunt tried to comfort her sister.

"No, honey, it's not," Ivy said, smoothing Rose's disheveled blonde hair. "Kids do things like climbing trees all the time. It's a part of being a kid, and this is just one of those crazy accidents that sometimes happen."

"No," Rose said. "It wasn't an accident. Earlier, he was wanting me to come outside with him, and I didn't go." She uncurled her fist and held out her hand. "He was wearing this. He figured it out, found it all by himself. It must've been hidden in the tree."

Emily took a step closer as she and Ivy stared into her sister's open hand. She saw the sparkle of gold and silver—a familiar locket, and a key engraved with "338" that was unmistakably real.

CHAPTER 32

As soon as she got home, Claudia tried to call Kyle to tell him about what happened to Alex. He didn't answer his phone, though, and the receptionist at the station told her he wasn't there. *Probably on patrol again,* she thought. Even though she felt anxious and unsettled, and her thoughts kept drifting back to the horrible image of the little boy lying unconscious in the grass, she finally decided to head into Rutland as she had planned.

At JCPenney, Claudia found some cute shirts and a new pair of running shoes, but as she paid for her things and looked out of the storefront into the mall, she was forced to admit that, after Alex's accident, her heart really wasn't into clothes shopping. She still needed to stop for groceries, though. The inside of her refrigerator was looking pretty empty, and the big Hannaford supermarket had a nice salad bar and a better selection of produce than the small grocery store in Mill River.

Maybe it was because she was so concerned about Alex, or because she had committed the cardinal dieting sin of shopping while she was hungry, but when Claudia emerged from the supermarket, there was a box of Entenmann's cake donuts in one of her bags. Oh, she'd bought plenty of fruit and vegetables, too, but it had been such a long time since she'd allowed herself her favorite sweet. *I'll ration them out,* Claudia thought. *One each day, after exercising, and I'll keep the box in the car to avoid temptation.*

On the way home, she passed the King's Lodge, the fancy restaurant where Kyle had taken her for Valentine's Day. She felt warm and tingly remembering the wonderful dinner they'd had . . . and the unforgettable night together that had followed. It was a welcome distraction from her worry.

She was almost back to Mill River when she thought again of the vandalism complaint Kyle had handled. He'd said something about damage to Rose DiSanti's lawn, about the word "lush" being burned into it. She and Daisy hadn't made it as far as Rose's house, and she was suddenly curious to see it for herself. She felt a little silly acquiescing to the urge to gawk, but vandalism of any kind was such a rarity in Mill River. It would take her only a few minutes to drive by and get a glimpse of what had happened. *In fact, I can get a little something for Alex at The Bookstop while I'm over there,* she thought. She remembered that Rose had mentioned how much he liked to read, so a couple of books would be the perfect get-well gift.

As she came into Mill River, Claudia turned onto Maple Street. The Bookstop was on one side of her car and Rose's house on the other, and she slowed her car and peered out the window at the front yard. *Someone sure did a number on it,* she thought. Just as Kyle had said, the word "lush" was visible in the lawn, with the letters being formed by swaths of dead, yellow grass. Strangely, though, the grass surrounding the letters seemed to be dying, too. It was wilted, and patches were beginning to turn a brownish-yellow, although none was yet the same hue as the letters. It was almost as if someone had purposely poured weed killer over the whole lawn in an attempt to hide the word written there.

Claudia didn't want to pause too long in front of the house lest she raise suspicion of any kind, so she stepped on the accelerator after a few moments of creeping along at idle speed. She had only gone perhaps another fifty feet, though, when she slammed on the brakes.

Kyle's truck was parked along the curb right in front of Emily DiSanti's house.

Her first thought was that it couldn't possibly be Kyle's pickup, since he was still supposed to be at work. But, there was no mistaking that the truck was his. She stared at the familiar dent on the left rear fender, the result of a close encounter with a shopping cart. As she eased up on the brake and slowly passed the vehicle, she saw the Mill River Elementary bumper sticker pasted on the back, the one she'd sent home with Rowen last year. Right next to it was the green license plate with the number she knew by heart.

With her mind reeling, Claudia drove the rest of the way down the street and pulled over just before the intersection. She was craning her neck around to look back at Kyle's truck when Emily's front door opened. She gripped the steering wheel and stared, still not quite believing what she was seeing. Kyle came out, looked around quickly, and jogged to his truck. Slowly, certain other facts registered in Claudia's brain.

The sedan Emily had been driving earlier was parked right behind Kyle's truck, which meant that even if Emily had gone to the hospital in Rutland, she was home now.

Kyle wasn't wearing his police uniform.

Rowen wasn't with him.

Claudia pulled away from the curb, gunned the engine, and headed back to Main Street. She needed to get home, to process what she'd just seen.

Something's been going on, she thought as she pulled back into her driveway. She grabbed her shopping bags from the back of her car and slammed the hatchback. She barely made it inside before starting to cry.

If she hadn't seen what she'd just seen, she never would have believed Kyle to be capable of cheating on her. How could she have been so stupid, and so blind? There had to have been signs— maybe she'd missed them, or talked herself out of any suspicions. Obviously, she'd misjudged Kyle and underestimated her own naïveté. He'd been her first real relationship, her first love, her first everything. She should have realized that no one was as perfect as Kyle had seemed. No real relationship happened just like magic and worked out happily ever after, like a fairy tale.

Claudia pressed her back up against her refrigerator and slid down until she was sitting on the floor next to the bags of groceries. She glared at the stalks of celery and the crisp green lettuce that protruded from them. What was the point? All the hard work to change the way she cooked, to deprive herself of delicious things, to fight with herself over running every morning seemed to have been a huge waste of time. When she'd been fat, no one had been attracted to her. Now that she was a healthy weight, it seemed that the only men interested in her were stalkers like Leroy and cheating scumbags like Kyle.

What other reason would there be for him to be over at Emily's? she wondered.

Emily. Claudia felt a growing disgust as she thought back then to the first time she'd met her—at Josie DiSanti's wake. She'd felt such empathy for her, standing alone in Josie's living room while her older sister had the support of a husband and son. On the day Emily had moved to Mill River, she'd actually schlepped her belongings into her house. She'd offered to introduce her to her circle of friends. And just this morning, after Alex's accident, she'd hugged Emily in a genuine attempt to comfort her, never guessing that the redheaded harlot had apparently been doing some comforting of a different kind. Emily's behavior in the face of the kindness she had extended was especially appalling.

Sticking up from the grocery bag furthest from her, Claudia saw a white cardboard corner. Almost without thinking, she jumped to her feet and grabbed it. Before another ten seconds had passed, she was standing at her kitchen counter and had poured herself a tall glass of milk. She opened the Entenmann's box and began to salivate. There were a dozen donuts before her. Claudia's hand hovered just above the neatly stacked rings of cinnamon-sugar- and powdered-sugar-coated bliss. Her indecision lasted only a moment, and the powdered sugar won.

It had been so long since she'd allowed herself even a single donut. She couldn't remember the last time she had truly eaten with abandon, particularly of things that were not normally on her list of acceptable foods. She did not intend to stop with a single donut this time. Claudia chose one of the powdered sugar variety, broke off a piece, dunked it in her milk, and shoved it in her mouth. The soft sweetness was beyond delicious. It extended up around her teeth, down her throat, and out through her limbs. It was the perfect way to push away the hurt she felt, at least for a few minutes.

After she had eaten another three donuts, she paused to swig some milk. She didn't care that cinnamon and powdered sugar dotted the front of her shirt or that crumbs littered her counter and the kitchen floor. Perhaps it was because the huge infusion of sugar was beginning to kick in, but it felt *so good* to eat.

When the box was half-empty, the first daggers of anger began to make their way through her sugar high. Claudia began to chew a little more slowly. Now that she had wised up, she resolved to act quickly to keep the upper hand and preserve what remained of her self-respect. At the very least, she deserved an explanation, and she realized how fortunate it was that Kyle was unaware he'd been caught in the act.

Claudia sniffed and lifted a plain cake donut from the box. She would blindside him with the truth. Once she had eaten her fill—which she hadn't come close to doing yet—she would call Kyle. She would invite him, no, she would *demand* that he come over. And when he did, she would confront him over his visit to Emily.

Regardless of whether he spluttered an admission or tried to lie his way out, and even if he begged for her forgiveness, she would look him in the eye and dump his sorry ass.

ROSE SAT IN THE WAITING ROOM OF THE SURGICAL WING OF VERmont Children's Hospital at Fletcher Allen Health Care. The twenty-minute flight to Burlington had been her first helicopter ride, but she'd rarely taken her eyes off Alex. Her son had remained unconscious during the flight. She'd found herself straining to hear over the drone of the helicopter's rotors, listening for the rhythmic beeps of the machines monitoring Alex's pulse and respiration as reassurance that he was still alive. Immediately upon landing, the crew had whisked him inside, straight into an operating room that was prepped and ready for their arrival.

She barely remembered signing the consent forms for the surgery. The surgeon who had come out to speak with her had used terms like "intracranial pressure" and "brain resection," and she hadn't been given any specific estimate of how long the operation might take. "At least a few hours, but we won't know until we're under way," the surgeon had told her when she'd asked. Then, she'd been left in the waiting room, surrounded by a sea of impersonal blue upholstered chairs, emotionally exhausted and terrified of losing her only child.

The chair Rose occupied was in the far corner of the waiting room and well away from everyone else. She'd been sitting there for more than two hours now, and every minute that passed seemed like an eternity. Consumed by guilt and shame and fear, she closed her eyes and leaned her head against the wall. *What have I done?*

"You're an ugly drunk and a poor excuse for a mother," her sister had told her. And Father O'Brien's words from just that morning had been remarkably prescient. "So many times, an addict, particularly someone who is addicted to alcohol or drugs, doesn't ask for help until something awful happens," he'd said. "He or she ends up getting hurt or hurts someone else."

He was right, and so was Emily, Rose thought. *Alex is here because of me, because I wasn't doing my job as a parent.* Her face crumpled as she realized the truth of what she had been told. She did have a problem with alcohol, one that had caused untold pain for people she loved and threatened to claim Alex's life. "The doctors will save him," she whispered to herself. "Please, please, let them save him. Please, please . . ."

Rose didn't know how long she stayed in that position, but she startled when a hand touched her shoulder. She bolted up to see her aunt Ivy standing beside her, along with Emily and Father O'Brien.

"Did I doze off?" she said. "Was anyone looking for me? Did someone come to give me an update on Alex? Is he out of surgery?" Wild-eyed and slightly disoriented, she looked around the waiting room, but no doctors or nurses were in sight.

"We just got here, honey," Ivy said, "but it doesn't look like anyone's come out to talk to you yet. How long has he been in there?"

Rose glanced at her watch. "Going on two hours. You didn't have to come," Rose said, glancing back at the priest and her sister. "I didn't expect any of you to come."

"All of us love Alex," Emily said.

"And we love you, too," Ivy added, although Rose noticed how the comment prompted Emily's mouth to press into a firm, flat line. "Did you get ahold of Sheldon yet?"

"Yes, finally. He's trying to get a flight, but the only nonstop one left today doesn't leave until after ten tonight," Rose said. "Driving's the fastest way for him to get here, but even if he left right after we talked, he won't be here until—"

She stopped speaking as a man wearing scrubs and a surgical cap entered the waiting room. A white disposable mask was still tied around his neck, as if he had just pulled it down from his face.

"Ms. Frye?" the man asked as he looked straight at her. It was the same surgeon who had spoken to her briefly when she'd signed the consent forms.

"Yes? How's Alex?"

"He's out of surgery, and everything went well. He's heading into the recovery room right now, and you'll be able to see him there very soon. One of the nurses should come get you in just a few minutes."

"Is he going to be okay?"

"I wish I could give you a definitive answer, Ms. Frye, but it's too soon to say. We were able to elevate his skull fracture and remove the blood clots that were putting the pressure on his brain. We also stabilized the skull with a microplate and screws and inserted a drain before we closed him up. Alex will be transferred to the pediatric intensive care unit once he is out of recovery. If all looks good after a day or so, we'll slowly bring him out of sedation and attempt a neurological exam. Only then will we get a better idea of what kind of recovery to expect."

Rose was fighting tears again. "Do you think he'll recover completely?"

"He very well could," the surgeon said, "but, again, it's too soon to make any assessments or predictions. It's also very possible that Alex will have some permanent brain damage from the injury. You should prepare yourself for a range of potential outcomes."

Rose nodded. "Thank you, Doctor. Thank you so much, for all you've done for him." The room started to swirl around her, and she tried to stay focused on the surgeon's sympathetic eyes. He reached out and touched her arm.

"You know, I have a son and a daughter. I know how difficult this must be for you, and I want you to know that there are a couple of things that may improve Alex's chances. First, kids are resilient, and they heal quickly. And, time is always of the essence in cases like his. You got him here for surgery very quickly, which was crucial. It's lucky for him that you were there."

But I wasn't, Rose thought. *I wasn't.* She barely registered the surgeon patting her arm before he left.

"It's gonna be okay," her great-aunt said. She felt Ivy's hand on her back, but just then, a nurse came through the double doors.

"Ms. Frye?" she asked, and Rose nodded. "You can see your son now. Someone else can come with you, too, if you'd like."

Rose looked behind her, at Ivy and Emily and Father O'Brien. She met the priest's gaze and raised her eyebrows. He nodded slightly at her unspoken question.

"Could Father O'Brien come with me?" Rose asked.

"Of course," the nurse replied. "Please follow me."

Rose's breath caught in her throat when she got her first look at Alex in the hospital bed. He seemed so small and weak as he lay in the center of it. His head was wrapped in a white bandage that extended down over his forehead. Tubes protruded from his mouth, held in place by white medical tape below his nose and on his cheeks. Several electrodes were also taped to his chest. The only sounds in the room were the beeps coming from the equipment surrounding his bed and the quiet hiss of the ventilator.

She leaned over his face, looking for any sign of movement or awareness.

"Alex, baby, Mommy is here. You're in the hospital, but you're going to be just fine. Can you hear me?"

She got no response, no eye or facial movement. There was nothing except for the rhythmic sound of the ventilator breathing for her son.

"Alex." Rose bent lower over his face, low enough to brush her lips against his cheek. "I'm here, baby, and I love you," she whispered. She wiped her eyes frantically as she straightened up. *It always upsets him when I cry,* she thought.

"Rose," Father O'Brien said softly, "take my hand." The priest held his hand out to her. When she grasped it, Father O'Brien bowed his head and began to pray.

"Heavenly Father, watch with us over your child Alex, and grant that he may be restored to that perfect health which is yours alone to give . . ."

In that moment, as she stood with Father O'Brien, it was as if she were her seven-year-old self, dressed in a white gown ready to make her First Communion. She still remembered that day at the little stone church in Mill River. She had been a little nervous, standing up in front of the congregation. When it had been her turn to receive a wafer, the smile on Father O'Brien's face had put her completely at ease.

He was so much older now. What remained of his hair was sparse and white. His hand clasping her own was not nearly as steady as it had been when he had placed the first Communion wafer in her mouth. And yet, the kindness and warmth that had always emanated from Father O'Brien still reassured her as completely as they had when she was a child.

"Father?" she whispered. When he turned to her, she looked into his elderly face and felt a nonjudgmental, unconditional love. "Everything you said to me earlier today . . . was true. If I had been . . . if I'd been awake to see Alex leave the house, he wouldn't have gotten hurt. If he has brain damage, or if he . . . doesn't wake up, it will be because of me . . . because of my drinking." She took a deep breath, trying to keep her voice steady in Alex's presence. "I need help. I want to be a good mom." Her voice became quieter and raspy. "Alex might not wake up. If he does, if I get a second chance, I won't take it for granted. But I'm not strong enough to do what I need to do myself."

Father O'Brien smiled at her in the same way he always had. "Of course I'll help you. And, I have great faith that when your son wakes up, so will he."

CHAPTER 33

In the kitchen of her little house on Main Street, Claudia put her hands on the counter and closed her eyes. The glass of milk she had poured for herself was empty, and there was one plain donut left in the Entenmann's box that was open in front of her. She'd taken a bite from it, but she just couldn't finish it. Her stomach felt as if it would explode.

She closed the donut box and shoved it up into her cupboard. At the moment, she couldn't even stand the sight of it. She took a sponge from the sink and methodically wiped up the crumbs and powdered sugar that were scattered on the countertops and floor around her. When she was satisfied with her cleanup, she walked into her bedroom, pulled off the powdered-sugar-smudged shirt she was wearing, and took a clean top from her closet. Finally, she went into the bathroom to wash her face.

This is what gluttony looks like, she thought as she wet a washcloth and looked into the mirror. The tears that had run down her face while she was eating had mixed with cinnamon, powdered sugar, and bits of donut. The whole pasty mess had caked around her mouth and on her chin as if she had a white mustache and goatee.

Once she had washed away the evidence of her gorging, she picked up her phone and dialed Kyle's number.

"Hey, sweetie!" he said when he heard her voice. "I was just thinking about you. How was your shopping trip?"

"Fine," she said, trying to keep her voice as normal as possible. "I'm not feeling too good now, though."

"You're sick again? Is it the same thing as last night?"

"Um-hmm, I think so."

"Do you want me to come over?"

Claudia hesitated before answering. He sounded so genuinely concerned, and knowing what she knew, it hurt to answer him.

"Could you?"

"Of course. Let me see if Ruth can keep an eye on Rowen for a little while, and I'll be there."

It took him only minutes to arrive at her front door. When she let him inside, he kissed her forehead and immediately embraced her, but she stiffened in his arms.

"What's wrong?" he asked, stepping back and looking down at her.

She looked up into his face for the first time. "There's something we need to talk about."

"Uh, okay." He looked bewildered, and Claudia was impressed by his acting skills.

"I want you to listen to me without interrupting," she began. "This isn't easy for me. I never thought I'd end up in a situation like this with you, but here I am."

Kyle opened and closed his mouth as she held up a finger.

"I know about you and Emily." She was trying her best to sound stern, but her voice was halting, and she was on the verge of tears. "I've suspected something's been going on with you for a while now. The way you were talking to her at the police station that day, and I know you were over at her place to talk to her about the vandalism, even though you never mentioned that to me. I told myself I was imagining things. I almost had myself convinced of it, until I saw you leaving her house earlier today."

Kyle started to say something, but she cut him off.

"I don't want excuses or denials. I just want to know the reason you did it."

"Claudia, it's not what you think. There's nothing going on—"

"That's bullshit!" she yelled, and the tears began to flow. "Just tell me the truth. What was it about me that you didn't like? Was I not pretty enough or funny enough? Was there not enough sex? Or did Emily just rock your world in some other way?" She was starting to feel nauseous. Her stomach wasn't used to handling massive amounts of food, much less an overload of pure sugar and fat, and her emotional state did nothing to help.

"God, Claudia," Kyle said. "How could you think something like that? I love you, and I thought you felt the same way about me." He shook his head, and his brown eyes narrowed in anger. "After all this time we've been together, do you really not trust me at all?"

"Do you deny that you were at Emily's today?"

"No. And, quite frankly, I can't believe you were checking up on me."

"I wasn't," she retorted. "I decided to drive past Rose's house on my way home, to see the lawn vandalism you were talking about at the cookout, and there you were, coming out of Emily's house. It didn't look like you were there on police business, either."

"I wasn't," he said, with the same harsh tone that she'd used, but he didn't elaborate further.

Claudia raised her chin and tried to look determined. "Then I was right."

"No, you're not. In fact, you couldn't be further from the truth," Kyle snapped. He wheeled around and walked out through her front door, slamming it shut behind him.

With her stomach twisting uneasily, Claudia stood in her foyer long enough to hear him start his pickup before she ran for the bathroom. She barely made it in time to raise the toilet seat and lean over the bowl. She gasped and sobbed in between heaves, feeling as if she were disgorging more than the contents of her stomach. It was almost as though the wonderful memories she'd made with Kyle and the happiness that had warmed her soul for the past several months were being ripped out, piece by piece.

When she was finally able to catch her breath, she flushed the toilet and sat back against the wall. Losing Kyle was too much to think about right now, too much for her aching heart and roiling stomach to handle. Feeling empty in every sense, she closed her eyes and tried not to think about anything at all.

"How is he?" Emily asked as Ivy came out of Alex's hospital room. While Alex was being moved to the pediatric critical care unit, she'd gone down to the cafeteria and brought back coffee and sandwiches for everyone. She was the only one who had yet to see Alex after his surgery, but she feared how Rose might react to her presence.

"Still heavily sedated," Ivy said. "Kid, it's scary how fragile he looks, the poor thing. Rose is holding up, but just barely, I think. It'll be a good thing when Sheldon gets here." She looked with interest at the tray of cups and sandwiches Emily held.

Father O'Brien approached them. "I just found out that there's a Ronald McDonald House near the hospital. Since it looks like Alex will be here a while, I'll call over a little later, once it's open for the day, and see if there's any space available for Rose and Sheldon. In the meantime, they also operate a family room for parents and relatives of sick children over on the fifth floor of the Baird Building. You can get cleaned up or even take a nap over there."

"Thank you, Father," Ivy said. "I hadn't even thought about how long we might be here."

"Anything I can do to help," he said.

"I'm not sure Rose will want to leave Alex's room, but she'll need to rest at some point to keep her strength up," Ivy said. "Em, we can take that tray and sit down out here if you want to go on in."

"Sure," Emily said. She handed the tray to Father O'Brien and then took a cup of coffee and a sandwich from it. Ivy leaned wearily on her cane and started walking toward the waiting area. The priest didn't follow her aunt immediately, though. Instead, he turned to Emily with a thoughtful expression.

"Emily, do you remember the conversation we had yesterday? When I asked you whether you still loved your sister?" he asked in a quiet voice. When she nodded, he continued. "I think what's happened to Alex has had a profound effect on Rose. And, I think that if there's anything left of the love you once felt for her, she needs to know it, and feel it, now more than ever."

Father O'Brien held her gaze for a moment longer before he headed in Ivy's direction. Emily took a deep breath and quietly entered Alex's room.

Rose was sitting in a chair at his bedside. One of her hands rested on Alex's small arm, and her head was slumped forward until her chin nearly touched her chest. Emily tried to ease the heavy door closed, but the soft click of the latch startled her sister awake.

"It's just me," Emily said as Rose's head snapped up. "I brought you some things from the cafeteria." She approached slowly and handed Rose the cup and the foil-wrapped sandwich. "The coffee's not great, but I figured it was better than nothing."

"Thanks," Rose said. She set the sandwich on a rolling table next to Alex's bed and took a sip from the cup.

Emily stood staring at Alex. He was so still, other than the subtle rising and falling of his chest, and it was heart-wrenching to see his slight form connected by countless tubes and wires to so many monitors and other equipment surrounding the bed.

"Has there been any change?" Emily whispered.

Rose shook her head. "The doctors said there shouldn't be while he's sedated like this."

"Do you know how long they'll keep him this way?"

"At least a day, maybe more. It depends on what happens with the pressure on his brain." Rose reached up to Alex's face and gently stroked his cheek, then the bit of his forehead that wasn't covered by the bandages.

Emily nodded, although Rose's gaze didn't leave Alex to notice it.

"I suppose Sheldon should be here soon, right?" She saw a tear slip from the corner of her sister's eye and run down her cheek.

"Soon, I hope."

Emily nodded again, feeling awkward and out of place. She took a few steps back and was about to make a quiet exit when Rose spoke again.

"I understand now," she said. "What I took from you."

Emily froze. Rose slowly turned her tearstained face and looked up at her.

"Alex is the most wonderful, precious thing in my life, just like Andy was in yours. If Alex doesn't wake up, or even if he does and he's not himself, it'll be because of me. Just like Andy's death was because of me."

Emily felt her breathing becoming ragged as Rose's words went straight into her middle, slicing into a hurt that remained deep inside her.

"I *was* drinking that day, during the afternoon, before Mom asked me to pick up Andy. I'd been sleeping for a few hours before she woke me up, so I figured I was okay to drive. A deer did jump out in front of us on the way home. I don't know how fast we were going, but I didn't react in time. It was almost like everything was in slow motion. I swerved to avoid the deer, and then the car was flying through the air. I honestly wasn't sure whether the alcohol affected my driving or not. I'm still not. But it might have. I was afraid of going to jail, and I didn't admit anything after the accident. Why would I, when my blood alcohol level was normal when they tested it? Besides, the damage was done. There wasn't anything I could do to change things, to bring Andy back. I just told myself over and over again that it was completely an accident, hoping I could convince myself of that."

Emily was trembling as she listened to her sister. She was afraid of what she might say if she tried to speak. She wiped her tears with the heel of her hand and wrapped her arms around her middle.

"I knew, deep down, what I'd done," Rose said, leaning forward to smooth the blanket covering Alex's chest. "On some level, I knew I was responsible for Andy's death and for messing up your life. But, I didn't really acknowledge it. I pushed it away. For all these years, I've tried to ignore the guilt and go on with my life. I've been so selfish, and I never knew or even tried to understand how it must've been for you, losing someone you loved with everything in you."

"You still don't know how it feels, not really," Emily whispered, looking at Alex.

"Maybe that's true," Rose admitted. "I can hardly think about the 'what ifs' with Alex. I'm not as strong as you are, Em. I don't think I could survive losing him."

"For Alex's sake, I hope that's not something you have to find out." Emily turned and reached for the doorknob.

"Emily?"

She stopped, wanting desperately to leave the room and ignore her sister, but for reasons she couldn't comprehend, she turned back to look at Rose.

"I am truly sorry for what I did to you. And to Andy. For all these years I refused to acknowledge it, and what I am. I'm . . . I'm an alcoholic. Probably have been since high school. It was always easier to drink than deal with a problem, and then after the accident, it was the only way I could escape the guilt." Rose's body shook from the force of her sobs.

"It's pathetic that it would have to come to this for you to admit anything," Emily said. "You should've dealt with your drinking a long time ago."

"You're right," Rose choked. "I should've asked Mom for help. A couple times, I almost did, but each time, I convinced myself that she'd compare me to her own mother and turn her back. I'll always regret that I never reached out to her before she died. But, I did just ask Father O'Brien to help me get clean, because I want to be a better mom for Alex if . . . when he wakes up. He deserves that. Just like Sheldon deserves a better wife, and you deserve a better sister. So, I'm asking you whether you could find it in your heart to give me that chance. Is there any way you could forgive me for what I've done to you?"

Emily stared at Rose for a long, silent minute. "If I had been responsible for Alex's accident," she finally said, "would *you* be able to forgive *me*?"

Rose looked again at Alex. "I don't know," she admitted. "It would be hard, maybe impossible. I don't think there would even be a chance of me forgiving anyone for something like that unless I loved the person who did it just as much."

Does love really enable forgiveness, or does it make it harder? Maybe it does both, Emily thought.

Memories began swirling through her head faster and faster. Rose, sitting next to her in the seat on the school bus, yelling at the fourth-grade bullies to shut up after they'd made fun of her red hair. Rose yanking hard on that same hair during a squabble as she'd pulled on her sister's blonde hair at the same time. Rose reading to her at bedtime all those nights when their mother had been working late. She and Rose sitting in their room, both of them

covered in chicken pox and dabbing calamine lotion over the un-
reachable itchy welts on each other's backs. Rose secretly and me-
ticulously supergluing their mother's favorite mug back together
after the dishwasher incident. Rose "borrowing" her allowance
money without asking so that Linx could pick up a six-pack after
she'd snuck out the window. Rose teaching her how to put on eye
makeup and telling her how it felt to kiss a boy. Rose sobbing and
slurring on the phone while Emily had been trying to study for her
college midterms. And after that Christmas visit when she'd finally
brought Andy home to meet her family, Rose hugging her goodbye
and whispering how happy it made her to know she'd found such
a great guy.

When Emily closed her eyes, trying to make some sense out of
the emotional vortex in which she was caught, it was Father
O'Brien's face that appeared in her head. "You were inseparable . . .
you loved each other very much," he'd said, and of course it was
true. She had loved Rose, in spite of and because of their differences, through those years of arguments and tears before Rose had
left home, and afterward, until Andy had died. The question now
was whether any of that love remained. Father O'Brien's quiet, ancient voice echoed deep within her, "If you still love her at all, you
may not recognize it right now. But, I think you do, and that love
is the key to forgiving her for what she did."

The heavy door to the room suddenly swung open, and Sheldon burst in.

"Rose," he said as he rushed past Emily toward her sister and
Alex, and Rose stood up and fell into his arms. Emily caught the
closing door and slipped outside. Her continued presence would
be an intrusion, and she needed to be alone.

From Alex's room, she hurried through empty hospital corri-
dors. She encountered a door marked STAFF EXIT and pushed it
open. The fresh air outside provided exquisite relief. The hospital

was so sterile and stifling, and her swirling emotions seemed hell-bent on squeezing the last bit of oxygen from her lungs.

There was a park bench a few yards from the door, and Emily sat down upon it. The sky was a clear midnight blue and filled with stars, so much like the night of her first date with Andy. After dinner, late in the evening, they'd gone back to campus and sat on the red granite bench in the Ross Commons Courtyard. He'd kissed her for the first time under these same stars, with the same cool night air caressing her face.

Later that spring, he'd surprised her with a weekend getaway in a cozy cottage at Branbury State Park. They had planned to hike to the Falls of Lana or up through Rattlesnake Cliffs, but in the end, it had been impossible to tear themselves apart long enough to get out of the cottage. And again, Emily remembered, there had been the crisp nighttime breeze, flowing through the open windows of the cabin as Andy had made love to her.

Their future plans had fallen into place so quickly after that. "You can teach while I finish school," he'd told her as they had lounged together, his fingers drifting over the soft skin of her belly. "Once I start my own practice, we can get a house. Something old and beautiful for you to restore."

"Something big enough for kids," she'd said. "At least two or three."

"At least," he'd agreed, whispering the words against her mouth.

She'd dreamed of marrying Andy, having a family with him, nurturing and cherishing their children before sending them off into adulthood. Then, they would grow old together, playing with grandkids in that same house, watching the seasons change from its windows.

Emily trembled. With her eyes closed, she could almost feel Andy sitting on the bench beside her. The slight breeze carried a hint of his cologne, a whisper of his voice. He was with her.

And yet, he wasn't.

Despite the time that had passed, despite having had other relationships after Andy's death, her heart was still aching and empty, longing for what might have been. Even if she wanted to, how could she find in that heart the forgiveness to give Rose another chance?

NEARLY THIRTY-SIX HOURS LATER, IVY WAS THE LAST TO ENTER Alex's room. The little boy was still unconscious and on a breathing machine, and the surgeon who had performed the operation was bent over him holding a penlight, gently pushing back one eyelid, then the other.

"He has normal pupillary response, which is a good sign," the surgeon said. "His intracranial pressure has remained stable since the surgery, too. We've been tapering the sedatives all morning, and he's not receiving any at all right now."

"Why isn't he awake, then?" Rose asked.

"It'll take time for all of the drugs to clear his system," the surgeon explained. "We'll wait and continue to monitor him. If Alex regains consciousness, the nurses will immediately contact me or the resident on call."

"Thank you, Doctor," Sheldon said. He put his arm around Rose's shoulders as she kept her eyes on Alex. The surgeon gave a small smile and hurried from the room.

"Why don't you take a break?" Sheldon quietly encouraged Rose. "You've barely left this room since you got here. Get something to eat, or go take a nap in the family room. Just keep your phone with you. I'll call you if anything changes."

"That's a good idea," Ivy said. "You'll want to be alert and rested when he wakes up, but right now, you're just exhausted."

"I showered in the family room last night," Emily said. "It's a nice place."

"And I just came from there," Ivy said. "They've got private, sound-proofed rooms for sleeping, and I was able to reserve one for us. They've got some nice, soft couches, too, with TV and Internet access. Why don't you come take a look?"

"Well, I suppose I could go for a little while," Rose said, looking at Sheldon, "if you *promise* you'll call me if anything changes."

"I will," Sheldon said.

"I'll show you where it is," Ivy said. "Father O'Brien, why don't you come, too?"

"Thank you," Father O'Brien said. "I suppose I wouldn't mind sitting for a few minutes in a comfortable place."

"If *anything* changes—" Rose said again to Sheldon as Father O'Brien, Emily, and Ivy filed out of the room.

"Don't worry," Sheldon said as he held up his phone. "I won't leave his side."

Ivy held the door open, waiting. Rose nodded, leaned over to kiss Alex's cheek, and reluctantly followed her from the room. While needing to use a cane usually made her the slowest in a group, Ivy found herself leading the way as Father O'Brien and her great-nieces shuffled behind her. Of course, they were all exhausted, especially Rose. She only hoped that what awaited them in the family room would bring them some comfort, and maybe even joy, during such a trying time.

"Here we are," Ivy said as they arrived at the entrance to the family room. She checked in with the volunteer at the front door and led everyone down a hallway with several closed doors off to the side. "This is our room," she said before she took a deep breath and pushed the last door open.

The private sleeping room had no windows. There were two beautiful full-size beds, made up with crisp-looking white sheets and mounds of pillows and separated by a nightstand. A large sectional sofa was positioned in one corner. In the other corner, facing away from the door, there was a floor lamp with a reading light next to a large rocking chair. A lamp on the nightstand and the floor lamp provided the only illumination in the room. Ivy waited as Rose, Emily, and Father O'Brien followed her inside before closing the door behind them.

"This *is* nice," Rose said as she glanced around, but her breath caught in her throat as the rocking chair moved slightly. Ivy gripped her cane more tightly, watching as Emily and Father O'Brien followed Rose's gaze. The only sound that disturbed the shocked silence in the room was the slight creak of the rocking chair.

Slowly, Josie DiSanti stood up and turned to face her family.

CHAPTER 34

JOSIE TREMBLED AS SHE LOOKED UPON HER DAUGHTERS FOR the first time in months. They were as different and as beautiful as ever, even though both of them, especially Rose, had deep, dark circles under their wide-open eyes.

"Mom?" Rose choked. Her older daughter gave a small cry and took a step forward before her knees buckled. Emily quickly reached down, grabbed Rose's arm, and pulled her older sister back to her feet. Behind them, Father O'Brien made the sign of the cross and leaned on the doorknob for support.

"I know this is a terrible shock for you," Josie said. She rushed forward, eager to touch her girls, to show them that she really was standing there before them. Rose was shaking, and Josie reached out and pulled her close. "I know about Alex. I'm so sorry. I didn't mean for this to happen, for it all to turn out like this." The tears were running down her face now, and when she stepped back and took Rose's face in her hands, her older daughter's eyes overflowed as well.

"You're really alive?" Emily whispered. "You didn't die?" Her complexion was pasty white, and when Josie turned from Rose to wrap her arms around Emily, her younger daughter began to sob. Josie held her tightly, steeling herself for the onslaught of questions that she knew would soon begin.

Sure enough, after a few minutes, Emily pulled away. "I don't understand. We had a wake for you. Your ashes . . . Daisy spilled your ashes. But, that wasn't you?"

"No, baby, it wasn't," Josie said.

"Then . . . who?" Rose demanded. "God, there must've been a horrible mistake."

"Well, yes, and no," Josie said. "I swear, I never meant for anyone to get hurt."

Emily looked at her, blinking rapidly. "*You* never meant for . . . you mean, you wanted us to think you were dead? On purpose?"

Josie opened and closed her mouth, struggling for the right words.

Rose's swollen, teary eyes narrowed, and her breathing was ragged. "What the FUCK, Mom? Why would you ever do something like that to us? Faking your death? Really? Do you have any idea what you've put us through? We left our homes, came up here and put our lives on hold, and for what? There's obviously no inheritance." Rose put a hand on her forehead. "Did you do it to be able to see us set up house and torment each other? Or maybe so Alex could have an accident trying to help me meet your idiotic demands and end up in this hospital fighting for his life?" She whirled around to look at Father O'Brien. "Did you know about this?"

"I . . . I didn't," he stammered.

"Did *you*?" she asked, turning to Ivy.

"Unbelievable," Emily muttered as Ivy stared at her shoes. Emily's eyes drifted back and locked with Josie's. She was shaking, wiping away tears, as she struggled to articulate her words. "How could you be so cruel? Why would you ever do something like this to us?"

Ivy looked at Emily. "Your mother has some explaining to do."

"Yes, I do," Josie said. "It's time you knew everything."

"I think we should all sit down," Father O'Brien said. "At

least, *I* need to sit down." He walked to the sofa and lowered himself onto the end cushion.

Ivy leaned back against one of the beds and rested her cane beside her. Josie took a daughter's hand in each of her own and gently drew them forward, pulling them in the direction of the sofa. Rose and Emily sat together on one side of Father O'Brien, while Josie took a seat at the end of the sectional, facing all of them.

"I never meant for anything this bad to happen," Josie began. "I wanted you girls to believe I was dead because it was the only way I could think to get you to come together and finally work through your differences. Whether you realize it or not, family is everything. I learned that the hard way. I never met my father. My mother was never there for me, and I had no other family while I was growing up. Do you know how much better my life would have been if I'd had one loving parent, or even a single family member who cared about me?

"Your father didn't have many relatives, either—only an uncle and a few cousins on his mother's side. When we got married, we looked forward to finally having a family of our own. You girls were everything to us. When your father was killed, I was all you had left. It was up to me to take care of you. It's why we came to Vermont. The FBI said that we should leave New York, for our own protection, and that's what I did."

"What do you mean, the FBI?" Rose asked. "Dad died in a house fire. Why was the FBI involved?"

Josie began to feel jittery, as she always did when she recalled the day Tony died. "There are some things about your father's death that I've never told you," she said softly. "When it all happened, you were too young to understand. I was afraid to say anything later because I didn't want you to be upset. Plus, the special agent in charge made it clear that the less I said about it in the beginning, the safer we'd be.

"Just before Christmas 1983, I put you girls down for your nap and left to run some errands. Your dad was home that day, so he stayed with you. When I came home, I found our house on fire. I ran inside, screaming for all of you. I found him in the kitchen, propped up in a chair. I remember shaking him, trying to wake him. He didn't respond, because he was already dead . . . not because of the fire, but because he'd been shot in the chest."

Josie paused to gather her thoughts. Her daughters were staring at her, shock having replaced the anger on their faces, and her heart ached, knowing she was wreaking havoc with their emotions.

"When I realized he was gone, the only thing that kept me going was hearing you girls crying upstairs. To this day, I can still smell the smoke. The whole house was filled with it, and the heat from the fire was overpowering.

"Somehow, I got up the stairs to your room and wrapped you both in blankets. I was still wearing my heavy wool coat, and I put one of you on each hip and started back down. By that time, I couldn't see the floor through the smoke, and there were flames crawling up the walls to the second floor. You girls were screaming and coughing, and I just kept telling myself that that was a good thing. It meant you were still with me. We finally got down to the front door and outside, but I don't remember much right after that. It's still a blur of sirens and smoke. I woke up in the hospital a few days later. They told me that we'd all been admitted for smoke inhalation, but you girls were fine, and I was healing well. I cried then, being so happy about that, but also devastated, knowing that your father was gone."

"Why would someone have wanted to kill Dad?" Rose asked in a whisper.

Josie took a moment to steady her voice. "Your father worked as an accountant at a big jewelry import-export company in Manhattan. He was hired right out of school and did very well. In fact, he'd been promoted twice by the time you were born, Rose. As time went on, though, and your father became more involved with the company, he started to find discrepancies in the books. He was afraid to tell me much about it, only that he suspected the company was laundering money and dealing in black market diamonds, and that a lot of powerful people were involved.

"The night before the fire, he came home late and said that we had to take you girls and leave town. His company execs knew the FBI was on to them and planning to execute a warrant, and they were pressuring your father to 'play ball.' I asked him if they'd threatened him, and he clammed up, but he wasn't the kind of man who could be intimidated into doing the wrong thing. No, your father said we were going to go away for a few days, long enough for the feds to move in and clean house, and then he'd seek protective custody for all of us in exchange for his testimony. We packed up some things and planned to leave the next evening, at nightfall. I ran out during the afternoon to get some traveler's checks at the bank and more diapers for Emily."

Josie shook her head before she continued. "I didn't know if they'd ever find who was responsible for the fire and your father's murder. The fire destroyed everything, including any physical evidence that might have existed. That was back before DNA analysis and other fancy techniques were routinely used in criminal investigations, you know. All they could do was have your father's remains cremated and sent to me after we'd moved in with Ivy.

"I was scared for a long time after we moved to Mill River, worrying that whoever had killed your father would find us. I finally got a letter from the U.S. attorney a couple years later telling me that they'd made an arrest in the case based on testimony from another criminal as part of a plea deal. Peter Salvucci the guy's name was. He was eventually convicted of arson and first-degree murder, and he's still in prison today. The long and short of it is that someone in your father's company decided he couldn't be trusted, and a hit man, Salvucci, came for him while I was out. Either he didn't know you girls were upstairs napping or decided not to shoot you, but he did set the house on fire. It was a miracle I arrived home when I did."

Rose, Emily, and Father O'Brien were listening intently. Josie looked at each of them in turn as she spoke, and she was surprised when Emily, who was seated closest to her, reached out and took one of her hands.

"The witness protection program was fairly new back then," Josie said. "The FBI wouldn't take anyone into the program who wasn't testifying in a trial or a relative of such a person. Your father was dead, so he couldn't testify and we didn't qualify. But, with his killer still at large, the detective in charge of the arson investigation told me I should leave the city and not reveal to anyone that we were going or where we were headed. I was totally alone, terrified and grieving, with two little girls. Aunt Ivy's was the only place I could think to take us, even though I hardly knew her back then. Thank God she was there for me, for us, when we first came to Mill River. Without Ivy, I never would have been able to survive losing your father and raise you girls. She just reinforced my belief that your family is more important than anything."

"Family *is* the most important thing," Ivy said, her voice gruff with emotion. "I'm just as thankful that you and the girls came into my life. Before then, I was alone, too."

Josie gave Ivy a grateful smile and turned back to her children. "I've loved you girls from the day you were born. I worked until I was exhausted to provide for you and protect you, to give you a better life than I had." She looked down at her hand, still clasped tightly in Emily's. "I failed you both in so many ways. Rose, I blame myself for your getting involved with alcohol when you were a teenager. I should've recognized what was happening with you and put a stop to it. And Em, you were always the glue that held us together. But, that should have been my responsibility, not yours. I was so focused on working, on providing, but I was providing the wrong thing. We lived on a shoestring budget for so long . . . I went overboard focusing on making money when I should have given you more of myself. Lots of times, I wasn't there when I needed to be. But, I always tried to be the best mother I could. I hope you can believe me when I tell you that. It was a promise I made to myself when you were born, and one I've repeated almost every day since your father was killed.

"As time passed and you girls still wouldn't speak to each other, I got more and more worried. I suppose the icing on the cake was finding a lump in my breast this past winter. It turned out to be benign, thank God, but it really scared me. It made me realize that once Ivy and I were gone, there'd be little chance of you girls finding your way back to each other.

"At the last town meeting, when I saw how Mrs. McAllister found a way to reach out to the folks in Mill River after she died, I got the idea to try to bring about your reconciliation after my death. But, I had no idea when my time might come. Too many more years might have passed, years that would make it even harder for you two to reconcile your relationship. And if truth be told, I was also selfish about it. I wanted to see you acting like sisters again and know that my plan had worked, while I was still living, and not be lying on my deathbed wondering what would happen.

"I knew a deception like this would hurt a lot of people." Josie felt fresh tears well up in her eyes, and speaking suddenly became very difficult. "You're so right, Em. It was an almost unspeakably cruel thing for a mother to do to her children. But, I thought the long-term reward, if it worked, would be worth the immediate emotional toll." Josie looked at Rose, whose face was still blotchy and wet. "I never, ever thought that anyone would be physically hurt by what I planned. I thought you two would figure out where the key was hidden, and that Emily would be the one to climb the ladder to get it." She focused on her younger daughter with a pleading expression. "Growing up, you were always my little monkey, the one who did all the climbing around. I never imagined Alex might become involved and hurt himself trying to help."

"Just how in the hell did you get the key up in that tree?" Emily asked. "I've never seen you climb on anything taller than a step stool."

"Jim Gasaway's son runs a tree-trimming business. I've used him for years to get overgrown rural properties cleaned up before they go on the market. I asked him to come by and do a little pruning. He didn't mind putting the key up in the knothole for me, even though it was a strange request." She looked at her older daughter. "I figured you'd see the highlighted passages in that old copy of *To Kill a Mockingbird*, Rose, and recognize it as your clue."

Rose wiped at her eyes with a damp, crumpled tissue. "I might've, if I hadn't given the book to Alex to read. He ended up working out the whole thing on his own. I should have been supervising him more closely, but you know something, Mom? He and I never would have been up here in this situation if it weren't for you. If Alex doesn't make it, or if he's not . . . not himself when he wakes up . . ." Rose's voice trailed off as she looked at Emily, and Josie saw an unspoken communication, some sort of shared understanding, register in their eyes.

Emily tightened her grip on her hand, and Josie could see the anger rising in her expression. "Do you realize how devastating it was," her younger daughter said, "that night Ivy called to tell me you'd died? All these years you've wanted Rose and me to reconnect. *You* wanted it. Not us. Did you ever stop and think that maybe what you wanted wasn't what was best for us? What you did was inexcusable."

"Totally," Rose agreed.

"I knew it would be terrible for you both," Josie said, and her voice was barely audible. "I'm so sorry for what you've been through. I did it only because I was convinced that being a part of each other's lives would be in your best interests. I still believe that, but I see now that it was foolish of me to assume you would agree. And Father, I'm so sorry for what I did to you as well," she said to Father O'Brien. "We've been friends for so many years, and you've been there for me through the most difficult times in my life. I wanted to tell you so badly, but I thought things would have a better chance of working if you didn't know."

"That's some way to treat a friend," he replied with a grim expression. "So many people care deeply about you, Josie, and your supposed death was devastating to all of us. Have you any idea what poor Ruth Fitzgerald has gone through?"

Josie had never seen such anger and hurt on Father O'Brien's face, and the thought of Ruth being so upset cut to her core. Yet, the reactions were not unexpected. "I know," she said softly. "I anticipated that people would react this way. But, in deciding to go through with my plan, I asked myself whether there was anything I wouldn't do for my girls. The answer was always no. I also asked myself whether my children and my close friends would understand and forgive me for what I did. The answer was always 'I think so.' I suppose now I'm begging for forgiveness, from all of you."

Father O'Brien was quiet a moment. He pursed his lips and exhaled loudly. She thought she saw a softening of the anger in his eyes, but she wasn't sure.

"Josie, even if Alex recovers, if your family and friends forgive you, I can't help but think that this whole scheme of yours might be criminal," he said.

"It would've been," Josie said, "if the death certificate you saw had been filed. Not that it could have been, since all Vermont death certificates are filed electronically now. But, Dr. Richardson filled out and signed an old paper version as a favor, so long as I promised it wouldn't be used for anything other than to convince you girls I was dead. Filing it, or using it as the basis for any legal action, like collecting insurance proceeds, would've been fraud."

Emily snorted. "Some favor. He could still lose his medical license for doing something like that. Besides, you don't know him that well, do you? Why would he even do something like that for you?"

Josie looked back at Ivy, and her aunt rolled her eyes. "He actually did it as a favor for me," Ivy said. "And he gave me a box of ashes from his pellet stove, too, so we'd have 'em for the wake. Fred and I go way back."

"The ashes were just plain old ashes?" Rose asked, and Ivy nodded.

"What do you mean, you 'go way back'?" Emily said.

"We were . . . involved. A long time ago," Ivy said. "Now that we're fessing up our longtime secrets, I guess it's time you knew mine. Fred's the whole reason Thomas and I split up. He and I met after I moved to Mill River with Thomas. We fell in love. It wasn't something we saw coming, but once it happened, we wanted to be together. I broke things off with Thomas. Fred was all set to leave Jane, but then she found out she was pregnant. That changed everything. He wasn't about to divorce his newly pregnant wife. It just wasn't done back then, and he's not the kind who would've done it even if others did. So there we were, in love and trying to go on with separate lives in a little town where everybody finds out about everything, and here we've been ever since. Time mellowed the attraction we felt for each other. We're just good friends with a secret now, but we still sometimes wonder what might have been."

"And we thought you couldn't keep secrets," Emily said drily.

"I guess you never know, do you? I should've at least confessed to it," Ivy said, with an apologetic glance toward Father O'Brien.

"It's never too late," he replied.

"Right," Ivy said. "Maybe keeping that big bombshell inside for so long's the reason why everything else I hear just leaks right out. There hasn't been room for much else."

"You didn't say anything to anybody about Mom's plan, either," Rose pointed out.

"Well, no, I didn't, as crazy as it was. The truth is, I wanted you girls to make peace with each other as much as she did. I know what it's like to go through life estranged from my only sibling. The grandmother you girls never had a chance to know was my younger sister. Yes, she had lots of issues, including a serious drinking problem, but she was *my sister.* I loved her even after she ran away and cut off contact with me and the rest of our family. I still miss her.

"I decided that if there was any way I could help keep you girls from living the same kind of sisterless life I did, I was willing to do it. And, your mom needed someone to keep tabs on things and communicate with her in case of an emergency." Ivy looked at Rose. "I actually called her right after the ambulance carrying you and Alex left your house."

"Josie, where exactly have you been all this time?" Father O'Brien asked.

"In New York, in a little sublet apartment off Arthur Avenue," she replied. "I figured after almost thirty years, I could handle going back," she said, and she looked again at her girls. "Losing your father the way I did, having to leave so suddenly, I never had any closure. I felt like I needed to see where we lived, where the house used to be. And, I wanted to spend some time where I grew up." She smiled wistfully. "Our old house, the one that burned, was rebuilt, but the block looks pretty much the same, just older and more run-down. It was actually easier seeing it than I expected it to be.

"I had another reason for going back, though. I wanted to find something of your father to give to you girls." She stood up and went to the rocking chair, where her large purse was sitting on the floor. Josie grabbed it by the handles and carried it to the sofa.

"I managed to track down Leo Campanelli, your father's only uncle," she continued. "He's ninety-two and living with one of his sons in Brooklyn now. He's a little hard of hearing, but he still has his wits about him. Leo and your father weren't all that close, but he came to our wedding, and he saw you girls a couple times when you were little."

Josie reached into her purse and withdrew a large manila envelope. "Back when we all lived in New York, pictures were taken the old-fashioned way, with regular cameras and film. The fire destroyed almost everything of our lives together, including all our pictures.

"So many times over the years I've wished I had even one photo of your father to be able to show you. I've seen his face in my memories, and I've seen glimpses of him on your own faces, and in your expressions and personalities, as you grew up. But, you've never been able to see him."

Josie reached into the envelope with a shaking hand and withdrew several old photographs. "Leo still had a few pictures of him, of us, even after all these years," she said quietly as she held them out to her girls.

Emily was seated closest to her, and her younger daughter was the first to take the photos from her. Josie watched as her girls bent forward, their heads together, to look at them. The first one was a small copy of her and Tony's wedding portrait. It was a close-up taken just in front of the altar. Rose and Emily stared at the image of them, and especially at Tony's smiling face.

"His mouth and smile are just like mine," Rose said. "And, Em, you really do have his eyes."

After a few minutes, Rose passed the wedding photo down to Father O'Brien while Emily held up the second one, which was an image of Tony with both girls. He was down on one knee, with baby Emily nestled in the crook of his right arm. Rose stood on his left with her little hand clutching the silver wristwatch Tony had usually worn. "You were about two in that one, Rose," Josie said. "I couldn't get you to look up at the camera for anything. All you wanted was to hold your father's shiny watch."

"I still remember that watch," Rose said. "He used to let me wear it sometimes." She touched her finger to the tiny watchband in the picture.

Emily still hadn't said a word about the photos, but tears poured down her cheeks as she examined them. Josie knew that, unlike Rose, she had no recollection of her father at all. In the precious, yellow-edged images, Emily was seeing him now for the first time.

The last photograph was an old Polaroid taken in someone's backyard. She and Tony stood together, smiling, each holding one of the girls.

"Leo took that last one," Josie said. "It was from the summer before the fire. We all went out to Brooklyn, to Leo's son's place, for a barbeque. We had such a good time, and your father talked about it all the way home in the car. He wanted us to be able to get a place of our own like that, where you girls could play and we could have family over."

"It's a real family photo," Emily finally said. "I wish things had stayed like that, with all of us together."

"I know, baby," Josie said. She reached out and gently smoothed a curly red strand of hair from Emily's face. "I do, too. But, the times we had together with your father were happy ones, and a lot of the years after we got settled in Mill River were happy, too. I'll always be grateful for that time with you girls."

Rose stared down into her lap. "I'm too exhausted to think anymore. I've never been so happy and so pissed beyond belief at the same time." Emily nodded her agreement.

With her chin quivering, Josie took a deep breath as she looked between Emily and Rose's tear-streaked faces. "I only pray now that Alex will be all right, and if he recovers, that somehow, you two will be able to forgive me for what I've done to you, and make peace with each other, so that we can truly be a family again."

Her daughters glanced up at her and then at each other without answering. Josie looked at Father O'Brien, who sat unmoving at the end of the sofa. She turned to see Ivy shrug her shoulders and open her mouth to say something when the theme song from *Seinfeld* broke the silence in the room.

Rose startled and then jammed a hand down into her jeans pocket. "It's my phone," she said as she pulled it out, glanced at the screen, and answered it.

"Sheldon? What's going on?" Rose's eyes blinked tightly, and she let out a strange half-laugh, half-sob as she listened. "I'll be right there," she gasped into the phone. Josie's heart rose up into her throat as her older daughter jumped to her feet and smiled through fresh tears.

"Alex is awake," Rose managed to say, "and he's asking for me."

CHAPTER 35

ON HER KNEES ON THE WOOD FLOOR IN THE MARBLE MAN-sion, Emily paused for a moment to stretch her neck and back. All morning, she'd been crawling along the baseboard in the great room with an edge sander, removing the old finish on the floor where the large drum sander had been unable to reach. It was slow, painstaking work.

Still, it felt good to get back into her own bed and normal routine after those stressful nights at the hospital in Burlington. The physical labor of working in the marble mansion was more tiring than usual, given how the past few days had disrupted her sleep schedule, but it was cleansing, too. The exertion had helped purge the last of the stress she'd felt over Alex's accident and injury. It also gave her time to think about how she would handle her mother's despicable actions and what, if anything, she would do as a result of her conversation with Rose.

When Emily reached the corner of the living room, she switched off the machine and replaced the worn sanding sheet with a fresh one. But, rather than resuming her work, she sat back against the wall and ran her fingers over the smooth square of used sandpaper. What she wouldn't give to feel that smooth and serene on the inside, to be able to get over the hurt she felt after her mother's deception, on top of everything else. She felt far more rough and raw than even the coarsest sandpaper. She wished, too, that in this one way, she were more like Rose. Her sister would simply explode at someone in anger rather than internalizing her feelings and allowing them to build up and eat away at her.

Going back to her hometown, facing all that had happened, was supposed to get her life on track. She had counted on using her time in Mill River to come to terms with so many things and leave the past truly in the past. Instead, she was more hurt and angry and confused than she had been when she arrived. The anger, especially, scared her.

This time, though, she would not suppress it and allow it to simmer away at her insides. And, she was finished running away.

"Em? Emily, are you here?" Her mother's voice carried from the kitchen door through the house.

Emily frowned at her mother's uncanny timing.

"There you are, honey." Josie removed her sunglasses and stepped into the great room. "I thought for a minute that you might be gone for the day."

"Hi, Mom." She glanced up at her mother and fiddled with the palm sander. There was a long, awkward pause before her mother spoke again.

"Alex is doing really well. They moved him out of intensive care to a normal room. When I left this afternoon, he was sitting up in bed eating a normal lunch. No more broth and Jell-O. His doctor says all his brain function tests are normal, and he could be discharged in a week if nothing unexpected happens."

"That's great news," Emily said. "I'm sure Rose and Sheldon are relieved. How are they holding up?"

"Better, now. They're focused on Alex, on getting him well and bringing him home."

Again, the silence. Emily felt the anger flickering inside her ribs and ran a finger over the switch on the edge sander. She was tempted to turn it on, continue working, and completely ignore her mother. Her mouth curled into a half-smile as she realized that that was totally something Rose would do. But, even as angry as she was, she couldn't bring herself to treat her mother that way.

"Look, honey, I know you're still upset with me. I don't blame you, and I know you need time to think through everything and . . . decide whether you can forgive me. I just wanted to tell you again how sorry I am that I hurt you, and that things turned out like they did."

"I have one question to ask you," Emily said. She stood up and looked into her mother's tired eyes. "When you were planning your whole little disappearance, making arrangements to live in New York, writing the letter to us, planning your wake, did you even once really think about how it would be for me, or Rose, to get a call from Ivy to tell us you were dead? Did you really stop and think about how we would feel?"

Her mother opened her mouth to answer, but Emily didn't give her the chance.

"I don't think you did, not really. If you had, you would have realized how devastating it would be for us, and you wouldn't have gone through with everything. But, if you didn't put yourself in our position, well, that's even worse. You wanted a happy little family—*you* wanted it, not us—and you were willing to do anything for it. And that's just selfish and cruel."

"I did what I did for *your* future, Emily, yours and Rose's, not mine. It might not be something you can truly understand until you have children of your own, but try to put yourself in *my* position. I can tell you that it is pure torture for any mother to see her child hurting, and it's even worse when you can't take the pain away. And what happened with you and your sister . . . it wasn't something I could fix with a Band-Aid and a kiss. I watched you and your sister suffer year after year. As a mother, how could I not try to help you? I may have gone about it the wrong way, but I'd tried everything else over the years, and I wasn't going to give up on what I believed, and still believe, was the last, best chance for you both to find happiness again. I have *never* given up when it comes to you girls. What decent mother would?"

Her mother's chin was trembling, awaiting her answer. Emily felt hot tears prick the corners of her eyes. "If you really loved us—"

"—I'd have done what? Left you alone, to live out your completely separate, miserable lives? Maybe I should've, but I made a decision wanting only the best for you. It would've been wrong *not* to try.

"Deep down, I think you know how much I love you and your sister. But I'm not perfect. No one is. And even people who love each other more than anything can make horrible, hurtful mistakes. I did it, and so did your sister."

Emily didn't say anything.

"I know how it feels to lose the love of my life, and to try to go on living after that," her mother said in a halting voice. "But I knew your father would've wanted me to find happiness again, and I did that as best I could. Andy loved you so much, and he would've wanted the same for you. If you can't forgive the past to find happiness for yourself, you should do it for him."

Her mother quietly left the room. Emily stared at her tattered work jeans and steel-toed boots as tears left dark splotches on the sawdust-coated floor. It hurt to admit that her mother was right, and it was even more excruciating to think about what Andy would have wanted for her. Even after all the time that had passed, she still had his engagement ring and a folder of his silly stick drawings, and she could still feel his blue-green eyes gazing straight into her heart.

———

IN HER HOUSE NEXT TO ST. JOHN'S, CLAUDIA LAY ON THE SOFA IN front of the television. She'd spent most of the past few days there, moping, eating whatever she pleased, and ignoring the treadmill. She hadn't seen or heard from Kyle since he'd stormed out of her house. Other than one of her teacher friends who called to tell her that Alex had been airlifted to Fletcher Allen in Burlington, she hadn't spoken to anyone.

Watching one show after another for most of her waking hours had proved to be a decent diversion. Now, though, as she worked her way through a box of Junior Mints and flipped through the sorry late-night offerings, everything reminded her of Kyle. Old-time romantic movies, reruns of *Cops,* and even the ridiculous phone sex commercials . . . it was as if the television were taunting her.

Claudia turned off the television and closed her eyes. If she could only keep her mind blank and avoid thinking about him, maybe she would be able to fall asleep.

She must have drifted off, because a soft knock at the front door startled her awake. Or, had it been a dream?

Claudia sat up on the couch and listened. Another knock sounded at the door.

"Claudia?"

It was Kyle. She had no idea why he had come, but she had no desire to see him.

"Claudia, I know you're in there. Look, we need to talk. I don't want to leave things the way they are, and I need to explain some things to you. This is all a huge misunderstanding. Please, could you open the door?"

Claudia clenched her fists and jumped up. She hesitated before unlocking her front door, willing herself to keep calm, but once she was staring Kyle in the face, all the bitterness and hurt returned.

"There's no misunderstanding. I know what I saw. You can leave now."

Kyle gave an exasperated sigh. His expression was serious, but without the anger he'd shown a few days earlier. "You need to hear me out," he said. "Once you listen to what I have to say, if you still want me to leave, I will. But not until then."

It was so unlike Kyle to speak to her in such a firm tone. And she was a complete mess—no makeup, stringy hair in a lopsided ponytail, and a nasty case of indigestion. But, it didn't matter anymore what he thought of her. He'd betrayed her trust in the worst possible way. As much as she loved him, there was no way she'd take him back now.

"Fine. The sooner we get this over with, the better." He nodded once and pushed past her, heading toward the living room.

"Come sit with me," he said as he sat down on the love seat and patted the empty cushion next to him. His face was calm and devoid of anger.

She sat down on the corner of the sofa facing him and waited.

"I've been in Emily DiSanti's house three times," he began. "Once on that day when she moved in and we helped her carry some stuff inside. Once this past Sunday, when I spoke to her in an official capacity about the vandalism of her sister's yard. And once on the Monday after that, the day you saw me, when I went over to pick up this." Kyle removed a small box wrapped with a ribbon from his jacket pocket and set it on the coffee table.

Wonderful, Claudia thought. *He's going to try the presents-and-groveling approach.*

"She told me that the heavy box that she and I carried into her house on the day she moved in was full of glass. To my knowledge, *you've* never seen the studio she has set up in there. If you had, you'd know that Emily is a stained glass artist, a very talented one. I asked her when she came to the police station, the day you brought the surprise lunch for me, whether she could make something special, for you, for our six-month anniversary. I had something very specific in mind, and she agreed to try to create it for me.

"She finished it Sunday evening, and I had just gone to get it when you saw me coming out of her house. You should know that Emily wasn't even home at the time—she was still at the hospital with Ivy. The package was waiting for me on her dining room table. She called my cell to tell me that she'd left the door unlocked for me."

Claudia stared at Kyle. Nothing he'd said so far had been remotely what she'd expected.

"When Allison died," Kyle continued, "I really didn't think I'd ever fall in love again. At least, not in the same way I loved her. I always thought I'd raise Rowen myself and maybe date a few women, casually, once she was older and I felt like I was ready. I never expected to find anyone else I'd want to spend the rest of my life with. But then I met you, and all those thoughts of myself as a single father went out the window." He paused and looked at the wrapped box. "Before I say anything else, I think you should open that."

She looked down at the box on the table and then up into his brown eyes. The little gift was rectangular, a bit larger than a deck of cards, but it was far heavier than she'd expected.

"Go ahead," he urged. "Open it."

Wordlessly, Claudia untied the ribbon around the box and pushed back the lid. She stared for a moment, then reached inside and lifted out a tiny dark-blue stained-glass box framed in silver. The lid, though, was what truly took her breath away. It depicted a wintery scene, with a thin thread of silver wire separating white iridescent glass in the foreground from the deep blue glass of the background. Tiny, brilliant, heart-shaped crystals were embedded in the blue glass. *It's a snowstorm,* Claudia thought, and she had to blink back tears as she suddenly realized why Kyle had chosen this particular image.

"The blizzard we had on Valentine's Day," she started to say, but she stopped speaking as Kyle slowly moved forward, off the love seat and onto his knees in front of her.

"Look inside," he said in a low voice, and Claudia knew now what she was about to see and what was happening. She was crying again, and her nose was running, and she couldn't even imagine how red and swollen her face must look. She did her best not to think about that as she lifted the beautiful glass lid.

The box was lined with blue velvet in the same shade as the glass, with a sparkling diamond solitaire nestled in the very center of it.

Claudia gasped and tried to cover her mouth, but Kyle grabbed her free hand and trapped it within his own.

"Claudia, look at me," he said. She sniffed loudly and squinted into his face, and it made her cry harder when she saw how moist his own eyes looked. "I love you. I love the person that you are on the inside—your sense of humor and kindness, your intelligence, your dedication to children, and your love for my daughter. I love that even though you're so beautiful on the outside, you don't act stuck up or feel the need to flaunt it. I love your determination and creativity and sense of adventure. I really love your wild imagination, even though it gets you into trouble sometimes."

Her little laugh acknowledging the truth in his last statement came out sounding like a strangled gasp. She also realized that all of the other wonderful things he had just said about her were true as well, and that she was proud of the person she now was. What was it that Daisy had told her—that if you love yourself just the way you are, what other people think of you won't matter? That once she had started loving herself, she was happy most of the time? Remembering Daisy's advice only made the tears come faster. For the first time in her life, Claudia began to believe that she was worthy and deserving of love—Kyle's and her own. Was it possible that this whole horrible misconstruction on her part had happened to convince her of that?

Kyle paused a moment, waiting for her to collect herself a bit. "You've brought such warmth and passion into my life," he continued. "I want nothing more than to spend the rest of it with you. I can see how my actions might've looked to you. But, it about killed me when you accused me of cheating and then wouldn't even listen to my explanation. I've never lied to you about anything, Claudia, I don't want anybody else, and I'd never do anything to knowingly hurt you. What I need to know is whether you trust me, whether you respect me and love me enough to become my wife?"

"Kyle," Claudia choked. "I'm such an idiot. I'm sorry, so sorry." Those were the only words she could get out before she threw her arms around his neck and kissed him.

After a minute, Kyle put a hand up to her face and used his thumb to wipe the tears from one of her cheeks. He smiled a little. "You've been eating bonbons."

"Yeah," Claudia admitted. "Among other things."

Kyle laughed. His brown eyes were watery as they searched her face. "So, about my question?"

"Yes," she said, with a teary smile. She was visibly shaking. "I love you so much. Yes."

"I love you, too." Kyle squeezed her hand, reached over to the glass box, and removed the ring. Carefully, he slid it onto her finger and stood up, pulling her with him. Together, they examined her hand as she extended it and moved it from side to side so that the diamond caught and reflected the light.

Claudia smiled down at the ring. "I don't ever want to take it off."

"Good," Kyle replied, and he didn't give her a chance to say anything more. He put his hands under her jaw and lifted her face to kiss her again.

This kiss was different, more urgent, and Claudia was more than willing. She led him by the hand from the living room, into the bathroom, and turned on the shower. "Let's start here," she whispered as steam began to fill the air. "I've had a rough few days."

Kyle nodded and laughed softly. "So beautiful," he murmured in her ear as they undressed each other. He had that look in his eyes again, the expression that made her heart race and caused her to completely lose her train of thought.

With every movement of her hand, she felt the strange, wonderful sensation of the engagement ring on her finger. Claudia opened the shower door, stepped in, and reached out to Kyle for him to join her. Goose bumps rose up on her skin as she felt the warmth of his hands and the torrents of hot water rushing down her back.

"Closer," she said, but he was already drawing her to him and bending to kiss her neck. She shivered as he moved his hands lower, gasped and leaned against him as he touched her. The steam of the shower enveloped them, surrounded their embrace with its own. In that moment, as happiness washed away her misery of the past few days, they were the only two people in the world.

NEARLY TWO WEEKS AFTER ALEX'S ACCIDENT, IN THE LITTLE HOUSE across from The Bookstop, Rose quietly closed the door to his room and came downstairs.

Sheldon looked up from the sofa. "How is he?"

"Fine. He's sleeping," Rose said. She sat down next to her husband. "I stayed with him until he dozed off."

"That's good. The more rest he gets, the faster he'll heal."

Rose nodded and looked around the room. It was still a shock, seeing how the excess furniture had been cleared out and their belongings unpacked and organized. "I still can't believe what Mom managed to do in just a few weeks. It seems so much bigger now, and the décor is . . . well, it could've been professionally done."

"Your mom did it, so it *was* professionally done," Sheldon said. "But it is nice. Small, but inviting."

Rose nodded and yawned as she rubbed the back of her neck.

"Why don't you take a nap yourself?" Sheldon asked. "It'll feel good, after a week of sleeping in chairs and strange beds."

"Maybe in a little while," Rose said, "but first, I think I'd like to get some fresh air."

Even with Sheldon there, especially with Sheldon there, she couldn't bring herself to stretch out on the sofa. The last time she'd done that . . .

"I'll stay here, keep an eye on Alex," Sheldon said. "It's nice outside. Get some sunshine."

Rose looked at her husband, really looked at him, for the first time in a long while. His temples were grayer and the creases in his forehead were more pronounced. The dark circles under his eyes matched those under hers. He knew everything that had happened, including the reason why Alex had been outside alone and unsupervised. There was still much they had to work through as a couple, and that she had to do alone, if she wanted their marriage to survive. But despite his disgust and frustration with her drinking problem and horror over Alex's injury, here he was, looking back at her with eyes that were still full of love.

It was one thing that hadn't changed. On the night when she'd first spotted him in the audience of her ill-fated stage début, he'd stared at her in the very same way. She hadn't appreciated it until now, of course she hadn't. But she was beginning to understand how alcohol obscured so many truths. How she had ended up with a husband like Sheldon, one who loved her despite her many problems and imperfections, was a miracle she would never understand.

Rose touched her hand to Sheldon's cheek, holding it there a moment. "Maybe I'll go see Ivy for a little while. I'll just be across the street, if Alex wakes up." He caught her hand and squeezed it as she kissed his forehead.

When she reached The Bookstop, the door was open, but no one was in the front room. She knocked on the door that led back into Ivy's living quarters.

"Aunt Ivy?"

"I'm in the little girls' room, kid," her great-aunt called. "Sit tight, I'll be right out."

Rose looked around the room. The Bookstop was another thing that hadn't changed. The towers of books still rose atop the shelves, and the brightly colored beanbags were still in the Kids' Corner. On a whim, Rose flopped down onto one of them. She remembered the photo from the Shakespeare book, which had been taken while she and Emily had sat in the very same place.

"It's been a long time since I've seen you in that corner." Ivy had reappeared in the front room.

"Too long, I think."

"How's Alex doing?"

"Really well. He's sleeping now, but he'd probably love it if you'd come by later."

"I'll do that, sure thing." Ivy smiled. "Do you remember how you used to beat the heck out of the beanbags?"

"What?" Rose said. A faint, distant recollection was triggered by Ivy's question, but she couldn't quite bring it to the forefront of her mind.

"When you first came here, to Mill River," Ivy said, "you were so little, and so torn up over your dad's death. For the first few months, your mom and I didn't know what to do for you. You screamed at everybody, had problems sleeping, and you didn't always accept what she told you about the fire. We finally decided you needed a harmless way to vent your feelings, and I told you to come over and pound on a beanbag when you felt sad or angry. We even moved one of 'em into your mom's house for a while so you could get to it anytime."

"Huh. I sure could've used one when Mom showed up at the hospital."

"I'll bet," Ivy said. Her great-aunt set her cane against her desk and lowered herself into a chair. "Have you talked to her since you've been home?"

"Not yet. I don't know if she even knows we're back. And frankly, I don't know if I want to see her yet, not after what she did." Rose struggled to keep her composure.

"I'm just as thankful as you are that Alex is gonna be okay, and so is your mom. She was only trying to do what she thought would help you and your sister finally move past everything, that's all. She did it because she loves you both. Think about it . . . if Alex were miserable for some reason, if you'd watched him fall apart slowly, year after year, wouldn't you do pretty much anything in your power to help him? Your mom just wants you both to be happy."

"I know that. I know Mom would never do anything to hurt us, not consciously, anyway." She snorted and brushed the tears from her cheeks. "You know, the last time I remember feeling really happy for any length of time was when I was really young, growing up here with Mom and Em and you right next door. I never thought I'd say that about Mill River—never. But it's the truth. I'd give almost anything to be able to feel that way again."

"You will, honey," Ivy said softly. "You will. It'll take getting some help for the drinking, and you'll need to make your recovery, and Sheldon and Alex, your priorities. It'll be easier if you forgive your mother and can earn Emily's trust and forgiveness, if she's willing to give it. All of that will take time, but you have time. And you have people who love you."

Rose heaved a sob into her hands just as the screen door to The Bookstop swung open. Before she could jump to her feet and hide her tears from whomever had come in, her mother was bending down to her, smoothing her blond hair under a gentle hand, pulling her into her arms.

"Rosie, my Rosie," her mother's soft voice said next to her ear, "I didn't mean to eavesdrop, but Ivy's right. You *can* find happiness again."

As she leaned against her mother, Rose felt an immense emotional rush. It was impossible to fully put into words, but for the first time in a long while, she felt free.

"Mom," she whispered, but she couldn't get anything else out.

Her mother seemed to understand what she was trying to say. Rose felt her soft cheek press against the top of her head. "I love you, too, Rose, and I'll help you every step of the way."

Time takes away the grief of men.
                    - DESIDERIUS ERASMUS

EPILOGUE

A New Beginning

ON A BRIGHT SATURDAY MORNING IN MID-SEPTEMBER, a few miles southwest of Mill River, Emily turned down the radio and slowed her old Subaru as she entered the little town of Wallingford, Vermont. She was dressed casually, in jeans and a T-shirt, with her hair up in a ponytail. Gus sat in the backseat behind her, sniffing the warm air and occasionally poking his head out the window.

Emily turned left onto Church Street and then quickly into the parking lot of the Serenity House, where her sister was receiving inpatient treatment. Rose was already standing outside the building, waiting for her.

"Hey," Emily said through the open passenger's side window. Her sister's blond hair was pulled back with a barrette, and she was wearing her usual dark sunglasses. Rose raised a hand in greeting as Emily stopped the car. "You can just put your bag back there, next to Gus," Emily told her as she motioned behind her. "Just move my toolbox onto the floor."

"Okay," Rose said. Her sister opened the back door and made room for an overnight bag on the seat.

Emily glanced sideways at Rose when her sister got into the front. She was surprised at not hearing a nasty comment about Gus or at least seeing her lip turn up in disgust at the thought of her expensive bag being so close to the dog. Neither she nor Rose said anything as she pulled back onto the road, and the silence began to seem strange. Emily felt no hostility, only a growing uncertainty about the way that Rose sat so meekly beside her, familiar and yet somehow different. For the first time in her life, she didn't know what to expect from her sister.

"How are you feeling?" Emily asked as she turned back onto the highway.

"Fine," Rose said. "A little tired."

"Is it odd, being outside that place?"

"Yeah. The sun's so bright," Rose said. "And it's weird not being on a schedule, and being able to choose what I want to do next. Funny how a couple of weeks in that place can give you a new appreciation for freedom."

"Well, the program lasts only twenty-one days," Emily said. "Another week, and you'll be out of there."

"Except for the outpatient sessions," Rose reminded her. "But, I'll be back in the real world most of the time."

"Well, just focus on enjoying your time at home today," Emily said. "Alex can't wait to see you, and he's dying to open the 'surprise' you and Sheldon ordered for him. UPS delivered it a few days ago."

Rose smiled. "He's begged us for an Xbox for the longest time. He's such a good kid, and it seems like all the boys his age have them. We decided that a little bit of time playing videogames shouldn't hurt him."

"Everything in moderation," Emily said. "You know, he's so tickled that his hair's about grown back where they shaved it for his surgery. He's made some new friends in school, too. Sheldon worried about how he'd be accepted once he was enrolled in the gifted and talented program, but apparently the other kids think it's cool that he had brain surgery."

Rose rolled her eyes and smiled a little. Emily glanced at her sister and noticed that she was looking down at a small, worn photo of Alex in her hand. "I've missed him so much. Thinking about him is what's been keeping me going, especially through the first few days of detox. I haven't been clean this long since I was pregnant with him," Rose said quietly. "Now, I have two weeks of sobriety and a long way to go."

That's true for so many things, Emily thought.

"How's Sheldon been doing with Mom?" Rose asked.

"Fine, I think. She got him into the Realtor training course. He had his first class this morning, or else he would've come to pick you up himself. Mom says he's a whiz with the financial end of things, and he's been going with her to learn how to show houses. She doesn't think it'll take him long to start handling listings on his own."

Rose nodded. "I don't think he ever envisioned himself leaving New York, but he still hasn't found a permanent position, and he knows it's important to me to be here while I get better. Mom's offering him a job is just another reason for us to stay, for now at least."

"True," Emily said. "Besides, Mom can't work forever, even if she thinks she can. She'll need someone to take over the brokerage at some point. It'd be nice if it could stay in the family."

Emily exited the highway onto the smaller road that led into Mill River. Although the fall foliage wouldn't reach its peak color for another few weeks, the trees were already showing brilliant patches of orange, red, and gold. The road passed through the covered bridge over the river for which the town was named. When they reached the beginning of Main Street, they could see the McAllister mansion high on a hill in the distance.

"I've been working with Ruth and Fitz up there," Emily said, looking up at the white marble home. "It is just the most gorgeous house. They're doing some remodeling and updating to convert it to a bed-and-breakfast. If you want, after you're settled back at home, I'll take you up to see it."

"I'd love that," Rose said. "I've always wondered what it was like inside."

They were at the far end of Main Street now, passing by a variety of small, older houses and trailer homes. Emily startled as Rose suddenly pointed out the window.

"Is that Daisy Delaine?"

Emily squinted to see where her sister was looking. Up ahead, a short, stout woman was standing on the front porch of one of the trailer homes. The yard surrounding the porch was filled with ceramic animals, a large birdbath, and all manner of whirligigs. Daisy's back was turned to the road, but she was unmistakable as she hoisted a watering can above a large potted mum.

"Yes," Emily said as she slowed the car. "Why?"

"I need to talk to her," Rose said. "Could you pull over? I know everyone's expecting us, but it won't take me too long, and I need to do it."

"Okay." Emily eased the Subaru over to the side of the road and parked along the curb. They were just a few houses past Daisy's, and she watched in the rearview mirror as her sister walked back to the little woman watering her flowers. Daisy's mouth fell open as Rose spoke to her. After a moment, they went together inside the mobile home.

Gus stepped through the space between the front seats to press his wet nose to her cheek. Emily smiled and reached up to cup her hand around his soft muzzle.

"We're just stopping for a minute, Gussie-pup," she told him.

The weird sense of uncertainty was still with her as she gently pressed her cheek against the dog's velvety face. Rose's behavior was surprising, and she wondered whether it was a shallow, short-term phenomenon or the beginnings of something genuine and permanent. More importantly, if Rose really had changed, what kind of sister would she be? And, what kind of sister was she herself willing to be in return?

ROSE PUSHED HER SUNGLASSES BACK OVER HER FOREHEAD AND looked around at the inside of Daisy's small trailer. The furnishings in the living room, where they stood, weren't fancy, but the place was neatly kept.

"Would . . . would you like to sit down, Miss Rose?" Daisy asked. "And would you like something to drink? I've got some tasty mint tea in the fridge." Daisy bustled into the kitchen and removed a large mug from a cupboard.

"Oh, nothing to drink, thank you," Rose said. "It's very nice of you to offer, but I can only stay a few minutes."

Daisy nodded, but she remained in the tiny kitchen, clutching the mug and staring at her with round, curious eyes. Rose noticed that Daisy's little gray dog, who was sitting quietly on one of the chairs at the kitchen table, was looking at her with much the same expression. Rose followed the woman into the kitchen, pulled out one of the chairs, and sat down.

"Daisy . . . I owe you an apology . . . more than one, actually. I was wrong about so many things. I'm not even sure how to begin." Rose felt her cheeks start to burn, and she took a deep breath before she continued. "The way I treated you at my mother's wake was so wrong. It was incredibly inappropriate and cruel."

"Oh, Miss Rose—" Daisy began, but Rose raised her hand to stop her from speaking.

"I don't mean to be rude, but please, please let me finish everything I need to say," Rose interrupted. Daisy blinked and nodded. "I have no idea what's in your potions, but I've been told that people in town have bought them for years. I don't think people would spend money on something that wasn't worth it, so there must be something about them, something special, that I just didn't understand. I had no right to say anything bad about your potions.

"And the last thing," Rose said, fighting to keep her voice steady, "the most important thing, is the simple fact that without you, I would have lost the most precious person in my life. You saved my son, Daisy. If you had given up on apologizing to me for something that was purely an accident, you and Claudia wouldn't have found Alex when you did, and he probably wouldn't have survived his injuries. I owe you so much . . . so much that I'll never be able to repay you for what you did." Rose clutched her hands together between her knees as tears rolled down her cheeks into her lap.

Daisy was still listening quietly, her expressions alternating between childlike wonder and soft sympathy. When Rose finished speaking, she pulled out the chair beside her and sat down.

"Miss Rose," Daisy said after a moment, "you might not know this, but I didn't know who my mother was—not the mother who adopted me, but the one who gave birth to me—until the night she died. I got to know her as a person for about a year before that, though, and I still feel so lucky that I had that little bit of time with her. I don't have any children, but I know how special it was for me to be able to spend time with my mother.

"I didn't do anything special for Alex, Miss Rose. I guess it was by chance that I ended up being there to find him. I'm just happy he's all right, and that you'll get lots more time with your little boy. You don't owe me anything, though."

Rose looked into Daisy's kind, round face, but she couldn't speak.

"About the ashes," Daisy said, "I won't lie and say you didn't hurt my feelings, Miss Rose. I know I'm not like most people, and sometimes people get frustrated with me. They even yell at me sometimes. But, I have feelings just like you. When I feel upset about how somebody treats me, I remember what my mother told me. She always said that nobody's perfect. She also said I should always try to be kind and forgiving, and see the best in people, even when they can't see it in themselves. Since she died, I've thought a lot about what she taught me and I know in my heart that she was right." Daisy reached out a pudgy hand and patted her knee. "Everything's okay between us, Miss Rose. Let's just start fresh from now on."

"Thank you," Rose choked. "Thank you." She reached out to hug Daisy, and afterward, it took her a moment to compose herself enough to speak clearly. "My sister's waiting for me in the car," she finally managed to say. "And my mom is expecting us back at her house."

Daisy smiled. "I'll walk outside with you. I need to finish tending my mums. Just a few more days, and they'll be ready for harvest!" The woman opened her front door and ushered her onto the porch. "Chrysanthemum tea is good for lots of things, you know. It makes your skin glow, and it's good to help you get over a bad cold. In fact," she said, as her voice dropped to a whisper, "mum juice is one of the ingredients in my special Sick-Away Potion. But don't tell anybody, okay? It's a secret."

"Okay," Rose said. "Have a good day, Daisy."

"You too, Miss Rose." Daisy grinned at her and picked up the watering can.

Back in the car, Rose turned to Emily. "You wouldn't have any Kleenex in here, would you?"

"No, but there's an emergency TP roll in the glove box. Help yourself."

Rose opened the glove compartment, found a half-flattened

roll of toilet paper, and pulled off enough to blow her nose. "Mom's going to worry if she sees me in such a mess."

Emily snorted. "A little worry on her part's nothing compared to what she made us go through over the summer."

"Yeah, I know. I've had a lot of time at rehab to think about that. Part of me still can't believe she did it, but I do think her intentions were good. Anyway, I'm ready to put it behind me and move on."

"I finally told Mom last week that I forgave her," Emily admitted, "but I reserved the right to be pissed about what she did for a good bit longer." Her sister shot her a curious look and glanced back toward Daisy's trailer. "It's really not any of my business, but I'd love to know what went on in there."

"I'm trying to make amends for what I've done," Rose said. "It's part of the program, but I'd do it even if it weren't. Daisy is one of many people I've hurt."

"Oh," Emily said. Rose finished wiping her nose and dabbing her eyes. As she lowered her sunglasses back into place, she glanced over at her sister. Emily's hands gripped the steering wheel close together at the very top, and her gaze was fixed straight ahead above them.

"While we're talking about forgiveness, I've been wondering whether you have an answer to my question," Rose said softly. "The one I asked you in the hospital, right before Sheldon got there."

Her sister remained silent, methodically downshifting as they neared a stop sign. Before they entered the intersection, Rose reached out and grabbed her sister's hand atop the stick shift. She didn't say anything to Emily. She merely squeezed the hand under her own, letting the physical connection convey what words of any kind could not.

The old Impreza idled at the stop sign. Emily's eyes flicked over toward her before they resumed their gaze straight ahead and filled with tears. Several more moments passed before her sister spoke.

"I'm not at all sure that I can," Emily said. She shifted her hand to squeeze Rose's in return. "I can't promise anything. A lot will depend on you, and what you do from here on. But, if you're serious about changing your life, if you really make a genuine effort to recover and rebuild what we used to have, then . . . I guess I'm willing to try."

"THEY SHOULD BE HERE ANY MINUTE," JOSIE SAID TO FATHER O'Brien as she slid a covered dish of potato salad into the refrigerator. The elderly priest was sitting at her kitchen table with a half-empty cup of coffee before him. "They should just have time to change before we head over to the cemetery. I hope Sheldon's class lets out on time." She looked over at Father O'Brien as she washed her hands and dried them on a kitchen towel. He was holding up the teaspoon she'd given him with the coffee, moving it slightly as he stared at it.

"Father? Is everything all right? Don't tell me the dishwasher missed something on that spoon."

"No, no, it's fine. The spoon is perfectly clean. I was just admiring how it catches the sunlight so beautifully."

"Oh, thank goodness. I'd have been mortified if it was dirty," she said with a little chuckle. "In fact, my silverware is so old that I'm surprised it still shines at all."

"Old things may lose their good looks, but they can still be useful a lot longer than you expect them to," he said.

"That's true," Josie said. "And every once in a while, you come across a priceless antique that's still functional." She smiled fondly at the elderly priest.

He smiled in return and slowly set the spoon on the table. She watched as he patted the handle of it before picking up his cup.

It suddenly occurred to her that she hadn't seen or heard Alex in a while. "Alex, what are you up to?" she called. "Are you ready to go?"

"Yes, Grandma," he answered from the living room.

"Why are you so quiet?" She peered out of the kitchen to check on him. Alex was sitting on the love seat dressed in a smart navy suit. His blond hair was slightly shorter on one side, but the difference was hardly noticeable anymore. He held a framed photograph in his hands.

"I was just looking at this," he said as he came into the kitchen to show her. It was the photo of her and Tony and the girls from the summer barbeque. "Mom has the same smile as Grandpa did."

"Yes, she does," Josie agreed as she looked at the picture. "I think that one might be my favorite, but I'm grateful to have all three. I don't know that I could go through with a memorial service for your grandfather if I hadn't been able to get those photos."

"Even if you hadn't found the pictures or kept his ashes all this time, he'd still be with you," Father O'Brien said gently.

"You're right, Father. Of course you're right," Josie said. Her gaze shifted to the fireplace in the living room, and to the small metal box sitting on the mantel, but she was quickly distracted by the sound of car doors slamming out front.

She hurried to the front window and looked outside. Rose, Emily, and Gus were already on the sidewalk, watching as Ivy crossed the street to join them.

"Mom!" Alex yelled. He opened the front door and ran straight for his mother, and Rose knelt down to fold him into her arms. Emily and Ivy waited while they embraced.

Josie closed her eyes. "Give not a windy night a rainy morrow," she whispered to herself. *If only things work themselves out from here on.*

Father O'Brien seemed to read her mind. "It's still a little odd, seeing Rose and Emily together like this," he said quietly over her shoulder. "Maybe there's hope."

"Hope is a wonderful thing," Josie said. She touched the locket around her neck and smiled.

ACKNOWLEDGMENTS

On the surface, writing a book would seem to be a solitary pursuit, but that could not be further from the truth. So many people were gracious enough to help me with this novel in various ways.

First, I'd like to thank those individuals who kindly took time out of their busy schedules to answer my many queries for technical information. These people include Carl Chilstrom, research librarian at the Gemological Institute of America, who taught me about diamond prices during the 1970s and 1980s; Thomas Scott, unit secretary at Fletcher Allen PICU, for explaining the PICU setup and visitation policy; Andrew Costello, city attorney for Rutland, Vermont, who answered my questions about the process of municipal acquisition of real property; Dr. Steven Shapiro, chief medical examiner for the state of Vermont, for information about regional medical examiners and procedures used to file death certificates in that state; Alan Shelvey, city engineer and public works commissioner in Rutland, Vermont, for historical information about the municipal landfill and the city hall building; Jeff Wennberg, former mayor of the city of Rutland, for a wealth of information on the history, politics, environmental issues, and citizenry of the city and the surrounding county; Bonnie Hawley, owner of Hawley's Florist, for permission to mention her floral business in this book; Lucy Notte and Lisa Polcaro, for their detailed descriptions of Route 103 and other roadways in the area in which this story is set; Dr. Viviane Tabar, neurosurgeon with the Brain Tumor Center at Memorial Sloan-Kettering Cancer Center in New York City, for information on the diagnosis and treatment of pediatric epidural hematomas; and Anita Baiker-Buckholz, wonderful friend and Realtor extraordinaire, for her insightful and entertaining stories of properties bought and sold.

I must next thank my merry band of test readers, my dear friends Lena Ottusch, Michelle Johnson-Weider, Tim and Beverly Trushel, Elizabeth SanMiguel, Deidre Woods, Sherri Miller, Anita Baiker-Buckholz, Ruth Uyesugi, and Cynthia Webb, and members of my family, namely Linda Tomasallo, Carrie Tomasallo, Dennis Tomasallo, Susan Tomasallo, and Sheila Wheeler—I appreciate you so much. Your insightful and honest feedback made this book so much better. (I'd like to particularly acknowledge the special efforts of Lena Ottusch and Susan Tomasallo, who quickly and enthusiastically read every major draft of this story!)

I've learned so much about the publishing process from my friend and fellow author Elizabeth Letts. Thank you, Elizabeth, for being my "writer big sis," a great sounding board, and a real source of inspiration. Also, thank you to Jenny Bent, whose tweets about my writing gave me an early and unexpected publicity boost. To Hannah Elnan and Jenny Stephens, assistants to my editor and agent, respectively—thank you for everything you do. And to Jane von Mehren, I'm still grateful for your helping to give me the opportunity to work with so many lovely and talented people at Ballantine Bantam Dell.

I would like to thank my publisher, Libby McGuire, as well as Kim Hovey, Jennifer Hershey, and Kate Miciak. I can't tell you how much I appreciate all of your support, feedback, and enthusiasm. Many thanks also to my publicist, Lindsey Kennedy, and to Susan Corcoran in the publicity department; to my marketing manager, Maggie Oberrender, and to Kristin Fassler, who heads up the marketing department; to my copy editor, Briony Everroad, and my production editor, Jennifer Rodriguez; to Marietta Anastassatos, the artist who created the gorgeous cover for this story; and to the rest of the wonderful people at Ballantine, whose great care and effort have gone into the publishing and launch of this novel.

To my brilliant editor, Kara Cesare, thank you for making my first experience with the editorial process absolutely amazing. I'm still in awe of your talent for bringing out the best in a story, as well as the fact that we operate so much on the same wavelength and have since day one. You are truly my "publishing soul sister"!

To my patient, tireless, clever, funny, and wise friend and agent, Laurie Liss, thank you so much for everything. You alone were willing to take a chance on me in the beginning. You stayed with me through the roller-coaster ride that was my publishing journey and found me the perfect editorial match. Your advice and effort helped give me the day job I always dreamed of having. Two words: miracle worker!

Finally, I would like to acknowledge the members of my immediate family whose support and encouragement are constant and unfailing. To my mom, Linda, my dad and my stepmom, Dennis and Susan, my sisters, Carrie and Molly, my mother- and my father-in-law, Gloria and Robert, and my brother- and my sister-in-law, Titus and Erin, my husband, Tim, and my little dude, Gavin—all of you mean so much to me. You are my light and my inspiration. Love you always!

The
MILL RIVER
Redemption

A Novel

Darcie Chan

A Reader's Guide

DARCIE CHAN'S TOP SIX FAVORITE READS

I have loved reading all of my life. I found it very difficult to choose only six books as my favorites, as there are so many more that I could have included here! But, each of the following books is simply wonderful, and I hope that you enjoy reading them as much as I did.

Slow Way Home, by Michael Morris

This gorgeous novel is variously funny, gut-wrenching, frustrating, and uplifting. Like all the books on this list, I thought it was beautifully written. The characters are utterly real and compelling, particularly eight-year-old Brandon, from whose perspective the story is written. The plot focuses on his grandparents' struggle to protect him from their daughter, who runs off with her latest boyfriend and abandons him at a bus station. I'm the mother of a little boy, and Brandon's plight touched me deeply. My heart ached for him and cheered with him at the end. Also, I was impressed by the author's skill at pulling the reader into the story. The emotional resonance of the story is great, and I could almost feel the humidity of the South settling against my skin.

The Snow Child, by Eowyn Ivey

There are very few books that completely blow me away, but this first novel did. Apparently, it had the same effect on many other people, as it was a finalist for the Pulitzer Prize! In this story about a childless couple in 1920s Alaska, the author's choice of language is exquisite, and I was surprised at how skillfully the author wreaked havoc with my sensibilities. First, I was convinced that a wild little girl seen by the couple was a figment of their imaginations. But then, I started to believe the girl was real before being slung once again in the opposite direction. The answer is revealed in a moving, surprising ending. This story is unforgettable.

Modoc: The True Story of the Greatest Elephant That Ever Lived, by Ralph Helfer

I tend to read mostly fiction, but this is a nonfiction book that I absolutely loved. It is a captivating story of the lifelong bond between a boy and a female Asian elephant. The story takes the reader from Europe, through the exotic teak forests of India, and then to the circus in the United States. It's an amazing testament to the intelligence of elephants and of their ability to form lasting friendships with people.

Practical Magic, by Alice Hoffman

This story has so many wonderful aspects: a clever, creative plot, a cast of mostly lovable, oddball characters, and great humor, all wrapped up with a touch of whimsy. I had such a strong desire to pack up and move into the old Owens house—I could see it so clearly in my mind's eye—and to get to know its inhabitants. And, having two younger sisters myself, I could truly appreciate the bond between Sally and Gillian. This is their coming-of-age story, one that ends with each sister finally finding happiness. I've reread this book several times, which is unusual for me, and I've come to think of it as an old friend.

A Gift of Magic, by Lois Duncan

I first read this story as a preteen and it captivated me, so much so that I reread it as an adult and enjoyed it just as much! After all, who hasn't wondered what it would be like to be able to read other people's minds? This is a story about three children, each of whom is blessed with a special gift. I love the relationships between the siblings in this book, too, and I was constantly guessing about what would happen next. This is a suspenseful story with a heart-warming ending.

A Tree Grows in Brooklyn, by Betty Smith

This is my all-time favorite book. It was first published in 1943, and it provides a fascinating, in-depth look at a slice of American society in the early twentieth century. It is written with unflinching honesty, and many of the situations described are difficult to read emotionally, but the rewards of the story are just as great. Francie, the protagonist, is an incredible role model. This is her survival story, one with lessons that are still relevant today. What Francie achieves in the face of poverty and adversity is inspiring and exceptional.

QUESTIONS AND TOPICS FOR DISCUSSION

1. In the beginning of *The Mill River Redemption*, Josie DiSanti is traumatized and frightened. Over the course of the story, however, she becomes strong, self-sufficient, and confident. What do you feel is the single biggest factor in her transformation?

2. As a single parent, Josie tries to be everything to and provide everything for her daughters Rose and Emily. Given her situation, what do you feel were her greatest successes and failures as a parent? What might she have done differently?

3. Josie has to deal with an unpleasant boss in her first job as a single parent. Have you encountered a "Ned Circle"—i.e., someone who intentionally tried to make things difficult for you—in your own life or career? If so, how did you handle the situation?

4. As young adults, Rose and Emily DiSanti experience a terrible tragedy and become estranged, and Josie spends many years trying to help them reconcile. If you were in Emily's position, could you forgive Rose for what she did? If you were in Rose's position, could you ask Emily for forgiveness?

5. In your experience, is trying to forgive someone easier or more difficult if you love the person seeking the forgiveness?

6. Daisy Delaine repeatedly seeks to apologize to Rose for her perceived transgression at Josie's wake. Do you think Rose's response to Daisy is an expression of personal animosity or a result of the influence of alcohol?

7. How does Rose evolve from the moment she arrives in Mill River for the summer to the end of the story? Did your feelings toward her change over the course of the book?

8. Emily returns to Mill River to honor her mother's wishes and also to confront her own past. Despite all that has happened, do you think she still loves her sister? Does she change as a person as events unfold? At the end of the story, do you believe she will really be able to forgive Rose for what she did?

9. Claudia Simon struggles with feelings of insecurity, even though Kyle gives her no reason to doubt his feelings until she sees him coming out of Emily's house. If you had been in Claudia's position, what would you have done at that point?

10. Ivy's little bookstore is a labor of love and her life's work. How does it reflect her personality?

11. Josie is desperate to see her girls' estrangement end. Does she go too far in her efforts to force their reconciliation? Do you think that what she does is worth it in the end? What would you have done had you been in her position?

12. As a "recovering spoon addict," Father O'Brien manages to keep his compulsion under control in this novel. Do you think

that he will continue to refrain from stealing spoons, or do you think he will eventually relapse? Does his grief over Mary McAllister's death have anything to do with his newfound self-control?

13. Sheldon sees Rose at an experimental theater performance and is taken with her immediately. Do you believe in love at first sight? If so, is it the kind of love that can withstand the challenges inherent in most marriages?

14. Near the end of the book, Josie refers to Father O'Brien as "a priceless antique that's still functional." Is there, or has there been, an elderly person in your life who fits that description? Who is or was it, and what made the person so special to you?

DARCIE CHAN is the *New York Times* bestselling author of the eBook sensation *The Mill River Recluse* and the novel *The Mill River Redemption*. She has been featured in *The New York Times, USA Today,* and *The Wall Street Journal*. For fourteen years, Chan worked as an attorney drafting environmental and natural resource legislation for the U.S. Senate. She now writes fiction full time and lives north of New York City with her husband and son.

ABOUT THE TYPE

This book was set in Garamond, a typeface originally designed by the Parisian type cutter Claude Garamond (c. 1500–61). This version of Garamond was modeled on a 1592 specimen sheet from the Egenolff-Berner foundry, which was produced from types assumed to have been brought to Frankfurt by the punch cutter Jacques Sabon (c. 1520–80).

Claude Garamond's distinguished romans and italics first appeared in *Opera Ciceronis* in 1543–44. The Garamond types are clear, open, and elegant.

Chat.
Comment.
Connect.

Visit our online book club community at
Facebook.com/RHReadersCircle

Chat
Meet fellow book lovers and discuss what you're reading.

Comment
Post reviews of books, ask—and answer—thought-provoking
questions, or give and receive book club ideas.

Connect
Find an author on tour, visit our author blog, or invite one of
our 150 available authors to chat with your group on the phone.

Explore
Also visit our site for discussion questions, excerpts, author
interviews, videos, free books, news on the latest releases,
and more.

Books are better with buddies.
Facebook.com/RHReadersCircle

RANDOM HOUSE